3

CRY DANCE

CRY DANCE

KIRK MITCHELL

Bantam Books

New York Toronto London Sydney Auckland

CRY DANCE
A Bantam Book / March 1999

BOOK DESIGN BY JAMES SINCLAIR
MAP BY JEFF WARD

Library of Congress Cataloging-in-Publication Data
Mitchell, Kirk.
Cry Dance / Kirk Mitchell.
p.   cm.
ISBN 0-553-10810-7
1. Havasupai Indians—Fiction.   2. Indians of North America—
Arizona—Fiction.   I. Title.
PS3563.I7675C79   1999
813'.54—dc21   98-24412
                                                                                       CIP

Published simultaneously in the United States and Canada

Bantam Books are published by Bantam Books, a division of Random House, Inc. Its trademark, consisting of the words "Bantam Books" and the portrayal of a rooster, is Registered in U.S. Patent and Trademark Office and in other countries. Marca Registrada. Bantam Books, 1540 Broadway, New York, New York 10036.

PRINTED IN THE UNITED STATES OF AMERICA

BVG   10 9 8 7 6 5 4 3 2 1

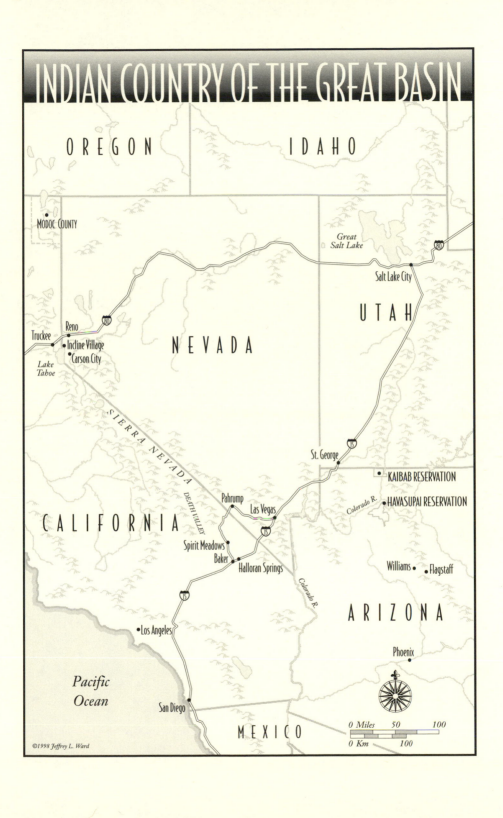

INDIAN COUNTRY OF THE GREAT BASIN

OREGON

IDAHO

MODOC COUNTY

Great
Salt Lake

Salt Lake City

UTAH

NEVADA

Truckee
Reno
Incline Village
Carson City

Lake
Tahoe

SIERRA NEVADA

St. George

KAIBAB RESERVATION

Colorado R.

HAVASUPAI RESERVATION

DEATH VALLEY

Pahrump
Las Vegas

CALIFORNIA

Spirit Meadows
Baker
Halloran Springs

Colorado R.

Williams
Flagstaff

ARIZONA

Los Angeles

Phoenix

Pacific
Ocean

San Diego

MEXICO

0 Miles   50   100

0 Km   100

©1998 Jeffrey L. Ward

CRY DANCE

Chapter 1

"You the BIA guy from Phoenix?"

The Bureau of Indian Affairs, United States Department of the Interior. In the last century, the same inflection would have been reserved for the cavalry. Emmett Parker had just locked up his government sedan and was studying the crudely painted sign at the trailhead on Hualapai Hilltop:

ENTERING THE SOVEREIGN NATION OF THE HAVASUPAI

"You Investigator Parker?"

Still silent, Emmett glanced skyward.

The snow was coming down harder than it had in Prescott,

1

where he'd grabbed a late breakfast while having his tires chained up. A soft, wet snow was falling all over northern Arizona. Lowering his gaze, he studied the vehicle tracks, not his own, that showed a U-turn in the slush. Boot prints were evident too, two sets. One was small enough to belong to a juvenile. On the way in along Indian Route 18, he'd noted the passing of only three other vehicles. A power company repair van. Then a Forest Service truck. The female employee driving it looked slight enough to have left the smaller prints. And finally, about ten miles back, a 1981 Ford station wagon with two figures seated up front. Their ages and sex had been obscured by the snowmelt the wagon's tires had thrown against Emmett's windshield.

Turning, he finally examined the Havasupai tribal cop. In his early twenties, the man had a scraggly beard. His straight black hair had been painstakingly coaxed into dreadlocks, and pinned to his khaki uniform shirt was a cameo of Haile Selassie. Pai youth turning to Rastafarianism. Emmett decided not to ask the young cop about it for the moment. He was back on Indian time again: Everything revealed in its own season. "Yeah, I'm Parker."

"Billy Topocoba. Ready for this?"

"Sure," Emmett said, flipping his parka hood up over his own raven-colored hair. He still had it cut boarding-school style—scalp showing through the stubbled sides of his head.

"Any luggage?"

"Just my evidence kit." Emmett slid the battered aluminum case from the car trunk.

Topocoba had tethered a string of two horses and a mule to a piñon pine beside the tumbling cliff that marked the end of the Coconino Plateau and the beginning of the lower Grand Canyon. The abyss was lost in swirling white. He walked a tired-looking gelding over to Emmett, averting his eyes as he offered him the reins. "You some kind of Apache?"

"No, Comanche," Emmett said. He brushed off the saddle before climbing into it.

"Don't recall meetin' a Comanche before."

"Never was many of us. Like you Havasupai, I suppose." Emmett paused, then asked, "You just bring somebody up the trail with you?"

"Nope."

"What about those footprints?"

"Forest Service made a pass-through while I was waitin' for you."

Emmett asked, "He or she?"

"She." That much was the truth.

"She get out of her truck to chat?"

"Yeah." Topocoba shoved Parker's evidence kit into a wicker pannier on the mule. He went on avoiding eye contact, which made Emmett want to check and see if his own horse's girth strap was tightly fastened. It was too early to get paranoid, even though Topocoba was possibly lying: The smaller of the boot-sole sets appeared to begin where the mule and Topocoba's horse were waiting. But, in all fairness, the prints had already melted out enough to confuse the heel and toe impressions; it was difficult to tell which direction the walker had headed.

"Anybody come off the reservation in the last day?"

"Nope." Mounting, the young cop started down the trail, leading the mule on a handwoven rope. Not a store-bought one. A poor people—the Havasupai, the Eastern Pai. Too far from any beaten track to profit from the Indian gambling boom. Emmett saw a blessing in that. His opposition to gaming, the criminal element it often brought into Indian Country, had made him a pariah with several tribal councils. But he remained convinced the boom would one day go bust.

Clucking his tongue to get the gelding going, he followed Topocoba.

3

He always disliked descending into the canyon. The soaring walls and narrow sky made him claustrophobic.

Six miles and two thousand vertical feet below lay tiny Supai, the only real village on the Havasupai Reservation. Maybe the toughest Indian settlement outside Alaska to reach, a nearly impregnable sanctuary for a fugitive as long as he could appease the clannish Pai. A place where the unspeakable could be done with only the cliffs for witnesses.

Emmett's office had arranged to hire a helicopter for him in Williams, but then the storm had swept in a day earlier than expected. Just like mid-December. But secretly Emmett preferred going in on horseback. He had grown up around horses. He missed them, living in the city, missed the freedom of taking a mount out into the sea of grass. His people had been the Mongols of the Southwest plains, measuring wealth and prestige by ponies. The rhythmic sway of haunches and creak of old leather could almost persuade him that this was a journey without something grisly at its end. It hadn't felt like that in his car on the race up State Route 89, the whine of the windshield wipers reminding him of a pathologist's bone saw. The worst part of witnessing a postmortem—the sound that saw made.

The rocks were slick under the slushy snow, and Emmett tried not to think about the plunging cliff that lined the trail. "Who found it?" he asked.

"My cousin."

"How?"

Topocoba twisted around in the saddle to face him. "Misty was lookin' for one of her lambs. And there it was up this cleft. Came home at a dead run. Grandma said she'd caught the spirit sickness and put her to bed right away. . . ." He gave an uncertain smile. Either he doubted such things or wanted Emmett's opinion.

Parker said nothing.

It was too soon to trust a man who, in the closed world of the Pai, claimed to know nothing about the gruesome discovery other than what his cousin had told him. And a man who might be able to lie with no apparent difficulty. "I'd like to talk to Misty."

"Can't," Topocoba said.

"Why not?"

"She's away at the Kotex hut."

Menstrual isolation. Emmett hadn't realized that the Havasupai observed the custom. "So Misty found it yesterday, and you called my office right away."

"I guess."

"Either you called or you didn't."

"I radioed," Topocoba said irritably. "The phone line went in a big rockfall. We got just a shortwave in the village now. Coconino sheriff phoned you for me."

Emmett's receptionist had said nothing about the call being relayed in this way. He glanced up again. The sky had darkened; they'd come down out of the snowfall into a steady rain. It popped against Topocoba's green nylon police jacket. The overcast had gone from a blank white to a curdled gray; the surface of the trail shimmered with rivulets of mud.

Emmett noticed that Topocoba's hands kept flexing on the reins. And the man looked all around each time the trail zigzagged.

"Any strangers come down to Supai lately?" Emmett asked.

"Just the usual."

"What's the usual?"

"Tree huggers. Sierra Clubbers." Then he added cryptically, "Babylon."

But someone or something else had been in the canyon. Perhaps it was still lurking nearby. A presence Topocoba found troubling.

Still, Emmett knew that it was too soon to lean on the man. With each passing day, the challenge expressed on the sign at the trailhead was becoming increasingly strident in Indian Country: Sovereignty was no longer a polite fiction between Washington and the reservations. Self-rule was a political ambition for many of the tribes, especially in regard to gambling. A flashpoint waiting for a spark. Federal and state efforts to curtail gaming were being compared to the slaughter of the buffalo. And recently the Havasupai had sent the BIA's uniformed cops packing, organizing their own tribal police force as another step toward political independence.

A sound was echoing up the canyon walls, a driving beat. Emmett couldn't make sense of it. "What's that?"

Topocoba just chuckled.

The two men rode down onto the unpaved main street of Supai. Now voices could be heard keeping the insistent beat. Bob Marley and the Wailers. The Jamaicans almost drowned out the rattle of rain on the corrugated tin roofs. Here and there, kerosene lamplight shone from windows of the houses, mostly shanties, although there were a few fairly modern ranch-styles, some with generators humming. The Pai cop led Emmett past a pole arbor made of twined sagebrush. Beneath it on a picnic table sat four sullen-faced teenagers. All wore their naturally straight Indian hair in dreadlocks. One was bending forward at the waist, using his chest to shelter a boom box from the rain dripping through the arbor.

Emmett waved. They didn't respond.

"Elders want to see you." Topocoba dismounted in front of a neglected Quonset hut. A sign tacked to it read EVANGELICAL CHURCH OF CHRIST, but felt-penned beneath those faded block letters was:

FUTURE SITE OF GRAND CANYON CASINO
AN ENTERPRISE OF INTER-MOUNTAIN GAMING

A frail boast, considering that the wilderness hikers and rafters who passed through this reservation didn't fit the profile of addicted gamblers.

The front door of the hut was open, but the interior was unlit. Emmett didn't explain to Topocoba that he'd already planned to meet with the elders before barging deeper into their reservation—simple courtesy. He hated sounding defensive. Dropping his parka hood, he flicked the beaded sweat off his hair, then climbed out of the saddle and followed Topocoba through the door.

It was too dim to see much at first, just human silhouettes in a circle.

"This here's Criminal Investigator Parker." The policeman raised his voice slightly. "He's from the BIA." Somebody grunted a soft hello, then Topocoba added to Emmett, "I got other business. Be back soon." He left.

Emmett didn't like having Topocoba out of his sight. He had the feeling that things were being orchestrated behind his back, alibis compared and tailored.

But then, he had etiquette to think about.

He slipped a pack of Havatampa cigars from the pocket of his flannel shirt. He'd bought them at a convenience market near Seligman and now passed them out to the five men seated on folding chairs around a hibachi. Havatampas for the Havasupai. The coals in the brazier were down to a throbbing red, but his eyes had finally adjusted enough to make out the faces turned toward him. Unsmiling. Skin textured like dried apples. At thirty-eight, he suddenly felt extraordinarily young.

A bank of video poker machines was gathering dust against a wall, mutely defying explanation of how they'd gotten down into the canyon. Helicopter?

"Sorry I had to come here," he began slowly, which accentuated his Oklahoma drawl. "I know that if this was Comanche country, I wouldn't want a stranger poking around. . . ." One

7

by one, the old men leaned up to the hibachi and lit their cigars off the coals. Nobody spoke. "But it's my job to get to the bottom of this. To find out the truth. I'll make sure your tribal magistrate knows as much as I do, so we all have an answer. Then I'll move on, so things can be like they were before." Finally, he asked for the very thing federal law said he didn't need from these people: "I'm asking for your permission to do my work here."

Silence.

After this quiet had breathed a little, one of the elders, a white-headed man in a faded U.S. Army Air Corps tunic, motioned for Emmett to sit. The only place left was an overstuffed chair. It stank of feline piss, and in a corner of the hut Emmett saw a bobcat-tabby mix glaring at him, a wild and unapproachable-looking creature.

"You see, Parker," the old man began asthmatically, "I left Supai in the forties for England. . . ." Emmett eased back, reminding himself to be patient, that this was different from listening to whites. Here meaning often hinged on context, not the words themselves. "We flew so high, a fella freezes to death in minutes unless he wears an electric suit. Hamburg. Cologne. Berlin. Bombed 'em all. Flak bursts like thunderclouds. But it must've been hell for those poor people on the ground. . . ." Disturbance. The old man was talking about disturbance and violence. But he might well be referring to the present. "Still, when I got home in 'forty-five, nothin' had changed. Nothin' at all. Not even me. I put on my peace clothes and went back to tendin' my daddy's garden plot and flock just like the war'd never been." He shook his head sourly. "So it ain't us goin' out into the world that brings change. It's the things from outside what blow down the trail to us. . . ." For a second Emmett thought the old man was talking about him, the federal presence, but then the elder lowered his voice. "And this latest wind, it's worse than the Jesus Road—" Christianity, he meant.

Emmett was waiting for him to go on, when he realized Topocoba had come back.

The tribal cop stood in the doorframe, wearing a black slicker and holding a spare one under his arm. "Storm's gettin' worse, Parker," he said. "If we go, we've got to do it now."

Emmett looked to the elders, and they in turn deferred to the old airman.

"Go on, Parker," he said. "We welcome you." Yet, there was a cautionary glint in his eye.

"Thank you," Emmett said. His face betrayed nothing, but he'd been surprised by the unease that had passed through the old men with Topocoba's return. He was left with the feeling that they would cooperate if eventually they found him worthy. They'd make sure he understood what had happened here. For that reason alone, he'd use a light touch, pressure no one unless pressured first. He wanted to interview Topocoba's cousin Misty but would wait for a second trip, when her monthly was over. Besides, his own grandfather, if still alive, would warn him against contact with any female in menses. It'd weaken his *puha*, or personal power, and Emmett had an inkling he'd need a great deal of that in the coming days.

Outside again, he realized how full of cigar smoke the windowless hut had become. The air was sweet. The reggae music had stopped, and the picnic table was deserted. The four teenagers had vanished.

The dull gray glow of the sun through the clouds was quickly fading. Topocoba tossed Emmett the slicker, and he put it on. The rain was coming down at a brisk slant. Handing Emmett a big-cell flashlight, the cop said, "You'll need this when you go up."

So Topocoba didn't intend to go up into the cleft himself?

Emmett switched his beam on first, casually passed it over one of Topocoba's boot-sole prints. An aggressive diamond pattern. In addition to eliminating the cop's tracks at the crime scene, Emmett wanted to check where the man had ventured. And hadn't.

They set off down the canyon, their lights flitting along the muddy trail. The shanties, peach orchards, and fallow garden plots of Supai were soon left behind, and they threaded through a maze of willows and cottonwoods. The leafless branches seemed to be clawing at the darkening sky. Topocoba broke his horse into a canter, and Emmett dug in his heels to keep up. Havasu Creek, a brilliant turquoise in daylight, was glowing as if its waters were radioactive. It was a trick of the evening light playing on the mineralized streambed, but Emmett felt as if the entire canyon had been poisoned by what Misty had found. Or by the secret somebody on this reservation was keeping, the killer someone might yet be hiding. Could this grotesque thing have gone past the front doors of Supai with no one noticing? Not likely. But Emmett asked, "Any chance of making it up this creek from the Colorado, Billy?"

"Nope. Havasu Canyon's impassable below Mooney Falls. Flash flood buried the old trail to Kaibab."

Somebody knew the whole story. This man, most probably. Ultimately, Emmett would have to tangle with Topocoba. But let the fray come with the support of the tribal leadership, or nothing would be gained. And lately he found himself turning more cautious than he'd ever been as an investigator. He didn't want to be the spark to ignite Indian Country into the conflagration that had lain low, smoldering, since Wounded Knee in the 1970s. Still, there was no harm in getting Topocoba talking. "What'd be worse than the Jesus Road to your elders?" Emmett asked.

Topocoba drew rein, wiped off the rainwater that had collected on his chin. "Old farts," he said.

"You a Rastaman, Billy?"

"Yep," Topocoba said, starting down the trail again. Off to the left, Navajo Falls foamed luminescently through the darkness. Emmett kept pace, although his horse was less inclined to trot than Topocoba's. "What're you, Parker?"

Emmett had to think a second. "Catholic." At least, he'd once been one. Most Indians were Christians, not the mystical traditionalists whites imagined them to be, spouting lines that sounded suspiciously like Greenpeace dogma.

"Not a peyote eater?"

"No."

"I heard you Comanches are into that big."

"Some, not all." His brother had joined the Native American Church, but legal peyotism, like everything else, failed him in his fight with alcohol. Emmett supposed that he believed in a supreme being, although the Old Man had no doubt pulled out his hearing aid by this late date in human history. "You been to Jamaica, Billy?"

Topocoba shook his head.

"Then how'd you become a Rastaman?"

"Our God, Ras Tafari, sent Bob Marley down the trail to us."

"The reggae singer?" Emmett asked doubtfully.

"Yep. He was tourin' Babylon, and the Lion of Judah drew him here."

Before leaving Phoenix, Emmett had booted up some background on the Rastafarians on the Internet link in the office, just to be ready for this new phenomenon among the Pai. Babylon was how believers referred to Jamaica and, in a broader sense, the white world to which blacks had been exiled by slavery.

"What'd Marley have to say?" Emmett prodded.

"Get ready for the repatriation."

Emmett pretended not to know. "Where?"

"Ethiopia."

"We're not Ethiopians, least not in a couple million years."

"No, no," Topocoba said with vague contempt, "that ain't how it'll happen. Babylon's goin' to be destroyed by nukes and

11

toxic waste. Then all the black Rastas will go back to Ethiopia, and us Indian Rastas'll have the wilderness in the West to ourselves, just like the old days. Get it?"

"Got it." Classic millenarian movement. Unshakable belief in a cataclysmic transition to a golden age with no more poverty and oppression. The last big one to sweep through Indian Country had been the Ghost Dance of the 1890s. That had promised whitey would vanish down a big crack in the world. From the same miraculous rift would spring all the buffalo and deer of the past, all the departed ancestors cut down by war and disease. "When's this coming?"

"Soon."

"If you say."

Topocoba's shoulders stiffened a little. "Don't you want to see them get theirs?"

Emmett didn't answer. The Comanche had punished the whites enough for him not to feel much lingering resentment. "You married?"

"Three years, two kids."

"What's your wife think of this?"

"She's Kaibab," he said as if the fact that she was Southern Paiute from the other side of the Colorado explained everything. A skeptical people, the Kaibab. Like the Comanche, who'd never thought much of the Ghost Dance.

Emmett smiled to himself.

"This is it." The cleft, Topocoba meant. They were a few hundred yards below Havasu Falls, their low thunder backdropping the rustling of the rain.

They halted, but the young cop remained in the saddle, his face turned away.

"You coming?" Emmett asked.

Topocoba shrugged.

"Rasta believe in the sickness?"

"No."

"Can't catch what you don't believe in."

"Maybe."

Still, Emmett could see that the man had no intention of climbing into the crevice that snaked up into a spur of Sinyala Mesa. All at once Topocoba seemed less ambivalent about spirit sickness than before. Maybe he now figured that if his cousin could catch it from a troubled ghost, so could he. Emmett had no such worry. His own spirit was already sick and would remain so until he was forced to retire from this unhealthy line of work. Spirit sickness had become a way of life, manageable now that he'd quit drinking.

Yet there was something odd about the cop's reaction. He was inferring a belief in spiritual contamination without giving off any apparent fear.

"Okay, you stay with the stock," Emmett told Topocoba, who didn't argue.

Emmett dismounted, grabbed his evidence kit, and continued alone up into the steeply walled defile.

The storm had obliterated any prints, including Misty's, but this did nothing to dispel the sense that this thing had just happened. Most often, the aura of a crime quickly dissipated, along with the value of its evidence. But here there was still a strong sense of immediacy.

His breaths echoed off the walls around him. The needles of rain stopped streaking through his beam. He was being shielded by an undercut cliff, a black awning against the woolly sky.

The smell found him. Deceptively sweet at first, like wilted flowers, then ghastly. Unmistakable.

Topocoba's voice reverberated up from below. "Find it?"

"Getting close." Emmett almost retched. Very close. He began finding tracks in the protection of the overhang. Coyote. And then the girl's, headed downhill, widely spaced. She'd been running frantically at this point. At last, he was standing over the spot, a depression in the sandy floor of a narrow cave. The top of a human head was showing. A Havasupai grave, perhaps. Except that the Pai had cremated their dead with all their worldly goods. Before the missionaries, in an effort to ease their poverty, forced them to inter bodies in Christian cemeteries without possessions. And except that the hank of hair jutting through the sand was strawberry-blond.

He photographed the scene from several angles, the flashes reflecting in blinding dazzles off the rock face.

Then, returning his camera to the evidence kit, he positioned the flashlight on the ground so that the beam shone against the back of the buried head.

Steeling himself with a shallow breath, he started digging with his fingers.

The hair was long and fine, the neck thin and shapely. On one side of the throat was an elliptical bruise left by a thumb. On the other, the stripes of four fingers.

"You okay?" Topocoba called from below.

Emmett didn't answer.

He'd just found the apparent cause of death. A knife wound at the base of the skull.

The meter was running. He had a homicide.

"Parker . . . ?"

With the flashlight beam Emmett raked the ground surrounding the corpse. Only the small boot impressions left by Topocoba's cousin showed in the oblique light. The cop himself had not come up here. Why? Fear of spirit sickness? Or had he had no reason to make the climb, knowing full well what lay partially buried beneath the overhang?

Emmett shifted around and began uncovering the face.

The sand was heavy with congealed body fluids, and the smell made his eyes burn. Factoring in the dry, cool air in the shaded bottom of the cleft, he guesstimated that decomposition was only about two weeks along.

He suddenly froze.

The face wasn't there. It hadn't been chewed off by the coyotes, as he might have expected. It'd been sliced away in a jagged oval that showed numerous starts and stops of blade strokes.

"Jesus," he hissed.

The woman might have been flayed alive, twisting and turning in the murderer's powerful grasp, trying to avoid the agony of the knife. The spinal cord had been severed as an afterthought. The dusty, lidless eyes stared up at him, beseechingly: *Help me . . . don't let me start down the trail of death alone . . . give me the comfort of your company. . . .* The eyeballs were the same smoky color as the moon in total eclipse. The pathologists called it *tache noire*, dark staining caused by exposure to the air, especially dry air. Usually, it was limited to thin strips of the eyes not covered by the lids. In this case there were no lids. She had gone unburied several hours, if not days, before arriving here.

The teeth had been smashed out. All gone.

He switched off the light, gathered himself a moment in the darkness. Nobody came down the trail to Supai without clearing it through the tribal tourism office. Invitation only. Had a Pai murdered a guest? If that was it, the case would be quickly closed. And by the FBI, which investigated most felonies on federal trust lands. Emmett had escaped being accompanied by the resident agent in Flagstaff today only because the man had taken his wife on a cruise to Acapulco.

He flicked the light back on and took a gardener's trowel from his evidence kit before continuing to dig.

She'd died in a blue dress. Tight-fitting, even given the effects of putrefaction. Nothing anyone would wear to ride a mule down into the canyon. The corpse had been left sitting in the fetal position, and propped over the knees were the chalky-looking hands. The last joint of each finger had been snipped off. On what remained of the third finger of the left hand was a paler band of skin that had been kept from the sun by a ring.

One thing was for sure.

Her killer had wanted her to go nameless, at least for the

time being. But destruction of teeth and fingerprints would only delay identification. The killer had also left a contradiction behind. Flaying was a distinct message, yet the messenger had been buried on the back side of nowhere.

Emmett went on digging.

Chapter 2

The Southwest Airlines flight from Phoenix arrived five minutes ahead of schedule.

Fortunately, Anna Turnipseed had given herself a little extra time to cross town from the FBI building on Charleston Boulevard to McCarran International Airport. The Strip was jammed by the five o'clock shift change at the casinos, plus the Christmas Eve shoppers darting from mall to mall. And all the locals knew the alternate streets that ran down the east side of the big hotels. Anna found a space on her third spin through the parking garage, then sprinted for the elevator to the terminal, her handbag banging against her hip from the weight of her 9mm pistol and handcuffs.

Most of the passengers had already disembarked by the

time she reached the gate. But the BIA man must have been sitting near the tail of the jet. He was bigger than any Comanche she'd ever seen, well over six feet and thick-chested, with a deceptively languid stride, for within ten paces he passed a dozen tourists impatient for the slots. "Investigator Parker . . . ?"

"Yeah." He offered her a smile, appealing but swiftly gone. "Special Agent Turnipseed?"

"Anna . . . yes."

They shook, and she tried to put as much force as she could into it. Still, her small hand was lost in his.

"Luggage?"

"Just this carry-on." They started walking, and she almost had to jog to keep up. The silence went on a moment, another moment. Parker seemed distracted all the time they strode toward the parking garage, and she thought that he'd already forgotten about her, when *the question* came with the predictability of an exchange of astrological signs in a singles bar. "What tribe are you, Anna?"

"Modoc. I mean, my father was Modoc. Mother's half Modoc, half Japanese." She was babbling. Unusual for her. And her heart was trip-hammering. She didn't even run this fast on the weekends along the dirt road behind her condominium.

"How'd that happen?" he asked as they boarded the elevator.

"What happen?"

"A Japanese get in the woodpile."

"Oh, there was an internment camp up our way during the Second World War. Grandma worked in the sugar beet fields with one of the internees. Fell in love, though he split after the war. . . ." Enough, she told herself. He was just asking for the *Reader's Digest* version. "And you're Comanche, right?"

"So Mama told me."

That explained the middle initial of "Q" he used when signing his rather terse reports. Quanah Parker, the half-breed

Comanche chief and son of a white female captive who'd helped his tribe keep west Texas perilous for settlement for more than a quarter century. So Emmett Parker was at least part Caucasian, however distantly. She herself was reminded of her ambiguous ancestry every time she went into Indian Country and flashed her credentials: "Well, honey, I'm FBI too—Full-Blooded Indian." A mixed blood was called an apple, red on the outside, white on the inside.

The elevator doors slid back for them. Through the open side of the garage, the lights could be seen bumping on along the Strip. They blotted out the last band of day shining behind Charleston Peak. She struggled to think of something pertinent to say. Nothing came to mind.

"You got a hard copy of the PCR results?" Parker abruptly asked. Polymers chain reaction—a DNA test.

"In my car. You mind if we slow down?"

He dropped his pace a click, and she began catching her breath for the first time since leaving the gate. "Sorry," he said, smiling again, "I just want to get on with this." But by the time they'd reached the row in which she'd parked, he was in full stride once more. "What happened to the victim's government vehicle?"

"Still missing."

"What was it?"

"Blue Dodge, two years old."

"Definitely didn't take her personal car?"

"No, her husband still has their Audi."

Parker said, "So it doesn't look like she was abducted from town here."

"Doubtful."

"And what were the traces of 'sodium borate compound' the lab found inside her shoes and in her clothes?"

"Borax."

"Not consistent with that sample of Havasupai sand I sent in?"

"I don't believe so. Was it milk white?"

"No, yellowish," he replied, "like decomposed granite."

She opened his door for him, got in herself, then reached into the backseat for her attaché case. A trophy from Quantico—number one in academics of all her academy class. If only it hadn't been just eight months ago. She was what was called a "first-office" agent, bureau-speak for rookie. Still, Parker had yet to let her know that he'd be calling the shots. Not that he hadn't reminded other FBI agents of the Las Vegas field office that he'd already been a veteran of Oklahoma City P.D. Homicide when they'd been squeezing zits, that with a dual bachelor's degree in criminology and anthropology he was indispensable to any investigation in Indian Country. She didn't want to tell him that hers was from Berkeley in sociology with an accounting minor.

"And what the devil was that dead bug they found hung up in her dress?"

She blanked on the Latin genus and species. "Um, some kind of saltwater mosquito."

"Havasu Creek must be more than three hundred miles from the Gulf of California."

"*Saline* mosquito is a more accurate term, according to the forensic entomologist. It's endemic to seasonal alkaline marshes around playas here in the Southwest."

"Still," Parker said, "no salt lakes on the Pai rez I know of."

Anna paused, then ventured to add, "Maybe she didn't die anywhere near the burial pit."

"That's a safe bet. Especially with her eyes darkened by *tache noire*."

"Safe bet," she echoed. She'd caught his insinuation that it wasn't an inspired guess either.

This wasn't going to be easy.

For some unfathomable reason, the U.S. Attorney in town had designated BIA the lead investigative agency in this hurriedly assembled task force of two. Anna's boss, Burk Hagiman, said that the director of Indian Affairs had probably gone to the secretary of the interior, sniveling that they were always sucking hind teat to the FBI. Burk had also warned her to keep an eye on Parker: He had the disagreeable habit of forgetting which side he was on.

She gave Emmett the report, then merged into the bumper-to-bumper line of cars headed for Tropicana Avenue. "Want to grab a bite?"

"No," he said remotely, riffling through the pages. "Let's go out to Henderson . . . talk to the husband."

Her blood sugar sank further. She hadn't eaten since breakfast. Just a granola bar.

"Christ almighty," he muttered. "Ten days to get this—while I've been sitting on my hands in Phoenix."

"Week and a half is pretty quick for a DNA test, especially on hair."

"And an eternity for every Pai on the reservation to figure out where he *wasn't* when the body was dumped."

She let the argument slide, tried to sound constructive. "You think somebody in Supai was in on it?"

He looked up at her, stared inquisitively. She had no idea what he was thinking. "You hungry?" he finally asked, glancing away.

"Famished."

"Mind takeout?"

"I guess not."

"Either you do or you don't, Turnipseed."

"How's that?"

"Everybody who works with me speaks his *or* her damned mind. You up to that?"

At first she was stung. He didn't like her. He was going to ask her boss for another agent, and this would be held against her. But then her anger flared, almost uncontrollably, after all these months of subordination and conformity. She'd grown up free in the juniper hills and lava flows of Modoc County; she didn't like being hemmed in by expansive male egos. Burk Hagiman's was bad enough. Now some churlish Comanche warrior.

To hell with him.

She swerved sharply into a Burger King. Parker had to brace himself against the dashboard.

"What do you want?" she demanded, rolling up to the speaker.

"Coffee. Black. And maybe one of them Whoppers with bacon."

"Either you do or you don't, Parker."

He glared at her a moment, then laughed under his breath. It was a nice laugh, warm and easy. Yet, as soon as it died, he looked like somebody who could keep west Texas on edge. And infiltrate a radical offshoot of the American Indian Movement his first months as a BIA agent, going so far to preserve his cover as to endure the agonizing Sun Dance, suspended on tethers attached to his chest with bone skewers. Burk had mentioned that part of the Emmett Parker legend too—with obvious distrust of the Comanche's motives in taking part in the ceremony.

Stretching and yawning, Parker now said, "You must be kin to at least one of my ex-wives, Turnipseed."

"Not a chance."

But his mind had shifted back to the autopsy report. "And just a couple of petechial hemorrhages," he mused aloud.

Tiny blood clots in the victim's oral mucosa just beneath the gum line. Presumptive evidence of strangulation. "That's right."

He added nothing more.

Twenty minutes later they were sitting in a Henderson living room that made her feel very Indian. White drapes and plush, cream-colored carpeting. A Hummel doll collection in the maple hutch. Stephanie Roper's widower sat opposite them on a love seat, his pupils dilated. There was an unnatural airiness about the prim man in the Irish knit sweater, as if at any moment he might suddenly levitate above the quilted cushions and float around the room, laughing hysterically.

Anna suspected the influence of some designer drug.

A Christmas tree twinkled behind Roper's frizzy, graying head, and through the bay window she could see the black pyramid of the Luxor Hotel in the distance. An Egyptian tomb with rooms to let. She scolded herself: Her mind was wandering. Long day. Too much detail work, the victim's expense reports and receipts, too many reminders that she was digging into the irrevocable past of a fellow federal employee, a woman only five years older than herself. One particular find had gotten her down, a wrapped gift in the closet. Burk had approved her opening it. A coffee-table book: *Our Nation's Capital from the Air*. The inscription was in Stephanie Roper's flamboyant and now familiar script:

> *To Daddy,*
> *Keep me in line and we'll wind*
> *up here.*
>
> > *Happy Holidays,*
> > *Babe*

"We appreciate you seeing us, Mr. Roper," Parker said with vague impatience, "it being Christmas Eve and all."

"Please call me Teddy," he said as if nobody ever called him that, even though it was his fondest wish.

"Sure, Teddy." Ignoring the man's obvious drug intoxication, Parker had made Theodore Roper as comfortable as the man was going to get, having been informed just last night that his wife's savagely mutilated corpse had been identified using hair taken off the neck rest of her office chair. "I'm new to this case," Parker fibbed. "What exactly did Stephanie do for the Bureau of Land Management here?"

23

"Well," Roper began tentatively, "she's the special lands staff officer for the western region."

Present tense. Emmett ignored his lapse into denial. "The *entire* western region?"

"That's right," Roper answered, unable to conceal an uneasy pride. Still, Anna mused, a government service pay grade of even twelve or thirteen couldn't entirely account for this house, which backed onto a fairway of Henderson's Black Mountain Country Club.

Obviously, Emmett was thinking the same thing. "And what do you do?"

"Musician. Marimba, percussion."

"That must keep you busy."

"Not really. I helped organize the strike a couple of years ago, so I'm still being punished by the big hotels. I get a gig now and again, but mostly down in the Indian clubs in California and Arizona."

"I see," Parker said. "What does a lands staff officer do?"

Roper hesitated.

Anna could tell by the stillness that came over Parker's face that he'd been maneuvering the man toward such a reaction. Parker knew exactly what Stephanie Roper had done for a living.

"Well," Roper finally said, "I'm not real up on it, Emmett, but I know this much. You can't just write a check for public land you may want. However, you can swap another piece of property for it. So Babe is"—he caught himself with an embarrassed chuckle—"Stephanie's kind of a broker for the government. She processes land trades. Developers buy private real estate next to national parks and wildlife refuges and such. You know, land the government would like to set aside for posterity but doesn't have the cash to buy. Then the developers trade these parcels for the federal lands they want to build on."

"Does Stephanie give the final approval on a swap?"

"Mostly. Unless it's a really big exchange. Then it gets sent up to Washington. But they usually follow her recommendations."

"Sounds like a pressure cooker."

"Oh, it is." Roper nodded. "People are always after her."

"In what way?"

"You know."

"I'm afraid I don't." Parker's expression had hardened.

"It's a pressure cooker," Roper said weakly. "Like you just said."

"Were any particular folks strong-arming her?"

Roper looked completely flustered now.

Anna was sure Parker was going to zero in for the kill, but instead he changed the subject. "What'd you do when your wife didn't come home that Wednesday afternoon before Thanksgiving?" He looked to Anna. "What, the twenty-sixth?"

She nodded.

"Nothing at first," Roper said. "I had no idea."

"Is she late often?"

"Oh, yes. Her work keeps her lots of times, and she can't always call."

"When'd you get concerned?"

"Elevenish. I phoned Eunice, her secretary, and she said she didn't know of anything special Stephanie was on. Said everybody left the office at noon, including her."

"Anybody see your wife actually drive away?" Parker asked.

"I . . . I don't know."

"That's okay, Teddy. What happened then?"

"Eunice told me to phone the Henderson Police Department and file a missing persons report right away."

"Henderson P.D. contacted us two days later, due to the possible sensitivity of Ms. Roper's position," Anna interjected.

She felt the need—before Parker established a pattern of complete dominance over the investigation, something Burk Hagiman would never permit.

Parker gave her a cool smile, then turned back to Roper. "I hate bringing up something like this, Teddy, but was there any difficulty in your marriage we should be aware of?"

"Absolutely not," the man said hollowly, then chuckled again. "I mean, I know Stephanie's an extremely attractive woman, and I'm sixteen years older'n her. But no. No difficulty."

Anna asked, "Did she ever say how far up she wanted to advance in BLM?"

"Oh, yes," Roper said, solemnly now. "Babe wanted to go all the way to the top. Washington headquarters." He tried to smile but couldn't pull it off. As if it'd finally struck him that she was gone. "We'd live on a little farm across the river in Virginia, and I'd play at Wolf Trap summer evenings. . . ." He laughed quietly at the notion. "Like I'm a Juilliard grad or something. Not a broken-down cabaret musician."

"Do you know where her wedding ring is?" Parker asked.

Visibly, Roper came back to the present. "Why, no. I was hoping you people found it."

Anna started to respond, when Parker came to his feet. "That's all for now, Teddy. We'll keep you informed."

A beat late, she rose too. "Here's my card, in case you have any questions."

"Thanks," Roper said, accepting it.

At the door she shook hands with him again, realizing for the second time that her fingers were sticky from the ketchup off the fries. Parker was studying the wedding portrait of the Ropers on the foyer wall. She knew what he was doing—adhering the striking-looking woman's smiling face to the half-flayed skull she herself had examined nine days before and dreamed of every night since. While Anna was working, the horrific was manageable. Only at night did it threaten to overwhelm her. Only then did that initial shock return, convincing her that somehow it could have just as easily been Anna Turnipseed on that autopsy table. That one day she would wind up on that porcelain tray. The psychologist at the academy had warned her entire class: *Sooner than later you'll come face-to-face with a sense of your own mortality. A shocking sense born of intimate contact with death. And the first casualty of that intimacy will be the comforting illusion that a safe and long life is a given.*

"Take care, Teddy," Parker said.

They returned to her sedan in silence. Anna was relieved to be away from the fragile, rattled widower. "Drop you off at your hotel?" she asked Parker, speeding up Boulder Highway toward Las Vegas.

"No, BLM headquarters. Got a liaison?"

"Their head investigator."

"Name?"

"Washburn."

"Okay, let's phone Washburn and get inside."

"I'm already going through Roper's files."

"Then let's finish them." Parker reached down, fished a cold French fry out of her discarded packet. It was almost to his mouth, when he paused, his eyes fixed on some point far down the darkened highway.

"What's wrong?" she asked.

"I don't like it when it's too easy too quick," he said.

"What makes you think it is?"

Turnipseed had been right.

As the Bureau of Land Management dick, disgruntled at being called away from hearth and eggnog, unlocked and flung open the door to Stephanie Roper's office, Emmett nearly groaned. Almost every square inch of desktop and floor space was covered with folders. "There's more in basement storage," Turnipseed said, threading her way inside to the small leather sofa, where she sat wearily. "But all these are pending approval, so I decided they deserve first look."

"Well, I'm going to shove off." Washburn seemed delighted to dump the mess on the BIA and FBI. "You still have the alarm code?" To get out the doors without bringing Las Vegas Metro on the run with guns drawn.

"Yes." Emmett sank into the chair behind the desk.

Frowning, Washburn said, "I didn't see you write it down."

Emmett recited the nine digits back to him.

Washburn hid his surprise with a shrug, then turned and went down the hall, whistling "White Christmas."

"How'd you do that?" Turnipseed asked.

She was small but shapely, with an oval face that was all eyes. Big, liquid eyes with just a hint of the Asian to them, although she looked more Latina than anything else. Emmett was drawn, which irked him. With three divorces under his belt, he was ready to become a law enforcement monk, one of those middle-aged workaholics who'd start looking again just before retirement. No Indian women. His last wife, a Kiowa, had put him off them for good. And no soul mates. Some uncomplicated companionship would do. "How'd I do what?" he asked, annoyed.

"Memorize the code like that."

"Didn't learn to read till I was eight."

"So . . . ?"

Yawning, Emmett said, "If you don't see words in writing, you can play them back inside your head. I just played Washburn's voice back. Jesus, don't you know anything about your own oral tradition?"

She bit her bottom lip, then said, "There's something I didn't want to mention in front of Mr. Roper."

"What?"

"Take a peek inside the pencil drawer."

He slid it open and brought out Stephanie Roper's gold

wedding band. "Well, that raises an interesting possibility, doesn't it?"

Turnipseed didn't reply.

Was it now sexist to suggest that women were as capable of infidelity as men?

Sighing, Emmett dropped the ring back in the drawer and at random opened the closest file. The thick application was from the North Las Vegas Water District, seeking to trade a patented mining claim they'd acquired inside Great Basin National Park for an aqueduct right-of-way from Lee Canyon to their overgrown suburb. Water. Reason enough to kill for in a dry land. But he had the numbing sense that each of these folders contained a reason for murdering Stephanie Roper. Personal fortunes and the prosperity of entire cities had depended on her decisions.

Turnipseed was watching him. "How can I help?"

Whatever intuition she had was untested by experience. Useless, then. But he forced himself to start somewhere with her. "Roper's secretary, Eunice . . ."

"Gone back East for the holidays. She'll call me as soon as she returns. Unless you want one of our Boston agents to interview her?"

"No, we can wait for the time being." Emmett paused. "How about you?"

"Pardon?"

"Don't you have to be somewhere for the holidays?"

She shook her head.

"No family?"

"Mother. But she wouldn't know me if she saw me. Rest home in Alturas."

"Where's that?"

"Northeast California."

"Oh, yeah, Modoc Nation."

"I don't think a couple of rancherias make a nation."

In his mind's eye he again saw the sign at the trailhead:

ENTERING THE SOVEREIGN NATION OF THE HAVASUPAI. They were no more numerous than the Modoc, but the Pai were certainly flexing their political muscle. Organizing a tribal police force. They weren't alone. In states like California, where federal law gave criminal jurisdiction to the county sheriffs, some reservations were insisting on policing themselves. But it was bigger than justice issues. A confederation was quietly taking shape, uniting the 550 tribes throughout the country in a way they'd never been unified before. Gaming had done it.

"Whatever, Turnipseed—tribe, nation." Emmett heaved himself up out of the chair and went to the window, raised the blinds. Immediately, he wished he hadn't. The city was on fire with jarring neon. He didn't like a place that refused to get dark at night, that resisted silence and introspection. How often had Stephanie Roper stood in this very spot, gazing out? Thinking what? Long ago Emmett had believed that the dead could speak to the living, that their spirits could be summoned by merely uttering their names. He no longer believed such things. If anyone, he was worthy of communion with the murdered dead. He was out to avenge them, to see that they rested easy. But Stephanie Roper would never appear to him, tell him where in the desert Southwest she'd been knifed to death. It hadn't been in that shallow cave above Havasu Creek. Emmett had known that as soon as he'd fully excavated the corpse and seen the pattern of postmortem lividity. The purplish mottling of flesh left by blood pooling in the lowest portions of a body at rest. Although barely visible due to decomposition, most of Roper's discoloration had been to her back. She'd been executed, then dumped in the trunk of a car for a long final ride to the Coconino Rim.

But how had she gotten past Supai?

The bringing of a murder victim onto the reservation would have been perceived as a virulent spiritual contagion affecting the well-being of the entire tribe. It would have been resisted. But the thing the white-haired elder had compared to

the Jesus Road had not been Roper's corpse. Emmett was almost sure of it. The old man had been referring to something
that still stalked the reservation. Something that could come
down the trail to Supai at will.

Turnipseed's voice brought him back to the room. "Roper
was on the take, right?"

"Maybe."

"Is that what you found easy . . . the intimation of corruption here?"

Turning toward her, he held down a smile. *Intimation of
corruption.* How old was she? No more than twenty-five. She
seemed smarter and surer of herself than most rookie agents.
But he reminded himself that she was a neophyte. It was his
duty to test her, see if she could withstand pressures from
within the system before outside pressures cost her her life.
And, of course, she was FBI. He'd withhold his approval to
keep her in check when the inevitable squabbles began. Why'd
the U.S. Attorney always insist on marrying the FBI to the
BIA? Of course, the law gave the FBI jurisdictional edge, but
Emmett had more practical homicide experience than the
whole Las Vegas FBI office combined. He didn't believe that
he had an unreasonable hatred for the agency; he'd even at-
tended its national academy for allied law enforcement personnel. Maybe it was Catholic boarding school that had left him
with little tolerance for authoritarian bureaucracies. He quietly
explained, "I don't want to call in the IRS auditors yet. That'll
only force Ted Roper to circle the wagons, destroy evidence,
and get himself an attorney to protect the assets Stephanie left
him."

Turnipseed stifled a yawn.

"Go home, lady, I can manage by myself."

"No, I'll help." She sat straighter. "Tell me how."

"We've got to find the application that shouts at us. It'll be
distinctive for some reason. Have Roper's attention written all
over it. That's where we begin." He could see her racking her

brain, but then she frowned as she scooped several folders up off the floor.

Emmett returned to the desk.

By three that morning they had found nothing distinctive. "Enough for tonight," he admitted.

He had her drop him off at Circus Circus, one of the few hotels in town with a rate still within the government per diem. He'd been asleep less than an hour, when the phone rang. Groping, he knocked it off the nightstand with his first grab, and finally had to turn on the light to find it. "What?"

It was Turnipseed. "I forgot something."

Chapter 3

Emmett was waiting in front of the hotel when Turnipseed pulled up. The blaze of casino signs made it impossible to tell if dawn had broken. "How far out there?" he asked, getting inside her sedan.

"Less than a hundred miles."

He'd told himself that the rookie would seem less pretty on second sight. He stole a glance at her, then almost winced from a growing sense of weakness. She was no less attractive.

They dropped by BLM headquarters again, waited ten minutes for Washburn. The investigator arrived in the family van, unshaven and out of sorts, but let them inside Roper's office once more. Turnipseed scooped up a file labeled DEATH VALLEY CHEMEHUEVI RANCHERIA and then the gasoline and motel receipts that had made her suddenly think of the land exchange application. It'd been made by a tribe based in Halloran Springs, California. Stephanie Roper had gotten gasoline at the Chevron station in Halloran Springs several times before her disappearance. And for two nights in early November she'd stayed at a motel in Baker, thirteen miles west along the interstate. Only an hour and a half's drive from her home in Henderson. Emmett found that peculiar, although in keeping with her having left her wedding ring in her office.

"Got everything we need," Turnipseed said, but then nearly swore when they reached the security console downstairs. The BLM investigator had already left.

Emmett punched in the code, resetting the alarm.

"That's witchcraft," she said.

"You can do it too." He opened the door for her. "Just stop letting the written word clutter up your mind."

"Blame the Head Start program. I started reading when I was four."

"Rotten federal government," he said.

She swiftly negotiated the freeways through town, and within minutes they had left the last cluster of casinos behind, the Disneyland-like amusement hotels along the south Strip. The freeway climbed toward the state border. Darkened sagelands enveloped the car. Still, no hint of sunrise along the ranges in the east.

"I don't see what makes you think there's a connection," Emmett said, beginning to think he'd been dragged out of bed for nothing.

"Twenty-Mule Team," Turnipseed replied sleepily. "What Grandma used to scrub the soles of my feet with in summer."

"Grandma did what?"

"My feet used to get stained from the red volcanic ash in our country. She used borax on them. Borax is mined around Death Valley, isn't it? And Roper's clothes had traces of sodium borate compound in them."

Emmett resisted giving her an approving nod. So she was bright. Like his second wife, a Kiowa-Apache and math professor at his alma mater, Oklahoma State, who'd tried to introduce structure into their chronic marital strife, even though booze and parliamentary procedure didn't mix. The Kiowa-Apache were skillful persuaders. Ethnically Apache, they'd managed to convince the Kiowa that they, too, were Kiowa and should share their lands. She'd come close to convincing Emmett that he was wrong about most everything. But she'd been petite and good-looking, like Turnipseed.

All this brought to mind another obviously difficult woman. "Stephanie Roper wasn't liked much around the office, was she?"

Turnipseed sat up. "Why do you say that?"

"Nobody expressed any regrets when I phoned from Phoenix."

She passed a lumbering big rig. "Sour grapes," she said over the sound of the diesel engine hammering through the window.

"Really."

"She got promoted over the rest of the lands staff."

"Mostly male?" Emmett asked.

"So what?"

"You're telling me the consent decree didn't help grease her way up?" A court order to promote females.

"Yes." Turnipseed veered back into the right lane. "Prior to going federal, Stephanie was a licensed real estate broker. A good one, according to her former boss. She just knew the turf better than the rest of the pack at BLM."

Emmett gazed eastward. The horizon was beginning to brighten. "Well, she still had one possible use for men."

"What do you mean?"

"You don't stay in a motel ninety minutes from home to catch up on your reading. Any chance Roper's secretary knew she was having an affair?"

"I don't know."

"Put it on your list."

"Shouldn't we be looking harder at Teddy Roper?"

Emmett grunted as he imagined the musician trying to get his wife's body down into the lower Grand Canyon, asking the Pai if there were any snakes along the creek. But he asked, "Why would he do it? Jealousy?"

"Possibly."

"I doubt it. He made his peace with Stephanie's ambitions long ago. It beat working. What about life insurance?"

"Just fifty thousand through payroll deduction," Turnipseed said. "About ten grand less than what she made a year."

"There you have it. I'm sure Teddy's got an ironclad alibi for the entire time frame of Stephanie's disappearance."

"What if he contracted the killing?"

Emmett shrugged. It just didn't fit the man. Any more than Theodore Roper doing it himself. This killer was skilled at his brutal craft. That came from practice. If Roper, a longtime resident of Las Vegas, was responsible, this M.O. would now be a familiar one in the Southwest. No, the killer was an interloper in the region.

A few miles into California, Emmett took over the driving.

Turnipseed's eyes had narrowed to glazed slits, and she'd been gripping the steering wheel too tightly. She immediately curled up on the passenger side of the front seat, legs folded beneath her, and dozed off. Her face looked very Modoc in repose, sleek and symmetrical. A handsome people. And tough. Fifty braves, with their women and children, had fended off three thousand U.S. soldiers for five months from 1872 to 1873. Yet less than a quarter century passed between the Modoc's first encounter with the wagon trains trespassing over their lands and the tribe's total subjugation. Unlike the experience of the Comanche, who'd had two centuries to carefully observe European civilization and even exploit its riches. So the Modoc had been caught in an arrested state of culture shock. That might translate from the culture to the individual, especially the female individual, as a monumental hardheadedness.

Emmett found himself wide-awake. And tempted to steal another look at her.

It mystified him, this sudden and obsessive attraction some women produced in him. It had led to three disastrous marriages, yet time refused to relieve it. Genetic inheritance might be to blame. Quanah Parker had kept plural wives long after the old justification had passed away, the need for a hunter to have several women to prepare buffalo hides for the Comancheros, traders out of Santa Fe. When the Indian agent demanded that he send all away but one, Quanah was heartbroken at the prospect.

But then again, job stress might be the culprit.

That's what a fellow investigator at Emmett's office said. He was undergoing counseling after his fifth divorce, and his shrink claimed that some cops continuously fell in love as an antidote to the numbing brutality of their working lives.

Emmett turned off the headlights.

The sun broke from a bar of clouds hugging the horizon, and the desert floor emerged from shadow. The landscape was dotted with the shaggy humps of Joshua trees. Interstate 15 was nearly deserted. The stream of Angelenos wouldn't set out for the slot machines of Gomorrah until Christmas morning was reduced to piles of wrapping paper and ribbons. He tried to recall those long-ago mornings at his childhood home near Fort Sill, but all he inwardly saw was Teddy Roper backdropped by his Yule tree, branches drooping from the weight of ornaments. It seemed pathetically obstinate for him to have bought and decorated one, under the circumstances. *Was there any difficulty in your marriage we should be aware of?*

A half hour later, Turnipseed sat up and yawned.

She looked ridiculously young—no doubt one of the reasons why Burk Hagiman, her boss, had assigned her and not one of his experienced hands full-time to the task force. Payback for the Las Vegas U.S. Attorney not making the FBI the lead agency in this investigation. And, of course, she was three-quarters Modoc. White supervisors, Hagiman especially, believed that all Indians had a conspiratorial affection for one another, centuries of intertribal war notwithstanding.

So what was Burk's hidden agenda this time?

Turnipseed cupped her face in her hands. While she looked young, she also seemed older than her years. A puzzling anomaly about her.

"How much you got on the proposed swap itself?" he asked without preliminaries. She'd rested long enough.

She rubbed her eyes, then reached back for her attaché case and fished out the folder. "Give me a minute."

The sunlight touched the far mountains, made them sparkle like brown sugar. There was a stillness to the desert too deep to last. High cirrus clouds, pinkish at this hour, told of wind on the way.

Turnipseed cleared her throat. " 'Death Valley Chemehuevi Rancheria Incorporated, a federally recognized Indian tribe, is offering several riparian holdings along' "—she flipped to the next page—" 'Black Tank Wash in Coconino County and upper Robinson Wash in Mohave County, Arizona, in exchange for six hundred and forty acres of BLM land along Interstate Fifteen here in San Bernardino Coun—' "

"Repeat that first."

"What?"

"*Where* in Coconino County?"

"Black Tank Wash."

A tributary of Havasu Creek. Which ran through the middle of the Havasupai Reservation.

Unconsciously, Emmett let up on the gas pedal, and the sedan began to coast down the long, straight grade from Halloran Summit. From the instant he'd seen the top of Stephanie

Roper's head jutting from the sand, he'd sensed that he'd been intended to find her. If not, why hadn't the murdered BLM officer been hidden miles away from even a chance discovery? The Apaches had concealed Cochise's body, and after more than a century of hunting for it, no one had yet found his mountain grave. The desert surrounding Las Vegas harbored the mummified remains of mob hits no one would ever uncover. And God only knew what rested at the dark, silty bottom of Lake Mead. In this country, discovery was seldom an accident. And there had been something else about the scene in the cave. Coyote tracks—but no evidence of scavenging. That could mean only that the animal had loped past the pit *before* the head was partially uncovered. Uncovered by whom? A terrified shepherd girl seemed an unlikely candidate.

"What's wrong?" Turnipseed asked.

He pressed down on the accelerator again. "We go slow today."

"Why?"

How could he explain it to her? Fresh out of the academy, she hadn't had time to develop an instinct for the hidden dangers in an investigation. "Black Tank Wash ties it in with the Havasupai." He tapped the folder on the seat beside him with a finger. "And I'll bet those holdings the Death Valley Chemehuevi bought belonged to individual Pai who lived just off the reservation on ancestral lands. Don't you see?"

"No," she admitted.

"Everything's falling into place too quick."

"Isn't that good? Aren't we making progress?"

"That's what jackrabbits think—till they realize they've been driven into a brush pen." He'd tried not to sound too sarcastic. How could she know? And what he himself knew was close to inexplicable, the aggregate experience of hundreds of cases. And not a single one of them had started with the strong connections that were seemingly tumbling into their laps with this investigation.

"Then what should we do?" Turnipseed asked. "Go back to Vegas?"

"Of course not." Taking the Halloran Springs off-ramp, he pulled into the Chevron service station. It was closed, but a sign taped to the inside of the office window promised an opening before noon on Christmas. He got out of the car. Something was making a loud flapping noise. He strolled around the building. The chill bit into his neck, made him snap up his jacket collar. The desert was a cold-blooded creature, entirely dependent on the sun for its warmth. He continued past a tamarisk, a Middle Eastern exotic that was crowding out many of the West's native trees. The breeze was sighing through its lacy foliage, but he saw the cause of the flapping across the freeway: a tattered wind sock at a small landing field with a hangar.

He turned and bumped into Turnipseed.

"Sorry," she muttered, stepping back.

She looked so apologetic, he was tempted to pat her on the arm. But he didn't. She was FBI. Sooner or later Hagiman and she would start chucking monkey wrenches into all his works.

Exhaling, he scanned Halloran Springs.

It consisted of the gas station and three wooden shanties strung out along a gravel road that wound up to a mountain of bluish-green rock. Nothing resembled a tribal headquarters. The setting didn't even feel Indian, what with mining scars all over the surrounding hills. "Where's this section of land these Chemehuevi want so damn bad?"

"Right there." She gestured at the flat acreage that began within the curvature of the off-ramp and stretched north to a boundary of flagged stakes. "It's apparently a checkerboard reservation"—meaning a patchwork of Indian holdings among federal and private lands—"and those flags mark the beginning of forty acres with a well owned by the Chemehuevi. Only sweet water in these parts, and they already have it. The rest is alkaline. Pure poison."

"So the tribe wants six hundred and forty acres to go along with the forty they already have here."

"Right."

"Water. Freeway access. And an airstrip," Emmett noted under his breath, then started back for the sedan. Turnipseed followed, her shoes scuffling over the rough cement. "You're a Californian . . ."

"Twice a native," she said.

"Ever met any Death Valley Chemehuevi? They'd be a branch of the Southern Paiute."

She didn't even have to think. "No."

"Me neither. Met me a couple Mojaves. Tough folks. Headhunters, some say. They told me they pretty much wiped out the Northwestern Chemehuevi years before the Mormons came down into this country from Salt Lake. So how the devil does a whole tribe get resurrected?" They got in, and Emmett sped up the gravel road to check each of the shanties for signs of habitation. All were windowless, long abandoned. One had a sign advertising wholesale turquoise from local mines.

"Back to the freeway," he decided.

She opened Stephanie Roper's folder again. "Tribal offices are listed as Box Four, Star Route Two."

"Mailboxes could be anywheres out here. We'll go into Baker for directions. Hit the motel. What's the name?"

"Owlshead Inn."

He could see the pit stop of a town at the foot of the grade, straddling the isthmus between two dry lakes. Windblown dust off these playas obscured most of the structures, although above the pall rose the crowns of twin golden arches.

Five minutes later he braked the sedan in the McDonald's lot and waited for Turnipseed to get out.

"What?" She didn't budge.

"Get yourself some breakfast. I should be back in about twenty."

"Where are you going?"

"The motel."

"I'm going too."

"Wrong."

"Like hell, Parker. I'm not sitting on my ass over coffee while you work *our* case."

"Fine, Turnipseed," he sighed, "*you* go to the motel and I'll sit on *my* ass over coffee."

She glared at him, unblinking, for several seconds. Then, in a less sharp voice, she asked, "What do you mean?"

"First, one of us should hang back in the event he *or* she can do some good here undercover if the need arises. Second, you happen to notice the Owlshead Inn on our way down the main drag . . . ?" Her look turned slightly sheepish. But only slightly. "If you sit in the restaurant, you'll be able to see the motel from the front windows. I want a description of anybody who leaves in a hurry while I'm inside the office."

At last, she got out, slamming her door.

It took Anna two cups of coffee and a Sausage McMuffin to calm down. Not that she hadn't been warned about Parker. BIA's law enforcement division was peopled by manly, controlling types, and Parker was reputed to be the most insufferable of the lot. Some of his fellow workers prayed for the day of his retirement, but it was a faint hope: The man owed too much in alimony to ever go off full salary. Still, he seemed to back off a little when confronted. That made her wonder if, in the declining years of his career, he was getting by on the myths he himself had created. *Have to see him with his shirt off . . . have to see those alleged pectoral scars from the Sun Dance . . .*

Abruptly, Parker barged from the motel office. He hurried

down the porticoed walkway. Anna reared up from her table to keep him in view. Something glinted in his hand. It proved to be a key, which he used to open the room at the far end of the row.

He went inside and shut the door.

She eased down again in her seat, pulse racing. He hadn't acted as if he had expected to encounter anyone. Still, he'd wasted no time covering the distance between the office and the room.

A white car whooshed past on the street. Only as it began to slow for the motel did she realize it to be a San Bernardino County sheriff's cruiser. The rear amber light flashed dimly through the dust off the playas. The deputy parked directly in front of the room Parker had just entered.

That was enough. Anna scooped up her pistol-weighted purse and bolted from the table.

She got no farther than the front sidewalk, when indecision crept over her. She'd agreed to stay inside the restaurant until Parker returned for her. She sidestepped behind a fan palm. The deputy had gone into the motel room, leaving the door ajar behind him. She glimpsed Parker sitting inside on the bed, alternating talking to the deputy and leafing through what looked to be a phone book. At last he dialed.

A minute later a voice inquired from behind, "Miss Modoc?" She whirled around. The rattling of the palm fronds in the wind made her believe that she'd misunderstood the young man in the white cap. The fact that he was the assistant manager was embroidered in gold on his blue shirt. "Are you Miss Prudence Modoc?"

"Yeah," she grumbled, eager to keep an eye on Parker.

"Call for you inside."

As soon as she let out a breath into the receiver, Parker barked, "What do I got to do to keep your goddamn face off the street, Turnipseed!"

43

She knew instantly that it sounded lame: "I thought there was trouble."

"There is. Register says Stephanie Roper checked into this room on the afternoon of November twenty-sixth."

"Her expense records don't reflect that. Why document her two-night stay earlier in November and not this one?"

"That was business *and* pleasure," Parker replied. "The twenty-sixth was probably just pleasure, so she had the good sense to pick up the tab herself. But let's keep mum about this for the time being. If she didn't come here in the performance of her official duties, we lose our biggest jurisdictional card."

"I realize that. Does the manager remember her?"

"Vaguely. Seems there was an envelope waiting for her. Night clerk accepted it, but he quit last week and moved on. Address unknown." Parker paused. "Anybody leave while I was in the office?"

"No."

"Then maybe the trail gets cold from here." He sounded almost hopeful. "Deputy Gonzales of SBSO is with me. He's kindly agreed to seal the premises till your I.D. technician gets here from Vegas. How soon can that be?"

"I'll phone right away. My guy's usually prompt. But this is within our Los Angeles division. They should handle—"

"Turnipseed, I want the closest possible tech—*now*. Do you understand?"

"Okay," she said.

"Have him collect fibers and hair. I don't imagine Roper was killed inside here, but I want the whole room doused with orthotolidine, if necessary. . . ." A test for blood traces, she recalled from her academy classes. "And then get yourself ready on the double."

"What for?"

"We're going to the Nation of the Death Valley Chemehuevi."

• • •

Reaching the Halloran Springs turnoff again, Emmett noticed that the gas gauge needle showed three-quarters empty. He swerved into the Chevron station. "Your plastic, please," he said.

Silent, she handed over her government credit card.

"Turnipseed." He spoke very clearly, "The only reason I'm driving is because Deputy Gonzales gave me the directions." She offered no response, so he got out and went inside the station office, where a teenage attendant hugged an electric heater and read a baseball card catalogue. His studied indifference almost passed for poise. Emmett asked him, "By chance, you remember a woman gassing up her blue government Dodge here in late November? Good-looking gal with reddish-blond hair."

"You a cop?"

"Yes."

"Last of November?"

"Right."

Emmett thought that would be the end of it, but instead the boy lowered the catalogue and said indignantly, revealing a front tooth that had been silvered over, "That's about when some son of a bitch stole my Firebird."

Emmett feigned mild interest. "From the station here?"

"Yeah, when I was workin' nights. It was parked next to my uncle's truck around back. He had a flat on an inner dual, and I was goin' to fix it in the mornin' for him. Same asshole lifted his acetylene rig and some aluminum flux."

"Your uncle a welder?"

"Uh-huh. The rig I can see. But how many guys need to weld aluminum?"

Emmett handed over Turnipseed's credit card. "Pump five."

Outside, flying grit came in a wave across the access road, and Emmett shielded his face against his shoulder as he inserted the nozzle into the tank. Aluminum flux was bouncing around the edges of his thoughts. He motioned for Turnipseed to crack her window. "Want a sodie?"

"A what?"

"A so-*duh*," he enunciated, wondering what it would be like to go home to Oklahoma and not have to explain his colloquialisms anymore. "It's colored sugar water with fizz in it."

"No, thanks."

"Nothing out the way we're going except rocks and chuckwallas."

"I'll manage." She rolled up her window.

The nozzle clicked off, and he went back inside the office. "Aircraft," he said right off to the attendant.

"What?"

"Tell your local deputy most aluminum welding is done on airplanes. Your uncle probably knows that, but it's important for the deputy to know it too." Amazing how commercial burglary cases left you with a wealth of industrial trivia.

"I will," the boy promised, suddenly eager to assist the law if it meant he might get his Firebird back.

Inside the car again, Emmett followed the gravel road northeast, past the last shack, up onto a ridge covered with creosote bushes. The spindly branches were flailing against the ground, and the sky was flecked with airborne trash off the freeway.

"Answer me something," Turnipseed said, lifting her chin.

"I'll try."

"If Stephanie Roper was having an assignation here—"

"A what?"

"A romp."

"This isn't a payback for that *sodie* business, is it?"

Turnipseed persisted. "If Stephanie was having a romp, why'd she register in her own name?"

"I doubt Teddy cared, as long as she didn't rub his nose in it."

"So you still don't think he's worth interviewing again?"

"I didn't say that. We'll see."

Emmett braked at the top of the ridge. Below, a broad valley swept up to a contorted sedimentary range in the north. Not his kind of country. Too parched and desolate. He liked grasslands, an orange sun sinking into an ocean of green wheat. Plumes of white powder were spewing from open-pit mines along the base of the range. Borax, he suspected. And off to the east lay something equally troubling: a playa showing the glints of shallow pools left by the recent rain. Places saline mosquitoes could have bred in the rushes during the temperate autumn at this low altitude.

"*Culex erythrothorax*," Turnipseed suddenly said.

"What?"

"That's the name of the mosquito the lab found in her clothes." And then the significance of all this struck her, for she asked tensely, "My God, it could have happened somewhere out here . . . couldn't it?"

He didn't answer, although he felt that she was closer to understanding his mounting apprehension. He struggled to find the words that would fully explain it. Something clear out of his past. Long ago, a Lakota friend, a pilot—a brother, even, before the law separated them forever—had flown him over the rolling hills at Little Bighorn, telling how Crazy Horse had drawn Custer on with just forty warriors, lured him on with the promise of sudden opportunity until there was no going back. It seemed like that now. A setup based on a quick and easy solution to Stephanie Roper's murder. A Comanche of the last century would have called this inner buzz a vision. A veteran cop might justify it as a hunch. Emmett felt stranded in between, and instead of trying to explain he simply asked, "You got a shotgun, Turnipseed?"

"In the trunk."

47

"Get it."

"Is something going to happen?"

"We'll be the first to know. Get the scattergun."

Fine sand gusted inside when she opened her door, whorled around the interior, and made Emmett squint. It left his lips tasting of salt. Just when he'd begun to think that there might be some comforting randomness to this investigation, he once again sensed that he was operating according to someone else's plan. Turnipseed let the boiling sand in one more time, then slammed her door and nestled the shotgun between her knees. Her fingers trembled as she checked to make sure no round was seated in the chamber, then that the magazine was full. Still, she seemed familiar enough with the weapon.

She was peering at him again, her eyes even larger than usual. No doubt her entire police combat experience consisted of role-playing at Hogan's Alley, the academy's simulation of Main Street, U.S.A. Emmett had come to the alley as a veteran. He'd thought there was no way to duplicate the terror of a firefight, no way to know what you'd do. Until it happened.

Slowly now, he drove down off the ridge and into the arroyo. The dry wash was cobbled with rocks worn round in some ancient time when this land had flowed with water. *Before there were men* . . . How many Indian creation stories began with that phrase? He hoped that there were no men out here, waiting for them.

Wind-driven sand flowed around the rocks like a restless brown flood.

He kept losing the road, it was so poorly defined, and had to back up several times. Turnipseed was pressing her face nearly up to the inside of the windshield, trying to be of help. The chassis lurched violently beneath them, making their seat belts click off with every jolt. "Must be what the deputy meant by 'unimproved,'" Emmett commented, voice jiggling.

"It'd be a superhighway in Modoc County."

"How'd you grow up—barefoot with burrs in your hair?"

"Almost."

Like Turnipseed, Emmett leaned forward. The last thing he needed was to run the front axle up over a boulder. "Watch for the first branch to the left." *And for anything resembling an ambush*, he wanted to add but didn't. This is how most feds died in Indian Country, alone, cut off from ready help. When he dreamed of his own death, it was always like this—groping blindly ahead in a flurry of dust or snow.

"There," Turnipseed announced five minutes later.

Emmett jinked the wheel to make the sharp turn—and still almost hit a Joshua tree.

This fork of the road passed over hard-packed sand, and the ride finally smoothed out. But then, approaching the northern edge of the valley, they came to switchbacks that zigzagged up a worn limestone ledge. Emmett found it difficult to concentrate on both the drive and a question that had nagged him since he'd come out of that cleft above Havasu Creek: What had drawn Misty Topocoba up there? Certainly not a stray lamb, as her cousin Billy had said. There'd been no sheep tracks at all. Emmett had wanted to return to Supai to ask her, but his supervisor had ordered him to devote his time to other pending investigations in the expectation that the faceless Jane Doe case would be turned over to the law enforcement agency at the point of the actual killing. That, most likely, would be a police or sheriff's department in Arizona, Nevada, Utah, or even here in California. But he hadn't known Stephanie Roper's identity then, or the fact that she was a federal employee.

"Something's standing in the road," Turnipseed said anxiously.

"What?"

"I see legs in the road."

Emmett glided to a stop rather than tap the brakes, setting

off the taillights. He slipped his .357 magnum from his holster and held it across his lap. Turnipseed jacked a shell into the chamber of her shotgun.

Then, just above the howl of the sandstorm and the engine noise, Emmett heard braying.

Reholstering, he inched forward, scattering the band of wild burros that had been sheltering in the lee of the limestone cliff. "Relax," he told Turnipseed.

"I thought—"

"You thought right for the split second you had to think." Then, more gently, he added, "Don't apologize. You saw them before I did."

As Deputy Gonzales had indicated, the road almost doubled back on itself before striking east toward the line of open-pit mines Emmett had glimpsed from the ridge above Halloran Springs. They went on, filling the air with white dust.

"Sodium borate compound?" A bit of self-congratulation broke through the tension in Turnipseed's voice.

"Keep a sharp eye," Emmett said. "We can hand out commendations later."

Something square loomed alongside the road. A sign:

D.V. CHEMEHUEVI RANCHERIA
No Trespassing
Patrolled by Tribal Police

Yet, nothing barred entry, so Emmett continued on. He glanced at the dashboard clock. Only eleven A.M., but it felt like evening twilight. He had to run the wipers now and again to clear the white sheen of borax off the windshield.

"There," Turnipseed said again, pointing.

A second later Emmett caught it: the square flickering of a window light. Again he coasted to a stop, but this time he killed the engine and tossed the keys under his floor mat. He reached up and switched the selector so the dome light wouldn't come on when they opened their doors. "See where I put your keys?" he asked.

She nodded.

"Now let's get out without shutting our doors. The sound carries like a shot."

He led her away from the road, up onto an outcropping of crumbly borax. Between the blinding gusts, he could make out a small cabin in the ravine below. A light was showing from the window, and smoke leaked from the stovepipe. This was the only structure, although the roofs of several others could be seen out in the brush, their walls having collapsed from dry rot long ago. No vehicles anywhere. At the upper end of the ravine was the first open-pit mine in a line of the gouges that marked the wave-cut shore of a primeval lake.

He had to raise his voice more than he liked to be heard. "I'm going down to the cabin."

Her watery eyes flared. "What about me?"

"Come running if something flies through that window."

"Like what?"

"Like me." He winked.

But she didn't rise to it. And she was shivering as she held the shotgun. "You explain nothing."

"Everything explains itself in time." He took off his jacket, wrapped it around her shoulders, then started down the slope toward the glow of the window.

Chapter 4

"Are you a witch?" Wuzzie Munro demanded as soon as Emmett stepped inside.

The second woman to accuse him of that today. But witchcraft was a bit too oblique for the Comanche disposition. "No, Grandmother, I'm a policeman."

"Indian police?"

"Yes. My name's Emmett Parker."

"You sound Mojave." Wuzzie spat out the last word.

"Comanche." Emmett ran his eyes over the interior of the single-room cabin. He and the old Chemehuevi woman were alone, which surprised him somewhat. He slipped his revolver back into his holster. He'd had it out again, holding it behind his right leg. When he felt sure that Wuzzie was truly blind, as

Deputy Gonzales had said, he'd consider shouting out the door for Turnipseed to join him.

The old woman sat placidly at her table, gazing into the lighted hurricane lamp set at its center. "What's your name again?"

"Parker." There were two windows, one facing south and one north. He glanced out each of them, but saw nothing. The swirling gray-white gloom took over within a few yards.

The lamplight accentuated the folds and wrinkles in Wuzzie's shrunken face. Her eyelids drooped over irises milky with glaucoma. Yet, she had a lantern going, so her blindness wasn't total. She brought a hand-rolled cigarette up to her mouth and inhaled. The smoke smelled like willow bark, although that could have been from the cookstove. "Want to sit down, Parker?" She coughed.

"Thanks." He eased into the chair across the table from her. On the windowsill next to him was the hand-tinted photograph of an Indian youth in the dress blue uniform of a World War II marine. "Who's this in the picture?"

"My son." She coughed more phlegmatically. "I don't say his name no more."

Dead, she meant. "In the big war, Grandmother?"

"Yes."

Emmett calculated. She might well be pushing one hundred years. Hunched, nearly blind, she looked scarcely to have the vitality to shuffle around this cramped room, let alone get to a mailbox miles away. There'd been none on the drive in. "Do they deliver mail out here?"

"Oh, no."

"A friend brings it to you?"

"No friends left. All gone. Over the chasm." Wuzzie pursed her lips fatalistically. "The county lady comes out now and again."

Emmett's look softened. He'd been there a thousand times before, all over the Southwest, sitting in a hovel heated by

53

wood and lit by kerosene at the end of the same century in which men had walked on the moon. Winnowing baskets hung on the clapboard walls. Drying herbs dangled from the open rafters like an upside-down garden. Below the hem of her long skirt she wore foot mittens made from the entire skins of two ground squirrels. "The dust outside is terrible," he said.

"Yes, Parker, the borax." Her eyes suddenly snapped to life, and with her head tilted back she squinted at him from under the lazy lids. "You don't come to open the mines again, do you?"

"No, I'm a policeman."

"I told 'em—don't let the miners dig here. They'll let the poisons out of the ground. This was all a poisonous lake before Coyote turned the north shore into hills so Raven would have a place to rest. But the elders let the miners come, and everybody got sick. Went away to die in Barstow. The lunger hospital."

"You didn't get sick?"

"No. I cough a little. But that's all."

"Where are the others?"

"Others?" she repeated absently.

"The rest of the Death Valley Chemehuevi."

She stubbed out her cigarette in a ceramic ashtray that had SHOSHONE HOUSE OF GAMES and FULL NEVADA-STYLE CASINO in embossed letters around the flat rim. "Let me see your face." Before Emmett could protest, she'd reached across the table and was reading his features with her leathery fingertips. "Your ears aren't pierced," she said, kneading the lobes.

"Is that bad?"

"You can't cross the chasm to the other world unless they are."

"Who says?"

"Coyote." Her hands fell away and slid back across the tabletop. So death was a chasm to this branch of the desert Paiute, perhaps because the Grand Canyon had been the only barrier to the Chemehuevi's travels. Emmett thought she was ignoring his question about the rest of her tribe, when she answered it in a roundabout way. "It's a problem. Nobody of blood is left to do my Cry Dance. . . ." The ritual comprising her funeral or—more properly, according to some anthropologists—marking the first anniversary of her death. She was telling him that no other members of the Death Valley Chemehuevi remained. "Didn't plan for this, you know." But someone had included her in their plans. Someone knew that in the eyes of the law a band of one was as much a federally recognized tribe as the 230,000-strong Navajo. And how convenient. Wuzzie Munro was both tribal chairperson and tribal council. Her signature automatically became Death Valley Chemehuevi policy even if she didn't comprehend what was being done in her name. It angered Emmett more even than Stephanie Roper's brutal murder. Only slowly was the BLM bureaucrat becoming a person to him. But he felt as if he had known Wuzzie all his life. Her voice was already inside his head, whispering the things grandmothers whisper to the sons of their sons. "Coso would do the dance, sure," Wuzzie went on. "But he don't know the old songs. And there's never been enough time to teach him. Coso comes and goes so fast. Never know when to expect him."

Emmett's pulse quickened. "Coso?"

"Yes. At first I thought it was him when you knocked."

"Why?"

"He's a witch like you."

"But I'm not."

"Coso denies it too."

Emmett paused. "I've never heard that name."

"We share it. Us and the Shoshone." No sour look this time, so apparently she was on cordial terms with the neighboring tribe to the north of her.

"Does it have a meaning?"

"To us—a wisp of steam. To the Shoshone it means fire."

"Does Coso live in Spirit Meadows?" The tribal headquarters town of the Western Shoshone Reservation, which was tucked under the southeast corner of Death Valley National Park. Maybe thirty miles from Wuzzie's cabin.

"A little ways outside."

"What makes you think he's a witch?"

Wuzzie grinned at his naivete, showing her toothless gums. "Sometimes Coso comes as Coyote, other times as Wolf. Who else 'cept a witch can do that?"

"I don't know, Grandmother," Emmett replied.

Many tribes viewed the cosmos as a duality, half of it personified by Wolf, the responsible but stolid brother who labored endlessly so people would live well. The more creative and mercurial brother, Coyote, tended to the darker half of existence. Coyote had brought death to mankind, but he was also the giver of fire, for no one knew the darkness better than he. "Is Coso's voice the same whether he's Wolf or Coyote?"

The old woman had to consider that. "Almost. I can tell it's the same blood."

The rasping of the grit against the windowpanes grew louder. No doubt, Turnipseed was miserable outside, but Emmett didn't care for how Wuzzie's seemingly opaque eyes tracked some of his broader movements. The rookie, however green, might be his only surprise for anyone lying along his path. He'd hold her in reserve. "Does Coso come here often?"

"No. But he don't have to come to leave things at my door. He just sends 'em through the air." She cackled.

"What things?"

She gestured in the general direction of a cardboard box on the floor.

"The county lady didn't leave these things, Grandmother?"

"Not this time."

"Mind if I look?"

She seemed puzzled by his request, but said that it would

be all right. He had an honest face. Inside the box, Emmett found only groceries, simple staples, plus a pack of Zigzag cigarette papers and finally a cash register receipt partially jammed under one of the pasteboard seams. It was from the Spirit Meadows Market, dated two days earlier. "When'd this arrive?" he asked.

"Last night."

Only last night. Although it was still shapeless, the danger seemed very close. Maybe, in a way of reckoning, he was dealing with a witch who'd learned to take things from one place and deposit them in another, hurling both groceries and corpses through the air with equal ease. "Grandmother, did a white woman ever come here?"

"Just the county lady."

"No, this would be another. Around a month ago. A young woman who worked for the government."

Wuzzie smiled mischievously. "You're too interested in women, Parker."

"Why do you say that?"

"I read it in your face. How many wives have you had?"

"Two," he fudged.

"Oh, more than that," she corrected him with an incredulous scrunch of her nose.

Emmett rolled his eyes, but then said, "I have to ask you about something, Grandmother. . . ." A shadow fell over her face, and he realized that she knew what he was going to ask. "It's about the land down along the interstate—"

"No."

"I'm sorry?"

"I don't talk about that."

"Says who . . . Coso?"

She'd crossed her arms over her breasts and turned her head. But then, visibly, she thought of something, for her right hand fumbled along the windowsill, deftly missing her son's framed portrait but coming away with a business card from a stack of them. She held it out to Emmett. "Talk to him. . . ." *Leonard Wine & Associates, Attorneys-at-Law, Carson City, Nevada.*

"You know Mr. Wine, Grandmother?"

"No."

"Does Coso?"

Silence. Through it, Emmett heard someone running toward the cabin, shoes thumping against the soft ground. He looked out the north-facing window and saw Turnipseed making for the door.

"Parker!" she cried.

After Parker went inside the cabin, Anna returned to the car and exchanged his huge jacket for her own. She buttoned up, pocketed her pistol, then decided to find a place from which she could keep an eye on him through the window next to the shanty's door. She had to climb to locate such a vantage point. Parker was sitting at a table with somebody, but the flue pipe to the woodstove blocked her view of this person's face. Whichever way Anna shifted, the pipe frustrated her.

Maybe there was a window on the opposite side of the cabin. She began working her way around the margins of the ravine. The shotgun was heavy in her hands, but she drew comfort from it.

A tingly sensation on the back of her neck kept making her believe somebody was trying to steal up on her. There was no sound except the wind whipping through the brush, yet without warning she sensed rapid movement behind her.

She spun around, forefinger on the trigger.

Nothing. Except vague shadows flitting by at the edge of visibility—either ragged pieces of flying trash or eddies of borax powder masquerading as human forms.

"Hurry up, Parker," she muttered.

Climbing, she began to make out a grid of dirt lanes among

the tumbledown roofs. The rancheria, now reduced to a single cabin, had once been much larger. She peered around, scanning for movement. The clouds of dust parted briefly, and atop the most distant ridge to the north she glimpsed some sort of wooden mining structure. It seemed like a gallows frame in the split second before the stinging pall sifted over her again.

Conversation.

She halted, thinking that she could hear conversation. Just under the howl of the wind, men exchanging shrill and chaotic instructions in the last minute before action. But the voices were so faint, she quickly made up her mind that she was imagining them.

"Come on, Parker."

There was indeed a window on the north wall of the cabin, and at last she had an unobstructed view inside. Emmett was alone with an old woman, and Anna could tell by the inclination of his head that he was listening carefully to her.

Then a roaring gust blanked out the sight.

Staggering, disoriented, Anna thought for an instant that someone had shoved her. But the blinding dust clouds ebbed once more, and she saw that she was by herself—although only two strides from a fall into the open-pit mine.

She crept over to the precipice and peered down.

The bottom was covered with little dunes. But then she spotted something that didn't belong among these curving wind sculptures: a perfectly straight edge about five feet in length. She waited impatiently for the wind to dissolve it, to leave behind a more natural contour. But the seconds ticked away, and the linear oddity remained. Finally, she found a ramplike slope into the pit and vaulted down it, digging in her heels to keep from pitching forward.

She waded knee-deep into the dunes and cautiously approached the edge.

Shouldering the shotgun, she reached out with her free hand and began digging. The angularity crumbled, and blue-painted sheet metal was revealed. Attached to it were chrome letters: *ODGE*. Anna balled up her hand to steady it, then unflexed her fingers and scooped away a remaining chunk. *D*.

An unlit taillamp lens showed a dull red.

Before she could think, she'd reeled and was sprinting for the shanty. She tried to slow down, to hide her excitement, her fear, but it was useless. She heard herself crying out for Parker.

He stepped through the door and quickly shut it behind him. "What?" he said angrily.

"You've *got* to see this."

Thankfully, he glowered for only a moment, then followed her back up the road toward the pit, head bent against the buffeting wind. "Better be worth it," she heard him grumble.

"It is," she said, becoming angry herself.

"You scared the shit out of that old woman."

"I just scared the shit out of myself . . . all right?"

His steps shortened as they neared the trunk of the blue Dodge. Then he halted altogether and shielded his eyes from a gust with his forearm. The front of his shirt was pasted to his chest and the back was rippling wildly. After a moment he uncovered the white U.S. Government license plate. He faced Anna. His eyelashes were frosted with borax. "Will your radio reach Vegas?"

"The repeater's just to the east of us on Clark Mountain. Maybe."

"Try," Parker said. "Give your I.D. man directions here— even if he's just reached the motel in Baker. Have ATF roll a bomb tech."

"Do you think the car's booby-trapped?"

He ignored the question, and from that she realized that her tone had been slightly panicked. "Leave the shotgun here and get me a flashlight," he said. "My jacket too. And keep a sharp eye. There's a good chance we're not alone."

"You mean the old woman?"

"No." He straightened and slogged deeper into the drifted powder toward the driver's side of the entombed sedan.

Anna raced for her car.

It felt good to run, as if she were escaping something frightful. But once she was behind the wheel she found that she was too breathless to talk. The old woman's window was now dark. Probably retreating within herself in the face of trouble, just as Anna's own mother had done so often. Turn out the lights and go to bed. Oblivion had been the answer to the unspeakable occurring under her own roof. *Forget that. Concentrate on the work at hand. You took this job to forget all that.*

Keying the mike, she tried to raise the communications center at Clark County Metro. All federal law enforcement offices were closed for the holiday. She was answered on the second try, the dispatcher's voice a thin crackle above the static. Speaking slowly and distinctly, Anna repeated the instructions Parker had given her, then asked that they be relayed to the on-call FBI supervisor.

"Sergeant's dialing right now," the dispatcher acknowledged.

Anna sat a few moments longer, feeling something warm and buoyant worming up through her shock. It was pride, she finally realized, satisfaction that she'd found something of enormous evidentiary value. And of all the places to kick off the investigation, she had suggested this one to Emmett Quanah Parker. She fought down a smile as she bundled up her flashlight in his jacket.

He had burrowed through to the driver's window by the time she got back. He had a shovel. His hands and face were chalky, and he sneezed repeatedly as he reached for his parka.

"Where'd you find the shovel?" she asked.

"Next to the sedan."

"Was it used to bury the car?"

Parker started to sneeze, but the blow failed to materialize. Putting on his jacket, he said, "I figure it was used to partly uncover the Dodge."

That made no sense to Anna, but she felt as if she had to say something. "What about fingerprints on the handle?"

"No latent's going to survive contact with borax," he said irritably. "Latents are made of body oil, and I'll guarantee a mineral used in hand soap will dissolve them."

Then his spin on the presence of the shovel hit her. "You mean, somebody tried to *unbury* this car?"

Scowling, he gestured with an arcing sweep of his hand. "See the big horseshoe-shaped dent in the borax pile? Wind didn't do that. . . ." He shook the shovel at her. "This did."

"But *why*?"

"Not my immediate concern, Turnipseed."

"What the hell is?" she insisted. She had to be at the center of this. Especially now.

"When somebody teases you on," he said, "they got a surprise waiting. Come closer. . . ." She slogged over to him. "They cover triggering devices at Quantico?"

"Yes." Then she hedged: "Sort of."

"Either they did or they didn't."

All of a sudden everything she'd learned over those long months seemed utterly inadequate. She had never dreamed that she'd face an actual improvised explosive device, or she would have paid closer attention. But Emmett's ominous tone of voice was pissing her off. "Just go ahead," she told him. "I'm listening."

"I was thinking trip wire as I neared the vehicle. A mono-filament line strung underneath the borax here . . ." She glanced back the way she'd come, cringed when she recalled how carelessly she'd advanced. "Now, as I examine the door," Emmett continued, "I'm thinking pressure release, a microswitch that kicks off as soon as you grasp the latch. If this boy's real clever, he rigged a temblor switch or two—if jarred, the whole car blows *Merry Christmas*, FBI."

"ATF's on the way. Why would we fool with any of this?"

"We're not!" Emmett barked. But he quickly controlled himself. "I'm acquainting you with a few of the ways of getting dead as you traipse around Indian Country. This isn't Vegas, Turnipseed. There's no backup around the corner. Fuck up out here—and you'll wind up like Roper." He seized the flashlight from her and shone it through the driver's side window.

His jaw muscles were rippling under the skin. She realized that his admonitions had been protective, but she wasn't about to apologize. After all, without her he might never have found the Dodge. He stepped back, tossed Anna the light, and motioned for her to take a look through a clear spot in what appeared to be a brown haze on the inside of the glass.

She knew that there would be no body. That had been found two hundred miles away along Havasu Creek. But what she saw in the icy light glancing about the Dodge's interior was almost worse.

"How tall was Stephanie?" Emmett asked.

She'd frozen, staring at the dried blood splashed copiously over the steering wheel and dash instruments. The keys, still in the ignition, were clotted with it.

"Turnipseed . . . ?"

"Uh," she said, trying to shake off her horror, "five-four, according to the autopsy report."

"Front seat's pushed all the way back. She didn't drive this into the pit. We'll search for blood spatters between here and the cabin."

"Why?" Anna managed to ask.

"There's no blood on the center portion of the dashboard or the middle armrest. The perp disabled her, dragged her out from behind the wheel, carried her around to the other side of the car. If he was alone, he probably had to set her down to open the passenger door. She lay slumped on that side of the seat for some time, judging from the stains on the dash. . . ." Anna could feel Parker's eyes on her, testing her.

"So much blood," she whispered.

"What's that mean?"

"I don't know." Saliva was welling in her mouth.

"Only a beating heart sprays volume like that."

Somehow, she'd known that Stephanie Roper had been alive when her face was carved off. But she hadn't imagined that the woman had lived for minutes after the mutilation, that the end had come only after the killer drove the sedan into the pit and turned toward her with knife in hand. She could almost feel the blade plunging into the back of her neck. "Oh, God."

"What'd you say?" Parker said sternly. A first-class prick in his element, and she almost hated him.

"Nothing."

"Look at the passenger-door latch button. See any blood on it?"

"No."

"So, Roper probably popped it. If the perp had, there'd be smearing. That supposes he came at her through her door, then reached across the front seat to unlatch the other side when he was ready to hide the car. That didn't happen, and I'll bet we find blood on the outer handle over there. What's it all mean?"

"I'm . . . I'm not sure."

"You drive around with your doors unlocked in the carjacking capital of Nevada?"

"No."

"So what's it mean?"

"She let the bastard in. She trusted him."

"That's my best guess too, Turnipseed." He picked up her shotgun, which she'd leaned against the trunk, and shouldered it. "Let's get busy. Staying busy keeps you from getting down, okay?" Unexpectedly, his tone turned sympathetic.

She nodded bleakly.

"We'll look for blood spatters on the ground," he said. "They'll look like brown, pea-sized balls of borax. That'll tell us where this sad mess began."

Chapter 5

Emmett sat up, shaking off his drowsiness.

Light snow was falling as Turnipseed turned into her condominium complex. It was one of those mock Spanish villages, with terra-cotta tile roofs and white stucco walls, that were rapidly covering the open range between the west side of Las Vegas and Red Rock Escarpment, the city's picture-postcard backdrop. Yesterday's wind had swept in a weak low pressure behind it, but the cloud cover was already breaking apart to reveal stars. Emmett glanced back: The tires left black streaks in the wet snow covering the parking lot.

He checked his wristwatch: 5:11 A.M.

Burk Hagiman, the special-agent-in-charge of the local FBI office and Turnipseed's boss, had insisted on a briefing before eight that morning, when he would meet with the regional head of BLM. Emmett had no desire to see Hagiman, especially with less than an hour's sleep in two days, but Turnipseed had volunteered her condo as the most convenient place for the three of them to get together.

She fished her garage door opener out of the glove compartment. The first press of her thumb did nothing. "Shit."

"Easy does it."

"Where'd you learn to say that," she snapped, "at meetings?"

"Yes," he said quietly.

So she was familiar with Alcoholics Anonymous.

The heat in her face rose. Ever since peering into the blood-drenched interior of Stephanie Roper's sedan, she'd been remote and irritable. Her way, doubtlessly, of hiding how shaken she was. Her first homicide. The world would never seem the same again. She drove into the garage, and the door lowered, leaving them in almost total darkness. "I'm sorry," she said. "I didn't mean anything."

"Not exactly a secret. Oklahoma state legislature passed a special resolution ordering me to abstain."

She could be heard unlatching her car door. But the dome light failed to come on, and she swore again.

Emmett reached for the selector. "I switched it off back there at the rancheria." He lumbered out and passed around the hood, which was steaming from snowmelt.

"Can you handle coffee this close to sleep?" She opened an interior door for him. It led to a tiny kitchen little different from his own. In fact, the place was nearly a carbon copy of his apartment in Phoenix. Bare walls, nondescript furniture, an air of minimal habitation. She snatched a granola bar wrapper off the breakfast counter and tossed it in a trash can under the sink. "I didn't hear an answer."

"Sure," Emmett said, "but only if you want some too." He saw that they'd both tracked borax across the linoleum. His skin was crawling from it, even though he'd beaten his clothes with his jacket before leaving the rancheria. "Dang, what a mess."

"No matter. Listen, I'm going to take a shower before Burk gets here."

"I usually shower *after* meeting with him."

She looked up while spooning Folger's into a cone filter. "How well do you know him?"

"Long story. Go get wet."

Then she said much too abruptly and earnestly, "I don't drink either."

He gave a shrug, and she pressed her fingertips against her forehead before sighing in embarrassment. "I'm whipped."

"Hit the shower, Turnipseed. I know how to pour my own."

"You mind calling me Anna?"

He pretended to think about it. "No."

"Okay to call you Emmett?"

"Sure."

She smiled at him before turning for the stairs.

While she showered, he sat on a bar stool at the counter, sipping his coffee, replaying the crime scene wrap-up in his mind. After a two-hour search, he and Turnipseed had found their telltale bloodstains—in the road dust beside the rancheria's no trespassing sign. Apparently, Stephanie Roper had been waylaid and savaged only twenty feet inside the reservation. Still, if it couldn't be established that Stephanie Roper had been even marginally performing some official duty at the time of her murder, or that interstate and racketeering statutes could be invoked, the homicide would be taken over by the San Bernardino County Sheriff.

Emmett tried not to be distracted by that possibility.

Wuzzie Munro knew everything and nothing: Vehicles and "putt-putt bikes" frequently came and went, but the old woman claimed she had no idea how a Dodge sedan had wound up in the open pit. The ATF man found no bomb in or around the sedan. So this hadn't been the rendezvous the perpetrator had intended for his pursuers. That was still out there, ticking. As Emmett had suspected, the effusive borax was so potentially damaging to the delicate oils of latent fingerprints, Turnipseed's I.D. technician decided to seal the car and have it towed to Las Vegas before getting to work. Emmett and Turnipseed escorted the AAA truck to the federal motor pool garage just to make sure the chain of evidence wasn't violated along the interstate. That had killed the rest of the night, leaving Emmett with an uneasy overview of a crime scene full of contrary impulses. Trust and betrayal. Concealment and uncovering.

"Didn't realize how itchy that crud was till I got it off me," Turnipseed said.

She'd come halfway down the stairs. She wore a white terry-cloth robe and was toweling her short brown hair. "You're next."

"I can wait." He kept his dust-inflamed gaze well above her bare legs. She was small but shapely. A smooth skin. His stirrings only irked him. She was Hagiman's minion. He detested the man. And the institution of the FBI, with its buttoned-up airs and hoarding of intelligence, even though he counted individual agents among his friends . . .

"I *said* you're next. Fresh towel's on the vanity." She went up the stairs again.

By the time he reached the landing at the top, her bedroom door was closed. He was both relieved and vaguely disappointed. Pivoting, he could see into the spare room, her study. Books lined one wall; a desk was pushed up against the other. Above the rolltop was a newborn's receiving cradle made of twined willow. Hers, no doubt. The only Indian thing in the entire place as far as he could tell; it pleased his sense of propriety that she kept this family relic away from general view.

A half-dozen Christmas cards had been propped open and

stood upright on the desktop. Did they mark the extent of her social circle? A strangely lonely young woman, although nothing on the surface invited pity.

He went into the steamy bathroom.

He thought to lock the door, didn't, and then felt foolish for having quibbled with himself over such a thing. He neatly piled his powdery clothes and holstered weapon atop the toilet seat lid and stepped into the tub.

Hagiman.

If he hadn't already, Burk would soon tell Turnipseed about that summer ten years before in South Dakota when he'd supervised Emmett's solo infiltration of the Sun Dancers, a rogue offshoot of the American Indian Movement supporting itself by a string of violent bank robberies throughout the Midwest. The group also assassinated its rivals for tribal offices and plotted hits on South Dakota state officials. The FBI-dominated task force—Emmett had been detached from the BIA merely "to blend in with the Indian community" and feed Burk Hagiman intelligence—had gotten its convictions, and the most prominent Sun Dancers were still in prison, but Hagiman had lacked the imagination to understand the changes Emmett had undergone during those months alone in the emotionally charged atmosphere of a full-fledged Sioux revolt.

Shutting his eyes, Emmett let the needles of hot water drum against the back of his neck, loosen the taut muscles.

Perhaps Turnipseed wouldn't understand either. But seeing that cradle had given him at least a spark of hope: The past, however irrevocable, could still touch her.

He'd no sooner dried off, dressed, and gone downstairs again than Hagiman arrived with a knock that shook the walls. The same bullet head, forced grin, and sardonic eyes. Burk had no feel for the style of man he was. His beautifully tailored suits seemed to have been flung carelessly on a body built for bucking hay. He'd been raised on a Nebraska farm. The upper plains. The incubator of the most virulent anti-Indian prejudice in the nation. Burk cleverly couched his biases in such a way that they appeared to be expertise in Native American psychology. He now looked from Turnipseed to Emmett, took in the fact that both had shower-damp hair, and apparently drew his own conclusion. "Been a while, Emmett," he finally said, not offering to shake.

Emmett just nodded.

"Anna tells me we're making some fast headway." Hagiman flopped heavily into the easy chair. "I like the sound of that." Turnipseed, in skirt and blouse now, hung her boss's jacket on the coat tree in a corner, then sat beside Emmett on the couch. At two that morning she'd phoned Hagiman from the Chevron station in Halloran Springs, but Emmett hadn't eavesdropped. As a show of trust. "So where do we go from here?"

"Carson City," Emmett told him, "first thing Monday morning."

"Oh?" Hagiman was either genuinely in the dark or had become an even better liar than he'd been a decade earlier. "Why?"

Emmett decided that Turnipseed hadn't told him. "Well, to a certain degree, Wuzzie Munro's been coached—"

"By whom?" Hagiman butted in. True to old form. Already he'd crossed a foreleg over a knee and was jiggling a foot.

"I don't know, Burk," Emmett continued. "But Wuzzie came up with this business card as soon as I started asking about the land swap." He took the card from his pants pocket, and both men cautiously leaned forward for the exchange.

Reading, reflecting, Hagiman absently ran a finger over his nose. The bridge was slightly flattened and skewed. Ten years before, Emmett had caused this deformity. Oddly enough, Hagiman had covered for him, telling the bosses in Washington that he'd slipped in the bathtub at the Rapid City motel

71

and bashed his face on the spout. No comradely feelings had come from this: Emmett figured that Hagiman only wanted to eat his vengeance cold. He was still waiting.

"Interesting?" Turnipseed finally had to ask. Emmett had been willing to sit him out.

"Maybe." Hagiman turned to Emmett. "You familiar with Leonard Wine?"

After a moment, he shook his head.

"If you have trouble getting a gaming license anywhere, you see Wine. Especially if you have known ties to organized crime. But you damn well better have deep pockets and friends in high places."

"Gambling dovetails in with what Emmett suspects," Turnipseed said. "This all might have something to do with the Shoshone tribal casino in Spirit Meadows."

Hagiman raised his eyebrows. "What makes you think that?"

"Injun intuition." Emmett yawned.

Hagiman smiled sourly. "Any indication whether Stephanie Roper was going to decide for or against the swap?"

"Not really." Turnipseed plucked a tissue from a box on the end table and swiped some borax out of the shell of her ear. "Washburn, the BLM dick, says lands staff officers have a habit of penciling in justifications for their final verdicts. But there were no notes like that in Roper's file."

"Well," Hagiman said, "she damn sure pissed somebody off."

Emmett had come to the same conclusion.

But it suggested only two possibilities so far, neither of which fit the intricacies of the crime, the teases strewn along the trail Turnipseed and he were following. The first was a jilted or disgruntled lover. While Stephanie Roper's secrecy about her destination on the afternoon of November 26 pointed to a tryst in Baker, the elaborate concealment of her body didn't jibe with the spontaneous character of a crime of passion. Star-crossed love most often ended in a roadside ditch, not eleven miles down a mule path into a remote Indian reservation. The second possibility was that Roper had disappointed some people who'd invested heavily in a favorable recommendation from her for the BLM to give up building-site acreage along Interstate 15 in Halloran Springs for two parcels of land in northern Arizona that could be tagged onto Grand Canyon National Park in the future. But that theory had its problems too. What was the sense in murdering a pliable bureaucrat when she might be replaced by somebody with scruples? Under civil service rules, Roper's position would be opened to qualified federal personnel from across the nation. Emmett couldn't imagine anyone, including Leonard Wine's well-heeled clients, having the clout to rig the outcome of that selection process. But still, he said, "I figure we can start in Carson City. . . ." If anything, he wanted to get in Wine's face for his part in exploiting Wuzzie Munro.

"Or we can start closer to home in Spirit Meadows," Turnipseed said, clasping her hands around a dimpled knee.

Hagiman smirked. "More Indian intuition?"

"No . . ." She repeated what Emmett had told her about the grocery receipt and the ashtray he'd seen in Wuzzie's cabin. "I think it's worth my going undercover there."

"Weren't you seen in the general area?"

"Parker kept me under wraps."

"I don't know, Burk. . . ." Emmett shifted uncomfortably. He was boxed in. The one person in the world to whom he could never explain his growing unease about this investigation was sitting across the room from him. The rookie had no idea what might be waiting for her on the Western Shoshone Reservation. Nor did she have the experience to deal with the criminal element drawn to uncontrolled gaming. And there was Coso, lurking on the fringes of this like Coyote—laughing, conspiring, patiently baiting his traps. "Her cover's probably blown."

"Bullshit," she said. "You didn't let me do a damned thing the whole day, Parker—not even sit in on an interview with a blind woman."

"Well," Emmett countered evenly, "you found a way to barge in."

"So she heard my voice."

"And maybe saw you. What's a totally blind woman need a kerosene lamp for?"

"All she knows is that you have a female partner," Anna retorted. "How would that get back to Spirit Meadows? The old woman must live fifty miles from there."

"More like thirty. And receives a Shoshone visitor named Coso quite regularly."

"Burk," she pleaded to Hagiman, "he's stretching it. There's no reason in the world I can't work the House of Games."

"You ever gone undercover before?" Emmett asked.

Her eyes tried to burn a hole in him. What was her interest in going covert? Did she think it would be glamorous?

Emmett silently counted to three. "I'm just saying we ought to talk to the lawyer up in Carson first. At the very least, we can get a sense of what we're up against."

"He might be right," Hagiman said, catching Emmett off guard. The man raised a hand for Turnipseed to be quiet when she tried to carry on the argument. "Let's see how Wine plays it, although I'd suggest starting your week, Emmett, with Investigations at the Nevada Gaming Control Board. Do your homework with them. I'll give you the name of a liaison. Used to work for me."

Great, Emmett thought. A Hagiman clone. Turnipseed was quietly fuming, but he was ready to let her. Better than having her end up like Roper.

"You mind going alone to Carson on Monday, Emmett?"

When he didn't answer after a few seconds, Hagiman hurriedly added that he wanted Turnipseed to submit a report on yesterday's progress, plus help their I.D. man inventory the evidence "before the paperwork backs up." Emmett let pass the insinuation about his habitual tardiness in filing. Reports were security blankets for supervisors; they had much to do with covering asses and little to do with solving homicides. "Sure, I can go alone, Burk . . . as long as it's understood Turnipseed's under my direction."

"I thought this was a cooperative effort," she said.

"It is," Emmett replied. "With me heading it till the U.S. Attorney says otherwise."

"I don't think it's necessary to shove that down my throat."

"I'm not shoving anything," he said, then his color deepened when she smiled impishly at his reaction to her choice of words. "I'm just saying I'm responsible for your safety." Then a bitter memory made him say with more force than he'd intended, "That's all there is to heading anything. The responsibility for the safety of others."

She let out a pent-up breath, but for the time being she'd apparently relented.

"Then it's settled." Hagiman peeked at his wristwatch. "I can drop you off at your hotel, Emmett"—his gaze shifted speculatively to Turnipseed—"unless . . ."

"Ain't no unless," Emmett said, coming to his feet.

Anna dreamed that she was back in Modoc County. The door to her parents' shanty was open to the evening. The place was scarcely bigger than Wuzzie Munro's. High summer cumulus was catching the last light. Movement drew her eye to the side of the sage-covered hill beyond the dooryard. A wolf and a coyote, prowling together, stopped mid-lope and gazed back at her without fear. Her father staggered drunkenly into view, rifle in hand. He braced himself against the doorjamb and fired, hitting the wolf. The animal fell in agony, died. Then her father swung the muzzle on the coyote and squeezed the trigger. The coyote howled but refused to die. Her father fired again. Still, the animal would not go down. "Jack . . . ?" Anna's mother called from somewhere, her voice quavering between fear and disgust. "Jack Turnipseed . . . ?"

Another shot, another defiant howl that became a low murmur of pain, and that somehow became Emmett's voice. He was telling her about Wolf Brother and Coyote Brother. But she wasn't in Modoc, and she wasn't in her car driving back to Las Vegas with Parker.

She was where a phone was ringing.

"Hello?" Anna eased up on an elbow. She could still see daylight in the slit between her blackout curtains.

"It's Burk. Sorry to wake you."

"What time is it?"

"One in the afternoon." Hagiman paused. "I want you to get down to the MGM Grand as soon as possible. Ask for Bud Shelby at the main cashier's cage."

"Shelby," she repeated groggily. "Why?"

"You're going to get a crash course in dealing blackjack. Shelby's a shift boss and owes me a favor. He'll also vouch that you worked for him."

"I don't understand."

"You're going into Spirit Meadows first thing tomorrow."

She rubbed her tired eyes. "Does Parker know about this?"

"Yes," Hagiman said.

Emmett awakened when his ears suddenly popped open. He raised the window shade. The Southwest jet was descending over Washoe Lake. Its waters were reddish from the declining sun, and the shoreline was ringed with fresh snow. Reno's south end slid into view, the tiny roofs of the houses dusted white. Emmett obeyed the seat-belt sign, then glanced across the aisle at a copy of Las Vegas's evening newspaper, *The Sun*, in the hands of a rancher-businessman who'd worn his Stetson the entire one-hour flight. The headline declared the discovery of Stephanie Roper's car in the California desert.

On the drive to Emmett's hotel after leaving Turnipseed's condo, Hagiman and he had agreed on what Burk's media representative would reveal.

He checked his watch.

It was almost four, but he fully expected Leonard Wine to wait as long as it took him to rent a car and drive the thirty miles from Reno to Carson City. The chief advocate and defender of Indian gaming, Wine had no wish to alienate federal law enforcement. Proof of this was the lawyer's willingness to meet with Emmett on less than five hours' notice the day after Christmas.

Emmett had slept three hours after Burk left him off at his hotel, then taken a taxi to McCarran International and boarded this flight. Burk still expected him to depart for Carson City Monday morning and meet with his investigator buddy at the Nevada Gaming Control Board. Emmett would do neither, convinced that Hagiman was already busy choreographing his stay in the state capital. For all he knew, the gaming detective might be on cordial terms with Leonard Wine, enough so to blunt Parker's aim of getting to the bottom of the lawyer's interest in Wuzzie Munro's rancheria.

He wanted nothing to stand in the way of that.

The jet bumped to a landing on the icy runway, and the engines roared in deceleration.

Twenty minutes later he was speeding down Highway 395 in a rented Ford Explorer, munching on a Whopper he'd picked up in the airport Burger King. It reminded him of eating with Turnipseed in her car two nights before. *I don't drink either, Emmett.* It'd gone unspoken until that awkward moment that morning in her darkened garage, the thing they obviously shared: protracted damage from alcohol. Hers probably came from her family, her father perhaps, which would account for her familiarity with AA jargon. Emmett's damage had been self-imposed, and he hoped he'd made that clear by admitting he still went to meetings. For some reason, he'd wanted her to know.

He passed a roadside tavern. A facade of ersatz logs with the brown paint chipping off the underlying concrete. The holiday lights framing the front window reflected off a sheen of ice in the parking lot. He had no conscious desire to stop, but the impulse tugged at his right foot, almost making him let up on the pedal.

From the beginning he'd consumed liquor only to get drunk. That was half of the equation. The other was the haunting sense that something fundamental to his happiness, his wholeness, had been taken from him. When sober, he couldn't name it. But when drunk, he could share it with others, usually his fellow inmates at the Catholic Indian boarding school who'd steal out with him onto the starlit prairie to get fucked up on cheap beer.

Saudade.

Maybe he did have a name for this sense of loss. In Portuguese. His first wife, the Comanche fashion designer who'd elaborated on a few meager Comanche motifs (to a nomadic buffalo-hunting society, art always came second to a full belly) to gain entree into the haute white world, had talked him into accompanying her on a sales trip to Europe. The first stop was Lisbon, where her buyer there, an urbane homosexual, had taken the Parkers out for a night of fados. Fate songs. Their plaintiveness struck Emmett, especially because these were the songs of a gold- and glory-hunting nation that had helped launch the seaborne assault which ultimately decimated the tribes of the New World. He asked the buyer what the lyrics meant, and the man explained, "*Saudade*, my friend . . . the presence of absence." And now Emmett liked going to AA meetings in reservation towns because it rekindled that juvenile celebration of *saudade*.

He suddenly realized that he missed Turnipseed.

It was the damnedest thing. He barely knew her, didn't even like her. Whatever, he was glad Burk had tossed cold water on her idea of going undercover. She didn't seem suited for it. While she was undeniably bright and even overly mature for her years, something had robbed her of the extroverted hyper-confidence associated with success in undercover operations. As if she were blaming herself for something.

The highway dropped down out of the Washoe Valley, and Carson City spread below, its lights just blinking on through the twilight. Despite a short strip of down-at-heel casinos, the city was more like smalltown America than any other state capital Emmett had visited. Especially now, under a frosting of snow and with artificial holly wreathing the lampposts.

Following Wine's directions, he turned off the main drag and then onto an elm-lined street of Victorians, one of them the governor's mansion. Directly across the street was a vintage house the equal of the chief executive's, the offices of Leonard Wine & Associates. The icicles hanging off the gingerbread and the stuffed Santa waving from the cupola window gave the place the unreality of a Currier & Ives holiday print.

Emmett parked in front, sat a few moments gathering his thoughts.

He'd been less than truthful with Hagiman by pretending not to be familiar with the name of Leonard Wine. But Burk had been untruthful with him in saying that Wine's clientele consisted of mobsters trying to worm their way back into the lucrative Nevada gaming market they'd spawned and then lost to the mega-corporations in the late 1960s. Wine had proved more visionary than that, realizing that the Families were never coming back to the Silver State. The lawyer had risked ostracism by the Nevada Resort Association by befriending Indian gambling from its outset in the early 1980s, weathered the storm, the snubs and threats, trusting that the big casinos would eventually see opportunity instead of competition in reservation gaming operations, especially those next to California's urban areas, a market Nevada had always had to entice over the border. At present, only Leonard Wine was positioned to broker fiscal marriages between the gaming corporations and the tribes. His victory had been signaled last year when the Nevada Resort Association dropped its opposition to Indian gaming. Now, as long as the federal courts upheld this aspect of tribal sovereignty, Wine was poised to make millions.

Emmett had known all this, and his heart had skipped a beat the instant he'd read the card Wuzzie Munro passed him.

He got out of the Explorer and went up the flagstone path through the chilly air.

In the foyer, a receptionist stood from her desk at his approach. A stout, middle-aged woman in a floor-length nineteenth-century dress. "May I help you?"

"Emmett Parker. Appointment with Mr. Wine."

"Oh, yes, Mr. Wine's assistant will be right with you."

And he was, a lithe young man with long white fingers who shook hands a bit too softly for Emmett's taste. "Mr. Parker, I'm Jerome," he said, maneuvering Emmett into the expansive room beyond in which three clerks dutifully worked at rolltop desks. The whole place reeked of bourgeois respectability. "Leonard begs for just a moment longer while he finishes a long-distance call. May I get you something to drink? Cappuccino?"

"Coffee, black. Everybody working late?"

"Oh, yes, always. 'Tis the season."

"For what?" Emmett murmured to himself, sinking onto a settee while Jerome scurried off. Before him on the burled walnut cocktail table was the model of a proposed casino complex on the Rincon Reservation in San Diego County, California. It rivaled Disney World. Another rug. Once again, Indian prosperity was being built on a rug that could be pulled out from under the tribes at any time the courts decided sovereignty was just a romantic myth. In the 1890s, the Comanche had been on the way to financial independence by leasing their vast grasslands to Texas cattlemen—when implementation of the Allotment Act stripped them of that pastureland and opened it to white settlement.

Emmett had yet to receive his coffee, when a diminutive but handsome man in his early forties emerged from the gilded doors of an antique elevator cage. Catching sight of Emmett, he smiled warily. "Mr. Parker, how are you? I'm Leonard Wine."

"Mr. Wine."

"Did anyone get you something to drink?"

"Coffee's on the way."

"Excellent." Wine turned to one of the clerks. "Please have Jerome bring it up to my suite." Then he ushered Emmett into the elevator, careful to guide but not touch. Inside, he punched a button and sighed. "I presume you're investigating the Stephanie Roper tragedy."

Emmett said nothing for the moment.

"Forgive me," Wine went on, "but I know everyone with the BIA's Indian Gaming Task Force, and unless you've been recently assigned . . . ?" He let the question trail off.

"No," Emmett said, "I don't care for that line."

"Religious objections?"

"Why do you ask that?"

"Well, generally, the opposition to gambling on the reservations comes from the churches, and we certainly respect their point of view."

Stifling a yawn, Emmett said, "My objections are practical."

"In what way?" Wine asked politely.

"The last time we were a one-industry people, we wound up squatting on piles of buffalo bones, eating stale army rations."

"I certainly appreciate that," Wine said noncommittally.

"Then I hope you'll appreciate this—gaming turns reservations into criminal enclaves. Cash is a big pile of manure, and you should see the white trash buzzing into Indian Country."

"I'm afraid I find that view a bit extreme, Mr. Parker. There's absolutely no proof gaming fosters undue crime. You know that as well as I. And the cash will enable the tribes to build infrastructure up to dealing with any undesirable element."

"Including their silent partners in the casinos?"

Wine's only reply was a subdued chuckle.

Emmett came at him from another angle. "You knew Stephanie Roper?"

"Only over the phone. This way, please." Wine led him out of the cage and down the second-floor corridor to a suite with its own receptionist. A Washoe woman, Emmett judged from her broad, pleasant face. Wine's inner sanctum had a view of the state capitol. The building's silver dome was catching the final streak of daylight in the west. "A real tragedy." Wine sat behind his desk, gesturing for Emmett to take a wing chair. "What's the world coming to?"

"It's been this way a long time," Emmett answered.

Reappearing with Emmett's coffee, Jerome flitted in and out like a shadow. By the time his assistant was gone, Wine's congenial mask had dropped and he was staring out the window. For the moment, his quiet air of mastery had deserted him. "My God, are the papers right—did you really find Roper's car on the Chemehuevi Rancheria?"

"Yes."

"Was she murdered there?"

"Yes."

Wine faced Emmett again. "I'm afraid Wuzzie Munro may have been manipulated."

"Me too," Emmett said, his anger rising to his voice for the first time.

Wine caught it. His shoulders stiffened a little. "Meaning?"

Emmett stared accusingly until Wine glanced away.

"If you're questioning our part in this, Mr. Parker—"

"Whose part?"

"This firm's and"—Wine hesitated for a split second—"and IMG's . . . Inter-Mountain Gaming."

The same company on the sign tacked to the Quonset in Supai, promising a casino there. "Which is?"

"A Nevada-based corporation that manages Native American gaming operations in California, Arizona, and Colorado."

"IMG retains you?"

"That's right."

"They honestly intend to open a casino for the *Havasupai?*"

Wine came close to simpering. "Well, perhaps a token operation on-site as a training facility. The trend at this time is for the tribes to think cooperatively."

"What kind of cooperative effort?"

"A single-venue casino run jointly by several tribes."

Located along Interstate 15 near Halloran Springs, California, no doubt. Emmett took a sip of macadamia nut–flavored coffee, pondered his next move. He was reluctant to draw attention to Spirit Meadows, but then reminded himself that Hagiman had kiboshed Turnipseed's offer to go undercover in the casino there. So he figured any possible harm to the investigation was minimal. Besides, it was the natural question to ask. Wine might turn leery if Emmett let it go unasked. "And IMG manages the Shoshone House of Games in Spirit Meadows?"

"Among other casinos, yes."

"Where else?"

"Kaibab, northern Arizona. A Ute resort in Colorado."

"Then they're the bastards pulling the wool over poor Wuzzie Munro's eyes."

Finally, Wine's carefully controlled temper flared a little. "I resent that."

"You resent it. Or IMG does?"

Wisely, Wine decided to sidestep that sand trap. "IMG takes its directions from the various tribal councils."

"Including the Shoshone?"

"Yes. And their interest in Wuzzie is both paternalistic and—yes—admittedly financial. Many Western Shoshone have Northwestern Chemehuevi blood, and Ms. Munro may be the last living link to that kinship. As far as we know. The council's hired a private detective to seek other Chemehuevi who may be rotting away in inner cities throughout the country. They, too, would benefit from the Halloran Springs casino."

"And bolster the notion that the Death Valley Chemehuevi are still a viable tribe," Emmett said dryly.

"They are."

"What standard will you use, blood quantum?" Meaning the percentage of Indian blood, which with some tribes could be as little as one thirty-second and still qualify an individual for membership.

"No," Wine admitted with a faint grin, "Wuzzie seems more interested in using a cultural approach. A demonstrable affinity for Chemehuevi values. You realize, of course, that the tribe has the right to set its own criteria for enrollment."

Emmett did. And without use of the blood quantum, Wuzzie's little patchwork of landholdings could become home in time to hundreds if not thousands of unrelated Indians and mixed breeds, if not white Indian wanna-bes. A tax-free employee housing complex for a casino on the interstate. "What's the financial interest for the Shoshone?"

"Not just the Shoshone. It may be the last opportunity for many of the Indians of eastern California and northern Arizona to survive as distinct cultures. You know that as well as I, Mr. Parker. The alternative is to watch them trickle away to the cities and drink themselves to death. Have you ever been to skid row in Los Angeles? Counted the Indian faces?"

"I'd like the names of IMG's corporate officers."

Wine was briefly expressionless, then said, "I can do better than that for you." He dialed a number from memory, using the cap of a fountain pen that quivered slightly in his grasp. Seven digits, no area code. "Nigel," Wine said after a little wait, "I'm down at the office with Investigator Parker from BIA. He'd like to talk to you if it's convenient." Emmett heard a bass voice rumbling from the receiver, then Wine gave the handset to him, explaining, "Nigel Merrison, president of IMG."

"Mr. Merrison . . ."

"Good evening, Mr. Parker." A West Indies accent. "I've been expecting you."

"Oh?"

"I'm tied up tonight, but how does lunch tomorrow sound, even though it's Saturday?"

"Where?"

"Leonard will give you directions." With that, Merrison hung up.

As Emmett handed back the receiver, Wine said, "You see, Mr. Parker, we're not opposed to legitimate law enforcement efforts to keep gaming clean. The industry can't afford faceless bodies littering the desert any more than you can."

Yawning, Emmett rose and stretched. "Well, Mr. Wine, I've got to say, you've been more helpful than I expected."

"Glad you see it that way." Wine took a file from a desk drawer, and from it a single sheet of watermarked bond. "Gaming is the surest means to Indian self-sufficiency. No madman's going to blow it for us, I assure you." He handed

Emmett the paper. "Mr. Merrison's press bio. With address. He works out of his home at Lake Tahoe. Take Lakeshore Drive to Incline Beach."

It was fully dark outside but for the security lights around the governor's mansion. Emmett sat motionless behind the wheel of his rental for a few minutes—until he could no longer contain his excitement. Then he slammed his palms down on the dashboard in celebration.

The fact that Stephanie Roper's face had been sliced off was an evidentiary detail that had never been divulged to the media.

Chapter 6

The westernmost of Las Vegas's far-flung bedroom communities, Pahrump was a scattering of mobile homes on a windswept plain straddling the state border. Anna sat on the edge of a bed in the Amargosa Inn, facing two middle-aged men on the adjoining queen. Both looked like high school football coaches—the same paunches and painfully intense expressions. Special Agents Nate Benjamin and Roman Crutcher were on loan from the Salt Lake City office and had served as undercover backups many times before. Crutcher was also a soundman, a specialist in electronic surveillance. "Your possessions'll be searched and analyzed for the slightest discrepancies with your cover story," he gravely told her.

"Count on it," Benjamin, also unsmiling, added with a Brooklyn accent.

"That's the only reason we went through your luggage, Annie," Crutcher said.

"*Anna*," she adamantly corrected the man. Her father had called her Annie. She still thought Benjamin and Crutcher's search of her suitcases had been an unnecessary indignity, although the twosome had betrayed no obvious fetishes while doing the check, and they claimed to have grown daughters of their own.

"And remember to tone down your vocab," Benjamin said.

"My what?"

"Your vocabulary, Anna. It's too good for your cover. Don't try to shine. Just blend in."

"All dealers are morons?"

"Pretty much."

Shaking her head, she asked, "What about a weapon?"

"We got a snub-nosed revolver bureau-approved for you," Crutcher replied. "Easier to conceal in the beetle's engine compartment than your nine mil." She'd been issued a pink Volkswagen bug, a DEA seizure from a Mary Kay representative who'd offered a special powder on the side. "Engine's in the rear of a VW."

"I knew that," Anna said. "What happens if I need the revolver in a hurry?"

"It's a tradeoff," Crutcher explained. "You're dead in the water if you're found packing heat. If you get anywhere close to the action, they'll search your car too. Expertly. All the crannies and compartments known to the drug trade. That's why we picked a place that's unobviously obvious."

Benjamin said, "We'll show you how to reach your piece before you shove off."

"When's that?" She was eager to get going.

"Hang on." Crutcher took a metal object from his coat

pocket. A compact. "You know about your drop. And using the telephone. Phone's your absolute last resort, always. This is your emergency lifeline. A battery-operated directional beeper. Technically known as a transponder. Developed and miniaturized to be included in the cash taken in bank robberies. When you hit this button . . . it"— with some difficulty he pried out the small powder tray to show her—". . . it transmits an alert tone to us."

"We've got a fixed antenna array on top of the Nopah Range," Benjamin said. "It'll find you as long as you stick close to Spirit Meadows."

"And a portable antenna in our carryall to track you if you're on the move." Crutcher reluctantly surrendered the beeper, as if he'd grown attached to it. He looked to Benjamin. "I guess that's it."

"Good." Anna rose.

The two agents followed her out of the room, although they would remain at the inn, posing as government geologists and awaiting her summons for help, if needed, from Spirit Meadows, twenty-nine miles into California.

There was a biting chill to the predawn darkness.

She could hear loose change and keys jingling in the trouser pockets of the two men as both jogged to catch up with her. "Be patient," Benjamin cautioned, "you're not going to discover everything in a day."

"You'll be lucky to have anybody's confidence within a month. Come closer, Anna . . ." Stooping, Crutcher opened the engine deck lid and, taking her hand, guided it around. "That's the fan shroud. Right behind it is a nice little pocket in the works. Deep enough so the piece won't ever shake out."

She could feel the holstered .38, but protested. "Roman, I have to be a contortionist to reach this."

"That's the idea. Only you will find it."

Exhaling, she climbed inside the VW. Her luggage was

already stuffed in the backseat. She cranked down the window for any final instructions, although her head was full of them by now.

"*Eye contact*, Anna," Crutcher exhorted.

"I know," she said with a singsong flatness to her voice, "look 'em square in the eye."

The two men just stared at her, faces strained by worry.

Did she seem that young and inept to them? Her self-confidence dropped a notch. She hadn't completed the FBI's undercover training component, but she wasn't the first agent to go covert without benefit of it due to some sudden investigative necessity.

"I'll be in touch," she said firmly, firing up the engine. But Crutcher, the more fatherly of the two, was so reluctant to let her go on alone, he shouted after her, "Remember to—"

"Bye!" She raised her window against the cold and veered onto the highway. The VW rattled up to fifty miles an hour, and the scattered lights of Pahrump soon faded in her rearview mirror.

She began to feel better. Chipper, even.

She tried the radio, but nothing quite suited her rising mood.

It was more than leaving the pressures of the bureau behind, she decided. She was leaving herself behind as well. No longer was she Anna Turnipseed, Modoc mixed breed and token FBI female. With a wave of a legal forger's wand, she'd become Ronnie Chavez, unemployed blackjack dealer, the vagabond she might have become had her mother not insisted that she go to college. And to make her feel even less like herself, Burk Hagiman had decided not to give her an Indian incognita. There was too much communication among the Nations, not to mention the computer database on tribal affiliation made available by the BIA. Besides, reservation casinos were chronically short of dealers, and her only test of acceptability would be with the cards.

Which she dreaded.

Four hours wasn't much time to learn a new trade.

The eastern sky was brightening, but the highway curved southwest and down into a canyon, where night still lingered. There were no oncoming headlamps for as far as she could see, just the dim cone of her own lights fanning out a few yards into the Joshua forest. A breeze made the spiky beards of the trees quiver, blew ribbons of sand across the asphalt.

The miles began to feel long.

She checked her odometer: She'd gone only twelve of them since leaving Crutcher and Benjamin. Their worrying over her was starting to feel less annoying. They'd wanted to stay somewhere closer to Spirit Meadows, but there was no such place. The town was surrounded by rocky wilderness.

Watch your mouth when you get there, girl.

She had the habit of speaking her mind when pressed. One of these blurts had already made the rounds through the field offices and resident agencies of the FBI. It'd come during the preappointment hand test to see if she had the strength to squeeze the trigger of a revolver a dozen times in quick succession. A real teat buster, according to the old-timers who agreed with the late J. Edgar that the bureau had no place for female agents. She'd been grimacing by the time she got off the last torturous snick, and the evaluator frowned under his neatly trimmed mustache. "Sorry," she fired back at him without thinking, "I never got all that grip conditioning your male applicants got behind those locked bathroom doors."

She let up on the gas pedal.

Something was sparkling in the morning twilight, bobbing up and down. She strained to make sense of it.

A human figure materialized in the middle of the highway, a man waving a flashlight.

She looked for flares, wreckage, but there were no signs of an accident.

Braking, she thought of her revolver.

The man held up a palm for her to stop. He had a thick chest and sepia complexion. Shoshone. He wore a khaki uniform with a gold star pinned to his Ike jacket. He'd apparently come from a Jeep station wagon that was parked just off the pavement. An emblem on the door glimmered in her headlights.

Pulling up to him, she lowered her window. "Problem, Deputy?" His hostile eyes stole the moisture out of her mouth, but she met them squarely with her own.

He shone his light around the inside of the VW. "I'm not a deputy," he said brusquely. "Western Shoshone Tribal Police. You're on Indian land. . . ." Disconcerting news. California was a Public Law 280 state: Even on reservations, the county sheriff had criminal jurisdiction. Crutcher and Benjamin would have to be advised of this illegal roadblock and possibly more of them along the other highways into Spirit Meadows. If she hit her beeper for help, the agents might have to come in on dirt roads to avoid these barriers. "Step out," he ordered.

She did so, but left the engine running. The cold air hit her moist palms. "Have I done something wrong, Officer?"

He ignored the question. Instead, he collapsed the front seat and began going through her luggage in the back. So much for the Fourth Amendment on Indian land.

She furtively glanced at the Jeep. He appeared to be alone. But she was alone too. Completely.

"Where you headed?" he asked without turning, still rifling through her things.

"Spirit Meadows." She realized that tension pitched her voice higher than usual, but she felt powerless to bring it down.

"Why?"

She wondered how Emmett Parker might handle this, then quit looking for inspiration there—the Shoshone cop was twice her size. And she doubted that Emmett was as ready with his fists as his legend claimed. "I'm looking for work at the casino."

He stood straight and confronted her, although casually resting an elbow on the VW's roof. "What d'you do?"

"Dealer."

"Prior experience?"

"Sure."

"Where?"

"MGM Grand."

"How come you're not workin' there now?"

She put on a smile, shrugged. "I got laid off when things got slow in October. Got tired of waiting around for my boss to call me back. 'Sides, I don't like big cities."

"What's his name?"

It was now light enough to see a fuzzy golden mantle clinging to the Sierra far in the west: an approaching storm. It was probably already snowing in the mountains. "My boss? Bud Shelby."

The cop was writing something in his notebook. At first she thought it was Shelby's name, but then he tore out the sheet and handed it to her. "See this guy at the House of Games. He does all the hirin'."

"Thanks," she said. *Cyrus Fourkiller, Casino Manager*, he'd written.

"You Indian?"

"No."

"You look part Indian."

"Mexican. Same thing, I guess."

"I guess," he said, smiling as he tucked the notebook back in his shirt pocket. He was starting to warm to her, and a wave of relief swept over her. "I'm Dan Beowawe."

"Ronnie Chavez. Nice to meet you, Dan." Her door had bumped shut in the wind, and he opened it for her. She slid behind the wheel, clenched it with both hands to keep them from shaking. She'd passed her first test. A small one, but she was pleased with her performance. Yet, her relief was mingled with the disturbing sense that she'd been bullied. "Is there some trouble in town?"

"What d'you mean?"

"Is that why you're out here?"

His mouth tightened. "You just crossed an international border, Ronnie. That's all. Welcome to our world."

Then Beowawe backed away from the VW and gestured for her to drive on.

The road wound down out of the canyon and banked along an overlook of a sprawling alkali basin. She could see Spirit Meadows just emerging from the mountain shadows. There was a long scar in the brush just to the north of the last houses. An airstrip. Already she could tell that the town was small and dusty. No vegetation except for a few tamarisk trees planted around the casino parking lot. The House of Games loomed above everything else. As she watched, its brushed aluminum walls glinted explosively in a sudden rush of sunlight.

The Sierra was socked in as Emmett climbed out of Carson City toward Lake Tahoe. Reaching Spooner Summit, he hit snow and had to put the Explorer into four-wheel drive. The flakes flew horizontally at his windshield, and any view of the lake below was whited out. The glare made his eyes ache, but thankfully he'd finally gotten some decent sleep. Leaving Leonard Wine the night before, he'd found a motel and turned in right away. He had made a point of not phoning Burk Hagiman with a progress report. Otherwise, today he'd no doubt find that an FBI agent out of the Reno office had beaten him to interviewing Nigel Merrison, president of Inter-Mountain Gaming.

He reached for his handkerchief and wiped the inside of his

half of the windshield. The defroster wasn't keeping up with the condensation.

Wine and Merrison were running scared.

If anything, Emmett had gathered that much from his meeting with Leonard Wine. Whatever IMG's plans, the murder of Stephanie Roper hadn't figured in them. Wine especially wanted to make that clear before the investigation went any deeper. Merrison might prove even more unnerved than Wine. *I've been expecting you.* The last thing anybody in the gaming industry admitted to law enforcement. Ever. The unexpected appearance of a cop always prompted mild consternation that a pillar of the chamber of commerce could be asked about such sordid enterprises as profit skimming and money laundering, the only reasons some parties invested in casinos.

Emmett made a right onto Highway 28, which ran up the Nevada side of the lake. Checking the dash clock, he saw that it was almost noon. He frowned and accelerated around a snowplow, fishtailing into a foot of unbroken slush.

He could finally see Tahoe through the pines. Its waters looked gray, cold.

Leonard Wine's slip about Roper's corpse being faceless— was it truly that? Attorneys in Wine's league didn't make gaffes that incriminating. Realizing this had turned Emmett's initial delight into puzzlement. He'd been pleased that he had reached the point in the investigation where he was reacting less to the suspect's lead and starting to exercise a little control of his own. But had Wine been hinting that he was ready to trade information for immunity? That's what puzzled Emmett, although this explanation made more sense than writing the whole thing off as a careless slip of the tongue. And it gave him all the more reason not to let the U.S. Attorney cut a deal that let Wine off too cheaply. The man would reveal everything only as long as he believed that it was the only way to save his own skin.

Emmett almost missed the Lakeshore Drive sign, it was so plastered with snow. Like most Pacific storms to collide with the central Sierra Nevada, this one was coming in pulses, waves of blizzard interspersed with periods of relative calm in which a light fall glittered down through the branches of the trees.

Emmett now drove through one of these brief calms.

Slowing, he crept into a neighborhood that looked like an alpine Beverly Hills. Cedar mansions stood where he imagined the Washoe had once camped. He tried to visualize those simple villages in the ponderosa forest, but the $60,000 Range Rovers parked in the circular driveways and the Mexican house servants shoveling the walkways made it difficult: This kind of wealth created the illusion that it'd always been there.

Nigel Merrison had done well.

Born and raised in Kingston, he'd worked his way up in Jamaican gaming from slot-change boy to vice president of operations. From there, Harrah's had tapped him to open and manage its resort in Laughlin, Nevada, a bait stop along the Colorado River until the hotel developers poured in. The casino prospered, as did Merrison, who soon looked to becoming his own boss. "Intrigued by the potential for self-sufficiency offered by gaming to Native Americans," as read the press biography Wine had supplied Emmett, "Mr. Merrison formed Inter-Mountain Gaming [IMG] around a cadre of proven industry professionals. Together with the progressive tribal leadership of the Ute Nation, they transformed a small-time bingo operation in western Colorado into a major destination resort. . . ." The rest was purported to be history.

Emmett had come to the end of Lakeshore Drive.

A private road took off from the cul-de-sac. The wrought iron gates were wide open, and a set of tire impressions showed blackly on the snow-covered lane. The tracks curved down into the mist that was scudding in off the surface of the lake.

Inching past the gates, Emmett cracked his door for a

closer look at the left-side track. Single cut. The vehicle had gone in. It hadn't come out.

Shutting his door, he picked up speed.

In a rush, the snowfall returned.

The road dived steeply through a stand of red firs, then leveled out across a putting green. The pin flag was snapping so loudly in the blizzard, he could hear it over the engine and defroster noise. Ahead, the mansion appeared through the snow, a kind of Viking castle with heavy timbers and brick turrets. A solitary second-story window was lit. A yellow Chevy van was parked outside the front door, facing Emmett. Its tailpipe was leaking exhaust even though the vehicle had been there long enough for the windshield to have glazed over.

Emmett punched up his high beams as he approached it.

The driver's door glided open, and a slender woman in a chef's uniform got out. Almost in the same instant, Emmett noticed on the van's side: INCLINE CATERING. He rolled down his window as the woman stepped unsteadily over to him.

"Have you seen Mr. Merrison?" She flinched against the flakes as if they were drops of acid.

"Why?"

"Well, I talked to him just fifteen minutes ago. He told me to ring at the front, and he'd let me in."

Emmett glanced over the upper-story windows. No hint of movement in any of them. "Merrison have servants?"

"Just a housekeeper-cook," the caterer replied, "but this is her"—she clung onto her hat as a gust billowed whitely all around her—"her day off. That's why Mr. Merrison asked me to do lunch for him."

"Stay here," Emmett ordered, bailing out.

He went around the south corner of the mansion—into three feet of hard wet snow that had slid off the copper-clad roof. He clambered over it and paused at the far edge of the house, surveying the grounds, which sloped down to the lake. Nothing, just shallow drifts and then the slate-colored waters fading into the mist. Something was whistling. Like the wind shrilling around a telephone or power wire.

A solarium was attached to the back side of the mansion, and its glass door was ajar.

Quietly, Emmett went through it, then on to the kitchen.

A teakettle was shrieking atop the stove. He left it on, passed into the dining room. Empty. As were all the vaulting rooms on the ground floor. The darkness at the top of the stairs made him finally draw his .357, although he held it behind his leg as he ascended to the second floor. Voices. He followed them down the unlit corridor to a square of light spilling from an open door.

"Merrison?" he called, promising himself that this would be the only time he'd ask.

No reply, although the murmur of voices continued.

Emmett spun around the doorjamb, his handgun clenched before him. The marble-tiled master bath echoed with his sharp breaths. A wall-mounted television was tuned to the Financial News Network, and a string of stock quotes crawled along the bottom of the screen. On the vanity, a neat row of toiletries was broken only by a razor and can of shaving cream. The razor was in the sink, and the can lay on its side at the far end of the counter.

The shower curtain was drawn.

Emmett whipped it back with his free hand.

No one.

There was a spray of white foam on the bathmat. He knelt to inspect it. Mentholated shaving cream, he determined with a sniff. It'd been shot off into thin air, apparently missing the cupped palm poised to accept it.

Swiftly now, he went through all six bedrooms. Nothing. Holstering, he went downstairs to the living room bay window. Memorizing the telephone number on the side of the van, he motioned for the caterer to leave. She drove off at a reluctant clip, her lunches undelivered.

Emmett turned off the kettle in the kitchen, gazed reflectively out the window into the storm. There was a possibility unrelated to the Roper homicide. Gaming executives were prime kidnapping targets, some even kept cash squirreled away for such an eventuality.

But this didn't feel like a kidnapping somehow. Maybe it was the absence of tire impressions preceding the caterer's down the long driveway. The usual abductor ran a portal-to-portal operation from the victim's home or business to the hideout.

Returning to the solarium, he checked the door for signs of forced entry. There were none.

Whatever had happened, it was only twenty minutes old. The caterer had talked to Merrison then. Emmett's chances for an easy solution were slipping away.

At the glass wall he looked for movement out in the swirling veils of snow, anything. He was thinking of driving back up to the cul-de-sac to check for any indication that a vehicle had parked there—when he saw them. A line of faint pocks in the drifts. Shoe impressions. They were partially filled in but distinct enough to suggest to him where two men had walked side by side toward the lake.

He bolted out the door.

The closer he came to the shore, the clearer the prints became. They turned west, following the beach. Above was a plunging hillside, forested and undeveloped. Somewhere up there was the highway that ringed Tahoe, for Emmett could hear the rumble of a snowplow blade scraping pavement.

He stopped.

The surface of the snow all around him showed fresh disturbance. Carefully, he raked away the topmost stuff—and his breath caught in his throat. Blood. It was just starting to freeze: He pinched an icy dollop between his fingers, and it ran redly into his palm. He crawled forward, digging deeper in an ever-widening arc. Frigid slurry filled his oxfords. He'd come dressed for lunch, not a winter trek. But the snow was more than deep enough to conceal a body, and he kept on working feverishly, pausing only to wipe his eyelashes on the shoulders of his herringbone jacket before they froze fast.

At last he was convinced that the drift held no victim.

Then, on the verge of rising, he found something. He thought it was an autumn leaf, a late-dropper still pale and moist from the tree. But then he saw it for what it was—a severed human ear.

He shot to his feet and plowed on, sprinting now.

Within twenty yards his confusion only grew. The two men were still walking abreast, even though one had just mutilated the other. Perhaps to quell a brief resistance? Blood spatters began to dot the surface.

Once more Emmett drew his revolver.

The tracks came to a sheer rock face and vanished.

He peered up at a soaring granite knob. There was no way around it except to wade the shallows. He thrashed into the water up to his knees, gritting his teeth against the fiery cold. It cut to the bone. He'd heard that Tahoe never froze, which seemed impossible at the moment. The frigid water was gin-clear, and he could see rounded divots along the sandy bottom. They led him around the bouldery outcrop and into a little cove.

There, a man floated facedown, spread-eagled and shrouded in a pink cloud.

Approaching, Emmett aimed his muzzle toward a chute in the hillside above. Through the slanting snow he thought he could see a single set of tracks zigzagging up this steep channel that had been gouged by a seasonal creek and swept partially clear of snow by the wind. He searched the storm-tossed firs on either side of it for a human shape, but there was no visibility after fifty or so feet. The falling snow was like a stinging curtain.

At last, he took a quick glance at the body.

Blood seeped lightly from where the ear had been—and from a knife wound at the base of the skull. Nappy hair shorn close to the scalp. Part African, for sure. Jamaican, perhaps. Nigel Merrison was still wearing a silk bathrobe and slippers, which meant that his captor had never had any intention of forcing him out into the weather except to kill him.

Emmett glanced upslope once more, then rolled over the body. The face was gone, crudely peeled away just as Roper's had been, revealing a grisly underlay of muscle and cartilage. And, as with the BLM woman, his teeth had been reamed out. For a split second a grotesque horror blanked Emmett's vision—the dripping of water over the eyeballs had given them the appearance of life. He gripped the already bruised throat, feeling for the carotid arteries. There was no pulse.

Again he scanned the long chute for the killer, who was undoubtedly climbing for the highway as fast as he could.

From far above came a clatter of falling rocks.

Swiftly Emmett indented one of Merrison's eyeballs with his thumb, just to assure himself that there was absolutely no life. The tissue was completely flaccid.

He waded ashore, dragging the corpse onto the narrow strip of beach, and started up the chute at a clumsy trot. He couldn't feel his legs. His temperature was dropping dangerously. Only vigorous motion would stave off hypothermia. Only movement would keep him alive. A voice within begged him to go back to the mansion, to call the Washoe County sheriff's office and let them handle it from here. But that was his fear talking. If he stopped now, the killer would get away. Within minutes of this spot, three highways led out of the northern end of the Tahoe basin. There were a dozen communities between Incline Village and Tahoe City where a fugitive could break into a vacation cabin and comfortably wait out the manhunt.

Emmett halted, gasping, lungs scorched by the cold. His fingers no longer felt as if they were his own. He tried to blow into his gun hand so his grip wouldn't fail. His pants legs were starting to freeze. He was now at least three hundred feet above the lake, and the chute had drifted over enough to show widely set boot impressions—incredibly, the man was still running.

Moving again, Emmett had to plant each step with all his concentration or risk slipping. Dizziness washed over him, and he used his free hand to steady himself. A hard blast made him sink to his knees, blinded, but as the wind began to ebb, he glimpsed a silhouette standing calmly in front of him several yards ahead. A human head and shoulders, he was sure, although the features were left blurred and coarse-grained by the whiteout. Cords—no, braids—flapped sideways of the indistinct head. He cried out for the figure to halt, but his voice was lost in the gale funneling down the chute.

And when he could see clearly again, the silhouette was gone.

He pressed on, one heavy step at a time, trying to pound sensation into his increasingly numb legs. The boughs of the young firs flanking the chute whipped his face.

He came to a ledge, rock debris jammed under a fallen log. It was as high as his head, but among the broken pieces of granite there were hand- and footholds. He pocketed his .357 for the moment and reached with his left hand for the nubbin of a branch. He was muscling himself up, when white-hot pain flashed through his brain. He began falling, but then the sharp thing that had impaled his hand to the log held him, pinning him to dangle helplessly with his toes just inches above relief from his torture. It was like the Sun Dance of ten years before: hanging suspended between heaven and earth, racked by prodigious suffering.

Growling, he fumbled for his revolver with his right hand, seized it, and fired twice over the top of the log.

The blade let go of Emmett's hand, and he plummeted.

At first he tobogganed headlong down the chute, shoulders

glancing off rocks, bracing for the blow that would knock him unconscious. But just before he lost his sense of up and down, he spun around, jammed in his heels, and skidded to a stop.

After a moment he raised his right hand. He was still clenching his .357. But his left hand was bleeding profusely. He formed a fist; the flow subsided slightly. His entire arm burned and twitched from the injury.

Scrambling to his feet, he left the chute and took to the young firs. Their branches formed an almost impenetrable thicket, but he made slow progress by scrambling over the tops, nearly swimming through the snow-laden foliage toward the highway guardrail he could now see above.

An engine turned over with a clangor. Eight cylinders in need of tuning. The sound quickly receded.

Then, only the wind could be heard.

Emmett heaved himself up the last few feet, leaving bloody handprints in the snow, and tumbled over the rail, falling hard on his side. Wheezing, he lifted his head. The car was minutes gone, but its tires had left well-defined impressions. The driver had made a sharp U-turn and headed west. Emmett crept on all fours over to the tracks, tried to fix the pattern in his memory over the distraction of his throbbing hand. He was desperately trying to do this, when a truck horn blatted at him. He lunged back. The huge curved blade of the Caltrans plow barely missed his legs.

When it had passed, the impressions had been erased, and only bare wet asphalt showed.

Chapter 7

He was soaking his feet in a basin of warm water when Burk Hagiman walked into his Carson City hospital room. Without knocking. He looked briefly at Emmett's bandaged left hand, then asked, "How is it?"

"Okay." The ER doctor had told him that the knife blade had nicked a bone but otherwise passed through flesh with little damage. Not counting the fifteen sutures closing each end of the wound.

Hagiman sat without being invited, but kept his overcoat on. A tan-colored trench coat. It seemed an affectation in the largely rainless Southwest, a declaration that all his ambitions pointed toward an eventual posting in the East. His bald pate was ruddy from the evening chill. This morning's snowstorm had passed east, and in the heavy stillness that followed, the temperature was plunging. Halfway across the room, Emmett could feel the cold penetrating the window glass. Lights were coming on across the grounds of the capitol, twinkling blue through the leafless trees.

"You going to lose some toes?" Hagiman asked disinterestedly.

"Doubt it," Emmett replied. For the past half hour a sharp tingle, painful but reassuring, had kept his mind keen. He already knew his next step, and it involved Leonard Wine. "Been frostbit before, and this ain't it."

Hagiman nodded. He was pressing his thumbs together, plainly building steam for a blow. Probably rehearsing what he'd say, no doubt having learned years earlier in a Rapid City motel room that there could be a big price for anger.

Waiting, Emmett lifted his right foot out of the basin and gingerly flexed his swollen toes. After missing the killer's getaway by minutes, and the snowplow by seconds, he'd run down the vacant highway to a convenience market and called the Washoe County sheriff's office. That quarter-mile sprint had probably saved his feet: He'd been sweating by the time he reached the phone, although his hand had started bleeding again.

Finally, Hagiman could wait no longer. "So . . . you came up here yesterday."

Emmett didn't know how he'd learned that, perhaps from the Washoe Homicide detectives, but admitted laconically, "That's right."

"Get a chance to meet with Nevada Gaming before closing time yesterday afternoon?"

"No."

"What led you to Merrison, then?"

"Leonard Wine."

"Meaning, you took on Wine without the benefit of a briefing from Gaming."

"Yeah," Emmett said, "I somehow managed to stumble through it."

"And what'd Wine say?"

"I'll put it all in the report."

"Wrong."

Emmett raised an eyebrow.

"I need to know *now*," Hagiman hammered on. "I've got some fence mending to do with the Gaming Board, thanks to you. And San Bernardino County too. The sheriff wants to know what we've got going in the middle of his desert, and I promised I'd advise him before we make a major move. And then there's my Los Angeles division. They don't like learning in the papers that the Las Vegas field office was playing in their backyard." Emmett slid his right foot back into the warm water. His body felt heavy with exhaustion, yet as soon as some more feeling returned to his feet, he was out of there. The rented Explorer was parked at the sheriff's substation up at Lake Tahoe, but he figured he could walk from the hospital to where he needed to go. "Gaming was closing in on Merrison," Hagiman continued. "The man had long-term ties to organized crime in Jamaica. The last thing they needed was you crashing their party."

"Too bad."

Hagiman repeated caustically, "Too bad?"

"I'm investigating the homicide of a federal employee, not Nevada gambling violations."

"*We're* investigating, Parker. Not just you. And we rely on the cooperation of allied agencies every step of the way."

Emmett almost laughed. Hagiman preaching the gospel of interagency collaboration when he was invariably the first to violate it. "Well, Burk, the Gaming Board can't look too deep into Merrison's background."

"Why not?"

"Five years ago they cleared him to operate a casino down

in Laughlin. Was he cleaner then than he was this morning? If not, it sure as hell looks like somebody's palm got greased."

That gave Hagiman pause.

Rising, Emmett stepped out of the basin and started across the room for the closet.

"What're you doing?" Hagiman demanded.

"Getting dressed."

At first Emmett thought he was going to argue. But instead, Hagiman asked, "Got anything to wear?"

"This 'n' that. Sheriff's office brought my things over from the motel."

"Your clothes looked pretty torn up in the crime scene photos."

"That they were."

"Never got a look at the bastard?"

"Nope." Emmett purposely unlatched the closet door with his left hand, just not to favor it. His lips thinned over his teeth for an instant, then he reached down for his suitcase. The doctor had said that had the back and edge of the blade been turned around, his hand would have been ripped in two.

"Washoe Homicide tell you their guess?" Hagiman asked.

"Jamaican mob." Emmett carried the suitcase back to the bed and snapped it open. "I walked right into the middle of a disciplinary hit."

"Makes sense. Merrison was being investigated. Careless of him. In the past, that's been enough to cut the ties that bind."

"They took out Stephanie Roper too?"

"I don't know. The two facial mutilations say yes, maybe. . . ." Hagiman sighed. "Damn if I understand this second one. The first, sure. The killer wanted to obstruct I.D. of Roper's body. But she was dumped a hundred miles from home. Why do the same to Merrison almost within sight of his house?"

Emmett had an idea, but he wasn't ready to discuss it with

Hagiman, who assigned all Indian motives to the realm of mindless superstition. Yet there might be some basis for a Jamaican connection. Particularly with much of the Havasupai Reservation running around in dreadlocks, playing reggae. Still, his instincts were resisting the Caribbean explanation: There was something ethnically familiar in this. The taking of faces. Was the motivation here related to that of taking scalps? Among tribes like the Lakota, the practice hadn't been based on any urge to desecrate the vanquished. It'd been predicated on the belief that the spirit of a man dwelled in his hair. A scalp was a dual form of reparation to the family of a slain warrior, containing the spirits of both the foe responsible and their departed loved one, which had been captured by that enemy in battle.

There was also something in this that brushed against the fringes of personal memory.

Emmett tossed his hospital gown in a corner and put on a fresh T-shirt. Wine had known about Roper's mutilation, but Emmett decided to keep that to himself for the time being. He felt Hagiman's eyes on his pectoral scars. It was always between them, that summer in South Dakota, a raw nerve waiting for the slightest touch to start buzzing again.

"Well," Hagiman said, "we'll find the bastard. Five law enforcement outfits are tearing the Tahoe Basin apart. He can't have gotten far. Though, it'd been nice if you'd gotten a vehicle description . . . other than just the possibility it's an older model eight-banger."

Emmett ignored the hint of criticism. He put on a pair of Levi's. "I want all reports of recovered stolens within fifty miles of the lake forwarded to me." He smiled while buttoning the fly. "But then again, maybe he didn't have a car."

"How's that?"

"Maybe he flew."

Hagiman remained deadpan. "Speaking of, I'm returning to Vegas tonight. When can I expect you back in town?"

"Soon." Emmett fought a shiver as he took out a flannel shirt. He was colder than he'd realized. It was as if the marrow in his bones had turned to ice. He'd been so close to dying on that hillside, and yet he'd been spared. Somehow, his numbing fatigue made him feel ungrateful toward the unnameable forces that had made that possible. On the ambulance ride down from Tahoe, he'd expected elation, plus anger toward the man who'd pinned his left hand to the fallen log with a knife. But that, too, was curiously absent, even though he could still mark the beating of his own pulse in the stab wound.

He asked, "How's Turnipseed doing?"

"Okay," Hagiman said casually.

"I need some reading material on the activities of Jamaican posses in California and Nevada."

"I'll put together whatever's available."

"Why can't Turnipseed?"

"She's busy."

And then it hit Emmett—why the man had been hanging back, not giving full rein to his usual truculence. His heart sank. "What's happened to her?"

"Nothing."

"Horseshit. Where is she?"

Hagiman stared at Emmett a moment, then said, "Spirit Meadows." He'd leaned forward in the chair, bracing his elbows atop his knees so that his forearms were poised to protect his face.

"*What!*"

Hagiman ponderously rose. "You heard me."

Emmett took a step toward him, came close to swinging, but miraculously stopped and didn't throw the punch. To his credit, Hagiman didn't flinch. Still, the two men remained within an arm's length of each other.

Emmett made himself slow down. Perhaps he'd misunderstood. "You don't mean undercover. Tell me you don't mean that."

"I've got two salts only thirty miles away from her in Pahrump."

"They might as well be in China!"

"Nonsense, Parker—thirty miles is nothing. Most of that summer in South Dakota we were a hundred and fifty miles away from you. Half the time we didn't have a goddamn clue where the hell you were."

"I knew the players, the situation. She knows nothing!"

"Has to learn sometime."

"Not in a snake pit like Spirit Meadows, you son of a bitch!"

Hagiman glared back at him. "You hit me again, and I'll have your ass," he said defiantly. "I'm not going to take another one for the good of the team."

Emmett recalled the intense satisfaction of watching Hagiman reel against the wall of the motel room ten years before, blood running from the man's nostrils and down over his chin. But now the voice of reason within him told him to keep talking. As long as he talked, he might not cross the line. "You tell San Bernardino S.O. she's in there?"

"No. Besides, the reservation's just inside Inyo County."

"But you promised the San Bernardino sheriff you'd tell him before you made a move, you lying sack of shit. You can lie to him and get away with it. But not to me!"

Hagiman wore his piece in a shoulder holster, and now exposed it as he brushed back his jacket flap to perch his hand on his hip. "Shut up," he said.

"You going to shoot me, Burk?"

"Control yourself."

"Because if you aren't, I'd cover up that pistol real goddamn quick!"

Hagiman glared a few seconds longer, then slowly sank into his chair, the front panel of his jacket sliding back over his weapon.

Emmett ached to seize him by the lapels and hurl him through the window. Once again, someone had usurped his personal responsibility for a subordinate's safety. The last time had been in Oklahoma City twelve years earlier, and it had ended fatally. Dress blues, white gloves, and a piper playing "Amazing Grace" on the far side of the cemetery.

But, finally, he forced himself to take a step backward from Burk Hagiman.

Then another.

He saw that his hands were still clenched, and he unfisted them. The injured one was throbbing. He withdrew to the bed, where he took his hiking boots from the suitcase and started putting them on, awkwardly, with his bandaged hand.

"I didn't order this to get back at you." Hagiman looked relieved despite himself.

"Right."

"Listen—sending Anna in was just the next logical step, based on the leads you yourself developed."

"Well, thanks for clearing it through me. I guess I got it wrong that the U.S. Attorney made me the ramrod on this one."

"It's a matter of expediency. I didn't have time to advise you of a sudden investigative opportunity. Just as you didn't with me in regards to Merrison. Happens all the time in joint operations. Besides, I'd think you'd be happy."

Emmett stopped in the midst of tugging on a boot. *"Happy?"*

"Sure," Hagiman said, "you never were a friend to Indian gaming. You've got too much sense for that. These two homicides could be the final nails in its coffin. Congress has been looking for proof that reservation gambling is an open invitation to corruption and racketeering. Here it is. In spades."

"Early for assumptions." Emmett returned to the closet, where the nurse had hung up his jackets. His herringbone was still wet from snowmelt and streaked with red from his hand wound. He bundled it up, tossed it across the room into his suitcase.

He was reaching for his parka, when Hagiman said, "Never seen you react quite like this. . . ." His tone the moment before had been vaguely conciliatory, which must have taken a toll on his pride, for now there was the hint of a smirk in his voice. A locker-room taunt. "Level with me, Emmett."

"What?"

"You fucking her? Is that what's behind this?"

Emmett's hands froze as he was threading his holstered revolver onto his belt. "If that girl's neck wasn't on the chopping block," he said hoarsely, "I think I could kill you right now, and live with the consequences."

Then he grabbed his suitcase and left.

At ten minutes to eight, Anna walked out of her sixteen-dollar motel room and started across the highway toward the Shoshone House of Games. She carried Ronnie Chavez's résumé, all of one page with two misspellings that lent authenticity to her alleged general equivalency diploma. The stars hung low in the sky, and a zephyr was blowing trash into the border of tamarisk trees. The casino's lights were garish but were still swallowed by the blackness of the moonless desert night. The rest of the buildings in town were barely lit, as if some ancient caution was still in force, one against big fires that might draw the notice of enemy raiding parties. She counted only five cars in the parking lot, two with Barstow license plate holders, three with Victorville—both cities were within two hours' driving time of Spirit Meadows.

Not exactly a destination resort.

She pushed through the heavy glass door, and a gust of stale cigarette smoke hit her. She took a moment before continuing down a gauntlet of video poker machines. Her heart was pounding. All day she'd felt as if she were whirling naked on a stage. If she stopped spinning, everyone would see her for what she was. A rookie federal agent with eight largely uneventful months on the job.

The House of Games logo, which appeared as the winning symbols on the slot reels, was a grinning Indian chieftain with a fat nose, maroon complexion, and huge feather headdress. Anywhere but here, a tribal casino, the mascot would have been protested as an offensive stereotype. Yet somehow it fit the House of Games. The entire place had an air of forced gaiety that had backfired and become a grim joke on itself.

"Hey, Ronnie!" Sal Baldecchi, the shift boss, spotted her from his station among the blackjack tables. "I think you're in luck." Sal was a gaunt, well-dressed man with big ears and a charming smile. Old Vegas gentry admittedly down on his luck: He'd been assistant manager of The Sands in the Rat Pack days. So far he'd gone out of his way to convince her that he was on her side. And that made her even more uneasy. In the world of gaming, everything came at a price. "Mr. Fourkiller just got in."

"Great."

"Mezzanine level, last door on the left. Knock first."

"You're a sweetheart." She lingered at the landing midway up the staircase, surveying the main room. More staff than patrons were visible. Each of the three on-duty dealers looked at her full in the face, making her wonder if job cuts were in the air. Earlier, Sal had confided in her that only the occasional tourist bus of Germans or Japanese on the way to Las Vegas from Death Valley was keeping the place afloat. No wonder the Shoshone were casting a covetous glance toward the Halloran Springs site along Interstate 15.

She stopped as her own reflection confronted her at the top of the stairs.

Benjamin and Crutcher had warned her to treat every mirror in the casino as if it were two-way. She decided that a quick check of her makeup and clothes was in order. That was the hardest part of this: trying to figure out what would appear natural. She examined her mascara, twice as much as she ordinarily put on. Still, her eyes looked small and scared. She was wearing the de rigueur white blouse and black slacks for dealers.

Light-headed, she turned.

The door at the far end of the balcony waited.

After four attempts today, this was the closest she'd gotten to Cyrus Fourkiller. Each time, she had been sent away with the explanation that the casino manager had yet to return from somewhere unspecified, although he was expected anytime.

Always *Mr. Fourkiller*, never Cyrus or Cy.

There was a judas window in the door. She knocked, and seconds later the tiny window snapped open, making her jump a little. Humorless brown eyes peered out at her. "Help you?" the woman asked.

"Um, my name's Ronnie Chavez. Mr. Baldecchi said I've got to talk to Mr. Fourkiller if I want a job here."

"Do you?"

"Do I what?"

"Want a job here?"

"Bad." Anna gave a meaningless laugh.

The eyes glanced down at her blouse and slacks. "Dealer?"

"Sure am."

"You have references?"

"I worked for the MGM—"

"Hold on a minute . . ." A deadbolt was thrown back, and then the door opened for Anna. The rawboned woman inside was Indian, but decidedly not Shoshone. She had a long, narrow face and an aquiline nose. Maybe some eastern or Canadian tribe. "Close the door and have a seat," she said, returning to her desk.

"You're working late," Anna observed nervously.

Ignoring the comment, the woman picked up her phone

and punched an intercom button. "Mr. Fourkiller, a Ms. Chavez is here to discuss employment opportunities with you. . . ." Pause. "Yes, sir . . . blackjack." She listened briefly, eyes blank, then hung up and said to Anna, "Go on in."

Closing the door behind her, Anna hesitated just beyond the threshold. She could hear a water tap running. The office was dimly lit, although neon spilled coolly out a side door onto the Navajo rug that covered the floor. To one side of the desk was a bank of television monitors, each spying on a different section of the casino. Behind the desk was a bay window. Through it Anna could track a Learjet taxiing down the airstrip, its rotating beacon flashing across the scrub.

"Why in the world would anybody want to be a blackjack dealer?" a smoothly modulated voice inquired through the side door.

"Beats honest work," she answered. She hoped for a chuckle, but none followed. "I need the money," she amended.

"That's better."

Shifting a few steps, she managed to see through the door into the small lavatory beyond. Cyrus Fourkiller, she presumed. He was hunched over the sink, washing his face. He had a broad, muscular back, and hanging halfway down it were two dark brown braids. "Tell me about yourself, Ms. Chavez."

"What's to tell?"

"Ever been arrested?"

"No way."

"That's a start." He stood erect and dried his face on a plush towel. She expected him to come out, but he didn't. Instead, he laid the towel on the vanity and began scrubbing his fingernails with a small brush. He was handsome in a remote sort of way. Like his secretary, he wasn't Shoshone. Plains Indian, judging by his angular facial-bone structure. "I wonder," he mused out loud, watching her reflection in the mirror before him, "what would things be like today if we'd washed after each contact with whitey."

"I'm sorry, Mr. Fourkiller?"

"Don't be. You're Indian, aren't you?"

"Well . . . Mexican."

"A Mexican is somebody who can't decide if he's an Indian or a Spaniard." Fourkiller rinsed his hands, shook the excess water off. "Microbes, Ms. Chavez."

"Pardon?"

"They decimated us with microbes, not bullets. We shook their hands—and died by the millions. That's how we catch most bugs, according to modern science. Hand contact. I always wash when I return from the company of strangers." At last, he emerged from the lavatory, a towering man in his late twenties with an incandescent stare. He switched on the desk lamp and took her in slowly from head to toe without apology. "The missionaries," he went on, rolling down the sleeves of his white dress shirt, "they gave us the key to survival, but wrapped it in so much mumbo jumbo, we couldn't grasp it at the time."

Sensing that he wanted her to show a little initiative, she sat on the sofa without being asked. "What key?"

" 'Cleanliness is next to Godliness.' " He took two gold links off his desktop and fastened his cuffs. Behind him, the jet roared up into the sky, but he paid it no mind.

"You got your own plane?" she asked.

"Belongs to our parent company." He held out his hand. "Pray tell, Ms. Chavez, is that a résumé you're clutching so moistly?"

Rising, she gave it to him, then darted back down.

He frowned as he read. "Bud Shelby . . ."

"Yeah?"

"He's an asshole."

Her heart skipped a beat, but she made herself put on some indignation. "He is not."

Fourkiller leveled his uncanny stare on her. "Maybe you don't know him as well as you think."

"Enough to know a pussycat when I see one."

"Pussycat." Fourkiller smiled and broke off the stare. "He'd get a kick out of that."

Was he bluffing, or did he really know Shelby? And if he did, could the MGM shift boss be trusted to protect her cover? She struggled to keep the worry off her face. "Anyways," she said, "I'm the one looking for a job, not Bud."

"True." Fourkiller took a leather jacket off the cushion of his chair, unfolded it, and spread it over the backrest. Anna saw that the shoulders and sleeves were wet. He sat. "But to be frank, Ms. Chavez—I just fired a dealer from Vegas, and I don't know if I want to take on another."

"Why not?"

"She had a cute little scam going here. Her druggie pals showed up with their cocaine profits, bought chips at her table, played a few hands, then cashed out, taking our nice, clean bills and a game earnings receipt away with them. So, forgive me if I worry that one or more of my employees might be drawing a paycheck from somebody other than me and Inter-Mountain Gaming. Should I worry about you, Ms. Chavez?"

She was afraid that the hammering of her heart was showing through her blouse. "No."

"Good, because not only did I fire the bitch, I turned her over to the DEA." A lie, Anna was sure, which calmed her down slightly. Hagiman said that he'd called around to all allied agencies, asking if they had had anything going in Spirit Meadows recently. No one had. Fourkiller tapped his bottom lip with his forefinger for a moment, then reached for his phone. "Yes, Ms. Lajeunesse—have Sal bring me a shoe and a chip rack." Hanging up, he tilted back in his chair and stared right through Anna. Before, she'd thought there was a spark of sexual interest, but now none of that showed, and his eyes were cold. "You related to anybody on this reservation?"

"No."

"Do you know *anybody* on this reservation?"

"No . . . except—"

"Except who?"

"Officer Beowawe. He stopped me on the way in, introduced himself."

"All right."

"Why's that matter?" she asked.

Fourkiller checked the surveillance screens. "The government has always excelled at pitting Indian against Indian. Crow and Pawnee scouts rode with Custer. Sitting Bull was gunned down by his own people, BIA cops. The White Mountain Apache got their thirty pieces of silver to track down Geronimo and the Chiricahua Apache. Flagrant examples. But sometimes the feds are far more devious. They turn your own brothers against you, and you don't know it until things have gone too far, until their conspiracy is rolling along like a juggernaut."

"What's a juggernaut?" she asked.

He smiled again, paternalistically this time. "Something that leaves you with your face in the mud. Now, I'll share a secret with you, Ronnie Chavez—I hate gambling. . . ." He chuckled as she widened her eyes. "That's right. Every part of it. The stink of cigar smoke and the slot machine bells. The poor white trash who come here night after night because easy money is the only dream they have. But I put up with it. Know why?"

She shook her head.

"Gaming is the means to an end," Fourkiller went on. "That end is self-reliance. Sovereignty, if you like. Since the House of Games opened, food stamp usage on this reservation has dropped by seventy percent. The Shoshone now run their own health clinic without outside aid, their own justice system. Still, the state and federal governments are pushing the Indian gaming industry into a corner. Well, any animal backed into a corner will fight to the death. We Lakota learned what surrender to the United States means. It means Wounded Knee. Frozen bodies in the snow—" He seemed to be visualizing this image, when a soft rapping turned his head toward the door. "Come in," he said.

So he was Lakota. Sioux. Anna had suspected so.

Fourkiller's secretary, Ms. Lajeunesse, opened the door for Sal Baldecchi, who held a chip rack and card shoe.

"On my desk," Fourkiller instructed.

"Surely, sir," Sal answered with his ingratiating smile.

"Deal to me, Ms. Chavez."

Anna's mouth had gone dry. She and some other agents had played poker on a long stakeout once, and even then she'd been ribbed about her clumsy shuffling. Failure was unthinkable, and yet she did think of it, seeing Stephanie Roper lying faceless on an autopsy table.

"I don't have all night," Fourkiller said.

She stepped up to his desk. It was covered with green felt, like a blackjack table. So this test was a regular occurrence in his office. He took a big handful of mixed chips.

Sal set the rack before her, pulled a fresh pack of cards from his inner coat pocket, and opened it. He fanned the deck into an arc for her. "Here you go, babe." He gave her an encouraging wink.

"Thanks," she said, going through the deck with her index finger to make sure that all fifty-two cards were there. This, Bud Shelby had warned her, was the first opportunity for a major gaffe. She was almost through the diamonds when she spotted it, yet she remained expressionless as she scooped the cards into a neat pile.

Fourkiller's eyes were riveted on her. "All set?"

"As soon as I get the jack of diamonds."

Sal laughed approvingly, slipping a second pack from his pocket. "I knew she was a sharpie."

Fourkiller said nothing, just kept watching her.

The second deck proved to be complete with no marks or printing imperfections on any of the back sides. After shuffling, she buried the top card. Fourkiller bet three chips and stood pat on two cards. She dealt herself a twenty in four cards, flipped over his sixteen, and collected his wager.

Fourkiller laid down his remaining chips, a tottering pile of jumbled denominations.

She was peeking under her top card, a ten, when he tossed the ace of spades and queen of hearts at her. "Twenty-one," he said.

The other pitfall Shelby had cautioned her about.

Even veteran dealers had difficulty multiplying a big bet by one and a half with any rapidity. So she now did what the MGM shift boss had suggested. She quickly sorted Fourkiller's chips, did some dead reckoning, and topped the payoff with a fifty-cent piece. Shelby had called the ploy "halving it," a fudge to appear accurate without being so.

She slid the pile over to Fourkiller.

Silence.

It went on so long, she was afraid he or Sal might actually count out the chips. But then, just when she thought she'd have to fight her way out of the office, Baldecchi laughed again.

"She'll do," Fourkiller said.

Sal clapped her around the shoulders. "Congratulations, babe. You're going to love working here."

She doubted that, but nevertheless gave him a peck on the cheek.

"Not so fast," Fourkiller said.

Anna let the smile drop from her face.

"You promise to run a clean table and obey the rules Sal will familiarize you with?"

"I will."

"Good," Fourkiller said wearily, his eyes dull and faraway now. "Because the House of Games isn't going to be the joint that shuts down Indian gaming in this country. Go, please, both of you."

Chapter 8

Leonard Wine lived up Ash Canyon Road in the heart of Carson City's upscale quarter, which was discreetly enfolded in the foothills of the Sierra Nevada above the hubbub of the casinos and state government offices. Most of the mansions along the way were still festooned with Christmas lights. It was less than a mile's walk from the hospital to Wine's estate, but on arrival Emmett found the house darkened. These were all horse properties, with deep, pastured lots sloping up into the hills, so he slipped around the side of Wine's place, avoiding the infrared sensors. He hiked toward the crest, scattering Wine's three palominos before him. The horses' ghostly shapes cantered back and forth across the face of the slope like restless phantoms.

The top offered a broad view of the neighborhood, wreathed in a soft haze of woodsmoke.

Sitting on his upended suitcase, Emmett waited.

Thirty minutes. An hour. Two hours passed in the ear-burning chill with no sign of the attorney.

He had considered asking the Carson deputies to make a welfare check on Wine. But then dismissed the notion. Somehow, killing two men miles apart over roadblocked mountain highways at the height of a blizzard was a tall order for even the knife-wielding creature Emmett had faced in that snowy chute.

Besides, he wanted to be the first to have a word with Wine. The man would give him one clear shot at the truth. Then he'd drop a legal curtain over himself and Inter-Mountain Gaming that the Justice Department would have trouble penetrating anytime soon.

Turnipseed, alone in Spirit Meadows. Her backup team cut off from her by a desert mountain range.

The thought made him feel angry all over again. And guilty. But for his and Burk's contentious past in South Dakota, Hagiman might not have sent Turnipseed in. That was the most plausible spin on it: an act of spite, making her a pawn in something that had begun when she'd been in pigtails, running barefoot through Modoc County.

Emmett made himself stop thinking about her.

Tomorrow morning he'd fly back to Las Vegas and take charge of the operation being mounted out of Pahrump, even if it meant a showdown with Hagiman before the U.S. Attorney. In fact, he'd demand just that, an irrefutable decision on which agency was leading. If BIA lost, he'd walk away from the whole grisly, disjointed mess in good conscience, go back to Phoenix.

But already he doubted that he could turn his back on this investigation. He'd staked himself to it, and there was even a peculiarly Comanche metaphor supporting his reluctance to leave the field to Hagiman. In the last century, members of an elite warrior society staked themselves to the ground before giving battle. Most whites found this practice fanatical or melodramatic, so Emmett had told few about it. Only a Sioux friend, estranged now, had glimpsed the utility behind it: Courage is the suppression of natural impulses, and of all those urges, flight is the most irresistible, especially when it masquerades as wounded pride. "Embrace death, and you're free of it," his percipient Lakota friend had observed.

Headlights flashed around the corner onto Wine's street.

Emmett stood as a sports car, possibly a Porsche, turned up Wine's driveway and parked alongside the house at what appeared to be the service entrance. The headlamps remained shining, even though the engine died.

Quickly, Emmett kicked his suitcase behind a piñon pine and started down the slope.

Across the smoky quiet of the canyon, he heard a door bang. Then something crashed, like glass shattering against a tile floor. Drawing his revolver, he ran. Wine's horses snorted in alarm and stampeded into the farthest corner of the pasture.

Lights came on and off inside the house as if someone were making a sweep of the rooms for prey.

He sprinted through the rear yard, vaulting over a low hedge onto the driveway. He reached the Porsche just as a light in the last room of a rear wing went on. It stayed on.

He threw open the driver's door, plucked the keys from the ignition, and pocketed them before going inside the house. Broken glass crunched underfoot as he made his way down a corridor to the kitchen, the greenish glow of the microwave clock drawing him on. A woman sobbed hysterically in a distant room. He followed her voice down a second hallway, painfully barking his shins on something overturned in the darkness.

Slowing as he neared the lit doorway, he gripped his .357 before him. He stopped, listened. The woman went on crying, yet she didn't seem to be imploring anybody.

Rounding the jamb, he cried, "Freeze!"

The woman stood petrified but screamed so loudly his ears were left ringing. Something fell from her hands. She'd been holding an answering machine as if prepared to hurl it against the wall. It spewed a glistening ribbon of tape across the carpet of Wine's home office. The sobbing woman shrank from Emmett, cringing, on the verge of collapsing. "Don't kill me too!" A strong Jamaican accent, which made Emmett shift the muzzle of his revolver back from a sweep of the room and steady his aim on her again.

"What'd you say?" he asked.

"Don't kill me," she wept pathetically, dropping to her hands and knees. He thought briefly that she'd fainted or pretended to swoon. But then she looked wetly up at him between her forearms, with which she was shielding her face. She was at least part black. A nap cropped close to her head.

"Keep your hands where I can see them," he said.

"What?"

"Just do it." He firmly grasped her by the back of the neck and made her go prone against the carpet. She didn't resist, and he patted down her floor-length ermine coat. "You got a handbag?"

"In the kitchen." She'd stopped crying now but had begun trembling. Little glints played on her cheeks from the shaking of her large gold earrings. "Please don't hurt me . . . *please.*"

"Got any weapons?"

"No, never."

"Don't lie to me," he warned.

"I'm not."

In her late thirties, she had an austere regality about her that would turn heads in public. Even though her chic elegance fit this house, he wasn't entirely convinced that she hadn't been sent to kill Leonard Wine. "Sit up. I'm a cop."

Now it was her turn to look unconvinced. "You're not a cop," she said, "and you know very well who I am."

"Who are you?"

A flicker of uncertainty in her eyes. "Jocelyn Wine." But then she went on in the same angry tone, "And you're here looking for my husband."

"You've got that much right."

"And when you find Lennie, will you murder him as you did my brother?"

Emmett holstered his handgun and showed her his credentials. "Investigator Parker, Bureau of Indian Affairs. Your husband was assisting me with a case that started on an Indian reservation." The body in the lake had had no face to compare to hers, but he asked, "You're Nigel Merrison's sister?"

"Yes." Her complexion had turned ashen.

"Water?"

She nodded weakly. "Bathroom, across the hall."

When he returned with a tumbler, she was still slumped on the floor, clasping her face in her hands. "My God," she said, then glanced warily at him as she accepted the glass. "That blood . . ."

He realized that the exertions of the last few minutes had loosened his sutures, and his parka was daubed here and there with red. "Mine."

"What happened?"

"The man who killed your brother . . . he did this."

"You saw him?" she asked with a kind of grim, vengeful hope.

Emmett decided not to reply. "Where's Leonard?"

"I don't know."

"I need to find him. For his own safety."

"I *don't* know," she insisted. Then the tears started again.

She gestured at the machine. "I was hoping he left a message for me. I was just leaving work—"

"Where?"

"The El Dorado."

"Reno?"

She nodded. "I'm vice president of casino operations. I heard on the car radio about Nigel. . . ." The pain of that moment came back to her, made her cover her eyes with a hand. "So I went by Lennie's office, but nobody was there." Then she added bitterly, almost accusingly, "And I knew he wouldn't be home. I just knew." She rose and went to an antique sideboard, where she poured a splash of amber-colored liquor from a crystal decanter. She drank. "Were you the one to find Nigel?"

"Yes."

"Did he suffer?"

He vacillated for only a second. Eventually, Wine would discover everything for her, including the autopsy findings. "Briefly."

She wavered on her feet, and Emmett caught her before she could fall. Nestling her face against his neck, she sobbed. The smell of bourbon gave him a twinge of craving. "We should never have come to this country," she said. "Should've stayed where we belonged. But Lennie can be so frightfully convincing."

Then the desk phone rang, and she backed away from him to answer it. "Hello . . . ?" Her fist tightened around the receiver. "I'm sorry. He's not here presently. May I take a message?" She glanced at Emmett before she reached for a notepad and jotted down three digits, a flight number perhaps. "I'll be sure he gets—"

"Tell Leonard I need to talk to him," Emmett interrupted loudly enough to be heard on the other end of the line. "His life depends on it."

She said nothing for several seconds, then reacted to the

voice on the handset. "Mr. Parker, BIA. He was watching the house when I got here . . . yes. I don't know . . . are you sure . . . ?" She motioned for Emmett to take the phone.

"Leonard," he said, "where are you?"

"Let her go, Parker," the attorney said. The background noise indicated a large public building. "She's in as much danger as I am."

"I can protect her. You too."

"Don't kid yourself. You should be running too."

"What do you mean?"

"Time, man," Wine snarled, "I have no *time* for you to complicate things."

"Why? What's going to happen?"

Silence.

"I'm going to hold her," Emmett finally said, keeping an eye on Jocelyn. She'd gone back for more whiskey, but stopped pouring to glare at him. "Material witness, intent of unlawful flight to avoid testifying." Then he added after a beat, "Unless . . ."

"Unless what, for God's sake?"

"You tell me where to look next."

Wine fell silent. A P.A. announcer intoned that it was against a Dade County ordinance to leave luggage unattended in the terminal.

"Is it Kingston?" Emmett demanded.

"Yes, no . . . hell, I don't know," Wine said crossly. "I don't even know if I'll be alive by morning."

"But you did know that Stephanie Roper had no face when I found her. Do I get airport security down there in Miami to hold you?"

"Don't, Parker," Wine begged. "Please, don't. I've got to get away until things become clear. I've got to get Jocelyn out of Nevada too."

"El Dorado's pretty close to Reno-Tahoe International. You couldn't swing by?"

"No time. I was being followed. I'm sure of it. I didn't want to bring the danger to her. This is the first chance I've had to call." His voice caught as he said, "Let her know that, okay?"

Emmett thought a moment. Wine was in Miami, which probably meant that he was headed for the Caribbean, Jamaica most likely. Why would he fly directly into the arms of Merrison's executioners? He wouldn't—unless he knew beyond the shadow of a doubt that the peril was coming from some other quarter. "Wine?"

"Yes?"

"Tell me how you knew about Roper's face, and I'll take Jocelyn to the airport myself. She could be on the way to you within the hour."

"I don't know . . . I just don't know."

"You were going to tell me anyways. Otherwise we both know you'd never have brought the mutilation up yesterday evening."

"That was before Nigel."

"So what? You'll be in Jamaica. With Jocelyn."

After another heavy lull, Wine said, "Put her back on."

Emmett gave her the receiver.

"Yes, Lennie . . ." She heard him out, then whispered, "I love you too." Hanging up, she turned coldly to Emmett. "This way."

He followed her down the unlit hallway to the master bedroom. There she clicked on a Tiffany lamp and pulled a corner of the carpet up, revealing a floor safe.

"Who'd Leonard win over first?" Emmett asked as she worked the dial. "You or Nigel?"

"Nigel. I was an unexpected bonus." A sad smile came and went. "At least, that's what Lennie always says." She tossed him a cassette. "There's a recorder in his desk, top right drawer. May I pack?"

"You can start." Emmett returned to the office and found

the recorder. A wire connected it to the telephone. Trusting soul, Leonard Wine. There was already a cassette in the machine, but there was nothing on it. Emmett punched in the one Jocelyn had just given him.

"*Leonard,*" an earnest-sounding voice said a few winds into the tape, "*this is Sam Yellow Gourd.*"

"*Sam,*" Wine said affably, "*how are you?*"

"*Fine.*"

"*How are things in Kaibab?*" The headquarters town of the Southern Paiute tribe in extreme northern Arizona that went by the same name.

"*Okay . . .*" But Emmett heard in Yellow Gourd's voice the Indian hesitation that went before mention of anything personal and unpleasant. "*I guess.*"

Wine had caught it too, for he asked, "*Something wrong, Sam? Everything going all right with your casino?*"

"*No, we had a pretty good month—*" Another long, troubled pause. "*It's Cyrus.*"

"*What's wrong with Fourkiller?*"

"*Nothin', maybe. But he's talkin' funny.*"

"*What do you mean?*"

"*I don't know . . . just funny.*"

Wine pressed, "*Is he dissatisfied with the corporation? The direction we're taking?*"

"*Fed up with somethin', I'm not sure what. I mean, it's crazy talk, Len. White folks windin' up without their faces and teeth, unless things change, you know, internally.*"

"*What things?*"

"*He wouldn't say. Maybe you should talk to him.*"

"*Maybe I should,*" Wine said. "*How long has this been going on?*"

"*Three months or so. Most of the time he's okay, like normal, the old Cy. But this stuff keeps comin' out. Somethin's really buggin' him, you know? Maybe it's just this damn business.*"

"*What about it?*"

Yellow Gourd laughed. On the surface, the laugh was awkward and embarrassed, but beneath it Emmett sensed a troubled conscience, perhaps even a moralistic bent. Not improbable traits in somebody employed by gaming. Many of Las Vegas's shift and pit bosses were practicing Mormons.

"I'll make sure to have a talk with him, Sam."

"Great . . . but don't let on I called, okay?"

"Of course not, this is between us. And Nigel?"

"Ah . . . how 'bout waitin' on that score? Merrison might not understand. It's kind of an Indian thing." Spanish explorers had dismissed the Kaibab as a shy and cowardly people. But that wasn't true. They were just cautious. A marginal existence in a hard land, living on lizards and roots much of the year, had ingrained caution in them.

"All right," Wine conceded, *"it's just you and me at this point."*

"Thanks, Len. That's all for now, I guess."

"Take care, Sam."

Jocelyn Wine was standing in the doorway, a suitcase in each hand. "Ready," she told Emmett.

Anna awoke with a secondhand tobacco cough and sore wrists. A ray of sunlight was slanting down through a tear in the vinyl curtains, falling warmly across her feet. She'd kicked off her covers in the breathless room. She'd spent the night dealing to a string of bleary-eyed truck drivers, Marlboro men mostly, with nothing much to say. Either exhausted or wide-eyed on amphetamines, they didn't seem to notice her mistakes, and fortunately her blunders tended to occur when Sal Baldecchi was turned the other way. Returning to her room from the casino at six that morning, she'd had the suspicion that her things were not as she had left them. Nothing overt. But it'd made her feel that her privacy, now more critical than at any other time in her life, had been tampered with.

Lifting her head off the pillow, she looked around for a radio alarm clock.

There wasn't one.

Nor was there a television set. Sixteen bucks didn't buy much, including cleanliness: The rug was so filthy she'd worn her shoes right up until the moment she tumbled into bed.

Cleanliness is next to Godliness.

As tired as she'd been earlier that morning, sleep had come hard. She'd lain awake, wired, filled with an almost overpowering excitement to report about Cyrus Fourkiller. Only in a dire emergency was she to phone a number that rang in the telephone monitoring room at the FBI's Las Vegas field office. Otherwise she was to use the drop, a mining claim marker back along the highway to Pahrump that would be checked Mondays and Thursdays by the BLM ranger in this district, for passing on routine intelligence. Even that entailed risks, should she be followed—and Crutcher had insisted that she would be followed at first. Just before sunrise, she'd realized how little hard information she had to offer Burk and Emmett. Just a few observations on a mildly obsessive-compulsive casino executive who may or may not prove to be Coso. With that admission, she'd finally drifted off.

She reached for her wristwatch on the nightstand and held it up to the dusty sunbeam: five after eleven.

She wriggled her feet into her shoes before crossing the gritty rug to the bathroom. Her eyes burned from the strain of counting cards all night. She braced herself before pulling the light chain.

"Holy shit," she muttered, quickly switching it off again.

Ten minutes later she sat in her Volkswagen in the motel parking lot, warming up the engine, wondering where to go for breakfast.

Lunch, she corrected herself.

Her stomach turned at the idea of eating at the café inside

the House of Games. Everything in the casino smelled and tasted of cigarette smoke.

So she just started driving, rolling down her window as she pulled out of the lot.

The day was warm and still, almost springlike, although the frigid altitudes of the deep blue sky were stitched with the contrails of jetliners descending on Los Angeles.

A block south of the casino, she spotted the Spirit Meadows Market. Greasy windows with sun-faded signs advertised pine nuts and venison. She went inside, smiling past the young Shoshone woman clerking at the front counter. There was a coffeepot next to the deli case and a selection of stale-looking pastries among the breads. In this store, less than a week ago, Coso had put together a box of groceries for old Wuzzie Munro. The Shoshone clerk might have seen his face.

Lingering over the pastries, Anna tried to think of some natural way to broach this with a total stranger. But her head felt thick from lack of sleep. And there was something else. Although her eyes were intent on the packages of doughnuts and danishes, she was seeing the blood that had been left behind in Stephanie Roper's car, congealed into tiny, rust-colored stalactites that had hung off the steering wheel.

Shaking off the image, Anna settled on an apple bearclaw and poured herself a large coffee before approaching the counter.

The clerk was wearing a gold and turquoise crucifix. "Oh, my, that's pretty," Anna commented.

A blush came over the woman's cherubic face as she began tapping cash register keys.

The Western Shoshone are usually reticent with outsiders, Anna reminded herself. *Don't push.* But she had to. She was here to find Coso before he killed again. That meant overcoming her own nature—wasn't an accounting minor in college proof of a reserved personality?—and being as forward as she could be without revealing herself. "Is that turquoise local?"

"I guess."

Halloran Springs had turquoise mines. "I once saw a Chemehuevi cross just like that."

"One sixty-nine," the woman said impassively.

Anna could think of nothing else to say.

On the highway again, she drove through town and then out into the open desert. The coffee lifted her spirits a little, but she still felt useless.

And uneasy.

Her growing uneasiness mystified her, for she'd begun to think about going undercover the instant Parker had groused in the McDonald's lot in Baker that one of them should hang back in the event he *or* she could be of some use undercover. And later, in her condo with Burk Hagiman present, volunteering herself to go into Spirit Meadows had felt good, the perfect way to declare her independence from Parker's dominance over their investigation.

But she hadn't imagined she would feel so exposed and alone out here.

Had there been a deeper motivation behind this decision? Something beyond the present? The Modoc recognized a certain kind of spiritual quest one was powerless to resist, no matter how dangerous the undertaking. To decline was to die by the inch, even if acceptance entailed a blind leap into the greatest darkness imaginable. To shrink from the opportunity was to remain trapped in one's own past. *Dear Mrs. Turnipseed,* the note from her high school counselor had read, *I think you should be aware of a problem that has developed concerning your daughter. Anna, a model student in every other regard, stubbornly refuses to disrobe for gym class.* . . . Then, as now, she'd felt as if the eyes of the entire world were boring in on her secret. In that case, the secret her father had bound her to for all eternity. A perversely holy trust.

Damn him.

A gravel road branched southeast into a range of warped

and buckled mountains. But the road soon ended at an over-look of a wash that wound down into the basin. The dusty cul-de-sac was probably a lovers' lane for Shoshone kids. Parking on the brink of the slope, she was surprised to see how close she still was to town. No getting away from it. No relief from the constant pressure of keeping her guard up. She'd be count-ing the days until she could return to Las Vegas. Her condo. Routine work. A life without deception.

"Shit." She flicked on the car radio, tuned in KNUU out of Las Vegas, hoping for some regional news to make her feel less isolated. The AM station kept fading in and out of a back-ground of static. She left it on, but got out of the car with her bearclaw and coffee. The day was utterly calm, noiseless. Dis-tance had no context, the snow capped far ranges looked like they could be reached in an hour's walk, although they were probably seventy miles away.

She sat on the front bumper, rested her back against the hood. Closing her eyes, she turned her face up into the sun as she finished the last of the bearclaw. Tomorrow she'd go back to the market, start winning the young clerk's confidence.

She could smell juniper woodsmoke. It reminded her of home, Modoc County, in winter.

A hawk screeched, fairly uncommon for a quiet bird.

She sat up.

A thin sheen of smoke broke over the ridge on the opposite side of the wash. Lazily, it flowed over the boulders, drifting downward through the still air before dissipating. On the sandy, flood-scarred bank across the wash, tire tracks vanished into a notch that cut through the ridge at its lowest point. She could see them only because of the elevation on which she stood and the low winter sun. The impressions would have been of no interest to her except that as they neared the gap, an attempt had been made to brush them out. The ground looked curdled there.

No more smoke appeared, but she dumped out her coffee and chucked the cup into the car through her open window.

She started down the slope from the overlook, digging her heels into the soft, powdery soil. It proved easier going than the arroyo itself, an expanse of boulders that called for more scrambling than walking. She reached the sandy bank but had to walk downstream to find a breach in its eight-foot height.

Climbing up, she peered back down the way the vehicle had come: a jeep trail that paralleled the wash down to State Route 127. From there, the driver could have gone north into Spirit Meadows, or south toward Baker.

She knelt over the tire impressions.

The weak front had blown through on Christmas night. Three days ago. These tracks lay on top of the dimpling left by those light rains, yet a solitary impression between them predated the storm. The knobbly furrow from a dirt bike's passing, she believed.

Rising, she followed the tracks up to the point where someone had begun brushing them out. But no. That wasn't how it'd happened. Off to the side of the trail, partly concealed in an animal burrow, she found a bundle of shad scale branches. The driver had started erasing the prints at the mouth to the notch, then worked his way down to this point. Here he'd hidden his makeshift broom. His boot-sole impressions disappeared where he'd stepped into his vehicle, a four-wheel drive judging from the softness of the trail, with lightly patterned all-season radials.

Yet someone had remained behind. And built a fire.

Missing her revolver for the first time, she continued on toward the notch. She was still well shy of its mouth, when she heard engine noise approaching. At first she feared that the sweeper was coming up the wash, returning from town. But the sound was breaking from across the arroyo, and when dust began rising off the gravel road, she realized that someone was pulling up behind her VW. She could see neither car over the rim of the overlook.

She began running, leaping from boulder to boulder across the wash. She was halfway up the slope to the overlook, when a stocky human shadow fell over her.

Halting, fighting for breath, she shaded her eyes from the sun.

"Where you been?" Dan Beowawe asked.

She started climbing again, giving herself a moment to calm down. "Nature called."

The tribal cop chuckled. "Hell, Ronnie—nobody to see you out here. You don't have to go traipsin' across the desert."

"Nobody 'cept ol' Dan."

"I didn't even know you were here till I saw a glint off your windshield," he said, backing up to his Jeep cruiser. He shut off his engine, then strolled up to her VW again, and gave her an idea how fast news traveled on the reservation. "Day off?"

"No. Just couldn't sleep." Once again she looked for more smoke spilling over the ridge. None. The brushed-out tracks might mean nothing: Secrecy was sometimes a mania with desert peoples. Soldiers, miners, and cattlemen had reduced the Western Shoshone to a handful of their former numbers by the turn of the last century.

Pivoting, she caught Beowawe taking in her hips and buttocks. He smiled and took a toothpick from his shirt pocket, began chewing on it.

"How come you aren't out on the roadblock?" she asked.

"Ain't a roadblock." Then he repeated what he'd said yesterday morning: "International border checkpoint." She thought that he might smile ironically this time, but he didn't. True believer. "We rotate. Fella can't take more'n two days on one of 'em before he goes stir crazy."

"International border checkpoint," she echoed. "Who're you keeping out?"

"Oh, it ain't that so much."

"Then what?"

"We just take care of our own problems."

She realized that her radio was still on. The weatherman was reporting that this afternoon's high in Las Vegas would be eighty-five degrees. Pool weather under a flawless sky. Never had her condo seemed so much like home.

"How you like the House of Games?" Beowawe asked, planting his boot on her rear bumper.

"Fine. One big family. But casinos make me feel closed in. That's why I came out here."

"Know what you mean. Busy last night?"

"Not really, but IMG must be doing great."

"How's that?"

"Well, flying its execs around in a Learjet and all."

Beowawe spat out the toothpick. "Ain't IMG's. Who told you that?"

"Mr. Fourkiller."

"Well, the company has a plane, but it's an old prop job sittin' broke in a hangar thanks to a berserk pilot who got himself fired for bein' reckless."

"Whose jet was it, then?"

"Leased yesterday out of McCarran. I picked Mr. Four-killer up at the strip last night and, believe me, that pilot was fumin'."

"Why?"

Beowawe stretched. "Had to fly in and out of Truckee Air-port in the middle of a blizzard."

"Where's Truckee?" she asked, feigning ignorance.

"North of Tahoe." He left off his stretch with a satisfied grunt. But when he'd finished, his eyes were pinned to hers. "I was wonderin', Ronnie . . ." She waited, interjecting nothing. "Where exactly in Vegas did you live?"

"You mean like my address?"

He dipped his head. A ponderous gesture, full of suspicion. She felt the paralyzing terror of a blank mind. It was like not being able to breathe. The office had supplied her with an apartment address where the manager, an FBI informant, would verify her prior residency. But it wouldn't come. "Why do you need to know, Dan?"

"We help the casino out with background checks on employees."

"Is there a form I should fill out? The casino never gave me an application."

He continued to stare. "Yeah, there's a form. I guess we can do it that way. Fingerprint you at the same time."

Another hurdle she dreaded. Burk had assured her that the bureau's computer system had been reprogrammed to do two things critical to her safety. First, report no prior fingerprint card on file if one matching Anna's classification came in. Second, automatically alert the Las Vegas office if anybody made a data inquiry regarding Anna Turnipseed—so the inquiring party could be investigated as a possible danger to her.

But sometimes computers failed.

Beowawe broke off his stare. "What you doin' for supper . . . ?"

She'd only half heard him. She was sure that the newscaster had just said something about Inter-Mountain Gaming. "Pardon?"

"You goin' to eat before your shift?"

"I suppose. . . ." Then she heard it in full as the reception improved momentarily. Nigel Merrison, president of IMG, had been found murdered near his Incline Village home. The fleeing suspect had then stabbed veteran Bureau of Indian Affairs Investigator Emmett Parker before eluding capture. She felt as if she'd been punched in the solar plexus, but through her shock came the realization that she must appear natural. What would this news mean to Ronnie Chavez? "Did he just say something about our company?" she asked innocently, although there was a slight quaver in her voice.

Fortunately, Beowawe had already leaned through her

open window to boost the volume. His face seemed strained as he stood erect again.

"Something wrong?"

"Quiet," he said.

The manhunt for the fugitive continued. Parker had been released from the Carson City hospital where he'd been treated. She struggled to hide her relief. Emmett was indestructible. Meanwhile, Nevada's senior senator was droning on over the airwaves about the need for comprehensive legislation to control the anarchic condition of Indian gaming. "Who's Parker?" she asked.

"Baddest son of a bitch in the BIA. Wouldn't be surprised if *he* whacked Merrison . . ." Beowawe looked like he was going to support his claim with an anecdote, but then said, "Come back to town with me, Ronnie."

"Why?"

"There's goin' to be a meetin' at the casino. We all got to show."

"But you don't work for IMG."

He smiled at her naivete. "Just come along, okay?"

It was the last thing she wanted to do. She needed to get to the drop, or even risk a call to Burk. Fourkiller had returned from Truckee last evening, a Sierra town less than twenty miles from Incline Village, where Merrison had died, Parker had been hurt.

Beowawe grabbed her by the shoulders, nudged her toward the VW. "Come on. This is important."

"What's the meeting for?" she asked, getting in behind the wheel.

"Reservation lockdown, I'm sure."

"What?"

"Fourkiller's goin' to seal off the rez. Nobody can come in or go out. Shut down the phones and mail too."

"But why?"

"We're at war," he said tersely, turning for his car.

Chapter 9

The shortest way to get Anna Turnipseed safely out of Spirit
Meadows involved a detour through northern Arizona. Emmett came to that conclusion on his second day back in Las
Vegas. By three that Monday afternoon he'd gassed up in St.
George, Utah, and was speeding southeast along the Fredonia
highway toward the Kaibab Paiute Reservation. The storms
that had vexed him on the Havasupai Reservation and again at
Incline Village had turned most of the side roads in Mohave
County into bogs of reddish mud. He'd tried to draw a four-
wheel drive from the FBI motor pool in Vegas, but in the end
had been forced to take a Chevy sedan. The last carryall had
been issued to a pair of "USGS geologists" working out of
Pahrump—in reality, Turnipseed's backups.

Burk Hagiman.

Last night he'd had a courier drop off a packet at Emmett's hotel. In it were the FBI lab report on the evidence found in Stephanie Roper's sedan and a DEA white paper on Jamaican organized crime—but no personal note from Burk. Still, sending the info amounted to declaring a temporary truce, and Emmett was willing to accept one for the time being. The only thing of real interest in the lab report was a nineteen-inch dark brown hair the FBI technician had discovered on the front seat in Roper's car. It was Mongoloid, meaning either Asian or American Indian. And the DEA was sounding warning bells about a particular Kingston-based posse, the Wild West–sounding name Jamaican syndicates gave themselves, which had muscled into the lucrative southern California cocaine and marijuana markets and was currently making more money than it knew how to launder.

On the last flight out of Reno on Saturday night, Emmett had decided not to force a showdown with the FBI in front of the U.S. Attorney. He might lose. Hagiman would argue that Emmett had been wounded by the suspect, leaving his objectivity in question. Lawyers were suckers for arguments like that, even though objectivity had nothing to do with finding Roper's and Merrison's killer. In fact, Emmett felt that he was now running almost solely on subjectivity. His instincts warned him to take the long approach to Cyrus Fourkiller rather than a head-on confrontation. But the government's attorney would be convinced by none of this and might bump Emmett from leading the task force.

Where would Turnipseed be then?

No, he would learn everything he needed to know at this point about Fourkiller from Samuel Yellow Gourd, the manager of the Kaibab casino, also an employee of Inter-Mountain Gaming.

Ten hours of wading through the databases had turned up nothing of value on Cyrus Fourkiller. He had no driver's license on file in either California or Nevada. No record with the FBI's National Crime Information Center. The Nevada Gaming Board maintained a second repository in Las Vegas, and Emmett had felt fairly safe in using it without worry that Hagiman's buddy at the Carson City headquarters would hear of his inquiry. Unfortunately, all Las Vegas had on Fourkiller was some résumé boilerplate put out by IMG, commending him as the innovative second-in-command of their Ute operation in Colorado, "a distinguished Harvard MBA with years of hands-on experience in Indian gaming." Harvard had no record of him. Neither did the BIA's Gaming Task Force. And a name search of the tribal affiliation lists, including the Western Shoshone one, proved fruitless. Grasping at straws, Emmett had phoned the California Department of Justice, only to learn that the state had yet to put a gaming commission in place. So, casino employees weren't necessarily fingerprinted and licensed, as in Nevada. It was up to the tribes. "Indian gambling here," the agent in Sacramento had explained, "is like a freeway with no speed limit. And we've got no idea who's behind the wheel out there. Any chance Fourkiller is an alias . . . ?"

Big chance.

Emmett slowed to eighty miles an hour as he went over the border. He'd already received his final brotherly warning from the state troopers: Next time he'd be cited, no professional courtesies extended. But the sooner he had a handle on Fourkiller, the sooner he'd order Hagiman to yank Turnipseed out.

He accelerated again.

Paddle markers whooshed past hypnotically.

He liked this country better than the shadowy, claustrophobic canyons just to the south. The terrain was rolling grassland with forested volcanic cones standing blue-green in the distance. The highway crossed into the reservation. Time to rethink this once more. To calculate what variables had been set into motion by his letting Jocelyn Wine join her husband in Jamaica. By surrendering the tape, Wine undoubtedly realized that Emmett would come here to Kaibab to interrogate Yellow Gourd. Would he keep that to himself? Or play both sides in a game for which Emmett still lacked a complete roster? But none of that ultimately mattered as long as Yellow Gourd could attest to having heard Fourkiller discuss a white victim buried in Havasu Canyon with no face and no teeth. If he could, and would—it was arrest-warrant time.

The casino lights glimmered across the twilit plateau.

Emmett was slowing for them when he decided to run through the parking lot of the Pipe Springs Motel first. There was a government sedan, but he paid it no mind. Indian Health Service. Then a dark blue Ford Bronco with a Hertz sticker and Nevada plates caught his eye. He committed the license number to memory, then turned for the casino.

A white security guard stood just inside the entrance. His biceps were straining his shirtsleeves, and his head appeared to sprout directly out of his deltoids.

"Where's the manager?" Emmett asked.

"Who's askin'?" A breathy grunt. There was a pink tint to his irises, and his hair was nearly colorless.

Emmett took out his credentials. "Criminal Investigator Parker, BIA."

The guard meticulously examined Emmett's I.D. photo. "Don't look like you."

"I was in a good mood that day."

"Stay here."

"Stay here *please*."

The guard glowered, then plodded off between the slots and down a back corridor.

The Indian dealers regarded Emmett with suspicion.

Not always a sociable people on first contact, the Kaibab Southern Paiute. A flourishing Spanish and then Mexican slave trade in girls of menses age had nearly wiped the tribe out. And then came the Mormons. They'd thrown up a fort around the only springs within miles, further stressing the Kaibab. They resembled the Navajo but were more closely related to the Chemehuevi. In recent times they were on fairly good terms with the Havasupai and Western Shoshone, the other points in this investigative triangle.

Emmett strolled toward the corridor the guard had vanished down. His near-brush with frostbite had left his toes sensitive, as if he'd clipped the nails too short.

"Twenty-one!" a white man with a John Deere cap and a sunburned neck hollered, throwing down his cards.

Emmett had the suspicion, unfairly perhaps, that the few patrons in the place were lapsed saints down from St. George for a little sinning among the Gentiles, although he wasn't entirely sure that Indians, the alleged descendants of the Lost Tribe of Israel, were held to be Gentiles by the Mormons. Whatever, they had been the most practical of the white invaders: Brigham Young noted that it was cheaper to feed the tribes than fight them.

The guard returned and said, "Sam can't see you."

"Who says?"

"Assistant manager."

"You saying Yellow Gourd isn't here?"

"I'm sayin' get out. I been told to order you off the premises, unless you got a warrant."

Emmett made himself keep his arms down at his sides, his hands unfisted. Short fuse. The past two weeks had left him with no patience. They'd stripped away a decade, leaving him as he'd been his first few years out here: mindless of the retirement check that awaited him as long as he suffered fools gladly. "Let me get this straight," he said, "the management is kicking out a federal officer?"

"That's right."

"In violation of the Indian Gaming Regulatory Act?" The

pinkish eyes shifted uncertainly. Actually, the summary right
to inspect casinos was in litigation, but Emmett doubted the
man read gaming law reviews. "Where's the head?" he asked.

"The what?"

"The toilet."

The guard pointed down the corridor.

"Can I use it?"

The man had to consider that, doubtless in light of the
sovereignty issue. "Only if I go with you."

"Lead the way."

Emmett knew what he was going to do as soon as they
reached the dimness of the passageway. The minutes he wasted
bickering here might never be recovered. Last night he'd
dreamed of finding Anna Turnipseed dead, her face peeled off.
It'd been stronger than a dream, almost a vision, and he'd
awakened upset enough to have wanted a drink.

He flexed his left hand. The bulky bandage had been reduced to two Band-Aids over the sutures.

"Make it quick," the guard grumbled as they neared the
men's room door.

"Okay." Emmett seized him by his collar and drove his
face toward the wall, jerking back at the last second to avoid
serious damage. Still, the man dropped, landing on his huge
butt, and sat dazed for a few seconds. Then, tentatively, he
explored his bloody nose with the back of his hand, although
his now-wary eyes never left Emmett's face. He seemed to
have completely forgotten that he had a handgun anytime he
wanted to use it.

Emmett stooped so they were on the same level. "Broken?"

Tenderly, the man pinched the bridge of his nose with his
fingers. "Don't think so."

"Haven't heard of me, have you?"

The man shook his head.

"Well, now you got a bona fide Emmett Parker story.

You're free to embellish it. Everybody else does. Where's Sam Yellow Gourd?"

"Ain't here."

Emmett reared back his fist.

"Honest—ask the assistant manager!"

"Why don't we do that?" Emmett helped the man to his feet: It felt like pulling a buffalo off the ground.

Clenching his handkerchief to his nose, the guard led the way down the last thirty feet of the corridor to a steel door. This he opened with a key. Inside was a one-room office with four desks pushed together to form a counting table. There, a priggish-looking young man was adhering a band around a stack of twenties, when he gaped up at the guard, his bloody handkerchief, and then Emmett right behind him. He might have thought that it was a robbery, or wanted to see it that way, for he began to reach inside the top drawer of one of the desks.

"*Don't,*" Emmett warned, spreading his jacket to show his own weapon. "You know damn well I'm BIA."

"Do I?" A British accent. Tortoiseshell-framed glasses.

For a second time, Emmett showed his I.D. "Who're you?"

"Graham Owen, assistant manager." The drawer slid shut; the man took a step back. "What do you want?"

"Sam Yellow Gourd."

"He's gone."

"Where?"

"I'm not sure."

"Take a walk," Emmett told the guard.

"Stay, Moby," Owen said sharply. He tried to regain some of his dignity by sitting in a swivel chair and nonchalantly propping one leg over the other. "I hope you realize this shall be reported, Special Agent . . . ?"

"*Investigator* Parker—I work for a living. Which part will

be reported? You refusing me access to your counting room . . . or me lawfully gaining it?"

"This is simply intolerable."

"You got that right," Emmett said. "How long you been with IMG?"

Silence.

"Where'd you meet Nigel Merrison?"

The assistant manager stared off into space.

"I see," Emmett said. "You a citizen?"

The glum eyes snapped toward him.

"That's right, Owen. You'd be astonished how far I'm willing to go."

The man's lips compressed as, apparently, his imagination plumbed the bureaucratic possibilities. At last, he exhaled loudly and dismissed the guard with a flick of his hand.

"I hope *Moby*'s a nickname," Emmett said as soon as they were alone.

Owen gave a grudging smile. "Afraid not. Stout Mormon stock though." Then he said defensively, "I'm in the process of becoming a citizen. Forgive my neophyte's understanding of the Constitution, Mr. Parker, but in the meantime I believe I'm afforded the same rights as a full citizen."

Emmett sat on a corner of one of the desks. "I'm here to find out who killed Nigel Merrison."

"Certainly you don't think—"

"How well did you know him?"

Instantly, Owen started weighing everything he said. "Well, by no means were we on social terms. He was the president of the company, after all."

"You like him?"

"Respected him. He knew this business better than anyone."

"How'd you meet?"

"My fiancée and I emigrated to Jamaica—"

"What'd you do prior?"

Owen glanced away. Sensitive territory, apparently. "I was an accountant with Lloyds."

"Of London?"

"Is there another?"

Emmett recalled a scandal several years before that had given the insurance giant a black eye, a scheme that had left hundreds of investors holding the liability bag. The kind of thing an ambitious young accountant might suggest to offset a rash of casualty losses. "Forgive me, I don't get out of the Southwest much. You leave Lloyds *of London* under duress?"

"Not in the least." Too much indignation to ring true.

"Your fiancée here in Kaibab with you?"

"It didn't work out. She went home to England, and I went to work for a casino in Kingston."

"Merrison's?"

"Yes. And then on to Laughlin with him before he formed IMG."

So Merrison, it seemed, didn't mind bringing someone with a tainted past on board. Was Fourkiller out of the same sort of grab bag? His educational background certainly hadn't stood up to even a cursory check. "Merrison have enemies in Jamaica?"

"Competitors, yes. Nigel is—was—far too careful to cultivate enemies."

"What about in this country?"

That made Owen weigh his words again. "As you probably know, there's resistance to gaming on all the reservations. Die-hard purists who want nothing the outside world offers. And the Christian fundamentalists, of course. But Nigel was a grand master at defusing these factions, getting on with the business of improving tribal life."

"What do you know about the Halloran Springs project?"

"Not a thing," Owen said, deadpan. "What is it?"

Emmett just smiled. "Is it possible Yellow Gourd would know about any intertribal projects?"

"Yes. He's in the developmental loop. I'm more a day-to-day-operations sort"—he gestured with an unsteady hand at the cash on the table—"as you can see."

"How long's Yellow Gourd been gone?"

"All week."

"Gone where?"

"Robinson Wash, I believe."

Turnipseed's voice piped up in the back of Emmett's mind. The land swap application she'd read to him in her car Christmas morning. Upper Robinson Wash had been one of the properties being offered on Wuzzie Munro's alleged behalf. "Where's that?"

"It winds up onto Kanab Point. Excuse me." Owen rose and went to a small sink in the corner. Clearly, he was still terrified, which puzzled Emmett. The two of them had come to a Mexican standoff of sorts, and the assistant manager had little left to fear as long as he told what he knew about Yellow Gourd's whereabouts. That could mean only that he had bigger worries than the BIA. The expulsion he'd ordered minutes ago, although carried out by the guard, had been a serious one from an accountant. After taking a drink of water and patting his glistening forehead on his sleeve, Owen opened the tiny window above the sink. Its panes had been painted over. "Sam's kin have a winter lodge in upper Robinson Wash, I'm told."

Emmett shifted so he could look over Owen's shoulder. The man had a view of the motel lot, which was the same as it'd been minutes before. Including the blue Bronco, which was still there. "What do you mean, you're told?"

"I've never been up the wash," Owen answered with a slightly wounded tone. "They use it for ceremonies." He shut the window and returned to his chair. Not the kind of white man to fit in on a remote reservation. "I've never been invited, quite naturally."

"Yellow Gourd say what ceremony?"

Whatever Owen had seen out the window, it seemed to embolden him a little. "Doesn't that fall under the category of religious freedom?"

"Might," Emmett said. "Certainly falls under obstructing a federal officer."

Owen shook his head, then said, "Soul Loss. Don't ask me to explain."

He didn't need to.

Emmett was familiar with this particular spiritual ailment: the sense that, under the influence of some powerful evil, the soul had separated from the body and wandered off. The cure, achieved with the help of a shaman, involved the pursuit and ultimate restoration of the soul. This was then confirmed by the tribal elders. Emmett would still seek their blessing for his brief trespass on their lands, but trusted that they were up Robinson Wash with Yellow Gourd. He was about to ask how far the winter lodge was from the casino, when Owen spoke first, almost plaintively. "Why not let me ask Sam to contact you as soon as he returns?"

"I don't have time."

Owen leaned back as if he'd resigned himself to something unpleasant. "Take the Antelope Valley cutoff out of here. Sign marks Robinson Wash turnoff. That's as close as I can get you."

"Thanks," Emmett said, rising.

But Owen's voice stopped him at the door: "Forgive my petulance this evening, Mr. Parker. I have this overwhelming feeling I'll be out of a job this time next week."

"Well, you were looking for a job when you found this one, right?" Emmett continued out onto the main floor of the casino. He patted Moby on the arm. "How's the nose?"

"Fine," the big man answered with no hint of resentment. A crust of half-dried blood ringed a nostril.

"Take care."

"You too, Mr. Parker."

The underappreciated utility of controlled violence, Emmett mused as he pushed through the door and into the parking lot. With some types, it was the only path to their sensibilities. And there was truth in the old locker-room maxim: They seldom remember what you do to them, but they *always* remember what you say to them.

The western sky was a fan of golden light, molten-looking where it touched the horizon. As always in this high country, dusk instantly sent the temperature plunging. He took his parka and hiking boots from his luggage in the trunk and tossed them in the backseat, just in case. If he failed to find Yellow Gourd this evening, he would check in the morning with the BIA uniformed cops assigned to this reservation.

He sped into Antelope Valley on an unpaved road that had only a few muddy spots. The land inclined toward the south, but he knew that the Grand Canyon lay just beyond the far ridgeline.

Yellow Gourd's Soul Loss.

A serious thing for a tribal leader to admit, akin to a white CEO checking himself into the hospital for depression. What was the source of the evil that had brought it on? Gaming? Perhaps. But Owen had been right when he said that resistance on the reservations to gambling came from either traditionalists or Christians. Yellow Gourd's job as casino manager made him less than a traditionalist, but his reliance on a shaman's cure didn't exactly put him on the Jesus Road. Yet, it seemed unlikely that the casino had sent the man's soul wandering. Emmett had heard it in the troubled voice on Leonard Wine's tape: the contamination of a far greater evil than gambling.

He slammed on the brakes.

The hard-packed dirt ended without warning, and the mud began. He was sure that he'd get mired, but the Chevy kept plowing ahead. The temperature must have already fallen below freezing, for the road felt firm beneath his tires. He continued to climb. Patches of snow began to appear where daytime shadows lay beneath the piñons.

A BLM sign appeared out of the darkness. Emmett slowed to study it.

Colorado River via Toroweap Point (No Bridge) 32 mi.

An arrow pointed straight ahead toward this fording. But he knew of other crossable shallows in winter's low water. One lay near the outlet to Havasu Creek, a route that avoided Supai. And that might have provided a back door to Stephanie Roper's burial site. But there was no road down to that crossing, and the descent into the canyon was arduous beyond belief. He dismissed the notion.

A second arrow on the sign pointed left up Robinson Wash.

Turning, Emmett pulled the automatic gearshift down into low. He yawned, wishing that he'd gotten some coffee before leaving the casino.

Within a hundred yards, aspens began flanking the road, which was narrower and rougher than the one he'd just left. A set of mud-and-snow-tire impressions led the way. Members of Yellow Gourd's extended family, he supposed. Through the winter-bare branches he looked for firelight in the upper wash. But the aspens were so thick, he saw nothing but a screen of green-white trunks. Here, the shade lasted most of the day, for the tracks ahead of him began cutting through drifts of icy snow.

His own tires started spinning.

He gunned the engine. The Chevy fishtailed, then side-slipped almost completely off the road into the trees.

"Christ almighty," he said, turning off the ignition and killing his lights.

It was the first night of the new moon, when Moon Woman was abducted by malevolent spirits and unable to show her face. A time of exceptional peril. The darkness seemed total until Emmett's eyes adjusted to it. Leaning into the windshield, he glimpsed a few stars through the canopy of branches. Shucking off his oxfords and reaching over the seat for his parka and boots, he told himself that Yellow Gourd had better make this worthwhile.

He despised putting on tire chains.

He grabbed the flashlight from the glove box and got out, wrestling into the parka as he made his way to the rear of the car. The usually dry air of the Kanab Plateau was cold and damp among the aspens.

Mist drifted through his beam.

He popped the trunk, moved aside the Remington shotgun so he could take the chains out of the axle hole in the spare tire. A chukar clucked in alarm somewhere out in the copse. It was only a slightly less menacing sound than the rattle of the chains as he spread them out in the slush behind the rear wheels. Something was coming, maybe just a coyote stealing into the aspens.

He was getting ready to try to back the car onto the chains, when the crowns of the trees lit up.

He switched off his flashlight.

Someone was driving down out of the wash. Samuel Yellow Gourd, hopefully, which meant Emmett could forego chaining up. He watched the vehicle, a dark-colored Bronco, finish negotiating a switchback and start down the wooded hillside toward him. Now he sensed lights behind him too. He didn't turn, thinking them to be a reflection off the snow. But then he heard the whine of a second engine below. Another vehicle had veered off the Antelope Valley road and was creeping up on him, hemming him in.

It hit him. What Graham Owen had seen in the motel lot. Or not seen: a second blue Bronco that had started this way while the first was still parked in Kaibab.

Emmett rushed to the trunk and pulled out the shotgun. Jogging forward, he opened the driver's-side door and flipped on all the Chevy's lights, including the hazard flashers. An undergrowth of wild rose clawed at his trousers as he ran into the aspens, but he kept moving deeper into the trees. The high beams of the upslope Bronco swept over the Chevy. Then brakes squealed, followed by the murmurous sound of two engines idling.

Emmett dropped and rolled on the downward edge of the copse, then spun around on his knees. As expected, the second vehicle was also a Bronco. The drivers had stopped fifty yards above and below Emmett's sedan. Car doors opened and slammed shut. Two men got out of the lower Bronco. A silhouette remained in the front passenger seat of the upper Ford, although the driver had stepped away from this vehicle. He was the only figure Emmett could see with any clarity. A tall man with a spray of dreadlocks framing his dark-complected face. Emmett's emergency flashers were visibly puzzling him. The man advanced cautiously from tree to tree, using them for cover until he figured that he'd gone far enough.

Then he stopped, lofted a pistol to eye level, and calmly emptied ten rounds through the windshield of Emmett's Chevy. There was a crunch as each slug penetrated the safety glass.

Finally, he quit firing.

Smoke and car exhaust sifted through the headlights, curled up into the branches.

"Does he still draw breat'?" a Jamaican accent asked from the vicinity of the lower Bronco.

The man from the upper Ford inched forward, peering

over the sights of his pistol at the sedan. Emmett's door was still ajar, and the man sprung it wider with his free hand before scanning the interior. "Gone," he reported. "Tracks, t'ey go t'at way!"

He pointed on a line that led directly to Emmett, then began firing randomly with his pistol into the trees.

The others joined in with automatic rifles, all except the figure who'd not gotten out. Most of their bullets thudded into the trunks, but one whizzed inches above Emmett's head. He jacked a cartridge into the chamber of his shotgun, but didn't return fire. With only five rounds, he figured he could fight his way out of the wooded glen, but any expectation beyond that was unreasonable. His .357 he would save for the long trek over the plateau, if he got out of the aspens alive.

"Come out, Babylon!" one of the men catcalled.

Another let out with a silly cannabis laugh that Emmett cut short with a blast from his shotgun. He rolled to the side, then pushed himself up off the snow and started running. He thought he'd heard a cry of pain through the echoes of his own report. But he wasn't sure, for they'd opened up with everything they had. Bullets sizzled through the air all around him. He was forced to expend another cartridge just to cut short this fusillade. He broke out of the trees and raced up an open slope toward an ancient lava flow, a curdled mass of black set off by the snow. Bullets splashed into the white around him, sparked and pinged off the rocks.

"Come back, Babylon!" And then the taunter said something to his fellows that—even more than the flying slugs—raised the hair on the back of Emmett's neck: "Any you dreads speak Comanche?"

Chapter 10

"Sorry to wake you . . ."

Anna thought she was still asleep and Cyrus Fourkiller's voice was echoing around inside her dream, the recurring one that dragged her back into that autopsy chamber where Stephanie Roper lay in arrested decomposition, faceless, dusted with borax.

"Listen, I'm tied up right now," the casino manager's voice went on in the telephone receiver, "and could use a favor."

She'd answered on the first ring, one-quarter awake.

She sat up in bed and clumsily switched on the nightstand lamp. A blinding moment passed before she could read her wristwatch. Almost four A.M. Around midnight, a call from Sal Baldecchi had startled her out of an exhausted sleep. He'd told her to come into work at eight in the morning. The Las Vegas media, aware that the casinos in town were their biggest advertisers, were smugly reporting that with the reservation shut down, the upstart House of Games was closed, inferring that it was for good. As damage control, Fourkiller had ordered Baldecchi to run the day shift, even though the reservation lockdown would keep out any white patrons.

"Is something wrong?" Anna asked, her voice raw from sleeplessness.

"No," Fourkiller said, not convincing her.

Things were terribly wrong. There were face-offs at each of the three roadblocks between Shoshone tribal police and the local sheriff's office, with a handful of federal marshals to keep them separated. The attorney general in Sacramento, long opposed to gambling in any form, was threatening to force a reopening of the state and county roads that crisscrossed the reservation. In Washington, support was gaining for a special investigation into the influence of organized crime on Indian gaming. Fourkiller had a dozen understandable reasons for being tied up by the crisis he himself seemed to have brought on. "I really do appreciate your support, Ronnie . . ." Following the meeting at the casino two days before, most of the non-Indian employees had speedily taken advantage of Fourkiller's offer to leave Spirit Meadows before the lockdown. So had a number of antigaming Shoshone, despite the support the council had given its casino manager *to resist any unjustified assault on tribal sovereignty.* "I feel I can trust you to do something for me, Ronnie."

His familiar tone suggested that he'd known her for years. "Like what?"

"Pick up a guest at the airstrip. Drive him back to the motel."

"When?"

"About twenty minutes."

His words were a shade slurred. He'd been drinking. That

explained his sudden friendliness toward her. Unless it was a ploy to get her to lower her defenses before he dropped the bombshell that he knew who she was. "Do I have to turn on the runway lights or anything?" she asked.

"No, no—the pilot can do it with his radio." He paused, and in the lull Anna could hear the CNN theme playing in the background on a television set. "When this is all over," he continued, "I won't forget who my friends are."

Was there an opportunity here? Or was he just baiting her? "You sound beat," she said carefully, "and blue." She didn't expect him to volunteer anything, but he surprised her.

"Thinking of my brother tonight. Haven't done that in a long time."

"Where is he?"

"Dead."

"I'm sorry."

"The war."

"Vietnam?"

"Yes," Fourkiller said, "and Wounded Knee."

"I don't understand. . . ." She reached for the pen and pad on the nightstand, but her hand was too agitated to write legibly. Besides, what if these notes were discovered? "Vietnam *and* Wounded Knee?"

"He flew in 'Nam. Little fixed-wing plane. Forward observer for artillery. Got home, went to the Wounded Knee killing ground, and understood for the first time what he'd done to those people over there. The fire he'd called in on them. People just like us. He shot himself in the head."

"I'm sorry," Anna repeated, figuring that poor, banal Ronnie Chavez could do little better than that. She tossed the pen across the room in frustration. She was screwing it up. Fourkiller was on the verge of revealing something. Something potentially useful to the investigation. She might never again catch him drunk.

"Well," he said philosophically, "*who fe do.*"

"What's that mean?"

"We all have to play the hand we're dealt. Right?"

"I guess," she said, realizing that the somber and almost defeated way he said this would stick with her.

"I'll let you get going, lady."

She said hastily, "Mr. Fourkiller . . . ?"

"Yes, Ms. Chavez." All at once he sounded sober. The words came out crisply enunciated. Unless it was just her imagination.

"Uh . . . nothing. I'll get going."

"Fine."

"Bye for now."

"Bye." Hanging up, she sat thinking a minute, clasping her bare feet in her hands. Her feet were cold. As were her fingers, she noted as she touched them to her face.

At no time in the past two days had she felt it safe to get a message out: Officer Beowawe, she suspected, was keeping tabs on her movements. Her sense of failure over this was now eased somewhat by Fourkiller's unexpected show of trust in her. His having been in Truckee the day of Merrison's murder was no doubt important, but less circumstantial information might come her way shortly.

She quickly dressed.

The Milky Way was visible from the parking lot, a thick, frosted band stretching from horizon to horizon. The Volkswagen balked a little at starting in the frigid air. The balminess of a few days earlier had been replaced by a blustery cold that made the old Shoshone women bring out their woolen kerchiefs and serapes. With the reservation lockdown, the dusty, windswept streets of Spirit Meadows had instantly taken on the atmosphere of a siege. Few people ventured out-of-doors. The chrome-colored cube of the House of Games seemed like an abandoned temple set among the hovels of a less prosperous age.

She turned on the car radio for news, but only talk shows

filled the airwaves at this hour, each host trying to sound more reactionary and disgusted with the federal government than the others. As she veered onto the highway, her headlights sparkled over the brushed-aluminum facade of the casino. On it in fresh red paint were a six-foot-high cross and the crudely sprayed words:

GO HOME, LAKOTA!

That's all I need . . . to be caught in the middle of a civil war here. But was that necessarily bad? Things were coming to a boil in Spirit Meadows, and a protracted stay here now seemed unlikely. *If only I can make it through the next few days.*

Driving north out of town, she watched the skies. If Dan Beowawe was to be believed, Fourkiller had lied about the Learjet being IMG's. Why? And something else had put her on her guard. *Guest.* The way Fourkiller had unconsciously euphemized the word made her think of her revolver in the engine compartment. Who would have to come onto the reservation under the cover of darkness? An Indian activist, almost certainly, and perhaps a dangerous fugitive.

She could still retrieve her handgun and conceal it under the front seat.

But no.

It was too soon to think about guns. Things might come to that before she got out of there, but not now. Besides, she was getting traction with Fourkiller, gaining his trust. It was proving easier to worm her way into his confidence than into a Shoshone store clerk's. That young woman still refused to open up about the man who had shopped for Wuzzi Munro, although in fairness to the clerk, Anna had never mentioned Coso by name. To do so would tip her hand to the entire reservation.

Patience.

She met her own eyes in the rearview mirror. They reminded her of a wild animal's as it cowered in its burrow.

Taking the airstrip turnoff, she passed under the telephone lines into town. Fourkiller had ordered them cut, then had the GTE repair truck turned away at one of his roadblocks.

She parked well back from the strip, shut off her engine, and stepped out.

No sound except the wind in the brush. Hugging herself with her arms, she scanned the darkness all around. No red and green lights anywhere.

The Shoshone could thank the U.S. Army Air Corps for their modest airport. During the Second World War, desert Indian reservations had been convenient, if uncomplaining, sites for small fields to service aircraft being ferried across country.

Flying made her think of her father. Although she had no desire to think of him.

He'd wanted to be a military pilot. Had even started ROTC at Oklahoma State. But then he'd gotten drunk, stolen a car, and wrecked it the evening of the same day he'd been made lieutenant of his unit. *Why'd you have to be two different people, making either hate or love for you impossible?* She'd not mentioned her Oklahoma connection to Emmett. In 1873, 155 emaciated Modoc, who surrendered only after humiliating the U.S. Army in the field for five months, had been exiled to the Indian Territory, the extreme northeast corner of what would become the state of Oklahoma. The Turnipseeds had been among these exiles, and her father repatriated himself to the Modoc homeland only after serving a year in the Stillwater prison for car theft.

Jack Turnipseed had had a Sooner accent not unlike Emmett Parker's.

A nearby utility box started to whine. Then the runway lights bumped on, blotting out the stars. She pivoted toward the south end of the strip, but saw nothing there. She was facing north, when a blaze of landing lights fell over her. The tires of the jet chirped against the runway pavement, leaving behind a smell of hot rubber. The plane came to a full stop at the far end of the strip and began taxiing around.

She went back to the Volkswagen, flicked the headlamps on and off three times so the pilot would spot her. She left them on.

Guest.

Getting out of the car again, she stood in her own lights. She waved to hide her unease. The jet pulled up, and the pilot waved back through the windscreen. He seemed nonchalant enough, although God only knew what he considered to be a routine flight. She tried to memorize the long registration number on the fuselage, but it wouldn't stick in her mind. Everything seemed to be whirring past in a blur; nothing felt real. She was thinking of going for a pen in her purse, when the forward hatch lowered and became airstairs. A diminutive figure with a sun-bronzed complexion and a hooked nose crept down the steps. The old man stopped midway between the plane and the Volkswagen, holding his hat to his head with one hand and a duffel bag in the other. He looked around, his lips curled back, revealing an artificial perfection of false teeth.

No one else got off, and the hatch went up.

Anna walked over to him. "I'm Ronnie Chavez. Mr. Fourkiller sent me to pick you up."

The old man shook his head, indicating that he couldn't hear her over the buzzsaw roar of the jet, which was already taxiing again. A few scraggly white hairs glinted on his chin. They were over an inch in length, testament that he no longer had the vanity to pluck them, as a younger Indian male would. He had to be pushing ninety years, although his eyes were vibrant and his smile suggested that nothing could surprise him.

"I'm here to pick you up!"

He gave no sign that he'd heard her this time either, except that he began shuffling toward the VW. He wore a fleece-lined rawhide coat and new-looking blue jeans, the cuffs rolled up four inches to reveal silver Nike running shoes.

Darting ahead of him, she opened the trunk, took his bag, and squeezed it in. "Careful," he said, although his back was to her. A husky, breathy voice.

The jet climbed steeply into the darkness, its roar fading and its underbelly catching the first light that had yet to clear the mountains in the east.

She eased down the trunk hood. The old man's bag had exuded a riotous perfume of herbs, including wild sage and mountain pennyroyal, both familiar to her.

These were the trappings of a shaman, a man equally capable of healing and of causing harm.

He was already in the passenger seat, lighting a hand-rolled cigarette as he peered off toward Spirit Meadows.

"I'm Ronnie Chavez," she repeated.

He acknowledged her with a nod but didn't offer his own name.

"How was your flight?" she persisted. It'd be natural for Ronnie to blather.

"The son of a bitch flew through every hard patch of air in the sky." He picked a flake of tobacco off the tip of his tongue, then looked at her, his dark and glossy pupils reflecting the green dash lights.

Smoke from his cigarette wreathed her face.

When she'd been a girl of eight, a Sioux shaman had visited the Modoc at their sacred hill near Tule Lake. In those days, Lakota and Navajo medicine men had been the keepers of a flame that had been extinguished for many of the smaller tribes by the BIA boarding schools, which forbade any form of Indian expression, especially religion. The particulars of that evening in a crowded earth-and-timber ceremonial lodge had grown muddled in her memory with time. But she recalled the shaman's interminable singing, then his stopping and the abrupt hush that fell over the Modoc. She'd gazed through the press of bodies at the astonishing thing he had conjured. It hovered in the heavy air. An impossible thing. A phosphorescent tangle of tiny lightning bolts through which the faint outlines of a buffalo could be seen galloping in place. The vision still defied rationality, and four years at Berkeley had made the memory only less approachable.

Could this have been that shaman?

No. Unlikely. Impossible. She told herself that paranoia fed upon the slightest chance of coincidence. Even if it were the same man, he would never remember a small girl at the back of the lodge, one of thousands of sites he may have visited through the years.

She cracked her window to let out the tobacco smoke, then started her engine and steered for the highway. "You been to Spirit Meadows before?"

"Yes," he said, still watching her. "It's an evil shithole."

Emmett sat forward in his seat as the helicopter pilot banked toward the aspen grove along lower Robinson Wash. "Here we go," the man said over the intercom. The noon sun glinted off the fire-blackened windows of the abandoned Chevy. The car had been torched, something Emmett had known within an hour of his setting out on foot from the ambush. He'd avoided the roads on his twenty-mile trek back to Kaibab, keeping the North Star before him and the car fire to his back. At dawn, his shins bruised and bleeding from having tripped over brush all night, he'd finally stumbled into the BIA police office in the tribal headquarters building. He laid the empty shotgun on the counter and asked to use the telephone. Reluctantly, his first call was to Hagiman. Burk showed up three hours later on an Air National Guard helicopter with his SWAT team. Emmett arranged to rent his own chopper out of Williams, realizing that Hagiman's would spend the day in a futile search for the Jamaicans who'd set fire to the car he'd borrowed from the FBI. They were probably back in Kingston by now.

His pilot was a thin-faced Navajo with an infectious grin. His name was Gene Yazza, and they'd worked together before. Yazza'd take chances as long as the reason made sense to him. "Want me to set you down?" he asked.

Emmett had had three hours of sleep in the Pipe Springs Motel, but it hadn't been enough to wash the coarseness out of his voice. "Anywhere fairly close to the car, Gene."

"Why'd they burn it?"

"The radio. Didn't want me to come back and use it."

"Nice guys."

"Yeah." Emmett could see where the upper Bronco had skirted the flaming Chevy by plowing along the top of the ridge before rejoining the road. Yazza came in just over the tops of the aspens and hovered a foot or two above a small meadow. "I'll just be a minute," Emmett explained. "An FBI tech will be along in a while to do the I.D. work."

"Roger."

Emmett laid his headset on the seat and opened the side door. He braced his boots on the skids, then leaped down into the frost-browned grass. The shock to his sore feet made him grunt. Yazza promptly lifted off a few hundred feet so Emmett could hear himself think. He hiked into the trees, thrashing through the wild rose thickets. Last night came back to him in kaleidoscopic images and sounds. Dreadlocks. Muzzle flashes and echoing reports. The taunting. *Any you dreads speak Comanche?* They'd known who he was. He started to get angry all over again, but quickly made himself stop. Anger blunted thought, and now he had to rethink everything. He'd come to Kaibab believing that he faced one suspect, a man with braids, most likely an Indian not unlike himself. But he'd been bushwhacked by a host of foreigners from a part of the world he knew nothing about. His growing sense of progress had been shot full of holes in this grove.

He reached the road.

Spent brass cartridges glittered among the fallen leaves and atop the patches of snow. Avoiding the footprints left by the Jamaicans, he approached the burnt-out hulk of the sedan. His suitcase was still in the trunk, incinerated, too, no doubt. Only now was he beginning to feel the aloneness, the helplessness he'd suppressed all night.

Enough. Let the FBI tech deliberate over this place.

He strode back to the meadow and flagged his arms. Down came the chopper, and Emmett climbed aboard.

"Find out anythin'?" Yazza asked.

"Yeah, that I used up eight of my nine lives here last night."

"Know the feelin'. Where now?"

"Up the wash."

He was surprised to see that the tracks of the upslope Bronco stopped and turned around within a hundred yards of the aspens. Beyond that, there was no sign that a vehicle had ventured there since the two big snows had moved through.

He frowned.

So Sam Yellow Gourd had not come up in pursuit of his errant soul. And that morning Hagiman had attempted to grill Graham Owen, but the apprehensive Brit had swiftly circled the legal wagons around himself by calling the tribe's local attorney, who was driving in from St. George to attend the next round of questioning. Emmett had seen no point in zeroing in on the accountant. Everything Owen had related had been fed to him, and at no time had he claimed direct knowledge about anything concerning Yellow Gourd, who was now in hiding.

Or dead.

Yazza gained altitude. The south rim of the Grand Canyon

came into view, layered bands of red and yellow stone topped by a green fringe of ponderosa pines. Emmett could also see Havasu Falls across the Colorado, deep within the redoubt of the Pai. Close but so very hard to reach. Or was it . . . ?

Yazza interrupted his thoughts. "What're we lookin' for?"

Emmett yawned to pop his ears. "Winter lodge." His eyes ran over the piñons and aspens below, but his mind was trying desperately to make sense of last night. He wouldn't feel balanced again until he understood the chain of events that had triggered the attack.

It had started in motion with Leonard Wine talking in Jamaica. That much was now a given.

But, surely, the lawyer had no intention of becoming a permanent exile. Wine was in the Caribbean just to weather the storm, perhaps mend a few fences with a silent partner of questionable integrity. As soon as the clouds lifted, Wine meant to return to Carson City and go on championing the profitable cause of reservation gaming. Conspiring to assassinate a federal officer didn't jibe with that, so someone else had entered into the mix, perhaps distorting Wine's report in such a way that the Jamaican syndicate saw no choice but to take out Emmett when he showed up in Kaibab to interview Yellow Gourd. What could anyone have said that would justify such a risky operation? It was beyond reckoning. Emmett sighed into his throat microphone.

"What's wrong?" Yazza asked.

"Ever want to go off and just be an ignorant, one-blanket Indian?"

"Figured I was one."

Emmett smiled. Then it registered. He'd spotted a conical shape down among some piñons. "Spin around, Gene."

Two minutes later he was threading his way through the stunted pines toward the winter lodge he'd seen from above. It was round and big, fifteen feet in diameter, with four poles interlocking at the top, tepee fashion. The sides were covered with juniper bark and rushes from the marshlands in Antelope Valley below. The earth surrounding the lodge had been pressed smooth by the snows, although the drifts had now retreated to the shade farther up the hillside. No tracks were visible but for the inquisitive meandering of a white-tailed squirrel awakened by the recent warm spell.

Stooping at the east-facing entrance to the lodge, Emmett checked the interior. Yellow Gourd's family had not been there in a long time. And they'd no doubt vanished, wanting no part in the evil that had made its way to them. A prescient people, the Southern Paiute. They'd known centuries before Columbus that the world is round and that it spins, although their creationism had a twist: This world is suspended on a cord from another earth above it. Emmett wasn't sure what dwelt on that alter world of the Kaibab. Maybe demons capable of ripping the faces off the living. And that's what still confused him about all this: its overlay of an almost universal native belief. By losing their faces, Roper and Merrison had been deprived of their identities on the other side. They couldn't even transmogrify into fanged animals that might avenge their murders, for their teeth had been bashed out. They'd been condemned to endless wandering through the maze of death with no possibility of a contented afterlife.

Burk Hagiman's voice squawked from inside Emmett's parka pocket.

He took out the Handie-Talkie radio the FBI man had thrust on him as he and Yazza took off from Kaibab. "Go ahead," he said warily.

"*Clear to copy?*" Hagiman was asking if Emmett was alone to receive confidential information.

"Affirm."

"*My people ran down the Broncos . . .*" Emmett had given him the plate number on the lower Ford, the one he'd seen parked in the motel lot early last evening. "Registrations come back to a Hertz agency in North Las Vegas."

"Subjects fitting our description rent them?" Jamaicans.

"*Negative. Some freelancers were apparently hired to handle the logistics. Possible Italian, Clark County locals. Gave bogus addresses and I.D.'s. They used a corporate credit card, just reported stolen this morning. Vehicles aren't due back until the end of the week, but Hertz is already writing them off.*"

"Copy." Emmett strolled over into a patch of sunlight so Yazza could see him. He waved, and the pilot immediately started down. "What're you working, Burk . . . the road to Toroweap Point?"

"*Negative. We think the Clayhole Wash road toward Colorado City is a better bet.*"

Emmett acknowledged by pressing the mike button twice. He wasn't about to argue. That put the FBI completely across the plateau from him—with no sign, no witness statements to indicate that the Jamaicans had fled north. He was beginning to wonder if they had yet to make it out of the Colorado drainage. He climbed into the helicopter and strapped himself in. "Got enough fuel to take me down to the river, Gene?"

"Hope so," Yazza said.

The one remaining shift at the Shoshone House of Games ran from eight in the morning until five in the afternoon. Anna and the three other twenty-one dealers stood dutifully behind their tables, their unused card decks spread in fans over the green felt before them. The keno board still registered a game that had been called three days ago, and the slot-change girl dozed on her feet. For once, the shaft of sunlight penetrating the front glass doors was not passing through a haze of cigarette smoke. No patrons had showed, even though it was New Year's Eve, traditionally the busiest twenty-four hours of the year. Still, Cyrus Fourkiller had explained to the staff that under no circumstances would the management be cowed into closing the casino.

The only employee keeping busy in the place was the cashier, who was honoring checks from the tribal government for its personnel, cops especially. Anna wasn't sure why, but it seemed that the crisis had precipitated a second one concerning the tribe's solvency. Had notes been called in? Or did revenue loss from the casino have an immediate and devastating impact on cash flow?

She resisted glancing at her wristwatch. She'd done so only a couple of minutes before. One-thirty.

Fourkiller came down the staircase, swept past the tables. His light complexion, typically Lakota, only accentuated the dark circles under his eyes. He hurried by Anna, but then turned on his heel and came back. The juniper smell of gin clung to him. "Take a drive with me, Ronnie?"

"Is it okay?"

One of the other dealers sniggered, but Fourkiller cut it short with a sharp look. "Just for a while," he told Anna.

"Sure." She put the cover on her chip rack and locked it before trailing Fourkiller out front. One of the maintenance men had brought around a caviar-black Range Rover. Now he opened the doors for Anna and Fourkiller. She saw that the vehicle was fitted with all-season radials.

"Yours?" Anna asked.

"Company's," Fourkiller replied.

The interior reeked of lemon air freshener. He drove slowly across the empty lot. The tires rattled a steel plate that had been set over a hole, dug—some said—to gain access to GTE's buried cable. All telephone communications with the outside were now cut. Fourkiller's mood seemed pensive, and he said nothing as he turned south on Route 127. She hoped that he'd take her all the way to Baker, she was so eager to get out of Spirit Meadows, even temporarily. This reservation was beginning to feel like a prison to her, just as her Modoc rancheria had seemed to her in her teens. Maybe that is why she'd joined the FBI. Agents moved around a lot. Shed the skins of their exterior lives and transferred to a new field office or resident post.

The Modoc held that the snake was immortal because he shed his skin every year.

Fourkiller broke the silence. "I'd appreciate it if you'd keep it to yourself . . . what I said about my brother this morning."

" 'Course."

He smiled, eyes moist. The smell of gin was strong over the inside reek of lemon. "Thanks, Ronnie," he said with such a sudden frailty she mentally squirmed. She didn't want to like him, not in the least. However great her discomfort here, she didn't want Fourkiller to be the one to soothe it. He cleared his throat. "What'd you think of our guest?"

"Weird old guy. Relative?"

"No." But then he equivocated. "Well, in a sense, I suppose."

"He Lakota too?"

"Yes." He braked for a middle-aged Shoshone man who was walking down the opposite side of the street. Fourkiller motioned him over. Tight-faced, the man crossed to the Range Rover. His reluctance showed in every step. A council member, she realized as he drew close and nudged his gray felt Stetson higher on his brow.

Fourkiller lowered his side window. "Earl," he said, unsmiling.

"Mr. Fourkiller." The man gave Anna a reserved nod.

"How're you doing?"

"Okay."

"Not what I heard," Fourkiller said, his face pitiless. "I heard you're not happy at all."

The councilman refused to glance away, although he shifted his weight from foot to foot before leaning against the Rover and saying, "Not exactly how I put it."

"Then how did you?"

"I was just wonderin' out loud if we're jumpin' the gun on this lockdown and all."

"What's the alternative?" Fourkiller demanded.

"Well, what happens if we get an agreement from law enforcement not to disrupt casino operations while they do their investigatin' on this Merrison business?"

"Whose brainstorm was that?"

"Tribal attorney," the councilman said, obviously feeling a little like a snitch.

"Oh, how inspired. Law enforcement will agree to that in a minute."

The councilman shrugged. "Then there you have it."

"Problem is—which law enforcement?"

"What d'you mean?"

"Well, we're confronted with a three-headed monster, right?" Fourkiller's reasonable tone was contradicted by his incensed eyes. "Federal . . . state . . . local," he counted off on his fingers. "Just one head has to break that agreement, and the House of Games is history. Forever. Remember the federal treaty with your great-grandfathers, Earl? The one promising them all their ancestral lands between the Amargosa and Coso ranges . . . ?" Anna tensed involuntarily at mention of the word *Coso*—it'd rolled off his tongue so explosively. "What happened to that agreement, Earl?"

"Well, the Indian Allotment Act—"

"Fucking right. The Dawes Act let your lands be homesteaded and mined by whitey, until finally you Shoshone were squeezed here in this dry sinkhole ten miles square. Remember the water agreement with the state? That got trashed too, all so Los Angeles could suck up anything that flowed west off the Coso Mountains. . . ." Again, the word hit her like a blow. "Then, when the cavalry pulled out, there was that pact with local law enforcement not to intervene on the reservation without tribal permission. That went in the shitcan when Public Law Two-eighty was forced down your throats. The sheriff considers your P.D. to be a security force without legitimate police powers. Give him the chance, and he'll disband and disarm your cops. Fuck, yes, Earl, you should sit down, smoke the pipe with your white brothers, and get yourselves a goddamn agreement right now!"

With that, he slammed down the gas pedal and sped on. A block passed in a blur before he swerved into the lot of the Spirit Meadows Market and stopped, killing the engine by letting up too soon on the clutch. He stared forward without blinking. The veins stood out in his temples.

"Cyrus?"

Finally, he seemed to get a grip on himself. He shook his head and muttered, "Shit," then reached over and took hold of her hand. She was caught off guard by the tenderness with which he did this. He had a surprisingly gentle touch. Somehow, it made him seem even more frightening: that he could dissemble his true nature so effortlessly. Psychopaths were masters at it. Until they struck. "You all right, Ronnie?"

"Yes."

"Did I jerk your neck when I peeled out?"

"No."

"Damn. I'm sorry. This isn't me. None of it. Everything's gone insane."

"The council?"

"Just a part of it. They're such idiots sometimes." He faced her. "Doesn't Earl get it? He's a *leader*. The government has never broken the back of an Indian rebellion without locking up its leaders. I'd say they've done worse in some cases, except being hanged or shot is better than prison. Do you have any idea what being locked up does to us?"

"I guess not," she said quietly.

"Me neither," he acknowledged. "But I've seen what it can do. God, haven't I?"

She asked, "Have you?" As soon as a tiny paroxysm tugged at the corner of his mouth, she realized that the question had been too pointed. Outspokenness was an Anna trait, not a Ronnie one. The role of Ronnie Chavez was beginning to feel like a chintz dress two sizes too small. She changed the subject but mentally dog-eared his revelation for further scrutiny. What was he talking about . . . seeing what prison could do to an Indian? "You know, Cyrus," she said sincerely, "they're going to appreciate you here only after you're gone. That's just how people are."

He leaned back from her, slightly, in his bucket seat. As if taking her in more fully. With new eyes. "You really think so?"

"Yeah. It's always that way."

Softly, Fourkiller ran his knuckles down her jawline. "Who *are* you, lady?" She smiled, although a spasm of tension passed through her stomach. "Come on," he said, withdrawing his hand.

She followed him, looking at the back of his business suit. She hadn't seen him in the leather jacket since that first night, when he'd just returned from Truckee. He could probably wash minute traces of blood off his hands, but spatters on a porous material like leather were almost indelible. The U.S. Attorney could make the entire case on that jacket.

Inside the market, he ignored the clerk, the same reticent young woman as always, and picked up a cardboard box on his way past the front counter. Anna let him lead. He took a list from the inner pocket of his coat and began picking items off the dusty shelves. One of his first selections was a pack of Zigzag cigarette papers.

"You're not going to roll your own, are you?"

"They're not for me," he answered curtly, moving on.

She stood riveted to the floor. From memory, Emmett had recited everything he'd seen in the box of groceries Wuzzie Munro had received from this market. Zigzags had topped the list. As far as she knew, most marijuana smokers on reservations preferred pipes. Only the aged, who'd acquired the tobacco habit before the advent of tailormade cigarettes, used Zigzags.

Fourkiller turned at the end of the aisle and stared back at her questioningly. "What's wrong?"

"Nothing." She rejoined him. "What else?"

"Cornstarch."

When he'd filled the box, he went to the counter, but before addressing the clerk he asked Anna, "You mind handling this for me?"

"I guess not."

"Thanks." He pressed a fifty-dollar bill into her palm. "I've got to talk to somebody who lives just around the corner. I'll meet you back in the car in five minutes." He took Anna in once again as if she'd been transformed for him. She was more unnerved than flattered. Had she deviated from her role somehow?

Fourkiller was no sooner out the door than the clerk eyed Anna's white blouse and black slacks and asked, "You work in that place?"

"Yeah, just started."

"I'll pray for you," the young woman said.

Chapter 11

Emmett had Gene Yazza fly over the road to Toroweap Point as it struck southwest across the plateau. Yet, within less than a mile, it became apparent from the lack of any recent tire tracks that the Jamaicans who'd tried to kill him hadn't attempted to go this way. Puzzled, Emmett reflected briefly, then told the pilot, "Go back, Gene. Back to the junction with the Robinson Wash road."

"Roger."

Perhaps Hagiman's current hunch was right. They'd turned north after setting the Chevy ablaze. Returned to Las Vegas on Interstate 15 through southern Utah, then flown out of McCarran International hours before Emmett had reached the BIA police station in Kaibab. Yet, desert highways were gauntlets; seldom were there parallel side roads. Especially the I-15 corridor, which was pinched down into the towering narrows of the Virgin River. A convoy of Rastas in matching midnight-blue Broncos was bound to catch the eye of some state trooper. Emmett assumed that Hagiman had had his agents check the airport parking areas, but reminded himself to ask the man when they met later that afternoon at the motel.

"Here?" Yazza asked. They'd returned to the intersection with the Robinson Wash road.

"Right," Emmett said, "just circle around it a few feet off the deck."

The pilot swooped, and Emmett's heart floated up into his throat. The skids almost touched the brush. Emmett cracked his door, leaned partly out, and peered down. Below, the dark red volcanic soil turned to brown sandstone, an ancient dune petrified in place for eternity. The road traversed it for a distance of about forty feet, unnoticeable from ground level because the passing of countless vehicles over the years had stained the dune with a deposit of reddish dirt. "Keep on this heading, Gene," he said, shutting the door. He looked between his mud-coated boots, down through the lower curvature of the canopy bubble at the sandstone. Abruptly, the younger layer of volcanic cinders took over and the tire impressions appeared again.

Emmett asked, "See them?"

The pilot nodded.

The tracks led due south. They cut across low scrub, making them invisible unless the viewer was directly above. Savvy. These Jamaicans had proven remarkably savvy in their choice of a route across unfamiliar country. And at night too. That made no sense. Rock outcroppings and gullies should have forced them to backtrack at almost every turn.

The twin streaks topped a crest, a rounded bluff with the Colorado glinting far below, and started descending into the canyon.

"Where the hell they goin'?" Yazza asked.

Certainly not in the direction Hagiman and the rest of law enforcement in the region assumed. The highway to St. George and Interstate 15 were crawling with cruisers. "Got me," Emmett muttered, concentrating to keep on top of the Jamaicans' next move in this labyrinth of stone, sand, and brush.

At last they seemed to betray some hesitation.

The tire tracks made a loop atop the first of the many terraces forming a giant staircase that fell away to the river. In the darkness, no doubt, there had appeared no immediate way down this cliff, and the driver of the trailing Bronco had pulled alongside the lead four-by-four. Both vehicles had stopped here. Everyone had gotten out to consult, for the ground was pocked with boot prints. Two sets struck off alone, skirting the rim until reaching a breach in the precipice, a natural ramp down to the next terrace. This pair of men had come back to the Broncos at a hurried trot, for the prints were spaced farther apart coming in than they were going out. And the Broncos continued on.

"Put me down for just a second, Gene."

"Where?"

"Anywhere we won't erase those tracks with your rotor wash."

Yazza wheeled and touched down farther up the slope.

Jumping out, Emmett retraced the path taken by the two men. Two, not one. That meant something, for he'd already decided that only a local could have brought the Jamaicans this far, someone from the Kaibab Reservation familiar with the old trade trail to the Havasupai, abandoned and nearly forgotten now that everybody drove around the canyon. And when a pair of men does the work of one, it usually spells distrust. He recalled the silhouette that had remained in the upper Bronco, motionless all through the firefight.

Emmett knelt and compared the two sets of prints. One meandered more than the other. The scout's. The impressions were smaller than his own, and each of the size-ten indentations was deeper on the outer edge. This man had been trained to move quietly, and the simplest way to do that was to walk on the outside edges of the feet. The military taught that. So did Indian hunters. The man accompanying the first was a city dweller, a sidewalk traveler, for the heel strike was the deepest part of his print.

Emmett frowned: Hagiman was talking at him again.

He boosted the volume of the Handie-Talkie so he could hear over the whistling of the rotor. "Go ahead."

"You interview motel management this morning?"

"Briefly. Gal named Chloe."

"And . . . ?"

Unproductive. The on-duty clerk, a former Las Vegas dancer gone to sag and cellulite, had dealt with only one of the Jamaicans upon their arrival at the motel early yesterday afternoon. The other two—not three, which added credence to the possibility of an unwilling local guide—had remained in the Broncos while "John Rasta" registered and paid with cash. The clerk could recall only his "braided rug hair" and gold nose ring. The man had failed to fill in the vehicle license numbers on the registration form. She'd been under the impression that they were musicians on tour.

Emmett transmitted. "You might have one of your boys talk to her again, Burk . . . in case I missed something."

"Copy." Hagiman signed off with a hint of aggravation in his voice. No doubt thinking how much easier his life would now be if the Jamaicans had succeeded in eliminating Emmett Parker last night.

Emmett returned to the chopper. "I want to keep after them, Gene, if you don't mind. This trail will get cold real fast."

Yazza twitched his lips, the Navajo way of pointing, at the reloaded shotgun Emmett had wedged between the seats. "You got another piece?"

Emmett lifted the bottom of his parka to show his .357.

"Which one do I get?" Yazza asked.

"Whichever I empty first."

The pilot laughed and lifted off, only to plunge the rig down over the cliff. The terrace stood at a crazy tilt until he adjusted his stick and the landscape righted itself. They followed the tracks over another three terraces, down past the history of the world layered in rock, reaching a shelf of hard black schist less than a thousand feet above the Colorado River. Here, some long-ago fault had opened a narrow, seemingly bottomless fissure in the last bench. The pair of tracks vanished into it.

"Whoa, Gene."

"I see it."

"Go ahead and land. Shut off your engine to save fuel. I may be a while."

"Okay."

"Got a good rope?"

"Under your seat. Gold line. In case I accidentally auto-rotate down into a tree."

"Happen often?"

Yazza just grinned.

Grabbing a flashlight and the rope, Emmett bailed out as soon as the chopper set down. He paused at the point about fifteen yards from the fissure. The same spot where the Jamaicans had stopped and gotten out of their Broncos. This was marked by a clutter of boot prints, a flurry of activity that made sense only when Emmett stepped up to the drop-off and shone his light below. The black schist seemed to absorb the beam, but about twenty feet beneath him he caught a faint sparkling of chrome.

Yazza had come up behind. "Don't figure they just drove off into that, do you?"

It'd been moonless last night, and Emmett himself had nearly walked off a ledge into oblivion. But no, there were human tracks all around this site. A survivor of the fall couldn't have climbed out of the fissure. "Nope, Gene, it was just time to ditch the four-wheel drives. They walked the rest of the way down to the river." He glanced around for a tree, but there was none this low in the canyon except for some tamarisk along the Colorado. "But I still want a look inside one of them."

"Here." Yazza took an end of the gold line and jogged back to his copter, where he secured the rope to one of the struts. "Hey, Emmett . . ."

"What?"

"Remind me not to take off till you come up."

Shaking his head, Emmett looped the rope under his right thigh and across his body. He walked backward, taking the slack out of the line as he went, then stutter-stepped over the edge and bounced down the wall into the darkness. His sutured left hand stung, but he continued rappelling until his boots thudded against the rear hatch of one of the Broncos.

Yazza's voice echoed down: "You okay?"

"Yeah." He took the flashlight from his pocket and tried to shine it through the vehicle's rear window. But the glass was caked with dust. He saw that he'd come to rest on the trailing Bronco, which tottered slightly under his feet. The first was directly underneath it, the hood jammed between the rock walls.

The running lights on both vehicles were still weakly burning.

Descending a few yards more, he landed on the driver's-side door, which—as expected—was wide open. The vehicle groaned ominously under his weight, so he tightened his grip on the rope as he aimed his beam inside the cabin. A brush-wood stick had been propped between the underside of the dashboard and the gas pedal. And a length of twine, a shoelace perhaps, dangled off the automatic shift lever. It'd been used to jerk the transmission out of neutral. The key was still in the ignition, the fuel gauge needle on empty. There was blood on the passenger bucket seat.

No doubt, the big blotch in the upholstery fabric had seeped from a bullet wound that refused to stanch. An entry wound in the proximity of a kidney, judging from the position of the stain on the backrest. The cry of pain he'd heard in the aspens during last night's firefight had not been imagined. They'd come thousands of miles to murder him, him person-ally, and he'd made at least one of them pay for it.

The upper Bronco began to sway.

Emmett started climbing before it tumbled over and pinned him to the rock wall.

Yazza pulled him up the last few feet. "Well . . . ?"

"They're on foot. One of them has a punctured kidney." He followed the tracks downslope until he found what he was looking for, a tear-shaped blood spatter in the earth. Just be-yond that, the wounded man's prints formed a ragged semicir-cle, as if he were reeling. After that, his progress was marked by a two-pointed streak. Most likely, it had been left by the toes of his boots as his friends half dragged him under the arms.

"*Parker . . . ?*"

Again Emmett reached for the Handie-Talkie. "Go ahead."

"*We're not coming up with anything,*" Hagiman said. "*Just a precaution, but I'm going to have my people check McCarran for these vehicles. What do you think . . . ?*"

Emmett rubbed the H.T. against his forehead. A perverse time for Burk to turn considerate. He knew precisely what would happen if he told Hagiman that both Broncos had been ditched and the Jamaicans were now on foot. The FBI had a containment mentality—they'd want to seal the perimeter before doing a damned thing. Cordoning off the Grand Canyon could take the rest of the week, particularly with the Park Service and tourists involved, and if the FBI apprehended the Rastas, it was almost guaranteed that the Jamaicans would say nothing. His purpose in coming here had been to get a bead on Cyrus Fourkiller. That'd swiftly be overshadowed by the confusion of a massive, multiagency operation.

"Good idea," he said in answer to Burk's suggestion to check the airport. "I'll be out of radio communication for a spell."

"*Why's that?*"

Emmett decided not to stretch the truth completely out of shape. "Working the back side of Kanab Point."

"You on to something, Parker?"

"*Not sure. Will advise.*" Emmett signed off and turned back to Yazza. "Fire her up, Gene. Approach the crossing from upriver. Maybe the rapids will cover the sound of us coming."

"I doubt it."

"Me too."

Yazza followed the terrace northeast for a mile, then banked his copter down into the brooding confines of a high-walled section of the canyon and skimmed the tumultuous Colorado. Spray from a roostertail in Upset Rapids flecked the canopy. Then the waters smoothed out, and Yazza slowed for the fording. It was marked by a translucency in the coffee-brown flow through which the riverbed showed. "Want me to hug the north bank, Emmett?"

"Uh, yeah." He could see where the fugitives had come off a debris fan and crossed the sandy bank to a wide indentation partway up the beach. There, a raft had either met them or been waiting.

"South bank, Gene."

Yazza jinked the stick, and a limestone ledge spun past in a sulfuric blur until he straightened again. The south bank materialized out of Emmett's vertigo. His eyes traced the indentation in the sand up from the beach to a belt of tamarisk trees along the high-water mark in spring. He had Yazza land but told him to keep the engine going in case muzzles flashed on the shadowy cliff above. "If you take fire, Gene, lift off ASAP. Worry about me later."

"Say what?"

"I can swim, if need be, downriver a ways."

"I'll be pickin' you out of the Gulf of California if that current snatches you. Havasu Rapids start just around this bend."

Emmett shrugged and gripped his shotgun. "Okay . . . downriver a *long* ways."

It felt odd to run on sand. Spongy. He racked a round into the chamber and approached the tamarisks, peering over his sights, sweeping from side to side of the stand. Vaulting over a driftwood log, he nearly landed inside a small raft. Stenciled in black letters on one side of its inflated tube was:

HAVASUPAI WHITE-WATER EXPEDITIONS

The rubberized flooring was smeared with watered-down blood, which meant that the gun-shot man was still hemorrhaging.

Plan B.

Obviously, the Jamaicans had taken a precaution in the event Emmett somehow escaped death. They'd chosen to flee across the canyon instead of chancing the highways back to Las Vegas. The man who had provided this raft probably had been waiting whatever the outcome in Robinson Wash, for radio and cellular phone transmission were virtually impossible down here. Emmett lowered the shotgun, but watched the cliff for the slightest movement as he rose and followed the boot prints. A new pattern had appeared among them, a corrugation of diamonds. He kept to this trail only until it was evident that the party was headed toward the mouth of Havasu Creek.

Then he returned to the chopper.

"Where next?" Yazza asked.

Emmett didn't climb inside the cabin. "You're headed back to Williams. I go on alone from here."

"You sure?"

"Positive. You got something I can carry water in?"

"Here." Yazza reached behind his seat for a day pack. "My emergency kit. In case I got to hike out of some godforsaken spot because of mechanical trouble. Been known to happen."

"Appreciate it."

"What about your backups?"

"FBI will find me no matter what." Emmett threaded the pack straps over his shoulders. "Mind telling a fib in a good cause, Gene?"

"What's the cause?"

Emmett checked the time. It was almost three, and already there was no direct sunlight in the bottom of the canyon. "A Modoc girl's safety. FBI's got her all hung out to dry, and I need to get some answers to some questions quick."

"Shoot."

"Phone Burk Hagiman at the Pipe Springs Motel a couple of hours after you get back to Williams."

"Why don't I just get a little elevation and radio him now?"

"Well, that's part of the fib. I want you to tell Hagiman that after I spoke with him on the H.T. we found the Broncos. And I went in foot pursuit before we lost them."

"What about your handset?" Yazza really didn't like lying, even to the FBI.

"Won't work down here, Gene. This is up to you. I'll understand if you don't want to get involved."

But then the pilot said, "I'll do it."

"Thanks. Also, tell Hagiman I expect these people to try to come out of the canyon either at or within a couple miles of Hualapai Hilltop trailhead. A wider net won't mean a thing."

Yazza repeated the name of the place, then reached over, shook Emmett's hand, and asked, "You drinkin' again, Emmett?"

"Nope."

"Then get yourself to a singer."

"Why?"

"How well you know this woman?"

Emmett just grunted as he turned. But running along the beach toward the Havasu Creek opening, he smiled to himself. The Navajo seldom openly discussed witchcraft, but Yazza's warning was clear: Emmett could use the services of a healer to divest himself of any spell Anna Turnipseed might have cast on him.

Chapter 12

Anna examined her flatware, then wiped her fork with her napkin.

She'd grown up in a world of greasy spoons and food poisonings of varying severities. The worst had sent her and most of the other patrons of a grill in Alturas to the hospital in Reno, nearly two hundred miles away. Lesser episodes had meant a night of running back and forth from the shanty to the outhouse, for indoor plumbing had come to her rancheria only with federal housing in the early 1980s. Her mother had refused to eat anyone's cooking but her own until life at the nursing home made that impossible. Part of it had been fear of ptomaine. But there had been a deeper reason, one that bordered on paranoia.

Yet, was it paranoia if history gave cause for the distrust?

In 1852, a company of California volunteer militia invited the unarmed Modoc to a peace conference. The soldiers laced their guests' food with strychnine. When the fare was refused, the militia resorted to a more direct method. They shot forty men, women, and children. Twenty years later, Kintpuash—Anna's great-great-grandfather, known to whites as Captain Jack—invited Major General Edward Canby to a parley. Neither side was to come armed. Jack shot Canby dead under a flag of truce. The highest-ranking U.S. officer ever to be killed by an Indian.

So the key to incomprehensible native behavior was always the past.

Kintpuash.

Her own blood. Still, he was an enigma to her. Why had he fought so long and so furiously with no hope of winning? Was the answer in the photograph the army had taken of him in stockade pinstripes hours before his execution? He'd offered the camera a faint, unapologetic smile. Her father's smile. And hers too, she suspected.

Finally, listlessly, she began carving into her creamed beef on toast. When her shift ended at five o'clock, she'd planned to return to her motel room and come up with a way of coaxing Cyrus Fourkiller into letting her accompany him when he delivered the box of groceries to Wuzzie Munro. If he'd left already, she had to make sure that she went along on his next delivery.

That had been her intention.

But the prospect of spending another evening of the reservation lockdown alone in her shabby little room, with the lampshade that wobbled on its harp and the cigarette burns in the bathroom linoleum, had so depressed her, she'd decided on an early supper at the casino coffee shop.

There was danger in being with Fourkiller and Wuzzie at the same time. The old woman might remember her voice, her scent even, and then where would she be? Miles from the Volkswagen and her revolver, miles more from Benjamin and Crutcher in Pahrump. Her closest help would be in Baker, San Bernardino County deputies who had no idea that she was operating on their turf. Would her directional beeper even reach back to Pahrump from the Halloran Springs area?

But she could think of no other way to confirm that Fourkiller was Coso.

As he dropped her off at the House of Games after the trip to the market, she'd tried to wheedle an invitation out of him. But she did it so clumsily, he'd been left with the completely wrong impression. *I'd love to take a drive with you later . . . just to get out of here for a while, you know?* In character for Ronnie Chavez, but full of unsettling implications for Anna Turnip-seed. And there was little doubt from the way he slowly lifted his brows that he'd filed away the offer for another time. He'd even slipped her one of his business cards with a local telephone number scribbled on its back.

She closed her eyes against the overhead neon that seemed to bring out the grease on everything in the coffee shop.

A large hand squeezed her shoulder. "Ronnie."

She jumped a little, then looked up. "Dan." The evening chill clung to Beowawe's uniform as he took the stool next to her, his right knee touching her left. She shifted slightly to break the contact. "Been out on a roadblock?"

"All day." He overturned his coffee cup and held it out to be filled by the waitress. "What you been up to?"

"Dying of boredom. No customers again."

"That'll change," he said cryptically.

There were fresh red blisters on the pads of his left palm. Both hands, she observed. It blurted out of her, half-jokingly. "You been digging graves?"

He blew onto his coffee as if taking time to frame his answer, then looked at her. "We take care of our own problems." Pretty much what he'd said Sunday morning at the overlook.

She tested his seriousness with a smile, and he glanced away. When the waitress had moved on, he said, "Tomorrow's the day."

"What day?"

"You'll see."

"I don't understand."

Beowawe lowered his voice. "Folks from all the western tribes with casinos will be showin' up at the north roadblock on One Twenty-seven. Goin' to force their way through to us, even though the deputies might try to arrest 'em."

"On what grounds?"

"I don't know. Incitin' a riot, somethin' like that. It don't matter, with county mounties. Half of 'em can't even read. They arrest when they feel like it, and then the D.A. has to backpedal."

"What d'you think the feds will do?"

"Don't care. We're goin' to have a lot of people there. The press too. You comin'?"

She hesitated. "I just work here."

"That's the point." He rolled his wind-burned eyes, indicating the casino. "This joint is your rice bowl. All of ours. If whitey shuts it down, what do we have then?"

"But how can they?"

"They'll find a way," Beowawe told her knowingly. "Did it to the Pomos upstate. Infiltrated tribal government. Bribed the council. Hired hitmen to terrify anybody for gamin' . . ." Anna had read a more complicated intelligence report on the bitter and protracted civil war in Lake County, California, but Ronnie Chavez cupped her chin in her hands and kept an attentive expression. "It's like Mr. Fourkiller says, Ronnie. They *got* to try to derail us. For years we stayed in the back of the bus. Fat, dumb, and happy. But now we're movin' up to a better class. That's what gamin' is all about. Upward mobility. And that's what pisses 'em off. You should hear those cracker deputies out at the roadblock, sayin' how they're goin' to pile up our slot machines and burn 'em. It's *us*, they mean. Us they want to burn. Don't you see?"

"I guess."

He finished the rest of his coffee in a single gulp. "So you want to go or not?"

"Will things get violent?"

"I doubt it. Hot, sure. We've taken all we can. But nobody's stupid enough to cook off a firefight. Mr. Fourkiller has made sure we got just as many guns as they do."

"When'll it be?"

"Ten o'clock in the mornin'."

"Will Cyrus let me off work?"

"Sure. He's runnin' the casino bus out there for anybody who wants to join in." Beowawe paused. "He know you call him that?"

"Who?"

"*Cyrus?*"

On the spur of the moment she decided to hint at intimacy. "Sure." Beowawe frowned, but her mind was on the roadblock. Confusion. Federal marshals. The opportunity to slip one of them a message. "I don't know, Dan," she said, filling an unpleasant silence. "Riots scare me."

"Won't be a riot. It'll be a lawful demonstration."

"Still . . ."

"Suit yourself."

"But will it help the casino?"

"Could be the only thing to save it. And Indian gamin'."

Privately, she was one of the few federal officers in favor of reservation gambling. It was the only reliable way to offset dwindling government support for basic services in Indian Country. And as far as she could tell, the much-predicted, full-scale infiltration of tribal operations by organized crime had never materialized. The Modoc of old had enthusiastically embraced games of all kinds as a social control to make certain that wealth wasn't concentrated among the most skillful hunters and gatherers. But all this was beside the point. What would Ronnie do? "Well," she said, "I guess I'll go, if it's that important."

He clasped her around the shoulders. "Attagirl. I'll be lookin' out for you, okay?"

"Thanks." He was rising when she asked, "Dan, where does Cyrus live?"

"Noplace."

She smirked. "Nobody lives *no*place."

"He does." Beowawe eased down again. "Couple years ago, a casino manager down in Riverside County got shot to pieces right in his own bed. Nobody ever got tagged for it, but I figure Mr. Fourkiller took the lesson to heart. He sleeps in a different place every night. Sometimes here in his office on the sofa, sometimes with friends. Once in a while out in the desert."

"He just sleeps on the *ground*?"

"No, he's got a wickiup in—"

"What's that?"

His jaw dropped a little. "You honestly don't know what a wickiup is?"

She shook her head.

"It's an Indian lodge," he explained. "Kind of like a tepee. Except it's covered with bark or brush. Anyways, Mr. Fourkiller has one up in Eclipse Canyon. Rides his dirt bike 'round there to relax."

Picking indifferently at her supper, she asked, "Where's that?"

"You were there. That's where I found you the other day." He rose again. "Listen, I got to run. See you tomorrow, all right?" But he turned within a few strides. "Oh, before I forget—drop by the station Friday morning. We'll take care of that casino employee clearance form and fingerprint you."

"Going to run me through the FBI?" she quipped to mask her unease.

He peered at her in silence for a few seconds, then came back to her, leaned close, and whispered, "Better than that. One of our dispatchers has a cousin who's a file clerk with Nevada Gamin' in Vegas. We slip her our applicant's form and fingerprint card. If the applicant is clean with the Gamin' Commission, good enough for us."

Then, without another word, he walked out, his ebony nightstick bouncing against his thigh.

She expected a moment of mental paralysis, given the bombshell Beowawe had just dropped on her. But none came. Instead, a hard, bright clarity filled her. She had less than forty-eight hours to accomplish everything she possibly could in Spirit Meadows. *After that, assume your cover has been blown.* While the FBI data systems had been sanitized in regard to Anna Turnipseed/Ronnie Chavez, to her knowledge the Nevada Gaming Commission had not been alerted. No one, especially Burk Hagiman, had dreamed that the House of Games had access to Gaming's intelligence resources. The Shoshone file clerk would immediately discover that Ronnie Chavez, allegedly a former dealer at the MGM Grand, had no work card on file.

That would be the end of this charade.

She had to be off the reservation by Friday noon at the latest. In spite of the roadblocks.

Unless she could contact Burk Hagiman or Benjamin and Crutcher in the meantime. That would necessitate a telephone call. Impossible, with the lines cut. She had no cellular phone, knew of no one on the reservation who owned one. And, because of the lockdown, she couldn't leave an urgent message inside the mining claim marker that would be checked tomorrow by the BLM ranger.

She forced herself to slow down.

Maybe this was just a ruse to panic her into trying to contact the outside. Maybe she was already under suspicion, and Fourkiller had devised a way to flush her out.

But how was she to know for sure?

She shoved her plate aside. The creamed beef on toast looked revolting.

She made up her mind not to try to raise Hagiman or her backup team in Pahrump. She would somehow zero in on Fourkiller before Friday morning, then hike east into the Nopah Range. Once she was safely off the reservation, she'd hit her beeper. Hearing the transmission, Benjamin and Crutcher would set out at once in their four-wheel drive carryall to locate her.

What to do in the scant time she had remaining here?

The prospect of going back to Las Vegas empty-handed was galling.

Taking a five-dollar bill from her handbag, she noticed the business card Fourkiller had given her. According to Beowawe, he didn't have a residence in Spirit Meadows.

She considered that while paying for her meal.

Then she went to one of the house phones, the only lines still working on the reservation. She dialed the number, half afraid that Fourkiller would answer, even though she hadn't seen him come back inside the casino after he'd let her off.

On the fourth ring his voice answered. *"Congratulations, you've reached my phone. I can't answer right now, but leave a message and I'll get back to you."*

She hung up.

If Fourkiller didn't keep a residence, the answering machine was almost certainly in his office upstairs.

The blackjack tables were shut down, but she returned to hers, tore a piece of masking tape off the roller that was used to brush lint and cigarette ashes off the green felt, and concealed it in her left palm.

Turning, she bumped into Sal Baldecchi.

"What's the rush?" The shift boss was grinning, but his

eyes were hard on her fisted left hand. Did he think that she'd picked the rack lock and stolen some chips? "You okay, babe?"

"Sal, be honest . . . do I got dandruff?"

"What now?"

"Dan Beowawe just told me I got dandruff." She began dabbing the shoulders of her black sweater with the tape.

Baldecchi chuckled. "Beowawe's pulling your leg, babe. He's the biggest bullshit artist on this rez. You're perfect."

"Really?"

"Would I lie?"

"Yes." She gave him a peck on the cheek, then breezed past him toward the staircase to the mezzanine level. Her face was pale in the mirror at the top, but she didn't linger to let her unease grow. She was already short of breath. Her glance took in the pull-alarm marked FIRE just outside the female employ-ees' rest room.

She knocked on the door at the far end of the balcony.

After a count of three, the judas window shot back, and Anna was once again confronted by Ms. Lajeunesse's humor-less eyes. Fourkiller's secretary was indeed a Canadian Indian, an Ojibwa who seemed to have no existence beyond this office. Anna had never seen her on the casino floor or around town. "Yes, Ms. Chavez?"

"Mr. Fourkiller in?"

"Not at this time."

"Maybe you can help me."

"Maybe."

"Did Bud Shelby's letter come yet from the MGM Grand? You know, confirming my employment there?"

"I don't believe so." Ms. Lajeunesse opened the door and withdrew to her desk, where she began sorting through her in basket to demonstrate that she was very busy.

Anna remained outside. "Could it maybe be in Mr. Fourkiller's office?"

The woman looked questioningly at her for an eternity,

but finally went through Fourkiller's door, leaving it to glide all the way back to the inner wall. The knob hadn't been locked, for which Anna was thankful. Ms. Lajeunesse riffled through a handful of envelopes, sighed, then stepped back into the reception room. "Nothing," she reported.

In the meantime, Anna had taped the latch bolt on the outer door to its faceplate. "Sorry to put you through this trouble. It's just that Mr. Fourkiller said this afternoon that he hadn't got anything back from the Grand yet, and I didn't want him to think I was lying 'bout working there."

"I'm sure Mr. Fourkiller trusts you," the woman said with an utter lack of conviction, "otherwise he would never have hired you."

Anna muttered, "Thanks." On the way out, she gently closed the door so it wouldn't bounce open again. She felt as if she were sprinting as she made her way along the balcony to the pull-alarm. Almost impossible to keep her pace down to a brisk walk. Relying on her peripheral vision that no one was watching, she gave the handle a yank and ducked inside the rest room.

Bells began clanging throughout the casino.

She flipped down the commode lid in one of the stalls, sat, and waited.

Ten seconds later she heard the clip of Ms. Lajeunesse's heels approach and then fade toward the stairs. Anna doubled her legs against her chest and rested her shoes on the seat, held her breath. Almost immediately, she heard the door swing open. A male voice demanded, "Anybody in here?" A security guard, clearing the building.

The door whooshed shut, and she lowered her feet to the floor, started breathing again.

Far off, a wail rose as the tribal fire department responded from the station down the highway.

She ran back to Fourkiller's office, ripped off the tape on

the lock, and pocketed it. The door locked behind her with a click. Ms. Lajeunesse had flipped off the lights on her way out. Anna left them extinguished in the reception room, and made do with the glow of a digital clock on Fourkiller's desk.

The answering machine was beside it.

She was hurrying toward Fourkiller's lavatory, when she suddenly stopped, pivoted, and looked at the machine again.

Crutcher had decided that fitting her with a wire was too dicey for the minimal possible gain, given the poor reception across the desert ranges. But here, possibly, was a means to capture Fourkiller's voice. She could get the recording out of Spirit Meadows tomorrow during the demonstration. Then Emmett could play it for Wuzzie Munro.

That was it. The way to identify Coso.

Prying open the cover with a fingernail, which broke, she took out the tape and dropped it into the pocket of her slacks.

Questions about unlawful search and seizure began swimming around inside her head. But the theft seemed so petty, and the stakes so high. She continued on to the small closet in Fourkiller's lavatory and blindly rummaged among the clothing hung there for his leather jacket. Grasping for the pliable texture of fine cowhide. But everything felt like rayon, cotton, or wool.

Shutting the door, she flicked on the light over the sink just to be sure. No leather jacket.

She was biting off the broken piece of nail, when she noticed the prescription bottles atop the vanity.

Quickly, she went through them.

Most were common sleep aids, but a particularly large plastic vial caught her eye. There was no prescription information on the label, just a handwritten notation that it contained haloperidol. A heavy-duty suppressant for psychotic disorders.

Jesus, she thought, turning off the light, *he's medicating himself between murderous binges*. That accounted for his relatively calm demeanor in Spirit Meadows. But was a psychopath capable of constraining himself like this? Would he even want to?

Sirens were arriving outside.

Stepping back into his office, she parted the venetian blinds with her fingers and looked down on the parking lot. A ladder truck was pulling up. Right behind it was Fourkiller's Range Rover. Running from his vehicle, he beat the firemen to the entrance.

She took out her hankie and wiped off all the surfaces of the answering machine she'd touched, then the knobs to both doors on her way out, and finally the alarm handle along the balcony.

Then she came down the stairs toward Fourkiller.

He narrowed his eyes at her. "What're you doing?"

"Getting out of here, I guess."

"What kept you?"

"I was in the little girls' room when the bells went off." Two Shoshone in helmets and turnout coats swept past her to check the upper level. "Just wasn't a good time to get up and leave, you know?"

Fourkiller scanned the place. "Smell any smoke?"

"Nope." Her heart was pounding again. "False alarm?"

One of the guards approached him. "I can't find anythin', Mr. Fourkiller. Kitchen and generator room are fine."

"Okay, let the staff back inside. Somebody's fucking with us. He'll show his hand again, and then we'll get the son of a bitch." Fourkiller grabbed Anna's elbow. "Anyone else stay inside during the alarm?"

"I didn't see anybody."

His grip tightened slightly on her arm. "Had supper yet?"

"Yeah, before I visited the powder room."

"I have to talk to you, Ronnie."

"Now?"

"If you don't mind."

She let herself be guided up the staircase, his arm around

her waist. "Get to leave those groceries off?" she asked brightly.

"Sorry?"

She repeated it patiently, hoping she struck just the right note of naivete. "Did you take those groceries to your friend?"

"Just got back," he answered curtly.

All the more reason to have taken the tape, although the cassette now burned in her pocket—his fingertips only inches away from it. Ms. Lajeunesse caught up with them on the balcony, and Fourkiller dropped his hand from Anna's waist.

"What happened?" the secretary asked. If the episode had disconcerted her, she gave no sign of it.

"False alarm. Somebody just trying to rattle us. Had your dinner break?"

"No, sir."

"Go ahead and take it."

"I'm not—"

"Take it," he snapped.

Chastened, Ms. Lajeunesse withdrew, and Fourkiller unlocked the outer door. He pushed it back for Anna and then closed it behind them. He located her in the darkness of the reception room by feel, his touch light on the small of her back as he directed her through his own door and into his office. "Care for a drink?" he asked, tossing his keys on the felt top of his desk with a jingle.

"No, thanks."

"Mind if I?"

" 'Course not."

He turned on his desk lamp to the first setting, which left the room in low light. He checked his answering machine, found it unblinking. At this point she expected him to duck inside the lavatory to wash his hands. But he didn't. Instead, he went to an antique Spanish cupboard that hid a wet bar and poured himself a Beefeater on the rocks. At their first meeting on the night Fourkiller had returned from the Lake Tahoe area, he'd given her every indication that he had a hand-washing obsession. Perhaps he'd had a special reason for washing so meticulously that night. And not since.

Fourkiller switched on the surveillance monitors as he worked his way around the desk.

She'd gravitated to the window. His Range Rover was still parked before the entrance. The sides of the vehicle were covered with dust—no paved roads into Wuzzie's rancheria.

"Come here." He'd kicked off his shoes and sat on the sofa. "Relax."

She joined him, smiling, although she was in turmoil. He was drinking, and she was reminded of her father, recalled that wet blur of a face gaping at her, that frightening tenderness washing over him like a narcotic: *Come here, Annie . . .* No one would ever call her Annie again—and go unchallenged. She thought Fourkiller was going to reach out and stroke her cheek, yet the moment passed, and he draped his arm along the backrest. But his gaze remained direct, searching. "You have an interesting face, Ronnie."

"Me?" Her look of surprise was genuine. She found Ronnie Chavez a study in banality, and maybe that more than anything was what irked her about the undercover role.

"Uh-huh. At least that's what my guest says." She kept silent, assuring herself that even had this Lakota shaman been the one to visit the Modoc on that long-ago night, he would never recall a child's face. There was no way the old man could recognize her. Fourkiller took a mouthful of cold gin, held it a moment before swallowing. "He says you're Indian."

"Well, whatever a Mexican is, that's me."

"No. He says you've got a Klamath face, that you come from somewhere up there along the California-Oregon border."

The modern Klamath and the Modoc, occasional foes, were interrelated thanks to the enforced sharing of a reservation. She chuckled to keep her trepidation from showing. "What is this old geezer . . . a witch doctor or something?"

"Something like that," Fourkiller said, leaning his head back and shutting his eyes. She could almost feel his exhaustion, or dissipation, taking hold of him. And yet she had the uncanny sensation that he was watching her through his closed lids. "He has the power to purge evil," he added drowsily. "Evil that makes the mind sick."

She sensed that this was fertile ground for questioning, but felt trapped by being Ronnie Chavez. Unless the dealer's naivete gave her license to ask anything. "You mean you're like *crazy*?"

An amused smile. "Without a doubt."

It was natural to cringe slightly from him, she felt.

His eyes snapped open, and he seized her wrist, not painfully but firmly. "You afraid of being alone with a crazy Lakota?"

For once, honesty suited her ruse. "A little."

"Don't be. Please. I could grow fond of you, Ronnie."

"Why?"

"You are what you seem. You have no guile, and in my world, that's a breath of fresh air."

"What's guile?"

"Deceit," he whispered with distaste.

He shifted around on the sofa, then pulled her partly on top of him. She was so terrified he'd feel the cassette in her pocket, the fact that he was kissing her came to her like an afterthought. She tasted gin, and it disgusted her. She started to twist out of his grasp, but then instantly sensed the futility of escape in his coiled strength. The old defense came back to her, although it had lain dormant for many years. Anna's mind vacated her body, and what remained in the man's boozy clutches was Ronnie Chavez. Anna told her body to be Ronnie, and after a moment Ronnie dutifully returned Fourkiller's kiss.

Not passionately, but with a rising feeling Anna refused to claim as her own. It was strangely electrifying, to stand on the brink of something she'd never willingly done, to be unexpectedly free of all the unshakable baggage that alcoholic's shanty in Modoc County had loaded on her.

"When this is over," he said thickly, "we'll go away for a time."

"Where?"

"My country, the Black Hills maybe. In spring. You ever make love in tall grass?"

"No," she said, surprised that she wasn't stopping him from touching her through her slacks. Part of it was worry that if she brushed his hand aside, he might find the cassette. But the other part of it was unbelievable to her—she was actually pushing against his hand, her hips starting to undulate.

Then self-disgust crashed over her, and her body went to stone in his arms.

She was lying with a man who'd almost certainly murdered twice, who had wounded her partner. He, who was kissing her face, had sliced and ripped off another woman's face. Excuses and pleas raced through her mind. "Not here," she said, her forehead pressed against his neck, trying not to see Stephanie Roper's body in her memory. "Not like this, Cyrus. In tall grass . . . okay?"

He raised his head, studied her.

"Please."

"Don't beg." He sat up and took another quaff of gin.

"I just—"

"Don't you have any fucking pride?" he exploded, hurling his glass against the wall.

She left while she had the chance, not knowing if she'd have a job in the morning. Not caring either. Sal Baldecchi tried to ask her something, but she raced on between the tables and out the entrance.

The night's frigid air only reawakened the memory of

other headlong flights. Out into the snow. Out into the darkened lava beds, where her shame could cool into something like the coarse, pitted masses of rock around her.

Reaching her motel room, she bolted the door and, feeling sick and dizzy, ran for the bathroom. She vomited once, swiftly and efficiently, then rinsed out her mouth and brushed her teeth.

Lying atop her bed, she clutched the tape in both hands. Looking back. Remembering everything with an appalling clarity. Some of her strongest childhood recollections were of FBI agents coming onto the rancheria. The local deputies did nothing to stop the nightmare; they usually laughed at the drunk blanket-ass staggering around the yard and quickly drove away. However unpopular, at least the government officers brought with them an air of power. When they were present, Jack Turnipseed held himself in check, and her sense of helpless terror subsided for that brief time the serene men in the dark suits moved through the reservation. She had wanted that power for herself, she now realized, wanted it to keep her fear at a distance. And she'd hoped from her first day at the academy that the job would be a buffer between herself and the past.

What a joke.

Chapter 13

Time.

Emmett knelt in the powdery sand beside lower Havasu Creek and tried to reckon time. The darkness was almost total. The overhanging rock walls nearly touched; only a thin strip of stars showed between them. It had taken Gene Yazza and him less than an hour to fly from Robinson Wash to the last terrace above the river. But it might have taken the Jamaicans most of the night and much of the morning to cover the same trackless distance by vehicle.

After that they'd been on foot, a wounded man with them. A dying man, it would seem.

Twice since starting up the creek from the Colorado, Emmett had found evidence of uncontrollable hemorrhaging, large bloodstains where the man had lain on a sandbar during a halt. Whatever timetable the party had in mind for getting out of the canyon, it was now blown. The four subjects—two Jamaicans and a pair of locals, Emmett believed—were carrying and dragging the bleeding man up the slender, close to impassable gorge. Car-sized boulders wedged between the walls formed a steeplechase course of little pools and cascades. There was no trail around, so they'd been forced to scrabble up water slides and wade through shallows, reducing their progress to a crawl. The Jamaicans had probably chosen this last-ditch route thinking that it would throw off any ground pursuit by law enforcement. But a gun-shot man hadn't been factored in.

Yazza would have made his call to Hagiman around six o'clock. Already dark an hour by then. In all likelihood, Burk had formulated his plans and marshaled his resources, but the actual multiagency operation would certainly be held off until dawn. He'd never try to insert a tactical team into Supai on a moonless night, although hopefully the Coconino sheriff's office was already staking out the trailhead at Hualapai Hilltop. Even with daylight Hagiman might be uneasy about venturing into the remote heartland of the Eastern Pai with anything less than overwhelming force. In 1975 he'd helped investigate the ambush murders of two agents on the Pine Ridge Sioux Reservation in South Dakota. He knew too well how friendless the FBI could be in Indian Country.

Emmett pressed the glow button on his wristwatch. Midnight, straight-up. "Happy New Year," he whispered.

The men ahead of him had stopped again. He had heard no clattering rocks in over an hour.

By the last echoes he'd caught, he'd guessed that the Jamaicans were three or four hundred yards upstream of him, clambering over the boulders. He wasn't sure if they were aware of his presence yet, although they'd probably been near enough to the river late that afternoon to have heard Yazza's chopper.

He rested a minute longer to let a cramp in his calf wear off. He was soaked to the hips, but in the confines of the slotlike canyon the air felt warm. There was just a slight stirring created by the falling water.

Moving on, he breathed deeply, trying to get some oxygen down into his heavy legs.

He was soon forced to climb another rock barrier on all fours. Passage would be impossible in spring and much of summer, with the creek filling its channel from wall to wall. But he painstakingly worked around the edge of the flow, groping in the darkness for handholds in the smooth limestone. He used his flashlight sparingly, covering all but a tiny portion of the lens with his fingers when he did.

The darkness was no comfort to him though.

His path, the only one unless he could find a way out of the gorge, kept funneling him into cramped spaces that were perfect for an ambush. In any one of these, the men ahead, even without benefit of light, had a good chance of hitting him with a spray of automatic rifle fire.

Reaching the top of another cascade, he had to wade yet one more pool. He held the shotgun over his head for fear that he'd step into a pothole. His .357 had already been transferred to a plastic bag Yazza kept in the day pack to store emergency rations. Lingering on the far bank, he let most of the water drip off his Levi's. To keep from making sloshing noises when he continued. To keep from getting shot.

Dying in the dark.

He smiled, mildly chagrined with himself.

Maybe it was one of the few tribal superstitions to have survived the boarding-school nuns. The deceased can't complete the arduous journey to bliss if he's been mutilated, scalped, or lost his life in the dark. Mutilation. It was the Indian imprint on the two homicides that made the Jamaicans seem like miscast actors. Could the braids on his knife-wielding opponent above Lake Tahoe have been just two of a headful of dreadlocks? He replayed that snow-bleared memory and swiftly decided—no. Not dreadlocks. A pair of thick Indian braids. Yet this suggested a conspiracy that cut across all kinds of lines, and it was one of his strongest convictions that human nature abhors a conspiracy. With time and sufficient pressure, they all disintegrate into a welter of conflicting interests and cross-purposes.

He set out again.

Was it even remotely possible that Nigel Merrison's killer had been a Rasta? There'd been no sign of a struggle in his house—sudden interruption, perhaps, unless there was another explanation for that spray of shaving cream on Merrison's bathmat. But the sum of those impressions indicated some measure of trust between IMG's president and his killer at the outset of the confrontation. Had Merrison known the man in Kingston? Stephanie Roper, too, had offered no initial resistance, had even unlatched a locked door for her murderer to enter her car. But would she have known and trusted a Jamaican hit man?

Halting abruptly, Emmett swung the muzzle of his shotgun around.

The beam of a flashlight on a ledge upstream of him seemed like a burst of phosphorous in the darkness of the night. It swiftly blinked out, but before it did, the image was imprinted on his mind's eye: two silhouetted figures with dreadlocks easing another—the wounded man—down onto the flat rock, his head lolling. Another man had been standing on the edge of this tableau, holding the light, his face obliterated by its glare.

None of the men appeared to have any idea that Emmett was on their trail.

Sitting on his heels, he listened.

Muffled voices drifted down to him. Accents made the words indistinguishable, but they held the sharp tone of an argument.

A piercing hunger cramp almost made him grunt aloud. He hadn't eaten that day. Much of the previous day as well.

The Jamaicans were bivouacking, perhaps for the remainder of the night. So he could afford to slow down. Catch a nap before his fatigue and hunger made him careless. Then, rested, he would steal up on them, letting the creek cover the unavoidable sounds of his approach.

He slipped off the pack and quietly unzipped the flap. He took out the plastic bag, removed and holstered his .357 Magnum. The revolver was still dry. Then he opened a small cellophane package and munched on the unseen contents, a bar of some sort. Stale chocolate, dehydrated pineapple, and rice cake. He grimaced, but went on chewing, ruminating about the two sets of boot prints he'd seen on the north side of the river. Two men had struck out together to scout a way off the terrace. And, the night before, one figure had remained inside the Bronco. So it was possible—no, probable—that at least one of the men was a hostage. At any time his captors could have swung their guns on him.

That gave Emmett a problem.

Not only would he have to surprise the Jamaicans, he'd have to give himself time to sort out the reactions, read which were hostile or defensive, pick out the one that was relieved. And if there was any doubt in his own mind, he couldn't shoot.

Later. He would tackle this later. He leaned his back against a boulder and closed his eyes.

He tried to think of something pleasant, hoping it would make him drowsy. Nothing came to mind until he visualized Turnipseed coming down her stairs in that terry-cloth robe, toweling her hair after she'd showered away the borax dust. *Didn't realize how itchy that crud was till I got it off me.* And then she'd said, *You're next.*

"My ass," he muttered.

There was a clock within him, an internal mechanism that

somehow never slept, that never let go. He now reminded it to awaken him in three hours—or at the smallest hint of a sound over the rushing water.

It took two hours to cover the four hundred yards from his resting place to a flat stretch of creek just below the ledge. Overhead, the slash of visible sky changed completely in that time, with fresh constellations in view at the instant Emmett first caught the labored breathing of the wounded man. From there to the protection of the overhang beneath the party had been another long hundred feet, exposed and made more dangerous by the lime-white streambed against which he stood out as if against snow. But the trick had been in how he was seen: He kept his body rounded, took the distance in quick, silent rushes followed by minutes of complete stillness.

At last he melted into the black shadow under the ledge.

And tried to rest again. The effort had drained him.

But whispering above made him sit up and grip his shotgun tighter. A new voice, one without a Jamaican accent, a familiar Indian voice, said wearily, "All right, all right." Rustling noises followed. Men were rising, milling around. One of them urinated over the side of the ledge. The stream splattered onto rocks yards below Emmett.

Two or more of the men began hiking upstream, their tired feet scuffling over the ground. The sounds faded in the distance.

Then, from above, Emmett heard the distinctive *click* of a Zippo lighter being unhinged. Guttering orange light reflected off the opposite wall of the gorge. Someone inhaled deeply. Coughing followed, racking and painful-sounding. The flame went out. Pungent marijuana smoke wafted down over Emmett, who frowned in the midst of concentrating on these noises, trying to get a mental picture of what was happening.

As best as he could tell, the party had divided up. Three

209

had moved on. One man was remaining behind with the wounded Jamaican. A rear guard, maybe, although that seemed uncharacteristically selfless of a hit man.

Had he been spotted? Instead of sounding an immediate alarm, had their leader decided to lure him out?

"Had enough?" the Indian voice asked softly.

A second later, the marijuana cigarette arced past Emmett's eyes, sparking before it hissed out in the creek.

The Indian had begun to sing, low and mournfully. In the Kaibab dialect. Emmett didn't understand the words, but he recognized the tune. It was the Salt Song, performed for a dying person if the singer didn't know that person's own songs, the ones the spirits had given him in dreams. No Indian would do this unless convinced that he was alone.

With that, Emmett rose to a crouch.

The daylight was coming on, but the surrounding cliffs were at their blackest against the brightening sky. He crept around the ledge and came slowly up an apron of rock debris, inching along so his boots wouldn't overturn any of the stones.

Finally, he could see Samuel Yellow Gourd.

He'd already decided that the casino manager had been the Jamaicans' guide off the Kanab Plateau and had been left behind with the dying Rasta. Yellow Gourd was the only Kaibab with a direct link to Nigel Merrison. And, through him, most likely, the Kingston posse carrying out this increasingly grueling failed assassination attempt. The Paiute was kneeling over the prostrate man, his broad back toward Emmett. Yellow Gourd wasn't large but had powerful-looking shoulders and arms. He wore his hair shoulder-length and with a headband, like an Apache. The trilled consonants of the Kaibab tongue made his song eerily birdlike.

"Don't move, Sam," Emmett called softly in the dawn.

Yellow Gourd stopped singing. He spread his hands out from his body.

"Where are the others going?"

"To the horses," the man answered. "Saddled horses are waitin' on ahead."

"How far?"

"Two miles, no more." Then Yellow Gourd added, "I heard you comin' a couple hours ago. Didn't let on though." True or not, it was a smart thing to say. "You're Parker, aren't you?"

"Yes." The light was coming up fast. Emmett could make out the wounded man's face. The skin was a dusty gray, like cold wood ashes. He thought the Jamaican was dead, but then the sunken eyes found his.

"Back away from him, Sam," Emmett ordered. "And keep your hands in sight."

Yellow Gourd obeyed.

Emmett glanced up the gorge to make sure the others weren't returning, then approached the Jamaican and frisked him. The Rasta managed an unrepentant smile as Emmett plucked a pistol out of his waistband. He dropped the 9mm into his own jacket pocket. "Can you hear me?"

A tiny nod. The wounded man tried to say something, but it snagged in his throat. The ghastly breathing went on.

"He can hear all right," Yellow Gourd volunteered. "But his voice is goin'. Goin' fast."

"Turn around, Sam." Emmett patted him down. Finding no weapons, he said, "Sit."

Yellow Gourd did so, facing Emmett. A somber-looking man in his early forties with troubled eyes.

Emmett dropped to his knees with Yellow Gourd and the Jamaican directly in front of him. The approach to the upper gorge was on his far right. He kept it fixed in the corner of his eye.

The Jamaican watched him with a remote curiosity, the man who'd taken his life from him.

"Can you understand me?" Emmett asked him.

A sigh that sounded like a yes.

"Like Sam said, I'm Investigator Parker. Bureau of Indian Affairs." He paused, mostly for Yellow Gourd's sake, so the Paiute could later accurately testify to this. "You're going to die in the next couple of hours. I've got no way of getting you to help. I would if I could. But I just can't. So this is it. You understand?"

Another feeble nod. No apparent rancor. *Who fe do,*" the Rasta rasped.

"What?" Emmett asked.

"They say it a lot," Yellow Gourd explained. "Must mean somethin' like 'so it goes.' "

Emmett asked the Jamaican, "Why were you sent here to kill me?"

The man muttered something, but the accent and gurgling in his lungs strangled his words. Emmett gestured for Yellow Gourd to help out, and the Kaibab drew his left ear close to the man's chalky lips. The Rasta repeated himself, then his head slumped to the side.

Yellow Gourd sat up. "They were sent because you killed Nigel Merrison."

Emmett checked the impulse to laugh. "He honestly believes that?"

"That's what they told him."

"Who?"

"His bosses, I guess. He'll never name names, Parker."

"Why would they care even if I had?"

"He won't answer that either."

"Go on," Emmett told Sam Yellow Gourd. "He said more than just 'I did Merrison.' "

"You killed him to avenge the lady, your fellow government officer. Because you thought Merrison had somethin' to do with her."

"Stephanie Roper?"

"Roper . . . yes," the Jamaican said.

"Federal cops don't do revenge hits in this country. And what about this?" Emmett raised his hand, showed his stab wound. "I got this from the man who murdered Merrison."

There was another whispered exchange, then Yellow Gourd said, "He says you did that to yourself. To cover up your crime. And it's bigger than Merrison. You want to end Indian gamin'. Everybody knows you're against it, that you'd do anythin' to close the casinos."

"Short of murder," Emmett said, exasperated by the enormity of the lie.

"I'm just sayin' what he heard, Parker."

"Understood." Emmett took a moment. This dying declaration was tacit admission of the involvement of Jamaican organized crime in Inter-Mountain Gaming's operations. But the answer to the more pressing question still floated beyond his grasp—*who* had convinced the Kingston bosses of these absurdities? Who had elaborated on Leonard Wine's report? It had to be someone whose word was trusted by the Jamaicans, someone cunning and inventive enough to make this all sound plausible. "Are you still with me . . . ?"

The lusterless eyes slid open.

"Who sold your bosses this lie . . . ?" There wasn't much chance the man knew, and Emmett was courting inadmissibility of the entire statement by straying into conjecture. But he had to have some idea before leaving northern Arizona. Otherwise it might wind up a bloody and useless detour. "Who talked to them?"

The Jamaican shuddered. He was sinking rapidly.

Emmett heard the drone of a distant helicopter. It didn't sound like Yazza's. Probably the Air National Guard chopper with Burk Hagiman aboard, which would make horse travel difficult along Havasu Creek for the surviving two Jamaicans and their other local guide, the man with the diamond-patterned boot soles. Emmett had to get after them again. But he needed to do something before pushing on. Try to clear Yellow Gourd. He sensed that Sam would help him, ultimately. "Did you force Yellow Gourd to lead you last night?" he asked the dying man.

The Rasta considered the question, then seemed to realize the good he could do for the Kaibab, who made no effort to beseech him. "Oh, yes, man," he murmured, then added something so faint and garbled, Emmett motioned for Yellow Gourd to listen closely once more.

"He says I had no choice," Yellow Gourd related. "They were ready to kill me. You can hear it for yourself, Parker, if you get down to his mouth."

"No need," Emmett said. Dawn had broken. Morning alpenglow clung to the tops of the east-facing cliffs. "Where'd they find you, Sam? It sure as hell wasn't at the lodge up Robinson Wash."

"No." Yellow Gourd shook his head. "I just told the people at work that so nobody'd bother me. I was camped alone in Bulrush Wash. Been there most the week, fastin'. They found me just after dark last night. I don't know how, but I guess they got spies everywhere. They said they'd hurt my sister's kids unless I helped 'em." The man looked as if he'd been living outdoors for a week. His hands were dark with char, and there were bits of brush in his hair.

"You lie to Owen about the Soul Loss ceremony too?"

"No. I'm workin' up to it. Fastin' and prayin'."

"What makes you think you've lost your soul?"

The Paiute started to shrug noncommittally. Then he said, "Just an emptiness inside, I guess. Ever felt like that, Parker?"

Emmett had no time to reveal his own demons. "You been exposed to some powerful evil lately?"

Yellow Gourd averted his gaze. *Bingo.*

But Emmett put the question on the back burner for the

moment. "I heard what you told Wine about Cyrus Four-killer," he went on, scanning the upper gorge again. No one showed, although a raven had lifted apprehensively out of the shadows.

"How?"

"Wine made a tape of your conversation."

"I didn't know that."

"Yeah, well, there isn't much trust when it comes to money. Tell me about Cyrus Fourkiller, Sam."

"What's to say?"

"I can use a description."

"Tall. Like you. Good-lookin' kid. Long braids, dresses Ivy League."

"I don't know many tall Western Shoshone."

"Me neither," Yellow Gourd agreed. "Cy's Lakota."

A little pixel of light flashed behind Emmett's eyes, like a memory trying to burst free. "You say *a kid* . . . ?"

"Late twenties, early thirties. Somethin' like that."

"What about his past?"

"All I know is from him. Claims he was real political in the late eighties. Ran up against the FBI and left the country so the feds would stop harassin' him."

"Where'd he go?"

"Cuba, for a while. But that wasn't what he was lookin' for, so he went on to Jamaica. Never talked about that much, though I always got the feelin' Merrison and him went way back."

Emmett was torn between his growing excitement and the need to move on. "How long have you known Fourkiller?"

"Met him at a company conference up at Merrison's place on Lake Tahoe nine months ago. He really impressed me. We talked pretty regular on the phone after that. He's a lot younger than me, but knows more about the business, dealin' with the government. But then, maybe three months ago, I picked up on somethin' while we were talkin' on the phone. His talk was a little sloppy, and once I heard him pourin'. I sensed a problem, you know? I'm kind of tuned to that."

"Me too," Emmett said.

Yellow Gourd dipped his head appreciatively. "Anyways, sometime later—"

"When, Sam? I need to know exactly."

"November twenty-seventh."

The day after Stephanie Roper had checked into the Owlshead Inn in Baker. "How'd you remember that particular date?"

"I don't know," Yellow Gourd said unconvincingly. "I just did. Around Thanksgivin', I guess."

Emmett let it slide temporarily. "So Fourkiller called again."

"Yeah, and he was really plastered. Talkin' crazy. Sayin' how white folks would wind up without their faces and teeth unless things changed internally."

Internally.

On the tape Wine had had a problem with the same word. He'd probably assumed that Fourkiller meant IMG, its internal squabbles, but Emmett had an inkling that *internally* referred to something more personal than the firm. "Was Fourkiller hinting at his drinking problem? We both know there's a lot of hemming and hawing before an alcoholic starts down the recovery road."

"Maybe, Parker. I don't really know."

Emmett checked on the Jamaican. He was dead, his jaw slack and his eyelids half closed.

Yellow Gourd saw too. "Damn," he said.

Emmett forced himself to feel nothing. That would all come later, when he was alone. It would wake him in the middle of the night, send him to the medicine cabinet for something to settle his stomach. The spirits of the men he'd slain in the line of duty seemed to go after his gut. "Never knew I hit him till I saw the blood in the Bronco."

"He sure came a long ways to die."

Emmett refused to dwell on it. The time had come to make Yellow Gourd reveal the true source of his trouble with Cyrus Fourkiller, the reason the Paiute believed that he had lost his soul. "It was more than his drinking . . . wasn't it, Sam?"

"Well, that's a pretty serious thing."

"It is. But that's not what made you sick."

"No."

"Tell me."

The man took a deep breath, let it out. "November twenty-eighth. Around midnight, I guess. Cy showed up at the casino. Been drinkin' again. He said, *Come outside, Sam, I need your help*. We walked to the back lot. I thought he might've flown in. He'd talked Merrison into buyin' an old Beechcraft, but that didn't pan out. So he'd driven all the way from California in his Range Rover. . . ." Emmett stopped hearing the man's halting words, began seeing the event unfold. In the darkness of the parking lot behind the casino, Fourkiller had opened the rear hatch to his four-wheel drive. He had something bundled in the cargo area. He flipped up a corner of the tarp, revealing the body of a white woman. The memory still had the power to revolt Yellow Gourd. Fourkiller had told him that he needed help getting the corpse down to the Colorado that night. Dazed, Sam protested that he wanted nothing to do with it, but Fourkiller threatened him, said that much of the advice he'd given Sam over the past year could land him in jail, that this was a company matter and he was ordered to cooperate. He could phone Merrison if he wanted. The woman had crossed IMG by dragging her feet on the land swap, and now look at her. . . . "Then he turned her head so I could see that she had no face." The haunted stare Yellow Gourd gave Emmett was vacant. For that instant it seemed that his soul had indeed abandoned him. "I don't know what made me go along, Parker. My spirit was weak, I guess. Weak from caterin' to sick people at the casino all the time."

"How'd you get Roper's body down to the river?" Emmett asked.

"My cousin runs a pack string out of Grand Canyon Lodge in summer. For the tourists. Pastures them in winter at Pipe Springs. We trailered four mules as far as we could, then led 'em down over the rim."

"Just you and Fourkiller?"

"That's right."

"Same trail you used last night?"

"Pretty much."

"Same fording?"

"Yeah. Except I stayed on the north side of the river."

"Who brought over the raft?"

"Didn't see. I'd already started back up with the mules." Yellow Gourd wiped his lips with the back of his hand. Lying didn't come naturally to him, even if it was for someone else's sake. He could readily admit his own transgressions, but not somebody else's.

Emmett made another end run. "What happened to Fourkiller's Range Rover?"

"Pardon?"

"He left it at the casino, didn't he?"

"Yeah. This Shoshone cop named Dan must've picked him up on the south rim. Cyrus and him showed up at my place the followin' Monday for the Rover."

Time was wasting. The surviving Jamaicans, no longer encumbered by a dying man, would be moving fast. "Who met you at the river, Sam? I've got an idea, but I need to hear it from you. To tie this all up so the killing stops."

Yellow Gourd shook his head in turmoil. "Oh, God . . . I just don't know." But then he appeared to come up with an answer that fit his conscience. "You found me, Parker—you'll find him too."

Emmett realized what he was being offered. "On upper Havasu Creek?"

"No," Yellow Gourd said, "Little Coyote Canyon. That's where the horses are."

"Okay, Sam," Emmett said. The Jamaicans and their remaining guide were cutting west over to the next drainage. From there they'd avoid the law enforcement now thronging Hualapai Hilltop. They'd eventually link up with a driver and escape vehicle somewhere along Indian Route 18 on the Coconino Plateau.

"What do I do now?" Yellow Gourd asked.

"Go home."

"What about the law?"

"I'll arrange a meeting with the U.S. Attorney in Vegas. If you help us, he'll probably help you. But I can't promise that. He'll have to speak for himself, Sam."

"What's this attorney's name?"

"Ara Kasarjian." Emmett stood. "Can you use the raft to get back across?"

"No, I don't want to touch it. Touch anythin' that was a part of this. Guess I'll do the Kaibab crawl."

"What's that?"

"Stroke with the right arm, hold a log under the left."

Emmett smiled. "Good luck." Then he started up the gorge again.

Chapter 14

From Spirit Meadows, State Route 127 ran straight up an alluvial plain toward Eagle Mountain. Something in the highway between town and the peak looked like an aneurysm. As the casino shuttle bus crept closer, Anna saw red and blue lights spangling in the middle of this peculiar swelling. After another mile, she could make out the massed law enforcement vehicles, emergency lights running. And finally people. A couple of hundred of them, at least.

"Is that it?" Sal Baldecchi asked.

"I guess," she replied.

Sal sat beside her in the bus. Ordinarily, it brought foreign gamblers in from Death Valley hotels. That morning Cyrus Fourkiller had filled it with casino employees willing to participate in the demonstration. Nobody had declined, yet the Shoshone riders seemed pleased that Ronnie and Sal had joined them. The shift boss, well dressed as always, appeared chipper but slightly bewildered, as if he was on the way to an unfamiliar sporting event. He kept asking the veteran activists questions. Would a handkerchief help if the tear gas flew? Would the federal marshals restrain the deputies? Apparently not satisfied with the answers he got, he turned to Anna and said with a tight grin, "Well, I'm sure everything will be all right, Ronnie . . . aren't you?"

"Yeah." *If* she could pass Fourkiller's answering machine tape to one of the marshals.

"Ever been to one of these shindigs before?" Sal asked her as the bus began to slow.

"Oh, yeah."

"When was that?"

Lanna Turnipseed had marched in college, in support of affirmative action. But Ronnie Chavez couldn't say that. "Long time ago. Friends of mine got arrested, framed really."

"Well," Sal sighed, "that's two of us. Used to be open season on Italians in Vegas."

She patted his liver-spotted hand. "Got a notebook and pen?"

"Yes . . . ?"

"Take them out if the clubs start swinging. Everybody'll think you're with the press."

"You're a doll, Ronnie. If I was only younger . . ."

She looked out the window. The previous evening remained with her like a hangover. And that morning, as the employees lined up outside the casino waiting for the shuttle, Fourkiller had stared right through her. She'd felt terribly dirty. Although she told herself that she'd felt nothing like arousal, only fear that had masqueraded as sexual attraction, making her momentarily forget what he'd done to Roper and Merrison.

Yet, how had even such a brief lapse been possible?

The driver pulled off the highway. He parked at the tail end of a line of tribal police cruisers and opened the bus door. Fourkiller bounded inside, his shoes dusty and his face drawn. "This is it, folks," he said. Once more his gaze sliced through Anna without acknowledging her. "We will not start the New Year with violence. None. Zero. Do I make myself clear? But neither will we tolerate violence against us. Like any sovereign people, the Shoshone have the right to control their borders. An attempt to turn back our allies in this struggle for self-determination will be met with lawful resistance."

"What kind of resistance?" asked one of the coffee shop busboys, too young to feel uneasy.

"You'll be told what to do when the time comes." Fourkiller exhorted, "Courage, folks!" He raised a clenched fist to applause, then got off the bus.

Ms. Lajeunesse stood from the seat directly behind the driver. "Please file off in an orderly manner and wait behind our police."

Anna stepped out into the tepid sunshine with the others, but then stood alone, not quite knowing what to do. Between the tribal cops and the deputy sheriffs stretched a kind of de-militarized zone, about fifty feet wide. Here, equidistant from both lines, stood a reservation boundary sign. It was riddled with rusted bullet holes, but the dirt around its wooden post looked freshly tamped. The deputies wore helmets and gripped clear plastic riot shields. A sergeant held a white German shepherd on a leash. The bored dog sprawled on the pavement, his muzzle squeezed between his forepaws. Tarrying behind the S.O. line were four federal marshals in navy-blue windbreakers.

Suddenly, the dog bolted up as if he'd sniffed danger on the slight breeze out of the north.

Anna could see nothing coming from that direction.

A gangly man in the uniform of a BLM law enforcement

ranger was leaning against the grille of his Blazer. He, no doubt, was the one assigned to check Anna's drop twice a week. Unfortunately, the mining claim cairn for that purpose lay beyond this roadblock, and she'd never had a chance to use it before Fourkiller's lockdown. Had Burk Hagiman described her to the ranger? The minutes dragged by, and she couldn't catch his eye. He was keeping tabs on a small throng of white counterdemonstrators. Local ranchers mostly, who grazed their livestock within the pre-1881 boundaries of the reservation and felt threatened by the sovereignty movement, which called for a return to the original treaty. The ranchers had been confined to an area on the east side of the highway. There they'd circled their trailers and campers like the proverbial wagon train under attack. Now and again one of them took a swig of Coors and hurled a catcall at the "goddamn war whoops!" but the impasse had been going on too long now for anybody to get worked up.

Not without a special provocation.

And that was on the way in the form of five charter buses, each dispatched by a major Indian casino in California. Support from other states had been politely declined, according to Fourkiller in his preboarding speech, so no federal statute would be violated. He'd said that a sympathetic U.S. senator from California had promised to appear. But so far the senator was a no-show. Anna suspected that the FBI had taken the politician aside and given her just enough intelligence on Inter-Mountain Gaming to discourage the appearance.

Anna studied the marshals, hoping that she'd met one of them before. No luck. Strangers brought in from outside the region.

Sal brushed against her elbow. "Doesn't look so bad, does it?"

She was about to nod, when somebody on the Shoshone side yelled, "Here they come!"

That brought on a flurry of war cries.

223

Shading her eyes, she spotted five silver dots curving around the southern end of Eagle Mountain. Earlier that morning the buses had rendezvoused at Stovepipe Wells inside the national park, trusting that federal cops would be less likely to obstruct them than the local sheriff, who'd issued a warning through the press that Spirit Meadows wasn't going to become another Wounded Knee. It was assumed that he referred to the 1973 standoff with the American Indian Movement, not the 1890 massacre of over two hundred Sioux men, women, and children by the cavalry. To draw attention to that bloodbath, AIM had seized the small town of Wounded Knee on the Pine Ridge Reservation in what, like this, had been expected to be a brief protest. When it ended seventy-one tempestuous days later, two Indians had been shot dead and a federal marshal paralyzed.

"Are those cop cars around them?" Sal asked.

"I think so," Anna answered.

The convoy was escorted by two CHP black-and-whites, one leading and one bringing up the rear. The deputies appeared more unsettled about this than the Shoshone, perhaps believing that the state had broken ranks with them. They looked to their sheriff, a freckled, pear-shaped man. He was decked out in a Western-cut suit and a sweat-stained cowpoke's hat—just to let his ranching origins be known. Strutting behind his line, he pretended to be amused by the development, but his eyes never left the convoy until the CHP cars peeled off and parked a quarter mile away. Then he drawled sarcastically, "Well, the CHP's sittin' it out, as usual." According to Fourkiller, the sheriff had been a regular at the House of Games until his delinquent line of credit exceeded any possible political gain for the tribe.

The buses continued rolling toward the roadblock.

They whished past a white man in a business suit and hard hat walking along the shoulder. He held a device the size of a TV remote, halting every few yards as if taking readings.

Anna had the feeling she was being watched. A tingling on the back of her neck.

She turned.

The old Lakota man stood an arm's length behind her, his pupils the same lucent black as obsidian, the stuff of arrowheads. They were fixed coldly on her. Traditional Modoc spoke of injection sickness, the power of a shaman to invisibly shoot a lethal spiritual object into a victim. It felt as if the old man were doing that to her now. Piercing her flesh with his razor-sharp gaze.

She tore her eyes away from his. "Morning."

"Mornin'." His rawhide coat gave off the smell of juniper woodsmoke.

"I'm Ronnie . . . picked you up at the airstrip?"

"I remember." He pointed at the tampon box tucked under her left arm. "I got somethin' to relieve that."

She tried to rise to the joke, but couldn't. A smile wouldn't come. The old man seemed to be looking right through Ronnie Chavez and into Anna Turnipseed. His uncanny suspicion that she was from Klamath-Modoc country was the most dangerous threat to her cover yet, and she couldn't let it go unchallenged. Confrontation. Burk had told her that the key to staying alive undercover was to confront threats. Even if her reaction felt out of proportion. Screaming at the top of her lungs if necessary. The worst thing to do was clam up. "So you think I'm Indian?"

He puckered his lips indifferently, watching the buses slow to a smoky crawl as they neared the roadblock. "Maybe."

"Where are these Klamath from?" she asked.

"South part of Oregon."

"Never been there."

"I have." He watched some movement in the S.O. line. Flanked by two shotgun-toting deputies, the sheriff had ambled out into the middle of the highway and was holding up a pudgy hand. "Used to travel all over when I was younger," the old Lakota went on. "Met lots of diff'rent tribes in those days."

Brakes hissing, the buses stopped. The lead one only feet from bowling over the sheriff.

"And so you told Cyrus I look like a Klamath?"

"Or a Modoc," he said offhandedly. "I went to their country too. Sang in a lodge near a lake full of rushes."

Tule Lake, he meant. His dark stare now felt like ground glass on her face.

"Well, I'm Mexican-American," she said, her voice starting out low but tremulous. "I am *Chicana* . . . *Latina* . . . and damn proud of it. We Mexicans were building cities of stone and mapping the stars when you Sioux were eating buffalo shit. So quit telling me what you think I am, old man. I know what the hell I am. A goddamn beaner!"

He grinned, shaking his head skeptically, and the Shoshone within earshot turned in surprise to listen for more.

But Anna was out of fireworks. She felt too jarred for another outburst.

Fortunately, at that moment the sheriff ordered his bodyguards to pry open the bus door with the stocks of their shotguns.

Fourkiller stepped forward.

The deputies had about-faced to confront the buses, so they didn't see him coming until it was too late. Then all they could do was tighten their line after Fourkiller had passed through it. Some of the more nervy Shoshone women pushed their way through the shields when the deputies halfheartedly tried to stop them. Glaring, they covered Fourkiller's back as he tapped the sheriff on the shoulder. The crowd went silent. All but the white dog, which stood growling with fangs bared. "Pardon me."

Startled, the sheriff wheeled, losing his rancher's hat. He quickly picked it up to cover a bald head that gleamed as if it had been buffed. "What're you doin', Cyrus?"

"I was about to ask you the same."

"Orderin' this driver to turn around."

"On what authority?"

"I am the high sheriff—"

"I know who the hell you are, Walter," Fourkiller said. "What statute are you citing?"

"Section Four-oh-four point six. These people are engagin' in conduct that urges a riot."

Hands in his pockets, Fourkiller gaped whimsically all around. "What riot? I don't see a riot."

"Don't be smart, Cyrus—"

"I see five busloads of invited guests who have no intention other than to get into Spirit Meadows for lunch. . . ." More and more Shoshone were slipping through the S.O. line to approach the buses. The deputies looked increasingly frazzled. They didn't know what to do: interrupt their sheriff in the midst of a heated argument or stiffen the line on their own. Ms. Lajeunesse was quietly giving instructions, sending this group of Shoshone this way, another that way, to mingle among the white cops. Meanwhile, Fourkiller said in a voice that carried over the sound of the breeze, which had picked up and was wailing around the edges of the riot shields, "Is that the California Penal Code you're quoting?"

"You know damn well it is, Cyrus—"

"Want us to break the glass with our batons, Sheriff?" one of his bodyguards asked. This deputy and his partner had had no luck in prying the bus door open, and the Indians on board were laughing at them. Yet, the laughter eased nothing. If anything, it made the deputies more anxious, and Anna was reminded that in 1890 it was white anxiety that had left all those Sioux dead in the snow at Wounded Knee.

All it took was one rattled man with a gun. The involuntary crick of a single trigger finger.

"Hang on a minute, boys," the sheriff told the bus-door bashers.

"What relevance does the California Penal Code have here?" Fourkiller demanded before the man could gather his thoughts.

The old Lakota chuckled as he lit up a hand-rolled ciga-rette. The smell of his strong tobacco mixed unpleasantly with the bus diesel fumes and odor of nervous sweat drifting off the crowd. He winked at Anna. "Okay, you're a Mexican."

She gave him a go-to-hell look, but told herself to settle down. *You got in his face, and it worked. For the time being.* Then she saw. "You use Zigzag papers?"

"Yes," he replied, slowly shaking out his match.

The sheriff had started shouting, his tone strident enough to make a few of his men reach for their sidearms. "The turnin' back of these buses has been cleared by the district attorney!"

"Gee, I don't see the D.A.," Fourkiller retorted. "Anybody see the D.A.? Maybe he was misquoted." He had a gift for street theater, and rowdy laughter broke from the Shoshone. Fourkiller was scanning the crowd—when his gaze flickered over Anna and came back to her. His expression became sullen.

"I'm warnin' you, Cyrus. Stand aside, or you're goin' to jail!"

Facing the sheriff again, Fourkiller crossed his arms over his chest.

Anna asked the old Lakota, "Is this what you mean when you said Spirit Meadows is an evil shithole?"

"No, this is just foolishness. I was talkin' about madness."

"*Whose?*"

That got his full attention. "What do you mean, girl?"

"Personal or public madness?"

His look turned contemplative. Had she given herself away? But then the wrinkles beneath his eyes deepened in amusement, and he said, "One usually becomes the other."

"And what do you have to cure it?"

"Medicine."

"What works best"—she was recalling the vial of haloper-idol in Fourkiller's lavatory—"white medicine or Indian?"

"The white stuff just covers up the symptoms. Ours sucks out the evil that causes the madness."

His fleshy neck now a bright red, the sheriff was citing Public Law 280, which gave him jurisdiction even if he were inside the reservation, which he then claimed not to be.

And that, it became apparent, is what Fourkiller had been waiting for: "But you *are* inside the reservation."

"That's a crock of shit!" The sheriff glanced around in search of anyone who might be offended. When he went on, he'd lowered his voice. "I'm sorry, folks, but this is just flatass ridiculous."

"No, it isn't," Fourkiller calmly said. "Last night it was reported to our police that within the past week parties un-known have moved the tribal boundary sign on this highway."

The ranchers hooted at the notion, but Fourkiller pointed at the man with the hard hat, and everyone quieted to hear what he had to say. The man explained that he was from the U.S. Geological Survey. "And Mr. Fourkiller's assertion is fundamentally correct. We're over a thousand feet within Sho-shone tribal lands. I even found the posthole where the sign used to stand."

The Indians erupted into cheering, and once again Fourkiller glanced at Anna. For her reaction to his coup, it seemed. She had none. Her mind was on the old Lakota, the reason he'd come here with a bagful of healing herbs. She pretended to sound conciliatory. "So, you make house calls."

"In unusual cases . . ." the old man started to explain, but then his words were lost in the rustle of uniform cloth and the clatter of gear as the deputies shifted to confront a new prob-lem: The ranchers had left their enclave. They were bearing down on the nearest Shoshone, a cluster of young men who encouraged them to come on with gestures more Mediterranean than Indian.

The deputies scurried to form a line between the antagonists. Despite the rising breeze, perspiration was darkening their shirts. The heavier ones were gasping.

A punch was thrown by a rancher, and a dozen men tangled, mostly shoving one another. The deputies hosed them all down with Mace. Immediately, the scuffling stopped in a cacophony of choking, gasping, and sneezing. Everyone backed off, furiously rubbing their eyes, although a silver Coors can arced across the sky from the ranchers and splatted in a shower of foam at the feet of the Shoshone youths.

Anna asked the old Lakota to repeat himself.

But, wincing from the pepper spray, he shook his head. "It don't matter. I'm finished here. Time to go."

"Back home to South Dakota?"

"Yes."

"When?"

"This afternoon."

The ranchers were regrouping. "The plane?" she asked.

"If it comes."

She had never seen him at the motel after dropping him off that first night, never seen him at all until now. "Your medicine didn't work?"

He wiped his eyes. "Maybe, maybe not."

"What's going to happen here?"

"Nothin' good. But it's still got to happen."

The buses had started inching through the crowd. The few deputies in their way, those not already with their hands full pushing back the ranchers who were coming on again, braced, hesitated, then stepped aside.

"Fuck it," one of the cops grumbled.

For the first time, the federal marshals approached Fourkiller and the sheriff. Before this, there had been too much distance and too many bodies between the feds and

Anna. But now she had a new problem. She wasn't comfortable passing the tampon box right under Fourkiller's nose.

The sheriff had nearly forgotten the convoy. He was trying to justify his presence to the marshals, who listened impassively behind their sunglasses, and the news media, who'd formed a greedy ring of cameras and microphones around him. In truth, Public Law 280 lent credence to his claim of jurisdiction, but Fourkiller was arguing far more persuasively that the statute had never been ratified by the tribes. The massing of so many deputies on the border, he maintained for the cameras, was a provocation. "The sheriff is giving de facto support to the claims of these squatter-ranchers with this armed encroachment."

"I wouldn't call it an armed encroachment." The marshal in charge shifted a lime-green sucker to the other side of his mouth. "Let's hold down the rhetoric."

Fourkiller started counting the weapons in the hands of the deputies. The press ate it up.

"Okay, okay," the marshal groused as if he was getting a headache.

"Tell me," Fourkiller said, "what's the federal government going to do to enforce the terms of its treaty with the Western Shoshone?"

"Get us a copy, and we'll shoot it upstairs," another marshal, a black with a scrupulously knotted tie, replied.

"Christ, I'm trying to prevent violence here!"

"So are we, Fourkiller."

Anna heard Dan Beowawe's voice declare martially, "Line, march!"

The tribal police advanced, making it obvious to the now-befuddled sheriff that they had every intention of enforcing Shoshone sovereignty. "You goddamn rent-a-cops halt right this minute!" he shouted, but took two mincing steps backward. That gave a mixed signal to his men, and before any clear orders could be given, one line had melted into the other.

The tribal cops and the deputies mingled, warily, but were in such disarray, every man with a stranger at his back, no one seemed willing to start anything.

The buses had cleared the roadblock and were accelerating toward Spirit Meadows.

The sheriff gave Fourkiller the finger, then withdrew his men to their vehicle park. Even the ranchers were asking themselves if they should go.

Anna saw her only chance slipping away.

All but one of the marshals had sauntered back to huddle with the BLM ranger, who was probably being asked to spend another cold night at the roadblock. The black marshal remained among the tribal cops, chatting with Beowawe, who offered Anna a self-conscious wave.

"Excuse me," she said, stepping forward.

The black marshal turned, looked her over. "Uh-huh?"

"I'm on the job," she said quietly. Nearby, Beowawe and a few of the others were watching. She also sensed Fourkiller hovering on the edge of the scene.

"What's that, miss?"

"You heard me," she said. Her stomach was churning.

The marshal stared down at her, some high cirrus reflecting in his mirror sunglasses, then said, "Yes, I believe I did. What's that you're holding . . . a bomb?"

"No," she said loudly, "but that poor old sheriff got his ass chewed so bad by Mr. Fourkiller, I figure he can use some of these." She thrust the tampon box on him.

The Shoshone within earshot laughed uproariously, and even the marshal cracked a smile as he glanced at the label. "Okay, miss, I'll see the sheriff gets them. Shall I tell him it's from a secret admirer?"

"Yeah, do that."

She swept past Fourkiller without looking at him on her way back to the shuttle bus. Once beyond him, she peered around for the old Lakota, but he'd been swallowed by the thick dust raised by all the departing vehicles.

Sal was holding a seat for her. He looked wilted but relieved. "Well, that was sure something, wasn't it?"

Hagiman's copter was working upper Havasu Creek.

Minutes earlier, Emmett had actually spotted it, a beelike speck flitting across the face of the Coconino Rim. Miles away, searching in an entirely wrong direction. But Burk had accomplished one thing: He'd slowed the Jamaicans and their guide on their climb over the ridge between the Havasu and Little Coyote drainages. Following their tracks, Emmett kept coming across clusters of boot prints where the men had hunkered down, most likely scanning the sky for the pursuing helicopter. At times, the ricocheting echoes made it sound deceptively close. He had yet to glimpse the fugitives themselves, but felt that he was narrowing the distance with each stride he took.

He knelt again to study the tracks.

Once more he was resting where they had rested, perhaps only minutes before. He squatted in sunlight, for their trail had wound out of the gorge on an old rockfall and started up toward the divide with Little Coyote Creek. The air was balmy, almost stupefying, it was so pleasant.

Tired.

More tired than he'd been in years. His legs burned with fatigue, and a pinkish fluid was seeping from his knife wound. He'd been forced to use his hands almost continuously since starting the climb the previous afternoon. He reassured himself with the thought that it would be decided that day. Either he caught them, or they would reach their transportation on the plateau above. And they were just as exhausted as he.

He checked his watch: 11:21.

He was halfway up the ridge. Mooney Falls was visible

about a half-mile away, plunging whitely into its turquoise pools. Above them, although still out of sight, was Havasu Falls, near the cleft where Misty Topocoba had found Stephanie Roper's body. He took the Handie-Talkie from his jacket pocket and depressed the transmitter button. "Any unit receiving, this is Parker. . . ."

He waited.

Nothing.

He didn't try twice. The canyon walls still towered over him.

He studied the ridge above as he plodded upward again, watched for movement, suspicious shapes. With a helicopter working the skies, the two remaining Jamaicans and their guide doubtlessly realized they were being pursued on the ground as well. An ambush was waiting sooner or later, and Emmett suspected that they'd spring it before they revealed the place where their horses were hidden. His shotgun wasn't much good at ranges over a hundred yards. Regardless of that, in all his years he'd never dropped a man at long range. It had always been close-up, always with the absolute certainty that his own life was in peril.

His exhaustion made him lurch dizzily, and, recovering, he asked himself what he was doing here.

But he knew. Deep down, he knew. It was one of the few jobs left in which *puha*—personal power—mattered. A solitary man could determine the outcome. As long as he didn't let the Burk Hagimans of this world muddle the issue.

He noticed a staircase ledge nestled between the two bouldery peaks that formed the ridgeline.

He exhaled.

It was the easiest way to get over the divide into Little Coyote Creek. Too easy. He decided to skirt it, find another route over the heights.

He was traversing the slope, jumping from boulder to boulder, when a raven flapped up from the crest and glided down into the safety of the gorge. His scalp prickled. Without thinking, he threw himself down into the space between two rocks. In the same instant, a high-velocity bullet whirred just above his head.

The booming report followed a moment later. It dissipated into overlapping echoes, became a long, rumbly peal of thunder.

Emmett waited for another.

But two minutes passed in silence.

He began listening for the Jamaicans to come down from the ridge in search of his body. It wasn't what he would do in their place, but street hoodlums were taught to confront resistance, blow through it if possible. A culture of bravado he'd learned about from the gangbangers in Oklahoma City. The only sound was the breeze rattling the dried panicle of a dying agave plant. He held his breath. Still, no human movement could be heard in the lull that followed the single rifle blast, just the wind soughing through the canyon walls.

Emmett pushed himself to his feet and ran. He dropped down within ten paces, gritted his teeth together as he waited for the second bullet.

None came.

This time he jogged straight for the ridgeline. He kept to the boulders, avoiding their tops and crawling through the gaps between them. He came across the boot tracks again, which convinced him to tend more to the left, away from the stairstep ledge.

Reaching the divide, he flopped down.

The ridge proved to be a cuesta, steep on the side he'd just climbed but gently dipping toward the west. The reason for the shot was now explained by the terrain: They didn't want Emmett close on their heels as they'd made their way down the open slope to a screen of red willows, into which their tracks disappeared. This ribbon of growth widened around a spring that fed Little Coyote Creek. It was shaded in summer by a big cottonwood. As Emmett scanned the swale, a soft nicker drifted up to him. The horses were somewhere near the spring. He expected riders to burst from the willows at any second, but maybe the mounts needed watering. The guide had expected to reach them yesterday—not twenty-four hours later, thanks to a mortally wounded man.

For the first time, Emmett was high enough in the canyon to be surrounded by sky. He reached for his H.T. "Any unit receiving, this is Parker. . . ."

A shimmer of dust rose through the leafless branches of the cottonwood. The three men were mounting up, the horses prancing beneath them, made skittish by the long wait.

Emmett switched to the Arizona mutual aid frequency. He had to work up some saliva to coax more words from his dry mouth, but he had no time to unpack the water bottle. "Any unit, this is Investigator Parker, BIA. . . ."

After a moment, someone answered, but he realized it more from the elongated burst of static than a recognizable human voice. For all he knew, it could be Tucson P.D. "Station or unit responding, you're unreadable . . ." he said. The willows were very tall, for the dust was tending down toward the creek with no glimpse of either riders or horses. "In the blind for FBI Hagiman in the vicinity of Grand Canyon. I am in foot pursuit of three subjects, southbound up Little Coyote Creek Canyon. Repeat, Little Coyote, *not* Havasu Creek. . . ." They were slipping away again. Emmett jumped up and began jogging down the slope, holding the radio to his lips. His calf muscles were excruciatingly taut, but he kept moving. "Alert Coconino S.O. to shift some men farther west along the rim. . . ." He headed for a gully the springwater tributary had dug through some sandstone. The riders had to go that way to eventually follow the creek, or climb an exposed bluff. Emmett guessed that they'd keep to the dense cover as long as they could. "Subjects . . . two African male adults

. . . and one possible Indian . . . do you read?" He'd slid to a halt where the slope plunged steeply into the gully.

Silence.

"Christ almighty." Putting away the H.T., he went prone behind the shaggy trunk of a juniper. The riders must have found the willow thicket tough going, for they'd slowed again. Still, the range for the closest shot Emmett could take was well over two hundred yards. And they were plunging yards, which only increased the difficulty.

Wrestling off the pack, he took out the survival knife he'd seen inside. He ejected the cartridge already in the shotgun's chamber, then the four in the magazine. Double-aught buck, each a bevy of .32-caliber balls. But useless for the distance he faced. He held a round up to the sun, saw through the translucent casing where the buckshot met the wadding. Using this line as a template, he cut the plastic completely around, but not all the way through. He repeated the process three times, then fed the doctored cartridges back into the gun, followed by the two he'd not altered.

"Parker . . . ?"

It felt odd being pleased to hear Hagiman's voice. He fumbled for the radio. "Go ahead."

"Where are you?"

"Lower Little Coyote Creek. And you?"

"Five thousand feet over Supai. I've gone hoarse trying to raise you all night, for chrissake. Where along Coyote?"

"Find Mooney Falls."

"Okay, we see it." Hagiman's voice revealed the strain of a diving bank. "On that heading now."

"Look for a spring with a big cottonwood in the next drainage west. Subjects are on horseback in the willows leading down toward the creek. From there they can follow it all the way up to the plateau. And Highway Eighteen."

"Roger."

"Watch your approach. They've got the artillery to bring you down."

"*Copy. I've got my team on board.*"

Emmett watched the tops of the willows for the slightest twitching. But the three men had stopped altogether, having figured out that he was perched above the gully, waiting for them. No doubt, building the nerve to make a sudden dash. That encouraged Emmett. He was counting on the growing pessimism behind their hesitation.

He was also relying on Hagiman to utterly disregard the warning he'd given him.

Below, one of the mounts could be heard stamping a hoof.

Emmett called down, "Anybody speak Comanche?"

This time there was no laughter, just a morose silence.

Aiming high, Emmett fired once. As intended, the cartridge split apart in the barrel, and a flat-nosed, plastic-jacketed projectile was hurled into the willows. It howled wickedly as it tumbled through the branches.

He lowered his shotgun and waited.

Within seconds a Jamaican accent called, "We won't give it up to you, man!"

"Why not?"

"You'll kill us!"

Emmett raised the gun to his shoulder and fired at a granite outcropping on the hillside above the spot from which the voice had come. The projectile sounded like a flatiron glancing off the stone. "Who will you surrender to?"

"Anybody but you, Parker."

"FBI?"

"Sure, FBI."

The Air National Guard helicopter suddenly thundered over the cuesta, its rotor noise masked until the pilot had cleared the crest. Descending, he veered so that the automatic rifle muzzles bristling out the side door were trained on the willows. Emmett could see Hagiman in the copilot's seat, peering back at him through binoculars. Burk said something to the pilot, and the chopper skimmed the gentle slope behind Emmett at a slow walk, dropping off helmeted SWAT men. They rushed en masse down to an overlook of the gully, went prone, and aimed their M-16s at the growth.

The pilot then climbed to a few hundred feet, where Hagiman and he could watch over the entire scene.

The two Jamaicans, hands over their heads, stepped out to the edge of the willows. They looked beat, almost half asleep as they gazed apathetically into the gun barrels trained on them. The team leader began the felony takedown, barking orders through a small bullhorn. "Continue walking forward with your hands raised. Subject with the knit cap—show me your palms!"

Glancing up at the chopper, Emmett radioed, "See the third subject, Burk?"

"*Negative. He must be lying low.*"

Emmett didn't think so. Leaving the juniper, he trotted along the lip of the gully. The swampy bed below was carpeted with watercress; he could see where someone had squirmed through it on all fours.

"*Where are you going?*" Hagiman demanded.

"Stay on the Rastas," Emmett transmitted. "I'm after number three." He started sprinting.

But the third fugitive reached Little Coyote Creek two hundred yards ahead of him. His green nylon jacket and khaki trousers were already wet and muddy before he fell while splashing across. He immediately bounded up and took the far bank in three lunging steps, grabbing fistfuls of rock sage as he clambered for the piñons above. Emmett had his shotgun trained on the man's back all the way into the trees. He believed that he could have hit him with his last remaining altered cartridge.

But he needed to talk to Billy Topocoba.

Chapter 15

She needed a place to remove her revolver from the engine compartment of the Volkswagen. It couldn't be too obvious, such as the parking lot of her motel. But neither could it be too remote, so far out of Spirit Meadows she'd never be able to explain her presence. Anna decided on the open desert south of town, the stretch of highway just before the turnoff to the Eclipse Canyon overlook.

It was also where she needed to be as soon as night fell.

The sun was throwing the beetlelike shadow of the VW far out into the clumps of spiny hopsage as she pulled off the asphalt. The wind had risen, and a dark gray cloud mass was building over the Panamints. She grabbed the tool pouch stowed under the front seat, got out, and spread the wrenches and screwdrivers on the ground beneath the rear bumper.

The tools were cold to the touch.

Opening the engine compartment, she examined the various parts before unclipping the distributor cap, something she knew how to quickly put back on. She started to reach around the fan shroud—but winced as her wrist brushed something hot. Jerking back her hand, she was sucking on the burn, when she heard a vehicle nearing her out of the south.

The highway was busier than it'd been in over a week.

The casino workers had been given the rest of the day off, a paid holiday. The reservation roadblocks had been lifted, at least on the Shoshone side. At a luncheon for the tribe's allies, Fourkiller surprised everyone by announcing a deal he'd reached with the U.S. Attorney. The offices of the House of Games wouldn't be ransacked, or tribal sovereignty violated in any other way, as long as the casino manager honored a *duces tecum* subpoena and showed up at federal court in Las Vegas with specified business records. Fourkiller would cooperate with a homicide investigation, but never an inquisition into his casino's operation other than the National Indian Gaming Commission's annual audit. The feds had apparently bought it.

Something in Fourkiller's calculations had shifted. Something major. She didn't know what. Perhaps Emmett, working on the outside, would.

In any event, the Shoshone were celebrating the restoration of their freedom by taking to the highways, and she paid the approaching car no mind until it pulled alongside. Dan Beowawe stepped out of his Jeep cruiser. "Trouble, Ronnie?"

"Oh, it's just running funny. . . ." Why did he always find her when she strayed from town? It could no longer be dismissed as coincidence. "I kick the tires, cuss a little, and usually she gets going again."

"What makes you think it's female?"

"Curved on both ends, ain't she?"

He chuckled, then wet his lips with the tip of his tongue. "Where were you headed?"

"Baker."

"What's in Baker?"

"McDonald's. I been dying for a Big Mac."

"Hang on a sec."

She swore under her breath as he backed up and maneuvered in behind her. Craning, she checked on the revolver. And gritted her teeth. The holster protruded slightly from behind the fan shroud, a glimpse of basket-weave leather among the gray metal components of the engine. But there was no chance to shift the weapon.

"Okay . . ." Beowawe said, squatting beside her. She could tell by his discerning look that he knew something about engines. But he took his time. So much time, she began to wonder if he'd noticed the revolver.

Distract him. "Must be nice not having to camp out at those roadblocks anymore," she said.

"Tell me." He picked up the distributor cap in his large hands. "This fall off?"

"No, I took it off."

"By yourself?"

"Sure." They both fell silent, and he inspected the engine again. Obviously playing the diagnostician. She forced herself not to think about the revolver. Not to radiate her rising alarm to him. She thought about the roadblocks instead. They'd been thrown up weeks before the crisis brought on by Nigel Merrison's murder. And they'd been dismantled only when Fourkiller seemed confident that outside law enforcement wouldn't invade Spirit Meadows. What did that mean?

"How's it behavin'?" Beowawe asked.

"Kind of rattling and shuddering."

"That could be an engine mountin' bolt." And then, before she could stop him, he began reaching around the fan shroud.

His eyes widened, and he said, "My hand's too big to make the turn. Feel back there for the bolt."

After a light-headed pause, she did so.

"Is it tight, Ronnie?"

"Yes."

"Then I don't know. Want me to roll a hook for you?"

"I can't afford a tow, Dan."

"No, no—I can write it off to the department. You know, if I'm the one authorizin' it."

"I don't want to get you in trouble. 'Sides, I always get her going again."

Something reverberated across the basin.

Both she and Beowawe glanced to the northeast. The Learjet descended, its running lights twinkling through the dusk. Here to pick up the old Lakota?

Nothing could be gained without putting her neck on the line. If she played it completely safe in her few remaining hours on the reservation, she'd never learn what Cyrus Fourkiller was hiding behind his chamber-of-commerce facade. The jet had already taxied around and stopped by the time she figured out a way to frame a question about Fourkiller's flight last Saturday. "Dan, what tribe's in Truckee?"

Beowawe idly rolled the distributor cap between his palms. "No tribe."

"Then why would Cyrus fly there in the middle of a storm?"

"I don't know. Business of one kind or another." His fingers had locked around the cap.

She'd been too rash. She had to deflect his suspicion. "Maybe personal business?"

"Like what, Ronnie?"

She paused to watch the jet lift off. "Is he like seeing somebody up there?"

His words came slowly now. "You mean a girlfriend?"

She nodded. And checked her wristwatch on the sly: 5:05.

243

"You worried Mr. Fourkiller has a girl, Ronnie?"

"I wouldn't say *worried.*" She had to disguise her relief. He'd taken the bait, and the evidence was the sudden glitter in his eyes. His wounded male vanity. "I was just wondering, Dan."

"Why ask me?" he said, standing. He looked as if he was about to plead his own case, but then muttered, "I got to get back to town."

"Dan . . . ?"

He turned on the way back to his cruiser. "What?"

"You mind if we postpone that fingerprint stuff until next week?"

"Yes," he said, brusquely flipping the distributor cap back to her. "I expect you at the station nine tomorrow mornin'." Getting in the Jeep, he fired up the engine, then cut a sharp U-turn and sped for Spirit Meadows.

"Shit," she said.

So much for trying to buy more time here. The shadow of the western ranges inched over her as she watched Beowawe's taillights grow small. She felt chilled, but it was more than the onset of night. Another glance at her watch—5:09.

She knew what she had to do if she had less than twenty hours before her cover was blown.

All afternoon she'd been mentally reconstructing her academy notes on serial killers. Ted Bundy had been outwardly normal, even emotionally vulnerable when it suited his purposes. Like Cyrus Fourkiller on occasion. Others, too, had worn a convincing mask of sanity, although none had ever admitted he was out of control by medicating himself. Those who dismembered and mutilated often kept their grisly souvenirs. Ate them in some cases. The instructor from the bureau's National Center for the Analysis of Violent Crime had said that the trophy keepers did this mostly for sexual pleasure. But there was also an anthropological explanation, a tribal belief as old as mankind that the part taken could increase one's own power.

If a man took a face, Anna wondered, was it because he somehow believed that he no longer had one of his own?

It was 5:15.

She stood and pivoted toward the Nopah Range in the east. The raw wind cut through her jacket, and gooseflesh erupted on the backs of her arms. She rubbed them with her hands as she waited.

There.

Two faint flashes blinked from the highest peak in the range.

Where Benjamin and Crutcher had set up their fixed antenna array to track her directional beeper in the event of an emergency. The two agents were up there now. They'd just signaled Burk Hagiman's instructions to her. Her note in the tampon box had informed him of the threat posed to her cover by the Shoshone file clerk at the Nevada Gaming Commission. She'd asked for a beacon signal at 5:15 that evening from the Nopah Range. Two flashes would mean that the situation with the clerk had been resolved and Anna could remain on the reservation in the near term. Three flashes meant that she should get out at once.

The signal was repeated atop the peak.

Definitely two flashes.

Hagiman believed it safe for her to continue her work among the Shoshone. As far as she was concerned, that meant going up to the wickiup in Eclipse Canyon that night.

Kneeling again before the engine compartment, she quickly threaded her hand around the fan shroud and took hold of the revolver. Its heft felt good. She'd missed it, the sense of security it had given her on the job until coming to Spirit Meadows. No longer would she be helpless in the presence of Fourkiller. And that evening, while he feted his guests at a tribal banquet, she would find out what he was concealing in Eclipse Canyon.

She replaced the distributor cap and got back inside the

Volkswagen. She didn't want to go to the wickiup across that bouldery wash, find the awful things she might find within it. Home was only three hours distant by way of Baker. But she couldn't pull out. Not yet.

Night was coming on fast as she drove up the gravel road.

Emmett didn't keep after Billy Topocoba, even though the Havasupai cop's tracks made a beeline up Little Coyote Creek toward the Coconino Plateau. By three that afternoon Emmett had come to believe that the Rasta-Pai would double back and stay on the reservation rather than face the deputies and FBI agents now lining the rim. So he abandoned Topocoba's trail and turned for the Havasu drainage once again. By four o'clock he'd crossed the divide and could hear Havasu Falls. He soon located the mouth of the defile up which, nearly three weeks before, he'd found Stephanie Roper's grave.

But this evening he couldn't take the same route as then. Topocoba would never try to hide there if Emmett's fresh tracks showed on the path rising from the creek. And Emmett was betting that the cop would hole up in this defile until the manhunt widened away from the reservation. He'd taken pains to try to convince Emmett that he feared catching spirit sickness at the site. Yet, the fear hadn't fit him. Topocoba was no closet traditionalist like Sam Yellow Gourd. Even three weeks earlier he'd been planning for a possible second arrival of federal law enforcement.

In the rapidly failing light, Emmett searched downstream for another way around to the shallow cave.

He settled on a jumble of talus leading up on to Sinyala Mesa.

He started climbing.

He cleared the chambered round and used the shotgun as a walking stick. It'd been hard to turn away from the rim earlier, knowing that hot food and rest had awaited him up there. But he didn't want to spend the coming weeks hunting for To-pocoba while Anna Turnipseed played cat-and-mouse on the reservation with Cyrus Fourkiller. And if his hunch about the defile was wrong, Sam Yellow Gourd's brother-in-law would run law enforcement ragged trying to haul him in.

Over the long afternoon, Emmett had picked some pieces out of the chaos and started fitting them together. Billy To-pocoba and Sam Yellow Gourd were related by marriage. To-pocoba's Kaibab wife was Yellow Gourd's younger sister. That's why Sam had been so reluctant to name the man who'd gone ahead with the Jamaicans. He'd have to live with the consequences of this for a long time, certainly much longer than the criminal justice system would care about the murders of Roper and Merrison. And the system didn't strike balances in this country. Extended family did. The law came and went like a thin white cloud, while kinship endured. Besides, Sam had known that Emmett was going to catch Topocoba and the two surviving Jamaicans no matter what he said or did.

Emmett halted at the top, regaining his breath.

Below, he'd thought that the day was completely gone, but now he saw the cap of the mesa was bathed in a pale bluish light. He wanted to linger and enjoy the sense of openness. But swiftly now, he trotted across the rock flats, slowing only as he came to the fissurelike cleft.

To assure himself that Topocoba hadn't come by the same slope first, he went prone and peered over the lip.

Down thirty feet was the sandy floor of the cave. The over-hang curved too sharply beneath him to allow a glimpse of Stephanie Roper's burial pit. But farther down the cleft he could see the stretch of path he himself had used that rainy night. The ground was still heavily pockmarked, probably his own tracks and those of the mule that had packed Roper to the helicopter landing site in Supai.

There was no sign that Topocoba had beaten him there.

He looked for a way down.

The upper cleft terminated in a chimney, a narrowing of the walls to a three-foot width. He threaded the shotgun under the shoulder straps of the day pack and started descending, the soles of his boots pressed against one wall and his back against the other.

His leg muscles quivered under the strain.

Then a cramp knotted his right calf, and he slid down the last ten feet out of control, the gun barrel clattering against the rock face.

He wound up with his knees jammed against his throat.

The shock of the jolt slowly wore off, and he realized that he wasn't hurt. At least not badly. The skin had been abraded off the heels of his palms, although he couldn't recall having tried to slow his fall with his hands. He was lodged between the walls. The only way to free himself was to roll to the side and tumble headfirst onto the floor of the cave below.

Strangely, while building up to the fall, he thought of Turnipseed.

He would ask her out to dinner. Nothing more ambitious than that. No intimations of things to come, those almost imperceptible foreshocks of commitment. Just dinner someplace nice in Las Vegas, where he could give her hell for putting him through all this. She'd decline, of course, and that would make him mad enough to stop visualizing her in that terry-cloth robe.

At last he took the plunge.

He struck the sand with his right shoulder hard, leaving him dazed for a minute. Sitting up, he fumbled for the shotgun in the darkness. Only the yellowish sand seemed to give off any light. He found the Remington and quietly chambered another shell. He was slipping the flashlight from the outer pouch on the pack, when he heard something. Thunderous breathing coming his way, footfalls thudding up the path from below.

There was no sudden shift of pace to indicate that the approaching man had heard Emmett's fall.

Emmett stepped back up into the chimney, swung the muzzle on the silhouetted head that was just breaking the horizon of the sandy ledge. The entire figure appeared over the lip at a staggering run, then the man flopped down on his knees. He either gagged or vomited. He had reached his refuge. He was finally allowing himself to get sick.

Emmett let him be for the moment.

Out of the southeast came the whine of Hagiman's chopper. Landing in Supai, maybe. Or making one last sweep of Havasu Creek, having found nothing along the Little Coyote—including Emmett, who hadn't used his Handie-Talkie since the takedown of the Jamaicans at midday.

The man had sucked in a sharp breath at the first hint of rotor noise, but now his respiration grew normal. He spat the bad taste out of his mouth.

"It's over, Billy," Emmett said.

Immediately, a muzzle flash lit up the cave. Topocoba's terrified face reflected it, ghostlike, then vanished again. The revolver report sounded like a bomb going off in the confines. Emmett's own echoes had confused Topocoba, making him fire upward. After pulling the trigger, the cop had flung himself down into Roper's burial pit. The top of his head was just visible above the luminescent sand.

Emmett drew a bead on it, but said, "I need to talk to you, Billy, or you'd already be dead."

"Parker . . . ?" he asked, incredulous.

"Toss your gun out of that hole."

"No way."

"I can count your dreadlocks."

"No way, Parker." The man squirmed lower into the pit, the crown of his head dropping out of sight. "Not till I get some guarantees."

"Like what?"

"Safe passage out of here," Topocoba said, his voice shaky. "I want out of the whole damn country."

"I can't promise anything like that, and you know it."

"Then I'm keepin' my gun."

The thump of the rotor faded into the distance: Hagiman was calling it a day. Emmett knew that his might be just beginning. He had to guard against any impatience brought on by his fatigue. "Tell me about Cyrus Fourkiller, Billy."

"Get fucked."

"He your friend?"

"I used to think so." Topocoba said it bitterly.

"What happened . . . ?" Silence. "I'm trying to help you, Billy. What about these boys from Kingston you've been giving the deluxe tour?"

"Brothers." But then a chink showed in Topocoba's bravado. "They all dead?" he asked.

"Just the fella you left with Sam. Other two are in custody. Talking to the FBI by now, I'd imagine."

"Bullshit. Dreads don't talk."

"See it your way." Emmett squeezed deeper into the chimney. It angled off the cave, and the slight bulge in the wall might deflect a lucky shot. "Sam told me they threatened to hurt his sister's kids. Your kids, I'd guess. Is that the case?"

Another silence.

"We both know that'll count for something with the courts, Billy."

After a second, the cop said, "I don't want it to count."

"Why not?"

"Like I said, they're my brothers." Then he turned irascible. "Christ, Parker, you're not even goin' to Mirandize me?"

"Don't see where the warning applies in this case. I haven't taken you into custody, have I? And if anybody's been deprived of his freedom of action, it's me. You can back out of here 'most anytime you want. I got noplace to go but up, and I can't fly . . . right?" While Topocoba mulled this over, Emmett decided not to let the silence firm up. A prolonged silence would lead only to more gunplay. "One thing about these two homicides puzzles me and the FBI—"

"Roper and Merrison?"

"Yeah," Emmett said, encouraged by Topocoba's butting in. "Stephanie Roper had her fingertips snipped off. You saw that yourself the night I packed the corpse out of here. Merrison had the facial mutilation . . . understandable thing to do to an enemy . . . but his hands were okay. Now, there's the chance I came upon Merrison's killing too quick for the perp to finish the job to his satisfaction. But somehow, I don't think so, Billy. . . ." He waited, not expecting Topocoba to take the bait at first. It'd be a long night, but Emmett felt that time was on his side. "Well, maybe I got it figured all wrong. Maybe all this snipping is a Rastafarian thing."

"Bullshit," Topocoba said angrily. "We don't desecrate the figure of man. Ever. No trimmin' and shavin'. No tattooin'. No cuttin' of the flesh." Then he controlled his anger, but not enough. "Maybe the killer wasn't the guy to do the woman's fingers. You ever think of that, Parker?"

Emmett suspected from the quiet that followed that Topocoba regretted having said this. But he also sensed that Billy wanted to differentiate between the man who'd murdered and the man who'd cut.

"Well," Emmett went on, "it's a lesser offense than murder. Some sort of obstruction of justice or concealment of a crime, I suppose—*if* the U.S. Attorney doesn't see him as a co-conspirator. Never had anything quite like this before. How about you, Billy?"

"No."

"So that's the hardest we might go on Fourkiller. Obstruction or concealment. I can live with a plea to that, if it turns out Cyrus jumped in only after the fact."

"That's how it was," Topocoba said. "I'd swear to that much."

"Then how about giving up the gun, going back to Supai with me? We can hammer out a statement to that effect."

Four minutes passed, and just when Emmett thought Topocoba was on the verge of caving in, the man's voice came from the pit, small and troubled. "No. Statements to you feds always backfire. You'll slap me on the back, tell me I've done my civic duty, and then the U.S. Attorney'll use my own words to lock me up. Forever."

"That's true in some cases," Emmett admitted. "But without your corroboration, my problem with Fourkiller is simple. . . ." He waited, if only to get Topocoba talking again. The man was sliding into a funk, and Emmett was increasingly afraid of what he might suddenly do.

"What do you mean?" Topocoba finally asked.

"Well, Billy, would Sam Yellow Gourd lie?"

"No way."

"That's what I believe. And Sam swears Fourkiller showed up in Kaibab with Roper's corpse in the back of his Range Rover. Asked Sam to help him get it down to the river. He wanted nobody to see it. That's why she wasn't packed down the trail through Supai. A lot of trouble bringing a dead body up that gorge from the Colorado. But Fourkiller was willing to go through all kinds of trouble to make sure Stephanie Roper got hidden away good. Not exactly something you'd do even for a close friend. And that'll make a powerful impression on a jury, wouldn't you say?"

"Cyrus no more whacked Roper than you whacked Merrison," Topocoba said adamantly.

Emmett paused to digest this. There was something enormously significant at the heart of it, something bigger than the fact that Topocoba hadn't bought the line the Kingston bosses had. It eluded Emmett, frustrating him as he felt the opportunity to save Topocoba slipping away. Frightening, the number of Indians who chose suicide over prison when they saw no other way out, and Emmett weighed this against his ravenous curiosity. "You tell the Jamaicans that?"

"Yeah."

"They believe you?"

"I guess so."

"What'd you say to them, Billy? What convinced them?"

"Cyrus lied 'bout you killin' Merrison."

There it was. The embellishment on Leonard Wine's report to the Jamaican posse that had almost cost Emmett his life the night before last. "Why'd Fourkiller tell them that?"

"It doesn't matter, Parker. Nothin' matters."

"Your wife matters. Your kids."

"Where will I wind up?"

"Not mine to say, Billy. You know that. But I'd argue for someplace close. So your family could visit regularly." Over the minutes, Emmett had lowered his shotgun but now raised it to eye level again. Topocoba might bolt, letting Emmett do the deed for him. He didn't want to shoot a man in the back, but neither would he let Topocoba get away. In his state of mind, the man would kill the first deputy or agent he came across. "Wherever you wind up, Billy, it won't be forever. Nothing is forever. You'll come back here . . . and be free of Fourkiller."

Topocoba exploded. "Get off Cyrus! It's not all his fault!"

"Whose, then?"

"Fuck you." But the man was weeping now.

Emmett was tempted to start toward the burial pit, talking soothingly all the way. But he'd watched that gambit unfold once before, and it'd ended with an Oklahoma City P.D. officer dying. He shoved that twelve-year-old memory back into the recesses of his mind and tried to refocus on his questions. All the dangling questions. "The night I came up here . . . you still with me, Billy?"

"Yeah," he said dejectedly.

"That night I saw no lamb tracks. You told me Misty came up here after a stray."

"Don't bug her, okay? You'll figure it all out in time. You're a prick, Parker, and pricks make the best cops. Maybe that's why I'm not worth a shit at this. I just don't have the heart to serve Babylon."

"But you contacted me, Billy. Even though you helped Cyrus bury Roper. You blew the whistle. That was the right thing to do. You could've let it stay hidden, but you got hold of me."

"No, I didn't."

Emmett felt a low buzz at the base of his skull as, once more, the investigation shifted beneath his feet. *"What?"*

"I didn't make no radio call."

"The message I received was from you."

"My name got used, but I never radioed. Next thing I knew, Coconino S.O. was raisin' me, sayin' you were on the way."

"Who phoned?" Emmett demanded. "It came into my office as a telephone message."

But Topocoba said, "I'm tired, man. Let me alone. I've had enough, Parker." Then he began whispering a prayer: "So we hail our God, Selassie I, Eternal God, Rastafari, hear us and help us, and cause thy face to shine upon us thy children."

"Billy . . . ?"

Another blue flash filled the shallow cave.

"Billy!"

Emmett shone his light down into the pit. Topocoba was slumped forward, his head tilted to the side.

Cautiously, Emmett stepped down out of the chimney and approached him. Immediately, he saw the bright red arterial blood flowing over Topocoba's hands, still cupped around the inwardly turned revolver.

He'd shot himself in the stomach.

Dropping the shotgun, Emmett grabbed him under the

arms and dragged him out of the pit. The bloody handgun thudded to the bottom. "Billy?" Emmett directed his beam into the man's glazed eyes, and they flickered slightly in reaction to the light. He rested him flat on the sand, unzipped his jacket, and ripped open his khaki shirt, buttons flying. The entry wound was hemorrhaging in tempo to his pulse. Emmett knew that direct pressure with his hands would help, but that would only postpone the inevitable unless Topocoba could be helicoptered to the trauma care center in Flagstaff.

Digging through Yazza's day pack, he found the first-aid kit, wadded some cotton between his palms, and used it to plug the wound. For the first time, Topocoba moaned. The pain was penetrating his shock. "Reuben . . ." he said. At first Emmett thought he was delirious, but the eyes held his. "Reuben came down the trail with Bob Marley."

"Who's Reuben?"

Topocoba looked bewildered.

Emmett stood, tucking the flashlight in his pocket. "I've got to get you into Supai, Billy. My H.T. won't reach topside."

"I'm tryin' . . . to tell you, Parker."

"What?"

But Topocoba's eyes drifted out of focus.

Emmett hoisted him onto his back in a fireman's carry. Topocoba screamed, but mercifully fainted. Emmett started down the path, staggering under the man's weight. The beam shone straight up from his pocket, but enough light spilled downward to show him the plunging floor of the defile. Emmett's sore knees threatened to fold with every jarring step, but he willed himself to remain upright.

As they reached Havasu Creek, Topocoba stirred and murmured, "Reuben Dye . . . Reuben came down the trail with Marley."

Emmett stopped dead in his tracks. "You mean *Reuben* is Fourkiller?"

Chapter 16

By the time Anna reached Eclipse Canyon, light rain peppered the wind. There were no stars, just a gray restlessness to the sky as the storm blew in. She kept thumbing on her flashlight, but only long enough each time to pick her way through the boulders jamming the dry wash. One of her jacket pockets was weighed down with her revolver, the other with her compact-beeper, both a comfort as once more she caught a whiff of woodsmoke. She came to the embankment, but this time quickly found the breach in it and scrambled up. On top of the bank she scanned for tire impressions with her light. Time and weather had erased the dirt-bike track. But a recent set of mud-and-snow prints wound up to the point where, as before, they'd been carefully brushed out. The pattern was too aggressive to be from the all-season radials on Fourkiller's Range Rover. And the dual-cut revealed that the vehicle had come out.

Breathing a little easier, she continued on toward the notch in the ridge.

On the other side, she felt sure, was the sole place Cyrus Fourkiller felt comfortable in being completely himself. Only there would he keep anything even vaguely related to his crimes. But, because of that, would he post a guard on the wickiup in his absence?

The question made her halt at the notch.

She'd grown up in country where privacy was often safeguarded with extreme measures, including snares and mantraps.

She decided to leave the jeep trail.

Starting up the slope, she noted that the scent of smoke grew stronger as she climbed. Had Fourkiller, using another vehicle, come here in the late afternoon between commitments at the casino and lit a fire? Maybe. But it seemed more likely that the tire impressions she'd just seen belonged to Beowawe's cruiser, that he'd been returning from the wickiup when he had driven up on her alongside the highway.

Yet, there was a problem with that.

Why would Beowawe have felt the need to obliterate his tracks? A patrolman can go anywhere he wants.

All at once the rain came flying over the crest like needles. She flinched and buttoned her jacket collar. Still, streamers of cold water twined around her throat and down her neck. Plodding up onto the summit, she dropped to her knees, faced the wet blast, and squinted into the small hollow below. It was ringed by sandstone cliffs on three sides and the alluvial ridge on the fourth. Vehicle access was limited to the notch. At the center of the barren sink was something that made no sense.

Cupping her hands around her eyes, she strained to bring the apparition into focus. It looked as if strips of orange light had been piled into the shape of a cone.

She rose, drew closer.

She almost expected the flickering thing to levitate and vanish into the overcast. But as she neared the floor of the hollow, she finally saw it for what it was: firelight piercing the seams between the bark slabs of a wickiup. Nearby stood a large mound of earth. At first she thought it was a sweathouse, but the ceremonial bath lay dimly visible on the west side of the hollow. The dirt pile ran counter to what she'd heard about Western Shoshone houses. A seminomadic people, the Shoshone'd never gone in for subterranean construction.

There was also an outhouse built of corrugated tin. A powerful-looking dirt bike leaned against it.

Sheltering behind a rock, she decided to wait awhile. To see if anyone showed himself. And in the hope her pulse would stop racing.

She recalled how far off the pinprick of light atop the Nopah Range had seemed at dusk. Benjamin and Crutcher were at least twenty miles away.

Emmett stood on the edge of the clearing in the middle of Supai, watching the medflight helicopter out of Flagstaff lift off with Billy Topocoba. The rotor wash tore sagebrush twigs off the pole arbor under which the Havasupai teenagers had sat eighteen days before, listening to reggae. He'd pulled off his parka while laboring to keep the tribal cop alive and left it in the Quonset. He figured it was too saturated with blood for him to ever wear again.

Topocoba's wife and two sons, who'd also been watching the chopper wheel into the sky, turned back for their shanty at the end of the dirt street.

Something touched softly around Emmett's shoulders.

One of the elders, the old airman who'd learned fear while bombing Germany, had shuffled out of the hall and wrapped a blanket around him.

"Thanks," Emmett said, although he didn't have much voice left. He'd try to sleep soon. Find a warm place and sleep. Hagiman was spending the night in Williams. Commandeering the radio in the tribal office, Emmett had advised Burk of the essentials, including the probable true identity of Cyrus Fourkiller. That alone, Emmett felt, warranted the immediate recalling of Anna from Spirit Meadows, and he said so in veiled terms. Hagiman was as familiar with Reuben Dye as was Emmett. That summer ten years ago in South Dakota, Dye had even threatened Burk's life. But Hagiman responded over the radio only that he'd consider the recall, although he had received word from Turnipseed that all was well. She'd sent along some evidentiary material Burk would reveal as soon as they could talk over a secure line. His waffling over pulling Turnipseed out rankled Emmett, but suddenly there was nothing left inside him. He was used up. His ears had begun to ring, his personal alarm that he'd pushed himself too far, that collapse was imminent. Wasn't it the Navajo who believed that ringing ears warned a man he was about to die?

Through his mental haze he realized that the old man was still standing beside him, his white hair shining in the kerosene light seeping from the windows of the houses.

"Misty'll talk to you now," the elder said.

Emmett had asked for this interview almost as soon as he'd arrived in the village. But now he didn't think he was up to it. Yet, the quiet insistence in the old man's voice made him ask, "Where is she?"

"Inside my house. Come, please."

Emmett fell in numbly behind the old Pai, thankful for the man's arthritic gait. There were stars, but his eyes couldn't draw them into focus and they hung overhead like fuzz balls.

The last echoes of the medflight helicopter were gone.

The paramedic had said that Topocoba might make it. For some unknown reason, the severed artery in his abdomen had been pinched shut, otherwise he would have died on Emmett's back.

The old Pai, wheezing asthmatically, led him along a path through a peach orchard.

Like many reservation houses, his was a hodgepodge of tiny rooms, most added when this or that building material had become available. The floors sloped, and the walls weren't plumb, but it was clean. The elder's wife showed him to the kitchen, sat him down at the table, and offered him some coffee. He didn't want the caffeine, but the steam from the percolator on the cookstove smelled so good, he said yes.

He dropped the day pack to the linoleum. In it was the dead Jamaican's automatic. He'd left the shotgun behind in the cleft.

The elder brought Misty Topocoba in from one of the bedrooms, guiding her by the shoulders. No older than twelve. The girl's hair was in dreadlocks, and she was so bony, Emmett wondered if she might be tubercular. An application of mascara had smeared under the stresses of the evening.

She slouched into a chair across the table from Emmett, avoided his eyes as much as he tried to avoid staring at her.

Billy Topocoba had mentioned that their grandmother had put Misty to bed upon her return from the defile, dreading spirit sickness. He now wondered if this might be that woman, so he cleared his throat and asked the elder's wife.

"No," the old woman answered, "that's another."

Yet it was clear that she and her husband had some sort of kinship to the girl—and they would stay close to protect her from a stranger. The couple ignored Emmett's request that they sit. It wasn't an occasion for sitting.

He turned toward the girl, tried to smile. Winning her confidence seemed like a monumental task. His mind was blank with exhaustion. "Misty, my name's Emmett. I'm a BIA policeman from Phoenix."

Her eyes abruptly probed his. "Did you shoot Billy?"

"No. He shot himself. . . ." When she showed skepticism, he added, "He was afraid of going to prison. He lost his head."

She wanted to hear none of this. She wanted to be angry, and the facts were only frustrating that desire. "You're Parker, right?"

He nodded.

"Billy says you serve Babylon."

He took a sip of coffee. Delicious, invigorating. He had to hold himself back from quaffing it down. "I serve the law."

"Same thing."

"No, it isn't. Sometimes the law has been bad to people of color, I know that. But other times it's been the only thing to save them. Still, the law isn't for one people or another. It's just the law."

Thankfully, the elder stepped in. "Misty, tell Mr. Parker about the man who came down the trail to us."

"The witch?"

"Well," the old man said uneasily, "the man."

Emmett felt his blood quicken. "When was this, Misty?"

She hiked a shoulder.

"The last of November?" Emmett asked the elder. The same approximate time Yellow Gourd and Topocoba had helped Reuben Dye pack Stephanie Roper's corpse in from Kaibab.

"No." The elder shook his head. "More like the middle of December."

Just before he himself had come onto the reservation with Topocoba. That utterly confused Emmett, made him doubt he was in any state to unravel this. Still, the truth seemed so tantalizingly close. "What makes you figure this fella's a witch, Misty?"

"He just is."

"What'd he look like?"

"Big. Tight braids."

"Dreadlocks?"

"No, not that tight. And just two of 'em."

The figure in the snow came back for a split second, as did the white-hot pain of the knife slicing through his hand. "How old was he?"

"I don't know."

"Older than Billy?"

"Yes."

"As old as me?"

She considered this. "Older some."

Emmett shut his eyes. He'd sensed personal memory in this from the outset. He felt himself rising, drawn up into the sun, the flesh of his chest crying out for relief. Reuben Dye had been there at the Sun Dance, watching Emmett's transcendental agony with a clean, steady gaze that shifted every few seconds to the stoical figure dangling beside Parker. "What'd this man call himself, Misty?"

"Coso."

His fatigue vanished. He opened his eyes and leaned toward her. "How'd you meet him?"

"I don't know. He just showed up one mornin'. We talked some. He asked me why I looked so sad, and I told him the coyotes probably got one of my lambs."

"How long did he stay?"

"Well, he went away for a couple of days—"

"Down the river trail," the elder interrupted. "Go on, girl."

"Then he came back." Her voice turned grim.

Emmett asked, "What happened when Coso returned?"

"He told me he heard my lamb cryin'. He told me where to look, and I went runnin' . . ."

"And found the dead woman," Emmett finished for her.

Tears welled in the girl's eyes.

"Was the witch gone when you got back, Misty?"

"Yes."

"What'd you do next?"

"Told Billy."

"And what'd he say?"

"Billy wanted me to keep it to myself. He was even mad on account I told Grandma. . . ." She began to cry, and the words spilled out. "Billy said the witch cast a spell on me, made me see things that weren't there. So that's why I was supposed to shut up, because Coso put a curse on me, and Billy didn't want everybody sayin' I was crazy."

"You're not crazy, Misty. I saw the body too. I brought it back to Supai, and everybody saw it before the helicopter took it away to Las Vegas." Emmett paused, recalling Topocoba's excuse for Misty's absence that day: She'd been in menstrual isolation. "Where were you when I did that?"

She wiped her eyes with her fingers, further smudging the mascara. "Kaibab."

"When did you go there?"

"The mornin' you came."

"I don't understand."

"Billy woke me up. He said Parker from BIA was comin'. He was real mad and started an argument with Grandma, on account she didn't want me to go to Aunt Lavonne's. A big storm was comin', but Billy made me pack some stuff and go."

"What's Aunt Lavonne's last name?"

"Yellow Gourd."

Emmett took a breath, not realizing until then that he'd been holding it. "And you went up the trail with Billy?"

Snuffling, Misty nodded. "Auntie was waitin'."

That explained the shoe impressions Emmett had observed in the snow leading from the trailhead to the parking lot. Plus one of the vehicles he'd seen along Route 18, the Ford station wagon with two figures in it that had sprayed his windshield with slush. "Must've been a long drive around the canyon in the storm."

"We didn't get to Kaibab till real late," Misty offered, her face still crumpled. The horror of that discovery in the cleft was refusing to let go of her. It had the ring of reality in a child's anguish: the spirit of a murdered woman, confronted with the loneliness of the death journey, beguiling a companion to accompany her into the shades.

Emmett asked the elder's wife for writing things. He was given a used envelope and a stubby pencil. It took a few seconds for his memory to switch on, for the number to echo around inside his head. Scribbling, he said to the elder, "I want you to contact this doctor in Phoenix and make an appointment for Misty."

"I don't want to see no white doctor," the girl said stubbornly through her tears.

"She's not a white," Emmett said. "She's Hopi, and she knows how to help a wounded spirit, okay? That's what evil does, Misty. It wounds the spirit."

The girl glared at him, although her compressed lips were now trembling.

The old man said, "We got no cars, Parker. None of us."

"I know. I'll arrange for a driver from the Indian Health Service." The old woman accepted the envelope from him, and he faced Misty once more. "Did Billy ever explain why you had to go to Aunt Lavonne's?"

Her look turned cautious.

"Misty," the elder prodded.

After a moment she said, "The witch was doin' somethin', and it was best we stay out of the way."

"What thing, Misty?"

"Trick you into comin' here."

"Me?"

"You're Parker, ain't you?"

He ignored her insolent tone. "Why would Coso want to

do that?" he asked. But he knew now that the answer had been taking shape in the depths of his mind for days. Maybe he'd avoided bringing it to the surface.

"So Coso could meet you again," Misty said. "And kill you for lockin' him away."

Emmett rose, snugging the blanket around his throat.

The past was clamoring around him, a shouting face, the echo of a threat off courthouse marble, promising him death no matter how long it took, death without end.

He heard himself again asking the elder for the key to the tribal office. As if someone else were speaking for him. Someone at a distance. The ringing in his ears was deafening.

Then he was out the door, rushing toward the only radio strong enough to reach Williams. He tried to raise Hagiman on the federal channel, but there was no reply after repeated attempts. Finally, he was forced to leave a message with the Coconino sheriff's office. He needed to be flown out of Supai at first light, if not before. The dispatcher promised to phone Burk at his motel ASAP.

Waiting for a confirmation that the message had been received, Emmett rested his forehead on the edge of the radio console.

Anna's jacket and slacks were soaked through.

The rain had turned to snow flurries, but not before she was wet to the skin. At last, she had no choice—either investigate the wickiup, which still showed signs of a fire within, or return to the Volkswagen.

The wickiup was closer.

She approached it from the side opposite the entrance flap. Her hands were buried in her pockets. Her right one fisted around her revolver, forefinger tight against the trigger guard. Not once over the past half hour had she heard a sound from within the hut. Still, she'd come up with an excuse in case someone was inside. Her car had broken down on the gravel road, and she'd smelled the woodsmoke. Neither the hollow nor the wickiup was visible from the road, so a claim to have seen the firelight would never hold up.

Passing by the dirt bike, she noticed that a padlocked chain had been threaded through both wheels. The precaution would not prevent the motorcycle from being loaded into the bed of a pickup. So what was its purpose?

"Anybody home?" she called out.

She tried to peek through the cracks, but the slabs of bark overlapped, blocking a direct view inside. The flames must have burned low, for the flickerings had stopped.

"Anybody here . . . ?"

She crouched and whipped back the flap with her left hand. The right was still tensed around her revolver.

The interior was larger than the outside suggested, perhaps twenty feet in diameter. A fire ring of river rocks lay at its center, heaped with embers that filled the wickiup with an eerie caramelized light not unlike infrared.

Shivering, she ducked inside.

The air was thick with odors of habitation—of sweat, urine, and stale food.

The floor was earthen. Freshly disturbed earth. Yet, in what appeared to be the kitchen area, a seven-by-three-foot steel plate had been laid over the dirt. It was perforated with inch-wide holes that had been recently drilled, for the exposed metal still gleamed. Anna stepped onto the plate, her shoes making a hollow sound, and inspected the plastic bins that had been stacked and covered with a strip of plywood for counter space. Atop the counter was a Coleman stove, old spills congealed into dollops of carbon.

She glanced completely around, just to make sure she hadn't missed something. Or someone.

Two military canvas cots were shoved up against the rough, sloping walls, both without bedding. Beneath one lay a battered suitcase. Snaps closed. She stared at it, wondering how good her probable cause was. What would Parker do? Certainly not quibble with himself. She dropped to her knees and slid the case open. Inside were underwear, woolen shirts, and trousers, outdated gabardines and tweeds that looked like they'd come out of a Salvation Army store. All were wrinkled and speckled with mildew, as if some had been taken off wet and mixed with the rest. But no bloodstains.

And no leather jacket.

On a sudden thought, she moved to the fire ring.

Pulling a stick of juniper from the kindling pile, she raked the coals back and forth, looking through the ashes on the outer edge of the fire. The heat felt sumptuous as it wrapped around her neck and face.

But then she stopped sifting.

Something had glinted against the background of ash.

Moistening her fingertips, she fished out a pewter and faux mother-of-pearl button, set it on a rock. The kind of button used on Western-style shirts. She'd never seen Fourkiller in one, but had he come here immediately upon his return from Truckee and flung his shirt into the fire because it was stained with Nigel Merrison's blood? The white shirt he'd worn that evening in his office had looked crisp, considering that it'd been a long travel day for him.

She stood again, thinking. Had his leather jacket been burned too, eventually? She suspected so now.

Instrumentality of the crime.

An academy checklist harped at her, and she turned for the makeshift kitchen again. There were knives among some flatware in one of the open-ended crates. One looked especially wicked, a slender blade for filleting. The hilt joint could be tested for traces of blood even if the knife had been carefully washed. She reminded herself to take it just before she left.

Or should she?

She ran through her litany of probable cause.

The night of Merrison's murder, Fourkiller had been flown out of Truckee, only miles from the IMG president's home. That evening in his office lavatory, he'd scrubbed his hands, especially his fingernails, with obsessive care, as if he'd been aware of how cohesive minute traces of blood could be. And, just as important, she had not seen him wash since that evening. And he had shopped for Wuzzie Munro, who by now, hopefully, had heard Fourkiller's voice on the answering machine tape and could confirm that it was Coso's.

She had every right to gather all the evidence she could find here.

Or did she?

Would a gifted defense lawyer make this appear to be a ransacking in violation of every tenet of search and seizure? On a normal assignment, anything other than undercover, she'd have benefit of her own counsel, the U.S. Attorney, who could tell her how to proceed.

"Shit."

Her gaze rested on a cardboard box that had been wedged into one of the bins.

Frowning, she jerked it out. Inside were the groceries she herself had helped Fourkiller purchase at the Spirit Meadows Market. Including the Zigzag papers. So they hadn't been for Wuzzie.

A sinking feeling came over her. Maybe she was on shaky ground. Maybe she should just back out before she ruined any possible prosecution against Fourkiller.

She was returning the cigarette papers to the box, when someone whispered beneath her feet.

The ghostly murmur made her stumble back a step.

Then, motionless, covered in gooseflesh, she listened.

Silence.

It was just the wind shrilling through the cracks, mimicking human vocal cords. She was feeling foolish when it came again, stronger: *"Help me . . ."*

Before she could think, she'd reeled completely off the steel plate and was training her revolver on the grid of perforations at her feet.

Long, brown fingers snaked up through four of the holes, twisted to reveal jaundiced nails, bitten down to the quick.

"Who are you?" she asked, barely finding the breath to speak.

"*Help me* . . ." The dirty fingers straightened, then vanished.

She let her breath out with a hiss. There was a space carved out beneath the metal plate. She fumbled for her flashlight, shone it down through the holes. An eye peered back at her, bloodshot in its pronounced socket. *"Help me, girl."* The pleading in the voice calmed her a little, but now she had a new worry. She'd drawn her revolver for the first time. Hastily, she lowered it behind her left leg, hoping that the man hadn't seen it.

"Who are you?" she asked, squatting.

She heard a rustling, as if the man had flopped down onto blankets. "You one of Fourkiller's people?" Despite his weakened state, he spat the name with hatred.

"I work at the casino."

"Great," he said desolately.

She looked for hinges on the plate. She found three of them along the far edge. And, on her side, a hasp and combination lock had been concealed under a dishrag. She tested the lock with a tug. The shackle clicked but didn't give. "Who put you down there?"

"You know," he said.

She glanced up. A meat hook dangled from one of the pole supports on a stout rope. A means of holding the plate open once it was unlocked and raised, she preferred to think. "How long have you been in there?"

"Weeks, I guess."

"Can I call somebody for you?" she asked, reflexively slipping back into Ronnie Chavez like a suit of armor. "The police or something?"

"I'd be dead before they got here." He'd sat up, for the eye had materialized again.

She was tempted to tell him that she was a federal officer, but couldn't bring herself to do it. Not with Fourkiller and his cops directly between her and her closest help twenty-nine miles away in Pahrump. She shifted her beam. His long, dark hair—just beginning to show a few streaks of gray—flowed down his bare back, covering most of it. His face, although clearly Indian, remained shadowed.

The pit was lined with bedding, and he drew a sleeping bag around his muscular shoulders. "How'd you get here?"

"Car trouble," she said. "I smelled your woodsmoke."

"Where from?"

"The gravel road."

"Long ways to smell smoke." But he didn't sound overly suspicious. Just weary. And defeated.

"The wind must've carried it." She paused. "Please . . . who are you?"

"Oh, just a stupid ol' buck who saw too much 'round here to keep his freedom."

"Saw what?"

His eye vanished as he lowered his head, and her beam fell on the part in his hair. "Stuff I should've kept my mouth shut about. But I'm stupid." He growled with self-disgust, *"Plain freakin' stupid."*

"What's your name?"

"Paul . . . yours?"

"Ronnie."

"Hi, Ronnie. Nice to meet you, I guess."

"Are you thirsty?"

"Bad."

She stood again, furtively pocketed her handgun.

A canteen hung on its strap near the entrance flap. Grabbing it, she asked, "How do I get it to you?"

"Just pour it down one of the holes. That's how they usually do it."

"Here goes." She dribbled water down into his waiting mouth. She was reminded of a small bird, straining for nourishment. She uprighted the canteen, but he begged for more. She felt her own kind of greed. To know the truth. To be able to present it in the flesh to a court of law. The prospect was intoxicating, but she made herself slow down, not appear overly eager.

"*They?*" she asked when he'd had his fill of water.

"Fourkiller. And that tub-of-guts deputy of his, Dan-O."

"Dan Beowawe?"

"That's him."

So Beowawe's blisters were explained: He'd dug this jail pit.

"Yeah, Dan-O comes afternoons, Fourkiller nights." The intonation was folksy, the accent vaguely southeastern. "One or the other rekindles the fire, feeds and waters me."

"When does Cyrus come?"

"Any minute now."

Still, she made herself pause and think. How would Ronnie Chavez react to this? How could she express an interest in the things that had landed Paul inside this pit?

"Get out of here, girl."

"What?"

"Just skedaddle. Fourkiller finds you, you're as good as dead. I'm already a goner, so it don't matter."

His despair was palpable. "I want to help you," she told him.

"I know it, sweetheart, but it just can't be done."

"Where you from, Paul?"

"Florida. Don't have a smoke, do you?"

"Sorry."

"Yeah, Florida. I'm one of them swamp Indians. Full-blooded Seminole."

"How'd you wind up out here?"

"Lookin' to deal cards. Make a dollar. Our casino back home got burnt down by the Cubans, so I hopped the Greyhound and rode west last spring."

The answers were so close, but the last gulf between them and her seemed impossibly wide. "Paul, have you ever heard Cyrus call himself Coso?"

He chuckled knowingly.

"What is it?" she pressed.

"Hell, girl—keep talkin' like that and you'll find yourself down in here with ol' Paul yet."

"Explain." She heard herself sounding more like Anna than Ronnie and warned herself to back off. And kept listening for the sounds of an approaching Range Rover. How much time did they have before Fourkiller showed up?

He sighed. "I should've knowed better. Gamin's a rotten business no matter where you go. Us Seminoles borrowed money from some Cuban loan sharks, when we couldn't make the payments, the goddamn Mariels torched our joint. Fourkiller's in bed with some calypso niggers, and they'll do the same to his pretty new place. If they don't ice him and take it over first."

"What new place?"

"Can I have a drop more?"

"Sure." She dribbled water again through the plate. "What new place, Paul?"

"Halloran Springs," he said, wiping his lips with the back of his hand. "Fourkiller—or ol' Coso, as he likes his buds to call him—expects nothin' but fat profits. All as pure as the driven snow. But those niggers got other ideas. Coso's just too goddamn stubborn to see it. Them niggers need an Indian casino down there for just one reason. To launder all the cash their drug operations are suckin' out of Los Angeles. If he balks, he's as dead as that BLM gal."

She felt as if she was dreaming. "What . . . what's BLM?"

"Bureau of Land Management. That's why I'm in this fix, sweetheart. I went on a ride one night I shouldn't. Saw somethin' no man should ever see."

This was it. She had her witness. She had Fourkiller cold.

So what was giving her pause? Making her look this gift horse in the mouth?

"I don't know, Paul. I don't know what to do . . ."

"Get the hell out of here, sweetheart," he said bluntly.

Why chase her away . . . unless he trusted Fourkiller and Beowawe not to harm him? Wouldn't a man in his straits do anything to escape?

"You sure I can't phone somebody?"

He didn't answer.

"Well, good-bye, Paul."

But then the fingers of both his hands shot up through the holes and flattened whitely against the steel. "You're *not* with 'em, are you?" he rasped.

"No, not if they do stuff like this."

"You really did break down."

"No, but that doesn't matter now." Relief swept over her. His reluctance to ask for her help had sprung from distrust. Natural. "My car's just across the wash. We can drive to Baker, tell your story to the deputies."

"Then get me out of here, girl—quick!"

"How?" she asked, then waited for his answer. If he suggested using her revolver, mentioning it for the first time after all these minutes, he would remain where he was until she could return with help. It'd be flagrantly devious to delay bringing up something as remarkable as a handgun.

"The lock," he said.

"Yes?"

"Don't mess with it."

"How could I even if I wanted to?"

"Beat it with a rock or somethin'. But don't bother. It's a good lock."

"What about the combination?"

"Hell, girl, you think I got a safecracker's ear?" He exhaled. "Can you see the hinges from where you are?"

"Yes."

"Are there bolts in 'em?"

"I think so."

"Okay," he said, pausing. "One night Fourkiller felt like celebratin'. Said he'd just created some *upward mobility* in the corporation. Roasted venison shish kebabs for Dan-O and me on the fire up there. Look for the skewers, girl. Use one to drive out the hinge bolts, okay?"

"What night was that, Paul?" she asked, rattling through the knives and flatware.

"I don't know . . . last time it stormed?"

The evening Fourkiller had returned from Truckee. She found the skewers, picked out one, stooped, and began tapping her palm against the rounded eye of the shank.

The bolt gave with a screak, clattered against the plate.

"Good," he said, "keep goin'."

But she was looking down through the perforations at him. It was time to shed Ronnie Chavez like an old skin. This man had to realize that the bureau could protect him. "Paul, I'm with the FBI."

He said nothing for a few seconds. "You mean you're already onto Fourkiller?"

"Yes, and with your help we can put him away."

"Jesus." Exultation shot through his voice. "This must be my lucky day. The hinges, Ronnie girl. Quick. He's never been this late before."

She started on the next hinge. "He's got a meeting at the casino. It should keep him for quite a while."

"Don't ever count on Coso to do what you expect. Ronnie your real name?"

"No. Anna." Cathartic to admit it. There was no need to return to Spirit Meadows now. No need to be Ronnie Chavez ever again. The last bolt popped out of its hinge, and she stood back as Paul began to push against the plate. "Want me to help?"

"No," he grunted, "I got it."

His face was still in shadow when the red firelight slanted across his chest. He had pectoral scars. A Seminole had undergone the Sun Ceremony, which made her step backward in sudden alarm. The skewer dropped from her hand as the steel plate tumbled over, slamming down on the fire ring and bringing on an abrupt darkness. But she had glimpsed his face. An older version of Fourkiller's, warped by rage. She grabbed for her revolver. Too late by a split second. He'd seized the rope and swung up, his long legs whipping forward to kick the revolver out of her hands. Something whooshed past her eyes. A piece of firewood. She lifted a forearm to protect her face. She heard the cracking sound, then a crippling pain jolted from her elbow to her brain. The second blow landed on the left side of her head, and she felt as if she were falling from a great height.

Chapter 17

Emmett and Burk Hagiman stepped out of the elevator onto the top floor of the Bridger Law Building. They hadn't said a word since the FBI man had parked on one of the lower garage stories, hadn't said much since the Air National Guard helicopter had set down in Supai at dawn. On the rainy flight back to Las Vegas, Burk mentioned that the two Jamaicans, presently in the Coconino County Jail, had refused to waive their rights. They'd made their call to the best defense lawyer in Phoenix and placidly returned to their separate cells to await the attorney's arrival. Emmett responded, "That'll get things rolling." Hagiman asked him what he meant, but Parker had just looked out the window in the sliding door of the chopper, watched the rain bead back along the Plexiglas.

Still silent, they walked into the U.S. Attorney's outer office.

Hagiman chatted with the receptionist, who mentioned that the package he'd requested from his own headquarters was waiting for him. Emmett helped himself to the coffee service. He caught the reflection of a dark-eyed wild man in the picture glass covering the president's portrait. There'd been no opportunity to change, and most of his wardrobe had burned up when the Jamaicans torched the Chevy sedan three days before. He realized that he stank in close quarters. Probably just the comparison Hagiman wanted to present to the Las Vegas U.S. Attorney: He himself was rested, shaved, and showered from a night in a Williams motel.

Emmett didn't care.

He intended to stick around town long enough only to get a fix on Turnipseed's whereabouts, then drag her off the Shoshone Reservation. Even if he had to take her kicking and screaming. He'd remind Kasarjian that he himself had anointed Emmett the lead investigator in this, and it was the lead investigator's decision that the situation in Spirit Meadows was too unreadable and dangerous for a rookie agent.

"Mr. Kasarjian will see you gentlemen now," the receptionist announced.

Bolting down the last of his coffee, Emmett let Hagiman go in first. He tried to find his energy. It was buried somewhere deep within him, waiting for the right imperative. Turnipseed. Alone on the Western Shoshone Reservation with his bitterest enemy, a frighteningly organized psychopath who'd put no limits on his now-obvious fixation to get back at E. Q. Parker. Emmett desperately hoped that Turnipseed's link to him would remain a secret until he could get her out of there.

He went into the inner office, shut the door behind him.

"You look like shit, Quanah," Ara Kasarjian said. He delighted in calling Emmett by his middle name. Maybe there was a familiar Armenian consonant in it. A large and rotund man with warm eyes, he gripped Emmett's hand, shook it. "Like holy fucking shit."

"I feel like shit, Ara."

"And this guy wants me to support him for a congressional seat, Emmett." Hagiman took the chair closest to Kasarjian's desk, clutching the padded envelope the receptionist had given him.

"What, Burk, I'm too fucking vulgar for elected office?"

"I rest my case."

Kasarjian finally let go of Emmett's hand. "You get some rest after this one, Quanah. That's an order."

"Intend to." He sank into the only remaining chair. The building stood in a neighborhood of seedy motels just south of Fremont Street, the now-out-of-date downtown eclipsed by the southern end of the Strip. Winos drifted along the side-walks below. Although the rain had stopped, a cottony banner cloud clung to Charleston Peak. For a few disorienting sec-onds, Emmett didn't know if it was morning or afternoon. He checked his watch.

Morning: 9:16. Friday, January 2. Although it didn't feel like a Friday. No weekends in purgatory.

Hagiman turned to Emmett. "Before I forget, Placer County S.O. found a stolen Pontiac Firebird buried in a snow-bank a couple miles south of Truckee Airport."

"Registered owner?"

"Some guy in Baker, although the plates had been switched. I'll get you the teletype when we're finished here."

The young Chevron attendant in Halloran Springs, Em-mett realized. He also realized that Hagiman had divulged this info in front of Kasarjian as a show of cooperation.

His guard went up.

Burk began telling the attorney about the hit on Emmett in Robinson Wash, the search and ultimate apprehensions, which he credited to Parker's foot pursuit. The two men then speculated about the Jamaican connection, intimating that the blame for the Roper and Merrison homicides rested with it. Emmett found sitting still hard. He saw no reason to wade through any of this. They were barking up the wrong tree. He had more than enough to go into Spirit Meadows with two arrest warrants, as soon as Turnipseed was safely back in Las Vegas. "Listen," he interrupted, trying not to sound as impatient as he felt, "that Kingston posse got pulled on like a big boot. Let's forget them for the time being. I'm ready to make my collars in Spirit Meadows. Tonight, or sooner, Ara, if we can extricate Turnipseed in the next couple of hours."

"But collar whom?" the attorney asked.

Emmett sat back, made himself slow down. "I know now who Cyrus Fourkiller is. It's just an AKA. His real name is Reuben Dye. . . ." He could feel Hagiman staring at him. "Sioux. Met him years ago on a case Burk and I worked together in South Dakota. Reuben was just a kid, seventeen then, trying to prove himself to the Sun Dancers."

"The AIM splinter group?" Kasarjian asked, beginning to take notes.

Emmett nodded. "Bank robberies. Hits on two tribal leaders the Sun Dancers thought were in bed with Washington."

"What was their M.O. for these homicides, Quanah?"

"Decapitation by machete. Eyes and tongue cut out."

Kasarjian grimaced.

"We got six convictions," Hagiman boasted. Unconsciously, perhaps, he was stroking the flattened bridge of his nose with a forefinger once again.

Emmett struggled to find the straightest line through the turmoil of the past three days. "Reuben Dye transported Stephanie Roper's body to the Havasupai Reservation. Buried her there. On the night of November twenty-eighth and the morning of the twenty-ninth."

Kasarjian stopped writing. "How do you know that?"

"Reliable informant." But Emmett was determined not to

give Yellow Gourd's name. Hagiman would rip the man's life apart between now and the trial, thinking that intimidation would gain him even more information. If left alone, Sam would say exactly what had to be said when the moment came. No more, no less.

Hagiman gave a short, humorless laugh. "You're not going to tell *us*?"

"In time, Burk."

"It's not Topocoba, is it?"

"Who's Topocoba?" Kasarjian asked.

"Havasupai tribal cop who shot himself," Hagiman said. "Dead?"

"Still touch and go."

Kasarjian asked Emmett, "You get a dying declaration from him?"

"No, not him. I thought he'd make it, wanted him to, so I wasn't about to tell him otherwise just to qualify the statement."

Hagiman shook his head. "Topocoba's a crooked cop, for crapsake. What'd it matter?"

"It mattered," Emmett said. "And much of what he did was out of religious loyalty."

"Let's back up a little here," Kasarjian said evenly. "Quanah, when I just asked you about a dying dec, you said *not him* . . . meaning you have one from somebody else?"

"The Rasta I wounded in Robinson Wash."

"We'll recover the body as soon as the weather improves," Hagiman contributed.

"And what was the gist of that statement, Quanah?"

"The three hit men were sent after me in the belief I'd killed Nigel Merrison. . . ." Hagiman and Kasarjian traded a glance that made Emmett pause. "My hunch is the Jamaicans weren't so much concerned about evening the score over Merrison as what they felt I might do in the long run to their money-laundering operations through Indian gaming. Anyway, somebody sold the Kingston bosses a fairy tale to protect his own interests. That's the gist of it. My informant listened in on this as well."

"You mean somebody *else* was traveling with the Jamaicans?"

"Under duress, Burk."

"Thanks for filling me in," Hagiman said. "I'm sure it'll all be in your report."

Kasarjian frowned slightly for him to back off. "Go on, Quanah."

"Billy Topocoba tried to set the Jamaicans straight that I didn't kill Merrison. He didn't have to do that. It wasn't what they wanted to hear. But it was the truth, and Topocoba went with the truth that time. I'm sure those two dreads in the Coconino jail passed this along to Kingston. If the bosses bought it, Fourkiller's in worse trouble than we can ever give him."

Kasarjian asked, "Wouldn't two murder convictions, one federal and one in Nevada, be pretty serious trouble?"

"Fourkiller didn't kill Merrison, Ara. Roper neither."

"Then who the hell did?" Hagiman exclaimed impatiently.

"Paul Dye, I'd imagine."

Hagiman was blank-faced for a moment. Then, having digested this, he smirked faintly. The son of a bitch was sitting on something.

Meanwhile, Kasarjian had asked, "Paul is Reuben Dye's—"

"Older brother," Emmett said. "Much older."

"The ringleader," Hagiman explained. "Never got him for the two homicides he unquestionably ordered. But we nailed him for conspiracy. Ten years, if he had to serve the full term."

"Which should've run out about four months ago," Emmett said. "From what my informant says, I'm guessing Paul Dye showed up at Reuben's casino in Spirit Meadows three months ago. Put a lot of stress on his little brother, I'm sure. Got Reuben drinking. Paul isn't easy to get along with."

"Some people just have the knack," Hagiman muttered as he heaved himself to his feet. "I'll check on the release date if I can borrow your fax, Ara." Kasarjian gave a restless nod, and Burk hurried out, taking the envelope with him.

"Sam Yellow Gourd," Emmett said as soon as the FBI man was gone.

Kasarjian jotted down the name. "Occupation?"

"Manager of the Kaibab casino. Yellow Gourd's everything we want in a witness, Ara. Just don't let Burk push. I could've had Paul Dye for those hits ten years ago, if only Burk hadn't pushed my informants. He had no idea how to handle them. Most Indians are lousy candidates for the Witness Protection Program. That's the carrot he dangled in front of them. They'd rather get whacked at home than die slowly someplace strange."

Kasarjian put down his pen. "Then how do you suggest we move ahead?"

"Get Turnipseed out of Spirit Meadows before she gets hurt. *Now*."

"That could be perceived as being sexist."

"Rookies are no match for Paul Dye. Male or female. I took him on with years of hard experience under my belt, and he still nearly got me. He's not human. He's like a goddamn force of nature. And I'm not shortchanging Turnipseed. It amazes me she's survived in Spirit Meadows this long. . . ." How could he ever translate this reality and not make it sound histrionic? "You've got to know exactly who you are *before* you go undercover. Your sense of self has to be set in concrete. A sociopath's nest is no place to discover yourself. . . ." Emmett realized that he'd raised his voice. The last thing he needed was to appear over the edge. He took another second, then said, "Ara, I'm not overreacting. It's just that this is like a nightmare happening twice. Years ago they assigned a rookie detective to me in Homicide at Oklahoma City P.D. I went on a trip to Europe with my wife, and without my permission the rookie got detached to Narcotics. They dumped him in the middle of a buy situation even an old salt would've had trouble surviving. By the time I got home, he was dead and buried." Kasarjian was avoiding his eyes. "Yank Turnipseed, Ara. I don't want her on my conscience."

"God forbid anything should happen, but she's Hagiman's responsibility, isn't she?"

"You telling me I'm no longer in charge of this investigation?"

"Of course not," Kasarjian answered. "Other than pull Turnipseed, what else do you want to do?"

"Arrest Reuben Dye as soon as possible."

"But not for killing Stephanie Roper?"

"No. He cut off Roper's fingertips to delay I.D. Transported her body across state lines. But I'm convinced he didn't take out her or Merrison. For what it's worth, we got pretty close that summer in South Dakota. I don't think it's in him to kill coldly like that."

"Might he voluntarily talk to you?"

Emmett didn't like the sound of that. The chances for arrest warrants were slithering away. "Maybe."

For the first time, Kasarjian looked unsure.

He was about to ask something, when Hagiman burst in and announced, "Paul Dye was released this September. Served his full boat, most of it in isolation. *But*," he went on, "I think we should evaluate some intelligence from Turnipseed before we make up our minds which brother did what." He took a tape cassette and slip of paper from the envelope, handed them to Kasarjian. He also removed a folder stenciled CONFIDENTIAL across its front. This he kept for the moment.

Kasarjian read the note, then inserted the tape into a player on a corner of his desk. "When'd this get passed, Burk?"

"Yesterday morning." Hagiman eyed Emmett as he continued. "And she's doing fantastic. The marshal she passed it to reports Ronnie Chavez appears to be extremely popular with the Shoshone. I hate to pull her when she's getting quality stuff like this."

Emmett asked, "Like what?"

"Turnipseed has Cyrus Fourkiller, or Reuben, as you claim, returning from Truckee Airport aboard a rented jet the night after you found Merrison. We're already trying to run down the rental carrier. No flight plan was filed, of course, even though a Learjet normally cruises above the filing requirement of eighteen thousand feet. Still, we'll nail this lead. Thanks to Turnipseed." But then he admitted, "We had one little scare though. Somebody on the reservation apparently conned her into believing they had a Shoshone mole at Nevada Gaming who might blow the prior employment part of her cover. Turns out to be bogus. Not a single Indian works for the commission."

Emmett demanded, "But are you sure Fourkiller doesn't have a non-Indian plant there?"

"Reasonably," Burk said too easily.

Preoccupied with Turnipseed's note, Kasarjian seemed to have heard none of this. "She wants you, Quanah, to play Cyrus Fourkiller's answering machine tape for a Wuzzie Munro. To see if the voice on it is Coso's. Make sense to you?"

"Yes," Emmett replied. "But Reuben isn't Coso. And I think he's been running interference for Paul all the way. That would include getting his big brother out of the Tahoe area before we nabbed him."

"How about hearing the tape before you go out on a limb?" Hagiman asked.

Kasarjian punched the play button, and they all listened to the confident, well-modulated voice intone: *Congratulations, you've reached my phone* . . . Twice, they listened. Then the attorney asked, "Well, Quanah?"

"Could be Reuben. But maybe not. He was seventeen when I knew him. His voice was changing. This is a waste of time. Let's save it for mopping up, after the arrests."

"Reuben and Paul?"

"Yes, Ara. Sooner the better."

"I'll agree that we might be dealing with the Dyes here," Hagiman said. Most generous, Emmett thought, until the man tagged on, "But unfortunately, Ara, that brings into play another issue you should be aware of." He pivoted toward Parker. "Now, Emmett, I don't like bringing this up. But if it's the Dyes we're against, I feel I have no choice. As head of this field office, I've got to make sure Ara is aware of anything that might affect the prosecution." He laid the file on the desk squarely in front of the attorney.

"What's this?" Kasarjian asked.

"Transcript of a disciplinary hearing."

"Oh, Christ, Ara—skip to the last page." Emmett gripped his ankle to keep his right hand from forming a fist. "If that file's complete, it should be duly noted that the recommendation of that Department of Justice board was overturned on appeal by the Department of the Interior." Emmett could tell by the attorney's expression that this sheet was missing.

"That true, Burk?"

"Yes. But the facts as they relate to our present situation remain the same."

"Oh, Jesus," Emmett said, "you both want me off the case that bad?"

This time Kasarjian frowned for Emmett to quiet himself.

The prosecutor read, the only sound in the office the soft rustle of Hagiman's pants leg as he jiggled a nervous foot. Emmett wrestled with the irrational temptation to grab that foot and wrench it. Finally, Kasarjian looked up at Emmett. "Did you obstruct Paul Dye's arrest?"

"I did everything in my power to postpone an ill-conceived felony takedown in the middle of five hundred innocent Sioux who'd come out only for a night of singing and dancing."

"Which resulted in Paul Dye escaping." Hagiman spoke with more bitterness than he'd probably intended.

"That night. Escaping that night. Tell it like it was, you son of a bitch."

The skin over the flat spot on Hagiman's nose whitened. "Don't you call—"

"Paul Dye was apprehended a day later," Emmett went on to Kasarjian. "By me. Without incident and without innocent casualties. If that costs me a month on the beach without pay, I'll do it every time. You never cleared anything with me, Hagiman, you just showed up on the reservation with a goddamn small army!"

Now, instead of reddening as it usually did under stress, Hagiman's entire face blanched with rage. From everything he'd suppressed all these years, yet secretly tailored and rehearsed for this very moment. "Don't you dare suggest we overreacted!"

"The Sioux haven't seen that many federal guns since Custer came to town!" Emmett yelled. "And you're damn lucky the Sun Dancers didn't produce the same result—they had the capability that day!"

"What, with the help of their Comanche ally?" Hagiman sneered.

Emmett was starting to rise when Kasarjian snapped, "Hold it. Both of you." The attorney leaned back in his swivel chair, glowering, hands folded over his wide belly. Emmett sank into his own chair again. He knew that he'd lost, that the man wasn't about to inflame the present with the past, jeopardizing his fledgling political aspirations. "This is how it has to be," Kasarjian said. "Quanah, I want you to keep a low profile. Very low. At least in the short term. Now, that doesn't mean you're off the case. I won't bow to that kind of pressure."

"What pressure?" Emmett insisted.

"You've just been involved in a shooting, and that's an administrative concern."

"*What* pressure?"

The warmth left Kasarjian's eyes. "The National Indian Gaming Association has petitioned the A.G. in Washington to investigate you in regard to the Merrison homicide."

"That's just Reuben pulling strings."

"Might well be," the attorney said, "but in the near term it means Burk has to be our point man. Until things settle down. Besides, he's been in town most of this past week. He's up to speed on the situation we have on our hands. I've given my word to Cyrus Fourkiller—"

"Reuben Dye," Emmett corrected Kasarjian.

"I've given my word to *all* of Indian gaming, through him—whoever the fuck he is—that I won't run riot over their operations. If I let you pop Fourkiller right now"—he glanced at his wall clock—"as he sets out for court here . . ." He held up his hands. "Well, I don't even want to think about what that could lead to. Burk . . . ?"

"Yes, sir?" Hagiman probably thought he had a poker face, but he couldn't mask his glee. At last, he'd had his revenge.

"What are your instructions for Quanah? He and the BIA are to remain an active part of this investigation, or you'll answer to me."

"Understood." Hagiman took the cassette from the attorney's tape machine, offered it to Emmett. "Mind playing this for Wuzzie Munro . . . ?"

Everything within Emmett cried out for him to walk.

"If we can place Cyrus Fourkiller at that old woman's borax pit," Hagiman prattled on, "nobody will be able to argue against his arrest. That's all Ara is asking for here."

Oklahoma City P.D. would take him back, Emmett was reasonably sure of it. But he could kiss an adequate BIA retirement good-bye. Ten years bought only a couple of hundred a month. *Fuck retirement.* The life force had gone out of his namesake, Quanah Parker, while the old chief waited for government money promised to the Comanche.

"That's it, Quanah. I just want some gaps filled in before we run to the judge with a half-cocked affidavit."

Walk.

But Emmett knew that he couldn't right now, not with Turnipseed still in Spirit Meadows. He choked down his anger and accepted the tape. "I've got no wheels."

"I'm sure we can spare you another car," Hagiman said.

Thirty minutes later, Emmett was speeding south along Interstate 15 toward Halloran Springs. Rage kept twitching through the taut muscles of his arms and legs. Like lightning. He was approaching the off-ramp for Highway 160, which led west to Spirit Meadows.

Reuben Dye was heading into Las Vegas along this road.

Emmett suddenly spun the steering wheel, sending the sedan careening across all four lanes.

He barely made the exit.

Consciousness returned with a jolt.

One instant, Anna was deep within the merciful blackness, the next suffocating in a gray, nauseating light. More jostling followed, setting her head and right elbow on fire. She was being hammered along the ground at breakneck speed. Blows started in her shoulders, worked down to her buttocks, and finally let go of her body by making her bare feet bounce six inches off the surface on which she lay.

She cried out but couldn't hear her own voice.

Metal. She was strapped with a bungee cord under the arms to something that was pliably metallic. It sagged slightly beneath her. Her head was higher than her toes. She struggled to make sense of the platform without turning her face. It was making a sound like fake thunder in a melodrama. She made an attempt to feel how far it extended out to both sides, but only her left hand obeyed her command to move. There was no sensation below her right elbow. The left edge of the platform was as straight as a ruler, sharp enough to leave her wondering if she'd cut herself by taking hold of it.

Tin. She was riding on a sheet of corrugated tin.

The ground had smoothed out, sand perhaps, but she realized this only when it abruptly turned rocky again. Her head could take no more. It was going to burst.

"Stop!" she screamed.

Nothing happened for several seconds.

Then the jolts started coming at wider intervals. Still, each successive one pounded her harder until she almost slid into the blackness once again. She was poised on its brink, when all motion abruptly ceased. In the almost deafening silence she could hear the puttering of a small engine at idle. The sky quit vibrating, became an upside-down sea of gray clouds.

She raised her head. This slight stirring brought on a blinding pain, but when the pain had ebbed, she could see. The barren slope dipped down toward the basin in which Spirit Meadows lay. The town looked tiny at this distance. She was high in the mountains that had seemed deformed to her, layers of multicolored rocks contorted by primeval heat into strange arabesques and scrolls. In the gullies were dustings of snow.

Snow. Whitening a conical shape in a hollow.

What did that mean?

Legs strode into view. She shifted on her metal bed, although the effort made her gasp. The man's face was stern and hateful, vaguely familiar. He wore his hair in braids. They were tucked behind his ears, the ends tied off with red yarn. The effect might have been comical but for his eyes. They were animal-like in the dispassion with which they regarded her. She searched for the slightest hint of humanness in them. There was none. It was like staring into the pupils of a rabid coyote.

Braids.

That touched a memory she couldn't quite bring to the surface. Her head flopped back down, and she groaned.

"Quiet, Anna," he grunted, as if addressing a dog.

There was something frightful about his using her name. But what?

Anna.

Ronnie.

And then it all came back in a sickening rush of images. The wickiup. Pectoral scars. This man coming at her through the darkness. She lifted her head again, despite the pain. The man had fashioned a travois, a kind of Indian litter, out of a tin sheet, and hitched it with a rope to the rear shock absorbers of the dirt bike.

That was what she was riding on.

With her left hand she patted her jacket pockets for her revolver and beeper. Both gone. As were her wristwatch and shoes.

He stooped beside her.

There was nothing remarkably abnormal about his face, but it seemed oddly misshapen, as if, like the surrounding mountains, it had been twisted by enormous heat and pressure. "This'll be my only warning," he said, his voice flat, no longer the amiable Seminole. He was Sioux, and the resemblance was too striking for him to be anyone but Cyrus Fourkiller's brother. "One more act of defiance, and I'll tear your face from your skull."

"What act?" Ronnie Chavez's voice broke from her parched lips. "What are you talking about?"

"I can read your thoughts, *Anna*. You just thought of your snub-nosed and compact. Unlikely combination, even for the well-groomed agent. There's a possible connection between gunpowder and face powder. But that isn't it at all, is it . . . ?" He arched an eyebrow at her. "No, no—the link's more obtuse. Both are instruments of defense. The gun, obviously so . . ." He took her revolver from his pocket, twirled it around his index finger. "By the way," he chided her, "I borrowed a bullet to break the chain on Cyrus's bike. Owe you one. That little piggie went to market. But four little piggies stayed at home." He pocketed the revolver with its four remaining cartridges and brought out her compact. "I must admit that this had me puzzled for a while last night. Had to go back to my flying days to dope it out. This is a transponder, right?" Despite his ragged, bitten-down nails, he deftly removed the puff and powder tray to reveal the alert button. On the verge of pressing it, he suddenly shifted the lid mirror and showed Anna her face. "Smile—this is the first day of the rest of your life. . . ." She already looked dead, her eyes sunken in their sockets and her lips sallow. "And before I'm done with you, it'll feel like a thousand lifetimes." He palmed the compact, curled a finger into a talon, and poised it above the button. "Little Orphan Anna has crashed in the desert. Wonder who'll come running if I hit this?"

She shut her eyes. She was bait. That alone was keeping her alive.

"I have an idea," he went on, "and it makes me wish I'd had this gizmo from the beginning. Would've saved so much trouble. You know, setting traps is a pain in the ass. They've got to be far away enough from the beaten track not to seem like traps. But close enough to snare the prey. *This* is pure convenience. . . ." He stabbed at the button, then jerked his shoulders and said, "There. Done. But just a tease, for the time being. I'll disconnect the battery in a minute or two. The tape might have done it, but this clinches it."

"What tape?" she croaked.

He thrust his face within inches of hers. Up close, the unblinking, emotionless eyes seemed even more inhuman. "Cyrus told me somebody kyped his answering machine tape. I warned him. Some sharpie was getting the goods on him. But Cyrus can be such a fool. Not me. That's why they had to put

291

me away in isolation all those years, hoping the silence would leave me a blithering idiot. Well, it didn't work. Not then and not recently."

She felt she had to keep him talking. To pinpoint some weakness within him. "Recently?"

"Yes. The pit. In the wickiup."

"Why'd they—"

"I have the habit of wandering off now and again. But their stinking hole only gave me a chance to fly out of myself and see things from the feds' point of view. Why would they steal poor Cyrus's voice? To play it for somebody who might identify him. Now, who could that be? Why, Auntie Wuzzie, that's who. They'd be looking for a way to place Cyrus at the crime scene, where he liked to fuck the white bitch who left her face with me while she screamed off into the other side. Let me take you where it all began, Anna. . . ." He stood and started back for the bike. "But no bellyaching," he said matter-of-factly over his shoulder. "I have a way of tearing out a tongue so the windpipe comes with it."

Emmett thought that the Nevada highway patrolman was red-lighting him. He was doing in excess of ninety miles an hour. But the trooper swerved around him, siren yelping, and scarcely slowed a quarter-mile beyond for the tiny hamlet of Mountain Springs Summit. Emmett fishtailed on a patch of ice but kept on speeding west.

Reaching for the radio selector button, he switched from the federal law enforcement channel to NHP's, catching the tail end of a transmission, something about the Pahrump fire department ambulance arriving on the scene.

He accelerated, breaking a hundred as he rounded the final bend before Highway 160 straightened out and dropped into Pahrump Valley. The roadbed had been elevated because of frequent flash flooding, and several miles down this scar embossed on the desert floor he could see a dot of vivid orange. Rising from it was a spindle of black smoke.

He immediately knew what had happened, anything else would have been a massive coincidence.

Jamaicans. He began running the oncoming vehicles of the past twenty miles through his mind's eye. No Jamaicans had been in any of them, and he'd glanced over each, hoping to see Reuben Dye behind the wheel. But maybe that figured, after the debacle in northern Arizona. Doubtless, the Kingston bosses had local assets they could tap.

Emmett slowed.

Ahead, the patrolman had parked on the center line and was blocking traffic in both directions. Two fire trucks and an ambulance were on the scene, and a Nye County cruiser tore toward them from the direction of Pahrump.

A Range Rover had plunged off the highway, gouging the embankment again and again as it bounced downward before finally nosing into the alluvium below. It still smoldered under a coating of fire-retardant foam. The noxious tang of incinerated vinyl hung in the air. All of the vehicle's paint had been scorched off. The windows were crazed from the heat, but Emmett could still make out the bullet holes in the windshield. The driver's door was wide open.

Emmett pulled in alongside the NHP cruiser.

The trooper impatiently motioned for him to back away. Flashing his credentials, Emmett asked, "Where's the driver?"

"Ambulance."

But first Emmett jogged down the embankment to the Range Rover. Peering through the open driver's door, he searched the interior for bodies. Roaring flames could shrink and contort a corpse into something nearly unrecognizable. But not this time. No one. He worked around the vehicle. Stuffed in the cargo area were what appeared to be thousands of Chinese paper lanterns. Blackened. The rear hatch window had been blown out by the fire, and he reached through and grabbed one. A charred file folder. The pages inside were as dark as negatives, but he could make out the Shoshone House of Games letterhead. He turned. The sand around the burnt-out hulk sparkled with shards of wine-bottle glass. He picked one up and sniffed. Gasoline, motor oil, and soapsuds. The new and improved Molotov cocktail.

A Nye County deputy ran down from the highway, looking like he wanted to arrest Emmett for souvenir-hunting.

Once again he held up his credentials. "BIA."

"How'd you get involved?"

"Your victim named Cyrus Fourkiller?"

"Yes," the deputy answered cautiously.

"Then I'm involved." Emmett noticed the chunky barrel of a pistol sticking out of the sand near the driver's door. He brought it to the deputy's attention, then started up for the ambulance, trying to recall the face of the boy. Handsome but full of smarting pride. But that was nine years ago. It'd be changed now, fuller, perhaps impervious to emotional wounds at this point. But it would be damaged, for sure. Nobody got out of a fire that intense unscathed.

Still, nothing prepared him for Reuben Dye's face.

The paramedic had fitted an ambo bag over much of it, but what showed was either shiny black or in red tatters of loose-hanging skin. He also had a bullet wound to the upper chest. The medic was leaning on it with both hands, trying to stanch the bleeding.

"I need to talk to him." Again, Emmett showed his I.D.

"Make it quick," the paramedic said. "As soon as he stabilizes, we're out of here."

Emmett ducked inside, sat on the gurney opposite Reuben's. The scorched eyes fixed on him, flared with recognition.

"Long time, Reub."

The man gave a shudder that might have been a nod.

Emmett had expected to feel angry. The man had conspired to have him killed. But seeing Reuben's massive injuries somehow took the edge off his anger and made him remember the boy. "I know you tried to stop Paul by yourself. I made the same mistake back then."

Reuben reached for the ambo mask. His hands were a mess, the tendons and muscles exposed and gleaming. He clawed the mask off, exposing a face that had been burned down to bone in places. "Find him, Emmett," he rasped.

"We're trying."

Reuben shook his head. "I mean, just . . . you. You didn't have to kill him last time."

"I was lucky, Reub. Can't promise that twice."

"Please." His look changed, became softer. "Why . . . ?"

"What?"

"Why'd you have to turn out to be a cop?"

Emmett didn't want to wade into that again, the adoration of a boy, shattered. It was still there in the man's voice. He'd never forgotten how eighteen-year-old Reuben had glared down at him from the witness stand. On the street outside the courthouse, he'd threatened to kill Burk. But, curiously, he'd said nothing about Emmett. "Where's Paul, Reuben?"

"Gone. Kept running off. Finally had to lock him up. Just like you bastards did. I turned out to be no better to him than you were. Tried. God, how I tried. Got him a job flying for IMG, but he was too far gone."

"Where'd you lock him up?"

"Eclipse Canyon. Wickiup." His ruined face spasmed. He started wheezing. "So tired, Em. Tired of juggling . . . everything." The paramedic tried to put the ambo bag back on, but he brushed it away. "Paulie has a girl with him, I think. Tricked her into . . . helping him get away."

"What do you mean?"

"One of my dealers. Ronnie. Found her VW."

Emmett's blood ran cold. "Where's he headed with her?"

295

"Don't know."

Reuben's chest started heaving wildly, and the paramedic pushed Emmett back. "That's enough. We're rolling."

"One more minute."

"Out!"

But as Emmett stepped onto the asphalt, Reuben cried out to him—delirious, proud, even forgiving as he recalled the Sun Ceremony of that late August day: "I still see you two hanging up there, Em. You and Paulie . . . !" Then his words were choked off by the gurgling in his throat.

Emmett closed the rear doors.

The ambulance tore off for Las Vegas, but just before it reached the bend in the highway, the driver turned off his lights and siren and continued on at normal speed.

Returning to the car, Emmett sat motionless for a minute, then reached for the microphone. He had dispatch raise Hagiman's office.

Coming on the air, Burk sounded off balance, almost scared. Somehow, he knew too. "Where are you, Parker?"

"Turnipseed's in trouble."

"How'd you learn that?"

"Just give it to me, Burk."

"Our men in Pahrump received a short transponder burst about twenty minutes ago. They're out trying to get a line of bearing on her now. She's somewhere south of Spirit Meadows, that's as tight as they can zero in for the moment. Listen, I want you to coordinate with Benjamin and Crutcher before you do any—"

Emmett turned off the radio as he sped west.

Chapter 18

The man slowed the dirt bike once again.

This time Anna's head was clearer, less racked by pain, and she concentrated on her surroundings. He'd brought her to the divide between Eclipse Canyon and a broad, Joshua tree–dotted valley to the south. Just below lay Wuzzie Munro's tiny reservation. Lifting her head, Anna could make out the little cabin among the borax mines. One of its lamplit windows was shining through the late-afternoon gloom.

The man parked in the shadow of something big and square.

The sky was still overcast, but the ground immediately around her was darker than what lay beyond. Craning her neck, she glanced up at the structure, the gallowslike head-frame over a mine shaft. Decades of desert sun had turned its timbers silver. She thought she remembered seeing it, a speck on the distant heights. Christmas Day, when she and Emmett had come to the Chemehuevi Rancheria.

The man began untying the rope that hitched the travois to the dirt bike. Anna didn't want to look at him. There was something malicious in his face even as he went about the simplest task.

It had begun to snow.

She stared skyward.

Wet flakes were whirling down at her. They made her think of dying. She was floating helplessly, just as they were. He might well kill her in the next few minutes. She had served her purpose as soon as he'd found and activated her beeper. But that also meant Emmett might be on the way. Her only hope now was that Coso—or Paul, or whoever the hell he was—foresaw another use for her when Parker eventually showed up. As a hostage. A shield or even a bargaining chip.

When Emmett came.

Why did she trust so completely in that? It occurred to her that Benjamin and Crutcher would be the first to respond to her distress signal. But she couldn't visualize them getting onto Coso's trail anytime soon.

Emmett would.

A week ago, during their meeting with Burk, Emmett had made a point of taking responsibility for her safety. At the time, she'd found his tone arrogant and patronizing. But that seemed a lifetime ago. Emmett had known what could happen to her in Spirit Meadows. And of all the cops now closing in on the Shoshone Reservation, he alone, she was certain, could figure out who had abducted her and where he was taking her. Wuzzie Munro's. Her instinct said that everything would come full circle there. Meanwhile, she mustn't come apart at the seams.

Somehow, Emmett would find her.

But if he didn't?

Then she had to find the pitiless will to survive. She could do it. Captain Jack's blood flowed in her veins. With a handful of half-starved warriors, he'd kept much of the United States Army at bay. She had to learn how to get by on very little hope.

The man stepped over her, straddling her as she lay on the tin travois. She thought to knee his groin, and nearly wept when her legs refused to budge.

"You're shivering," he said without sympathy. "It's warmer below."

For the first time, she realized her clothes were damp from the soaking she'd gotten the night before while waiting outside the wickiup. Sensation was ebbing. Did that mean her will to survive was too? But she was thirsty. That was a good sign.

She turned her face to the side. The snow melted as it hit the ground, making the rocks glisten.

The man walked away from her.

He wheeled the bike into the headhouse, the enclosure at the base of the gallows frame, then emerged again immediately to grab the travois rope. He dragged her inside. Enough light spilled through the entrance for her to make out the rusted machinery and rodent middens, dry piles of feces and plant debris. "Can you stand?" he asked, dropping the rope and unstrapping her.

She tried but had no legs. As far as she could determine, nothing was wrong with them. The blows had come to her arm and skull, but these had been enough to disable her. Gingerly, she'd felt the jagged edge of bone just beneath the skin on her elbow and the puffy hematoma on the left side of her head.

She said, "I can't."

"Sorry I had to hit you," he said disinterestedly, "but you tried to shoot me." Then, without so much as a grunt, he picked her up from the sheet of tin and carried her into the cage, a kind of open elevator car. The motion of his stride made her dry-retch.

"Easy," he said, resting her on the floor.

The hoisting machinery was useless, and she wondered how he could lower the cage. Then he proved that he'd been there before. The pulley system had been jury-rigged to a manual one, and he released a brake and gripped the rope with his powerful-looking hands. Hands capable of tearing off a human face. He began pulling. The cage descended, sluggishly at first but then with increasing speed. Above, the square of daylight grew smaller. She tried not to wonder if she would ever see the sun again. He slowed the cage, then stopped it with a bobbing jerk, setting the brake.

The blackness was nearly total.

The beam of his flashlight danced around her before probing a side tunnel. It gaped like a dark mouth. Slipping his light into a pocket, he leaned over and again picked her up. His face was close to hers, and she wanted badly to go at his eyes with her fingernails. But he was grasping her neck with his right hand. She remembered the bruises he'd left on Stephanie Roper's throat, how he must have restrained her as he sliced off her face. The image left her angry, too angry to keep silent. The Modoc had never mutilated, except to scalp. "You'll be punished for this," she said.

"I've already been punished for this. That's why I'm free to do whatever I see fit." He took her down the tunnel, his light escaping from his pocket and flitting along the overhead. The cream-colored rock was laced with pale blue seams. Turquoise. She was in an abandoned turquoise mine.

"Parker will find you. Even if you kill me."

"That's fair to say," he said with a galling lack of emotion.

She needed to get a rise out of him, to discover his tell, the unconscious signal that came just before he lashed out. Knowing this might save her life. She'd learned one valuable lesson in her undercover stint at the blackjack tables: Nearly every human being signals intent before acting. Successful gamblers are careful observers of this.

Find this bastard's tell.

The tunnel swelled into a chamber.

He halted, letting her slide through his arms. She felt as if she were falling into her open grave. She landed on a heap of ore, knocking over a roll of primer cord that skipped off into the darkness. The space smelled of rock dust and stagnant air. He lit two candles atop an empty dynamite crate and switched off his flashlight. The glow failed to penetrate the far recesses of the mine, but she had the impression that the tunnel went no farther. There was only one way out, and he sat directly across it.

He stared at her. She had the sense that his eyes were tracking her without use of the candlelight. They were drawn to her body heat.

The time had come.

Her self-defense instructors at the academy had showed her how to parry a knife thrust. But what if the blade wielder were capable of operating a mine elevator by the sheer strength of his arms? And parrying required two hands. With a broken elbow, she had but one that was of any use to her. *Get him talking again. He might reveal something about the trap he's laying for Emmett, and in knowing that there might be opportunity. The chance to distract him.*

"How'd you meet Parker?"

He didn't respond.

"Paul . . . ?"

It was over in a stinging flash of the back of his hand. He'd slapped her hard. With no tell to warn her. Seemingly, there had been no synaptic bridge: The spark that incited him to violence had gone from urge to action in the same split second. Her brain roared with pain, and into this seeped his voice, dispassionate but insistent. "Paul's dead. The poor bastard shot himself right here. . . ." He spread the hair just above his right temple, revealing what appeared to be the puckered scar of an old bullet wound. "Coso's eternal!"

Locking onto his gaze, she snarled, "Don't hit me, you son of a bitch!"

She thought he would slap her again, but instead he chuckled and leaned back. "Criminal Investigator Emmett Quanah Parker," he said expansively. "How'd *you* meet him, Anna?"

There was no reason for anything but the truth. "We were both assigned to the Roper homicide."

"Just the two of you?"

"Yes."

"Who's lead investigator?"

"Parker."

"Was that the U.S. Attorney's decision?"

"Yes."

"Wrong," he said, gloating. "*My* decision. First I made sure the white cunt was buried in Parker's jurisdiction. Reuben wanted her dumped in the desert here in California, but I told him no over the phone. Not wise. Too many dirt bikers in this country. Weekenders from L.A. She'll turn up like a bad penny—"

"Who's Reuben?"

"My kid brother. Cyrus Fourkiller to you. Don't interrupt," he said tersely. "So I said to Reub—bury her at the ends of the earth. Among your old friends, the Pai, who can keep a secret." He chuckled again, but cunningly this time. "Truthfully, I didn't want it kept a secret. And I kept phoning the BIA office in Phoenix until I figured out the case assignment rotation. Amazing the dumb-ass Indians I can mimic . . ." He then did one, a guttural Navajo accent. "Anyway, I made sure Parker got the call to Havasu Creek. It was time for us to meet again."

Emmett had said after interviewing Roper's husband that it

was coming too easily. But this man's first strike had been at the Bureau of Land Management—not Parker and the BIA. She sensed that he wanted her to ask questions as long as they gave him a chance to boast. "I know not many people liked Stephanie Roper, but what'd you have against her?"

He took a canteen from the dynamite box and offered her a drink. Her thirst had become agonizing, but she was terrified of being drugged. She shook her head. "You sure?" he asked.

"Yes."

"Suit yourself." He tipped the canteen back and swallowed, then said thoughtfully, almost professorially, "For more than a century now, Native America has been screwed into a vise. One jaw is represented by you and Roper—"

"Us?"

"The fucking feds," he snapped. But he smiled. "I have nothing personal against you, Anna. You're misguided, particularly for an Indian. But as far as I know, you aren't leading Reuben around by his cock. Roper was, a fact my little brother refused to see. It's an ethnic failing. We believe we're manipulating whitey, when in fact we ourselves are being screwed. Royally." The smile thinned and died. "Roper just hadn't named her price yet, so Reub thought he was getting away with something. . . ." He stared off into the darkness.

"And the other jaw of the vise?" Anna asked, bringing him back. Keep him talking, her brain screamed.

"The locusts. They pretend to serve the needs of Indians, but wind up exploiting us. The whiskey peddlers. The oilmen and uranium miners who promised to pay us royalties on profits that never materialized in the sets of books they showed us. And last but not least, the calypso boys. They used their shill, Inter-Mountain Gaming, to dangle the carrot of a big casino on a major interstate in front of a few backwater tribes with dying slot joints on their hands."

Now she knew why he'd murdered Nigel Merrison.

But there was so much more she needed to fill in, even if it meant catering to his pathological ego. "I don't understand how this all began, Coso. I want to know."

"Fair enough," he said agreeably. "It began with an airplane ride down to Halloran Springs." Pausing, he visibly enjoyed her puzzled look. "See, when I got out of prison, Reub had plans for me. Get my commercial license back, fly IMG's corporate plane for them. I guess I freaked."

"How?"

He was gazing off again, but this time he roused himself without a prod from her. "Parker arrested me at the height of the Native American renaissance. Except for the usual quisling or two, we were all in total agreement on what it meant to be Indian . . . *a strict observance of tradition.*" He waited for her reaction. When she offered none, he asked, "Doesn't that mean something to you?"

She didn't answer.

"A return to what we'd been," he said, raising his voice. "That was our contract. Resurrect the past. Reuben argues that our people have always had a head for business, that during the Black Hills negotiations in the last century Chief Spotted Tail held out for enough cash for the Lakota to live off the interest forever. Reub points to that as proof of our financial bent. Bullshit. It's just proof of early contamination. Ten years ago nobody dared talk that way. My brother would've been laughed out of the Sun Dancers. . . ." A cramp shot through her legs, twisted beneath her. She gasped involuntarily. His eyes immediately clicked toward her. "You put people away," he continued pitilessly. "That's your stock-in-trade. But do you have any idea what it's like to be sentenced to a maximum security prison?"

"No," she said.

"Like going into deep space. The judge presses a button and you're blasted up into the silence, the darkness. Time and distance become so stretched out, you have no sense of motion. Einstein was right. A man in space travel ages slower than his contemporaries on earth. I landed four months ago, stepped out of my steel and concrete rocket ship to find that all my brothers—warriors only ten years before—had become white corporate executives. So I guess I freaked. . . ." He grinned, shaking his head. "I took all these Indian tycoons up in IMG's old Queen Air and scared the holy shit out of them. Got them puking on their power ties. Broke the landing gear strut, I set down so hard on the strip. Merrison grounded the whole operation right then and there."

"And Cyrus—Reuben?"

"Little brother was *pissed*. Turned to modern medicine, hoping to control me. Started slipping me something in my food . . ." The haloperidol in Reuben's lavatory, she realized. "Stuff makes your whole body go rigid. You can't do anything but blink and drool. He thought he had me under his thumb, there in the wickiup. Secretly, I fasted, and when the shit was out of my system, I took off. I had to make things right."

"How?"

"Walked all the way south to the interstate, stole a car at a gas station."

Setting into motion Stephanie Roper's murder. "How'd you get Roper out to Wuzzie's place?"

"Easy. I left a message at her office. Using the cute little code she and Reub had. Asking for a callback to a Mr. Purdy before Wednesday evening. Meaning, let's get together at that time."

"On the rancheria?"

"No, no—they did most of their fucking and sucking at the motel in Baker. The reservation was used for alfresco sex in good weather. Roper liked getting it outdoors. When she checked into the motel that afternoon, an envelope was waiting for her. A typed note from Reub telling her to come out to Wuzzie's. Telling her the old woman was being testy about the land exchange."

Anna visualized Stephanie Roper driving up to the rancheria. The instant of terrible confusion as she realized that the man with the braids getting into her sedan beside her wasn't her lover, but, rather, his crazed double. The rest Anna had imagined too often. Panic welled up inside her. She forced it down. Her options were few, but she had to find one that worked. "And then Reuben put you in the pit."

"That came later. I was on the road for a while, beyond his reach. When I finally phoned him from Arizona, he swore to kill me. But I knew he'd never do that. Or go to the cops. He'd never make me go back to prison. He hates the law almost as much as I do."

"Where'd you wind up?"

"Lake Tahoe," he said. "A romp in the snow with Emmett."

"What kept you from finishing off Parker then?" she asked.

"We're talking about one formidable bastard." He tugged something from his jacket pocket, a red bandanna. All four corners were joined in a knot. "And persistent. There's a saying about his people. A white man will ride a horse until he's played out. A Mexican will ride him another day until he thinks he's played out. A Comanche will ride him to where he's going. It was all I could do to reach the car above the lake and get away." He shrugged. His impassivity chilled her. "Besides, each time I went out with no more than this"—he took the filleting knife from his pocket, the one she believed she'd seen in the wickiup kitchen—"I was counting coup." Pointing it at her, he cut an oval in the air. Using her face as a template. With each jink of his hand, the blade sliced into candlelight. "Most sensation, especially horror, enters the spirit through the face. Does it not?"

She froze with terror.

But then he quietly put away the knife.

She forced her mind back to his line of reasoning.

Counting coup.

He was referring to the Plains Indian practice of tapping a fully armed foe with a lance or a whip, a way of proving one's courage. "And you called Cyrus—Reuben—from Truckee," she said, her mouth dry, "because you saw no way out of the area unless he flew in to get you."

"Very good, Agent Turnipseed. I was in a pretty tough spot. Cops everywhere. And I was sure Emmett had seen my face. Of course, I didn't count on Reub going medieval on me when we got back to Spirit Meadows. I counted on some more medication, and then, when things quieted down over Merrison, I'd give him the slip. Start the journey we're making right now."

"What did he do when he learned you killed his boss?"

He began unknotting the bandanna. "*That's* where the pit came in. He had Dan-O dig it and lay steel plating over the top. Admitted he was at a loss what to do with his big brother. One evening in the wickiup, he sat above me, holding his pistol between his knees. I waited for this little piggie to have its roast beef. And I waited. Finally, he put it away and wept. That was shortly before you dropped in."

"You had another visitor."

"Did I?" he asked vaguely.

"The Lakota shaman."

"That's right." The bandanna was undone, and he was studying some kind of small leather pouch within it. A medicine bag, perhaps. "Little brother Reuben decided I needed a cure."

"Did you?"

He glared up at her from his busy hands.

But she pressed, "What'd the medicine man say?"

" 'Coyote will be Coyote.' "

She felt close to the meaning of all this but was terrified his mood might swing into sullen rage once again. "Tell me about you and Emmett."

He'd started massaging the pouch, kneading it, but his fingers went still, as if he was struck by the request. "Betrayal," he said wistfully.

"How?"

"Betrayal's possible only if trust goes before it. You can't be betrayed by someone you don't love."

"Is that how it was between you and Emmett?"

"I loved him," he said with a childlike honesty. "It came back there in the snow above the lake. For a moment. Maybe that's why I didn't kill him. Of course, his bullets came close, and I had to get away. So much more to do."

"Did you expect Emmett to show up at Merrison's house?"

"Eventually. But not that soon. He got onto my trail a lot faster than I figured he would."

She resisted saying that her examination of Roper's files had put Emmett onto that trail. Another question, the most essential one, burst from her of its own accord. "What did this to you?"

"Acculturation," he said.

"You mean, we Indians should resist it?"

"If we know what's good for us . . ." When she started to retort, he held up a palm to silence her. "What'd the Nazis do to the Jews before gassing them? Shaved their heads, stuck 'em in uniforms, made them march. Turned them into good little Germans. Don't you see what's coming?"

"So you made up your mind to ward off this genocide." She kept her voice level, even though her mouth twisted with revulsion.

"And I shall, no matter how long it takes."

He intended to survive his coming encounter with Emmett. That was revealing. She might be able to use it against him. "How'd butchering Roper and Merrison help that cause?"

"I just told you, dammit," he said. "The jaws of the vise. The feds and the locusts. By killing some of both, I've made sure they'll pounce on reservation gaming. Crunch it down in their mighty jaws. Ending it forever. *But,*" he added, "awakening the struggle for genuine Indian sovereignty."

"Who will lead this struggle?"

"Don't belabor the obvious, Anna." Taking the pouch from his lap, he flattened it over a knee. It wasn't a medicine bag. Was it some sort of mask? Only when he spread it over his face and peered through the empty eye orifices did she realize.

The taste of bile burned against the back of her throat, and she nearly vomited.

"To tan something well, you need brain and oils from the same animal," he lectured impassively, staring out from where Nigel Merrison's eyes had once been, his hands stretching the shrunken tissue. "I made do with salt for a while, but then I got stuck in that pit. . . . Are you all right?"

She refused to give him the satisfaction of a reply. For a few moments she'd almost felt pity for him. He'd seemed human, but now that was over.

Lowering the flayed skin of Nigel Merrison's face from his own, he said happily, "But I had much better results with Ms. Roper's." He seized a candle, sprang up, and carried it to the far end of the chamber. The shadows danced over a workbench that stood there. No, it was more like an altar. He lit candle after candle until the bench seemed to be ablaze. At the midst of this conflagration were four wig stands made of Styrofoam. Three were blank. But to the far left one was pinned the parched oval of Stephanie Roper's face.

She vowed to herself that she wouldn't go meekly. When the end came, she would fight, even if struggling was futile. Captain Jack had resisted long after there had been no possibility of winning. And he'd made his enemies suffer mightily for their victory.

Coso began attaching Nigel Merrison's face to a Styrofoam head with pushpins. "Some Canadian tribes used to stretch the faces of the vanquished on hoops. *Trophies.* That's what the anthropologists call them. But that's not it at all. They're *windows*. Windows through which the victorious can glimpse the eternal torment of their dead enemies." Then, turning to smile at her, he added, "I'll keep Emmett and you with me always, Anna. I promise."

Chapter 19

Emmett was almost at the tribal police station in Spirit Meadows when he noticed the cruiser in the rain-slick parking lot of the grocery store. All four of the Jeep's tires were flattened; its radio antenna snapped in two. No other black-and-whites were in sight. He swerved in behind the disabled cruiser, got out, and nudged his jacket flap behind his revolver grips as he cautiously approached the vehicle.

Empty.

The keys were still in the ignition, and the engine was murmuring. The tires appeared to have been punctured with a knife.

He looked up.

The market's front door was propped open even though rain was gusting through it.

"In here!" a strained female voice cried from inside.

Were there hostages? Emmett decided to go through the back door.

He drew his .357 in the darkened service corridor, held his breath, and listened, straining to get a sense of how many people awaited him. Reaching a pair of swinging doors, he could see only two inside the store, a female clerk and a Shoshone police officer. Emmett's quiet entrance startled the young woman, but the cop was too far gone to care. His face was waxy. He sprawled in one of the aisles, his back shoved up against the pastry counter. Blood pooled beneath his outstretched legs. His holster was empty. He'd been shot in both kneecaps with a big-caliber weapon. Just above the wounds were makeshift tourniquets, pantyhose twisted tight with ballpoint pens.

Daniel Beowawe, his brass nameplate read.

"You with the ambulance?" the clerk asked Emmett, fidgeting a turquoise crucifix between her bloodstained fingers.

"No," Emmett said. "You already call for one?"

"Ten minutes ago."

"Call again."

As she scurried for the phone, Emmett holstered and sat on his heels beside Beowawe.

The man dully studied Emmett's face, then either smiled or scowled—it was impossible to tell which. "You're Parker."

"Yes."

"There's a deal with the U.S. Attorney. What're you doin' here?"

"All deals are off. Reuben Dye's dead."

Beowawe played dumb. "Who?"

"You know." Emmett began easing the man's tourniquets.

Weakly, Beowawe tried to push away his hands. "I'll bleed to death."

"You'll lose your legs unless you give them some circulation." The clerk had returned. "Loosen these bindings every few minutes," Emmett told her. "What'd they say about the ambulance?"

"It's comin'."

"Okay," Emmett said. "What happened here?"

"Leave her be," Beowawe said, the words garbled. His chin had sunk onto his chest and he was having trouble breathing. Emmett lifted the man's face, held it so the airway wasn't compressed. "They got Reuben?" Beowawe asked, incredulous.

"On the highway east of Pahrump."

"Had to be the same two bastards who snuck up on me."

"I agree." Emmett cradled the back of Beowawe's neck in a loaf of sourdough bread. His hands left bloody smears on the plastic wrapper. "What'd they look like?"

"Wops."

"*Italian* Italians?"

"No. Vegas guineas. Had my gun before I knew what happened. And then the motherfuckers shot me with it."

"What'd they want to know?"

"Nothin'." Beowawe's eyelids started to droop down over his pupils.

"Bullshit. Otherwise those holes would be in your head. They wanted to know what I do—where's Paul Dye?"

The injured man hesitated, but then all the implications of Reuben's murder seemed to hit Beowawe and the tribal cop said resignedly, "Gone."

"Don't lie to me."

"I'm not. Check for yourself."

"I will." Turnipseed couldn't afford a wrong guess on his part. No faltering steps in the coming hours. Beowawe's wounds started bleeding again, and Emmett reset the tourniquets without the clerk's help: She was back on the phone. "How do I get to the wickiup in Eclipse Canyon?"

"He ain't there."

"Not what I asked."

"I looked for his trail all mornin', man. Rained hard just before sunup." Beowawe exhaled dismally. "He's got this girl. Ronnie. I'm scared for her, all right?"

"Did Paul have a car?"

"No, but Reuben's dirt bike is gone."

Emmett couldn't imagine Paul Dye letting Turnipseed sit behind him on a motorcycle. It'd leave him too vulnerable, and she wouldn't be one to go along meekly. Did that mean she was already dead, buried somewhere in Eclipse Canyon? His stomach knotted. "How do I get to the wickiup?"

Beowawe's eyes squeezed shut.

Emmett heard a siren howl.

He was sure that it was the ambulance, until the wail ripped past the market's front door and continued past along the highway. Running outside, he reached the lot in time to see the emergency lights of a tribal cruiser dim into a curtain of rain. Right behind it was a government-plated International carryall. Turnipseed's two backup agents. The one in the passenger bucket seat held a radio-direction-finding antenna, a gunlike device, out the side window.

Emmett jumped inside his borrowed sedan, revved the motor, and gave chase. He reached for the microphone while sloshing through a flooded dip in the roadway. "Parker behind you."

The man holding the antenna brought it inside the carryall and rolled up his window before answering, *"We see you. I'm Crutcher. Benjamin's behind the wheel."*

"Do you have a fix on her?"

There was a pause, and the longer it went on, the more anxious Emmett became. *"Not in some time,"* Crutcher replied. *"Either she's stopped signaling, or we've got a problem with multi-path signal propagation."*

"Then what the devil are you responding to?"

314

"Tribal officer needs assistance," Crutcher said defensively. *"Shots fired in lower Eclipse Canyon."*

"Was Turnipseed's last transmission from that direction?"

"Generally."

Emmett flung the mike onto the seat beside him.

It was huge, empty country all around. Trying not to be overwhelmed by its vastness, he focused on the advantage that emptiness gave him. Nothing could pass through this landscape without leaving a sign, however faint, even during a rainstorm. And there was something else that made it probable he'd find Turnipseed in this discouraging haystack. Paul Dye had been luring him on from the moment he'd gone back to the borax pit to uncover Roper's car after his brother, in all likelihood, had so laboriously concealed it. And two weeks after the BLM woman's body had been squirreled away—forever, if that had jibed with his deranged but intricate plans, Paul had gone to the Havasupai Reservation and demolished Reuben's frantic damage control by sending Misty Topocoba up that cleft. He had never let Emmett stray too far from the trail, so why would he vanish at this point?

But the problem would not be finding Paul and Turnipseed. It would be avoiding the trap Dye had set for him. And Emmett still wanted to take him alive if he could. The arrest on the South Dakota prairie a decade earlier had been possible only because Paul had trusted him.

That, certainly, was no longer the case.

The tribal cruiser abruptly turned up a muddy jeep trail. It, like the carryall, had four-wheel drive. Benjamin braked, and Crutcher scuttled out to turn the hubs. Emmett had no hope of following them in the two-wheel drive sedan, but by the time he'd grabbed his Handie-Talkie and bailed out to join the FBI men, the International was splashing up the wash behind the Shoshone cop's unit. There was no ready place for them to turn around, let alone slow down in the clinging ooze. Even if

Emmett asked by H.T. "Christ." He was trotting back for his car through the downpour, when a speck atop an overlook of the canyon caught his eye. Pink. Inside the sedan again, he radioed, "Crutcher, describe her vehicle."

"*VW Beetle.*"

"Color?"

"*Pink.*"

Emmett jammed the shift lever into reverse and hit the gas pedal. Mud flailed against the wheel wells. He and the others had just sped past the turnoff to a gravel road.

He now took it.

Everything was entirely up to him. As he wanted it. Let the FBI run after erratic beeper signals all night. It'd keep them out of the way until he could close in on Paul and Turnipseed first, otherwise Hagiman would call in his hostage negotiation team. A couple of white negotiators would get nowhere with Paul Dye. He wasn't their normal dim-witted hostage-taker bargaining for two parachutes and a million dollars in twenties. He had a degree in aeronautical engineering. After his artillery-spotting aircraft was shot down over the Central Highlands of Vietnam, he'd survived a month alone in the mountains at the height of the monsoon, two steps ahead of the V.C. the entire time. Following his return from the war, he had shot himself in a fit of alcoholic despair, lived despite slight brain damage, then emerged from his depression to lead the Sun Dancers, the phantom radical group that brilliantly eluded law enforcement until Emmett had discovered that Paul was flying them from robbery to robbery.

Yet, his history didn't even begin to define Dye.

Perhaps the Sun Ceremony did. During it, he'd hung almost effortlessly from the sacred pole on his rawhide tethers, smiling eerily over at Emmett, hour after hour—until the bone skewers tipping the thongs cut completely through his flesh, at last releasing him with a spray of blood into the waiting arms of Reuben. Emmett, half delirious in his own agony, had never seen such a perfect expression of mind over body. But his admiration had been unfounded. Paul's stoicism proved to be something else. A distorted reaction to pain, a symptom of psychosis. A sickness of the soul so deep, no ceremony could cure it.

Emmett parked behind the Volkswagen, rushed out.

Turnipseed's car was locked. He popped the rear hatch and found the engine to be cold. There was no sign of a struggle around the car, and Turnipseed's small prints, barely discernible under the dancing rain, struck down the hillside into the wash. Across it, the Shoshone cop, followed by Benjamin and Crutcher, had come to an abandoned tribal black-and-white. Driver's door left open, it was mired in the wet sand below a notch in an alluvial ridge. Emmett quickly surmised what had happened. Following the shooting of Beowawe in the market, this officer had pursued the suspects here, where he himself had taken fire and put out his distress call.

The cop Emmett had followed in from Spirit Meadows began zigzagging on foot up the ridge with a carbine, the FBI agents running heavily behind him. Benjamin and Crutcher soon walked, although a rattle of gunfire from the far side got them trotting again briefly.

Emmett plunged down the slope into the wash.

He knew that Paul would never be drawn into a fight like this. His only interest was finding Dye's trail out of the canyon.

The Shoshone cop reached the crest and, going prone, began firing. Benjamin and Crutcher squatted behind him, handguns drawn but obviously too winded to do anything.

Emmett ran as fast as he could over the slippery tops of the boulders. Tracking would be a waste of time: Turnipseed had made it to the wickiup, and the trail took off from there. He waded across a ten-foot-wide swirl of waters that came up to his shins, and finally plodded up a steep-walled bank. Losing his footing, he hurled the upper half of his body over the lip. He squirmed the rest of the way up, then slogged on, unzipping his parka front to let a gout of mud flow out. He blew past the line of law enforcement vehicles. The laminated safety glass of the abandoned cruiser's windshield was a webwork of bullet holes.

He decided to climb the ridge farther up the canyon.

Reaching the top, he peered down over a sandstone cliff at the cop who'd somehow come through the ambush unscathed. Crouched behind a mound of earth, he was alternately pumping shotgun pumpkin balls into a red Nissan Pathfinder and a slab-bark wickiup. His partner, given moral support by the FBI, was now providing high cover from the ridgeline.

The suspects were inside the wickiup, for a puff of smoke spurted out of a crack in the bark, and the Shoshone officers answered with a fusillade that tore big chunks of juniper off the shelter. A voice from within shouted something, and after a few seconds the two cops held their fire. Reluctantly. The Shoshone enjoyed a scrap. They and the Comanche were distantly related tribes.

Crutcher peeked over the crest, his legs spraddled behind him.

A voice from inside the wickiup declared that enough was enough. When the Shoshone didn't agree right away, and started reloading, Crutcher butted in and started talking the suspects out. Two men soon duckwalked through the entrance flap, faces pinched by the driving rain as they held their hands over their heads. One had stylishly draped his cashmere coat over his shoulders, and it slid off into the muck. The other wore a camel-hair jacket and gold chains. Las Vegas's latest unemployed: low-level Mafia soldiers. Although law enforcement could take little credit for the mob's pullout from Vegas. Rules and regulations, CPAs, MBAs, inquisitive shareholders, and all the other trappings of modern business had made skimming profits too troublesome for the midwestern bosses who'd once been the gaming town's absentee landlords.

Emmett had little doubt that these two, seeking to ingratiate themselves with their new employers, had rented the Ford Broncos for the Jamaicans who'd ambushed him outside Kaibab.

He checked his watch. It was pushing three. Two more hours of daylight at most.

As the tribal cops searched and handcuffed the glum pair, Benjamin and Crutcher skidded down the ridge on their slick-soled oxfords and went inside the wickiup. If Anna was there, she'd be dead. Not wanting to think about that, hating the wait, Emmett began working his way around the U-shaped cliff. He scanned the hollow for any disturbed dirt. The rain would have smoothed a grave down, but he believed that he could still pick out one. A sheet of tin had been pried from an outhouse wall. He was contemplating that, when Crutcher emerged from the wickiup carrying the automatic rifles that had been used to kill Reuben Dye. Catching Emmett's eye, he shook his head.

It was good news for the moment. Turnipseed wasn't there.

Nor, as Benjamin established a minute later, was she inside the sweathouse.

The rain had tapered off to a mist.

Emmett searched the heights for dirt-bike tracks, but the sandstone protruded through the slopes and the rain had beaten down the shallow soil. Only one way in and out of the hollow. The water-cut notch in the ridge. Otherwise, a vehicle, even a four-wheel drive equipped with a winch, could never climb out of the sink.

But a motorcycle could wend its way back and forth up the broken ledges.

Hagiman's voice was coming from his pocket. Emmett's H.T. But Burk wasn't trying to raise him. The traffic sounded far off, and Hagiman was advising somebody that he was en route to the airport to be picked up by the Air National Guard. Soon, scores of cops, by road and sky, would pour into this big tract of desert.

And furious activity would masquerade as progress.

Emmett kept his eyes on the ground as he entertained this disturbing thought. The soft and grainy sandstone had been scored by something that had left lead-colored streaks.

He started off, away from the hollow and in the direction they pointed—south, up Eclipse Canyon. He took long strides, but quickly broke into a run.

The next set of streaks indicated the same trail.

And the next two hundred yards higher.

It came to him beyond the shadow of a doubt, yanking him to a stunned halt. On the other side of the distant divide lay the Death Valley Chemehuevi Rancheria.

He turned back for the hollow. The four men watched him in bewilderment as he scooped up a fist-sized rock on his rapid approach to the outhouse and then vigorously rubbed it against one of the sheets of tin. The metal left the same dull, silvery streak he'd seen on the trail above.

"What is it?" Crutcher demanded.

Emmett held his tongue. His excitement was tempered by knowing that Paul Dye had always been two steps ahead of him.

He stood dead still in the drizzle, thinking.

The man had not spoken for a long while, when he abruptly asked, "How're your legs?"

"What do you care?" Anna said.

He pinched the candles out and strolled away from the darkened display of faces. Only one candle flickered in the mine chamber, the one he'd set up on the powder box. He was holding her compact-beeper in one hand and his flashlight in the other. "I'm going out for a while," he said conversationally. "Promise to be a good girl?"

She glared spitefully up at him.

"No? Very well . . ." Then, with absolutely no warning, no change in his deceptively bland gaze, he brought the heel of his boot down on her right ankle. She heard the crack and thought for an instant that she could hold back her scream. But the pain strobed in her brain, and she cried out. Yet, quickly, she bit off her scream. "You insane prick!"

He stared down at her as if he had no idea what she meant.

His boot flailed out again, but this time it overturned the box. The last candle bumped out against the ore pile. Down came a darkness so total, her eyes refused to assimilate it. The blackness was aswirl with tiny specks of light.

He could be heard walking away from her.

His flashlight beam skipped along the dusty floor of the tunnel as he moved toward the elevator cage.

Her head sagged, and she dry-heaved again.

The cage rattled up its shaft, and the last vestiges of his light vanished.

Abandoned, her anger grew. It became stronger than her nausea. She vowed to be ready for him when he returned. But what if he didn't? No, he'd be back. He had more heads to fill with faces. He wasn't finished with her. As terrifying as that seemed, it offered more of a chance for survival than being left down here to starve to death.

She would never let her face be taken.

The night following Captain Jack's hanging, grave robbers or the army medical staff—it was never clear which was responsible—cut off Jack's head. Embalmed, the head wound up touring the country with sideshows. When she was six, Anna had gone to her first carnival in Reno, shrinking behind her

321

mother the entire time in terror of suddenly coming upon her great-great-grandfather's face leering at her from a big glass jar somewhere along the sawdust-covered lanes. And glimpse his deathless humiliation. Jack had lost his face, and each of his descendants since had drowned in facelessness. Except Anna. She would resist.

Not my face.

With her left hand she rummaged over the ore pile.

Most of the pieces were small and so crumbly, they disintegrated in her fingers. Where were the matches? Had he had them on his person? She couldn't recall. She went on clawing at the pile, visions of the bloody interior of Stephanie Roper's car stirring her anger. It was like a narcotic, this hatred for him. It made her feel hot and flushed, pulled her frayed nerves taut and steeled her against the pain. Her fingertips brushed against something brittle. Something sharp. A piece of turquoise, perhaps. She pried it out of the pile.

Could she get to her feet? She would have to stand to get at his eyes, his throat.

She pocketed the shard and crawled through the darkness, groping for the nearest wall. Her palm finally rested on stone. She scrabbled up with her usable hand and balanced her weight on her left foot. Her shattered ankle was racked by each beat of her pulse.

She took a tentative hop toward the tunnel.

Her head emptied of everything except a suffocating fog. She spiraled helplessly down through it.

When she came to, she was sprawled over the ore pile again, all her injuries on fire.

Kill him.

The voice within was her own. And, then again, it was too merciless to be her own.

Kill the son of a bitch.

If she must die, so would he.

She rolled onto her left side and began squirming toward where she believed the opening of the tunnel to lie. Somehow, she'd cut the rope to the cage, sending him plummeting to the bottom of the shaft with it. The image gave her a satisfaction so sumptuous, she almost laughed. She bunched her jacket pocket in her fist to make sure that the turquoise shard was still there.

This is what Captain Jack had felt in the final days of his resistance. Elation born of rage. Going down, but going down fighting. She fended off her pain with rage and crawled forward.

She reached the wooden platform. The floor of the cage abutted it when stopping on this level. She fumbled until she found a pebble wedged between the boards. She freed it, tossed it down the shaft, and listened, counting to herself. A falling body has a velocity of about thirty-two feet per second, she remembered from somewhere. A science course at Berkeley. Another world. The pebble clicked against the shaft walls for seven seconds, then made a distant splash. The flooded bottom was at least two hundred feet below. She would slice through the rope with the shard, fray it enough so that it'd snap under the weight of the moving car. Her good arm was searching blindly for the line, when the knowledge struck her: Her rage had become as irrational as his. Was she really prepared to die just to watch him streak past to his own doom?

Nestling her face against her shoulder, she began to weep. But soon stopped.

Kill him, the voice urged. *But survive.*

Fuse. She'd overturned a roll of primer cord when he'd dropped her upon their arrival in the chamber.

Turning around, she started back down the tunnel.

A sound echoed down the shaft from above, boots drumming the floor of the elevator cage. Gasping, grunting, she tried to use both feet to propel her along. Agony pulsed up her leg from her broken ankle and seemed to pool like magma in the small of her back. She choked off a moan before it reverberated up the shaft. He was descending toward her, the rope squeaking through the pulley. She crept back into the chamber but was certain she'd never have the time to prepare for him.

The squeaking stopped.

He had returned to her level of the mine.

She seized the metal roll. Unwinding two yards of primer cord, she severed the length with the shard. Then, rising to her knees, gnashing her teeth together to keep from crying out, she took a headlong lunge toward the workbench. Her landing was so concussive she almost fainted.

Do it, dammit, she told herself. *Or die trying.*

There was no more feeling in her ankle. Shattered bone had probably cut the nerves.

A diffuse light penetrated the chamber: his flashlight beam flitting down the tunnel.

Do it.

Gripping the workbench, she pulled herself up, overcame her revulsion, and batted off the Styrofoam heads. There was a curious look of surprise in Stephanie Roper's eyeless face as it tumbled away. Anna quickly wound one end of the cord to a bench leg and the other around her wrist. For a split second she was distracted by a plopping sound. A jagged ridge of blue-white bone had slit the skin of her right elbow. Blood was falling from the wound in driblets.

She tried to scoot backward on her buttocks, but her legs wouldn't drive her. Lying down, she squirmed and writhed on her back along the hard bottom of the chamber.

The beam invaded the space, played along the stone walls before freezing on the empty bench top. "What the hell do you think you're doing!" he bellowed. He ran for his heads, which had dropped behind the bench. He was within three feet of them when she gave the cord a fierce tug. His shoulder slammed against the wooden crossbar, and his light clattered on the ground, shone upward at a crazy angle.

"Damn you!" He wheeled around, crablike, without rising.

She waited for his face to come within range.

Crying out wordlessly, she reached between his hands, which were closing around her throat, and plunged the shard into his right eye. She kept driving with all the force she could bring to bear. He didn't scream, but his breath seized and he began to screech.

"Bitch! Filthy bitch!"

His hands fell from her throat. Before he spun away from her, she saw the blood spurting down his cheek from the ruined eye. He clasped his head in his forearms, growling like an animal. Somehow, she had to finish him, even if that left her no way to return to the surface on her own. She wouldn't die here. There was water in the canteen. And Emmett or the FBI search team might find her as long as the dirt bike remained inside the headhouse. She'd forgotten that, in her confusion. She had to think clearly.

Kill him.

His shins had snapped the length of primer cord in two, leaving her a piece about three feet long. She couldn't grasp it with both hands, but formed a loop and held it fast in her left fist.

He'd fallen silent. She heard the rasp of his breath.

Again, she waited, her heartbeats drumming in her ears.

After a time, he lowered his hands from his face, moving with a chilling slowness. His expression was lost in shadow, but she could see his thigh muscles flexing under his jeans, pulled tight by the coiling of his legs. He was getting ready to spring at her.

Leaning forward, she dropped the loop over his head.

He flailed so violently, the cord was ripped out of her fist. He backhanded her, knocking her flat and dazed. "There, bitch!" he bellowed. Rising, he began kicking her head. "There!" The blows felt far above her. She was insulated from them by an odd, expanding distance. She struggled to remain conscious, yet felt herself slipping under again.

Not my face. Kill me, you son of a bitch, but don't take my face.

Chapter 20

Stars.

She was floating in a deep black pool crowded with stars. In that waking moment she believed that she no longer had a body, just an insensible point of view on the desert night. But then a ripping jolt came through the travois, and all her injuries buzzed to life. Her head ached so badly she wondered if her skull was fractured. She wanted desperately to curl up against the onslaught of pain, but once again she was strapped prone to the sheet of tin. Her face was horribly cold. As if the skin were gone and each muscle exposed to the wind. Her eyes, tearless, were being seared by the frigid air. It wasn't possible, she told herself, to have her face taken from her and go on living. Yet, Stephanie Roper's heart had gone on pumping blood over the interior of that sedan until the bastard plunged his knife under the base of her skull.

She started to touch her face, recoiled from what she might find, but then forced herself to do it.

The skin was tight from swelling and knotted with hematomas, but it was all still there. Her elbow had stopped bleeding.

She started breathing again.

Suddenly, a massive shock passed through the travois. The tin sheet slewed and nearly overturned, then went still beneath her. They'd stopped. He had rammed a boulder in the darkness and lay tangled over the bike, cursing. The motorcycle's engine sputtered out, and for the first time she heard the wind in the Joshua trees. It had cleared away the overcast, leaving a blazing star map overhead. The polestar was over her right shoulder: He was taking her south. "Fuck!" he said. Rising, he retied a small duffel bag that had been knocked off the cargo rack.

She hadn't been able to kill him in the mine. That'd been asking too much of herself in her condition. But she'd managed to blind him in one eye, perhaps tipping the scales in Emmett's favor.

Emmett would come.

She didn't know what she would do if she quit believing in that, although she was afraid that her will to survive might become an equally powerful will to die. More than anything, she didn't want to give the man the pleasure of her death.

"Far enough," he said, seeming to gain control of his temper again, although there was nothing reassuring about that.

She braced for his approach.

But he walked away from her and the bike, then halted, a brooding silhouette against the stars. He appeared to gaze carefully below, his head inclined toward a tiny square of light in a ravine. He lifted a hand to his temple and held it there gingerly. So far, his only visible concession to the torture his ruined eye must be giving him. The starshine picked up something in his other hand. It glittered metallically. Her vision was blurred, but she suspected that he was clutching her beeper.

His head shifted toward movement in the distant west.

At first she thought the hazy yellowish dot to be Mars or Venus, hovering in the paler band of sky just above the horizon. But when the object moved, she decided it was an aircraft. Then, however, it dipped down across a black hump of land—a bluff, perhaps—and began weaving in and out of sight. There was no sign of it for almost a minute, but then it reappeared with an iridescent flash out of which the single glimmer became two: the headlamps of a vehicle following a switchback road.

She glanced back to the speck of light in the bottom of the ravine. And finally understood. She was looking down at Wuzzie Munro's cabin. The headlights were winding down off the limestone ledge on which she and Emmett had been spooked by the wild burros sheltering from the sandstorm an eternity ago, before they'd discovered Stephanie Roper's sedan.

The man watched, cupping his hand over the empty socket. He would have a blind side in the other world, a serious handicap for even a supernatural predator, she realized with a grim sense of satisfaction.

The vehicle reached the point where the dirt road nearly doubled back on itself before heading east onto the rancheria. It proceeded slowly, cautiously, just as Emmett would, fully aware of what was waiting for him. She dampened a sudden current of joy within her—before she cried out, drawing the man's wrath again. Emmett was on the way. He would find her. But joy was premature, for while she silently, telepathically, urged him on, she also feared for his safety. He would never have the advantage in this game of cat and mouse, and he'd already been wounded once.

There was a swish of clothing.

The man had hurled something down into the ravine. His hand was now empty. He'd flung away her beeper. It landed without a sound, possibly in one of the powdery borax pits.

The headlights winked out along a straight section of road.

The man barked a laugh as if he'd expected nothing different. "He's tearing apart the Mojave Desert for you, Anna. He has that Comanche thing for women." Then he strode back to the motorcycle, righted it, mounted, and started the engine.

She felt a neck-snapping jerk as he set out again.

They nearly capsized as he cut diagonally across the face of a steep slope. She cradled her broken arm to keep it from flopping along the ground. The slope leveled out, and he dragged ever deeper into the night.

She hadn't been able to hear the sound of Emmett's vehicle. Which meant he wouldn't catch the fading whine of the dirt bike. He would spend precious hours sifting over the rancheria, anticipating an ambush at every turn as he zeroed in on the mindlessly beeping transponder. Her hope faded again, and the darkness weighed down on her. Her heart felt swollen and pulpy inside her bruised chest.

The whish of smooth ground roused her.

But she didn't want to come back into the light. She wanted to remain tucked away in the darkness. Insensible. No nerve endings to telegraph her agony to her exhausted mind. Still, the inner voice scolded her: *Awaken and survive.*

She opened her eyes.

The man was pulling her at full throttle across the glazed flats of a dry lake. Its bed of salt crystals glistened under a sliver of moon in the western sky. She raised her head to get her bearings. The polestar wasn't too much farther along in the sky than when she'd last seen it. Hunched over the handlebars, the man was speeding toward a string of dots, some white and some red. It took a minute for her to decipher them. Vehicles going east and west on Interstate 15. The Chevron sign was just becoming visible. Behind her, a pencil of light probed down out of the night, rippling fluidly across the mountain-sides. A helicopter searchlight. It did nothing to cheer her. Hagiman and all the resources of the Las Vegas office were focusing on Wuzzie Munro's place.

Think, think, she ordered her sluggish brain.

How long would it be before they fanned out into the surrounding desert? All too quickly the man was putting the rancheria behind. The chopper pilot would probably work in concentric sweeps, ever wider until something was spotted on the ground. She couldn't let the man take her too far from the starting point of that search. *Stop him before he gets away with you . . . there will be no survival if you go along with him. . . .*

Tightening her jaw against the coming pain, she began rocking. Her skull felt as if it were breaking apart into razor-edged pieces. The tin sheet wobbled, slightly at first, but then with increasingly wild oscillations that whipped the travois from side to side. She was sure it was on the verge of flipping over, when the pitch of the engine changed. *Stop him . . .*

He skidded to a halt, spraying her with damp salt that made the cracks in her lips sting. He dismounted and thrust his face into hers, the ends of his braids brushing her throat. "Don't," he said.

Then his fist flew at her.

Her slitted eyes opened on an array of instruments and gauges. Strangely, she could read some of them by the flashing blaze that nearly blinded her. Horizon indicator. Airspeed. Pitch trim. Landing gear control. From somewhere nearby came a sound like an electrical short, a sinister hissing and snapping. She glanced down, although even that tiny motion brought on the fires inside her head. She was strapped to a bucket seat. She felt very small within herself, as if she'd re-treated into the tiniest and hardest grain of her being. Beyond pain. Caring. Beyond hope. Indifferently, she realized that she was in an airplane, and that made her believe she was in the sky. She turned toward the window at her side and tried to make sense of the blaze around the nose of the aircraft. Her mind couldn't unravel the mystery. She didn't even make an attempt. Nor did she cower from the apparition of a manlike being in a strange helmet. He was space-walking alongside the fuselage, fire squirting from one of his gloved hands.

The blaze went out, and the hissing subsided.

The manlike being stepped up onto the wing and opened the door beside her. She expected a gush of freezing air as the slipstream blustered into the cabin, but there was only an acrid-smelling stillness. No sound except for the hollow scraping of his boot soles on the wing.

He lifted the darkly tinted faceplate to his helmet, and the now-familiar leer confronted her. He seemed hideously unmindful of his collapsed eye, the dried blood and tissue smeared over his cheek. "Anna . . . can you hear me?"

Not really. Everything was far away, including his mocking voice. Let it all stay out there. On the fringes of knowledge. She was going to die.

"I'm going to teach you how to fly. Have you ever flown?" She refused to look at him. He no longer mattered. Nothing mattered. Even the pain in her battered body was laughable. She'd lost. "I've just finished welding the landing gear strut. It'll hold for one more flight. That's all I need to be free. And now I'm going to pretty you up. Make you look like you've never looked before. Then we'll take to the skies over Las Vegas. I'll drop you off at work, Anna. How does that sound to you, honey? From about five hundred feet. I'm sure you can hit the top of the FBI building from there, aren't you . . . ?" The words came and went, triggering no emotions until he said, "Parker . . ." She saw Emmett's face the way it had looked in her condo when he'd told her that he was responsible for her safety. ". . . he has no idea what he's in for—"

"Shut up." She waited for him to strike her, but she didn't tense this time. There were no defenses left to stiffen, and she wasn't sure from where that last spurt of defiance had come. She'd felt no anger, just annoyance with him. His voice was keeping her from something exquisitely pleasant. It kept bringing her back from the edge of some dark, nameless comfort.

Is this how Captain Jack had felt as he waited for the gallows trapdoor to drop? Yes. At last she understood her previously inexplicable ancestor. Understood him perfectly.

No blow came, and the man jabbered on. "But I can't put Emmett in prison. That was little brother's idea, but Emmett's way too clever to frame. So what's left?"

"You're an abomination," she said matter-of-factly. "And he's going to kill you."

"I'll turn his entire life into a prison," he continued, oblivious of her. "Wherever he goes, whatever he does, he'll be locked into an obsession—finding the mad Lakota who one fine night dumped his partner's body on top of the FBI building. . . ."

That was it, then. She felt a curious relief, knowing how it would end, realizing that it wouldn't go on forever.

"Death is oblivion," he went on. "That'd be too sweet a thing. I'll give him an endless chase instead. An itch that can't be scratched. A thirst that can't be quenched. And you're just the first, Anna. I'll take all his partners. One by one. Each and every one of them. Until being assigned to Emmett Parker always ends in screaming wee, wee, wee all the way home. So, let the hunt begin, Anna. . . ." He clicked some kind of igniting device, and the flame erupted, shot a few inches out from the torch nozzle he was gripping. The hot light turned, cobralike, and came toward her face.

"Nothing quite cuts like fire," he said.

•   •   •

Emmett had a long view down Route 127 of Baker's evening lights. The most prominent was the McDonald's sign. He read the dashboard clock: 6:28. Twenty minutes ago he'd parted company with Benjamin and Crutcher by continuing along the highway while they barreled east in the carryall down a gravel byway that would eventually link up with Wuzzie's road. They were eagerly responding to a new signal from Turnipseed's beeper, as was Hagiman. He was in a chopper that had appeared over the wickiup shortly after the two hit men were apprehended. Emmett had suggested that Burk fly over Dye's probable trail up Eclipse Canyon while he, Benjamin, and Crutcher drove around the mountain range to the Chemehuevi Rancheria. Surprisingly, Hagiman had agreed. But between Eclipse Canyon and the turnoff on 127 to the rancheria, Emmett had changed his mind about this plan. And impulsively split off from the two agents. For he felt that he had finally gotten inside Paul Dye's head.

A pilot, the man knew about emergency transponders.

And, eleven years ago, he'd nearly been caught in Colorado because of one. A bank manager in Fort Collins had inserted a wafer-thin beeper in a stack of bills, and police ground units would have boxed in the fleeing Sun Dancers had they not been able to abandon their stolen car and take to the sky, apparently vanishing into thin air once more.

Two San Bernardino County prowler cars shot past Emmett in a whoosh and a blur of amber lights. He was doing a hundred miles an hour, and they had been doing at least that.

There was no temptation to follow them. Turnipseed would not be found anywhere near Wuzzie's rancheria.

He slowed slightly for the back streets of Baker. The sand-pitted mobile homes and the dingy mock adobes streaked by. Bats flitted in and out of the streetlights, preying on clouds of moths hatched by the recent rains. He lifted himself a few inches and brushed off the seat. As it dried, mud from Eclipse

Canyon was flaking off his jacket front and collecting between his legs.

He couldn't stand to imagine that she was out there some-where, buried beneath the mud of some playa.

Swerving, he honked for a slow pickup to move to the side of the on-ramp. Then, with tires chittering, he joined the sparse traffic heading east along the interstate.

Turnipseed was Dye's bait, of course.

But the notion that he would hold on to her until he was surrounded at gunpoint presumed that he was irrational enough to want a confrontation at any cost. What if he didn't? It was the last thing Emmett, remembering all that had passed between them, expected—a vengeful Paul Dye to back off, vanish, and, waiting for the heat to die down, patiently prepare his next strike.

But, in being so unexpected, was it precisely what Dye intended?

Would he dispose of his hostage before he was out of the area? He wouldn't get far on a dirt bike, towing Turnipseed behind him on a sheet of outhouse tin. He could steal a car, as he'd done in Halloran Springs in late November, but the road-blocks put up around Lake Tahoe after Merrison's homicide no doubt would have convinced him of the futility of slipping away by vehicle once law enforcement was alerted to him. Hagiman had already enlisted all the regional agencies to cor-don off the main arteries out of the Shoshone Reservation. CHP was checking cars at the agricultural inspection station west of Baker, and NHP was stopping traffic at Jean, just over the border.

Dye would count on all of this.

Punching up his high beams as he topped the grade, Em-mett could see his last gamble: the hangar on the small airstrip across the freeway from the Chevron station. Almost his last gamble. If his hunch was wrong, he could always sweep up the unimproved road from Halloran Springs to Wuzzie's, hopefully pincering Dye between himself and Benjamin and Crutcher.

Inter-Mountain Gaming owned a corporate prop-job.

Yet, in that morning's meeting with Kasarjian, Hagiman had said that on the evening after Merrison was killed, Reuben flew from Truckee to Spirit Meadows in a leased Learjet. And he hadn't used IMG's aircraft to transport Roper's body to Kaibab, even though Yellow Gourd had expected Reuben to show up in an old Beechcraft instead of by vehicle.

That left an airplane unaccounted for somewhere.

Emmett took the Halloran Springs exit, but instead of driving directly to the landing field, he crossed the freeway on the overpass bridge and pulled in behind the Chevron station. He nosed into the foliage of the tamarisk tree there and parked. Getting out, he felt the breeze cut through his muddy clothes. He studied the airstrip and hangar on the other side of the interstate. The field looked deserted, and the building unlit.

The crescent moon was setting over Baker, but he decided not to wait for its light to go. He jumped the five-strand fence and started toward the other side of the freeway. No cars were coming in either direction for miles. He jogged across the median ditch, over the far lanes, and vaulted the final fence.

Beyond lay a caliche flat. It was dotted with tumbleweed sprouts that tugged at his shoes like Velcro. The open ground stretched all the way to the back wall of the hangar.

He slowed to a walk.

The wind sock flapped loudly, and he believed that it would cover the sounds of his approach.

No motorcycle tracks broke the crust on the stony soil, but Dye would have left the bike on the north side of the freeway and carried Turnipseed the last few hundred yards to the hangar.

She was there. Recalling the past made Emmett increasingly certain of this. Dye had always escaped by air. On that final day together, they'd been making their way across the prairie toward his concealed Cessna and were nearly to the abandoned army airfield, when Emmett said over the sights of his hideaway gun, *I'm a cop, Paul. . . .*

The wind shifted, and the sock swung around.

Would Dye smell him coming? The man's senses were that keen, that attuned to approaching threats. A force of nature.

He crept up to the wall and pressed his ear against the cold galvanized metal. He could hear the distinctive *click-click* of a welding rig being lit. This was confirmed an instant later by the muted roar of the torch flame.

He drew his revolver.

The station attendant across the freeway. The same night Dye had stolen his Firebird, an acetylene rig and some aluminum flux had been taken from his uncle's truck.

Emmett moved faster.

The hangar doors were chained, but the lock was unlatched. He peered through the crack where they joined, but the flickering blaze within revealed only the tip of an airplane wing to him. The smallest movement of the huge doors would alert the welder inside.

There was a human-sized door farther down the front of the building. He went to it and tested the knob.

Locked.

He hesitated, telling himself to slow down. But caution took time, and more than anything, he knew that he had no time.

He kicked.

The door took the jamb tumbling into the hangar with it. He lunged through the opening. His eyes raced to make sense of the scene through the ghostly, sputtering light. Dye—it was decidedly Paul Dye—was standing on the right wing of the two-engined Beechcraft, the face shield raised on the welder's helmet he was wearing. He was holding the flame on a figure slumped just inside the open cabin door. Dropping the torch to the wing, he began shedding his bulky gloves.

"Freeze!" Emmett cried.

Grinning, Dye reached under his welder's apron and dug inside his jacket pocket for something. He was bringing out a small revolver, when Emmett fired. He felt no conscious decision to shoot. He missed Dye's face. But not by much. The man's head snapped back as Emmett's bullet ripped the helmet away. It skittered across the concrete floor.

Recovering almost instantly, Dye squeezed his trigger. The sharp report joined Emmett's in echoing around the interior of the building.

Emmett didn't pause to ask himself if he'd been struck. He advanced and fired again. A puff of dust rose off Dye's jeans near his groin. But the man didn't drop. His underlit face registered no pain, just a triumphant rage that verged on ecstasy. He leaped from the wing to the floor, nearly collapsed on impact, but then stood erect and started limping toward Emmett. "Welcome, brother!" Blood was sheeting down over his left leg. And he was closing one eye, apparently to improve his aim. Emmett resisted the urge to empty his .357. Taking fire while giving it made for inaccuracy, and he had to slow down. *Make haste slowly.* Carefully, he let go another round, but Dye's muzzle flashed simultaneously. The slug whizzed close enough for Emmett to feel its heat on his right ear. The smoke from both revolvers blotted out his vision for an instant, and when it had cleared, Dye was reeling. His revolver barked twice more as he tumbled back and sprawled across the wing.

Time stopped and motion slowed for Emmett. His sight contracted into a long tunnel, and down it he saw nothing but Dye's open eye fixed hatefully on him. "Release me, brother, if you can!"

Gladly.

Emmett's next bullet did little more than tear a ragged streak in the man's leather apron, missing his exposed chin and

338

throat. Squirming farther back on the wing, Dye shifted the revolver to his other hand and aimed it through the yawning cabin door at the form slumped in the copilot's seat. Emmett was already applying pressure to his trigger when he saw that it was Turnipseed. Her head was lolling in semiconsciousness as Dye roughly tapped her temple with his barrel.

"Don't!"

"Don't *what*, brother?" Dye mocked.

Emmett eased his .357's hammer forward again but kept the sights trained on Dye's contorted face.

"Stay where you are," the man said, his attempt at a laugh seizing from the pain of his wounds. In addition to the groin wound, Emmett had gotten him in the left shoulder. "Or my last bullet's for her."

He himself felt no warm stickiness, no numb places, so he was reasonably sure he hadn't been hit. That allowed him to take quick stock of the standoff. The fallen acetylene torch had come to rest against the wing, but the flame jutted upward— away from the fuel stored just beneath the Beechcraft's thin aluminum skin. He tried to ignore the insistent hissing noise. Dye had not been squinting to improve his aim: His right eye was ruined, the socket empty and ruptured. Turnipseed. Emmett fought a surge of pride. He couldn't be distracted by any powerful emotions. Not now.

"You want to go out together, brother?"

Emmett ignored the question.

Four.

He had counted four rounds fired by Dye. The man was gripping a light-framed revolver with a two-inch barrel, most likely a five-shot weapon. He himself had also expended four cartridges. He had two left.

Dye gestured with his free hand at the deep red arterial blood flowing from his groin and down the metal wing. Emmett could hear the splatters plopping on the floor over the sighing of the torch and his own explosive breathing. "Well,"

Dye said with an exhilarated grin, "you've staked me to the ground, brother. No running today. Victory or death, what?"

Emmett said nothing.

If Dye believed flight was impossible, what was keeping him from shooting Turnipseed? In some perverted way, was he trying to think of how to make the most of his final moments of depravity? Emmett calculated the risk of taking him out with a head shot, the nearly unfathomable calculus of whether the man's dying impulse would be to jerk the trigger, send a bullet into Turnipseed's brain.

He didn't know. He just didn't know.

Meanwhile, Dye had picked up the torch with his other hand.

Emmett tightened his grasp on his .357 but was powerless to stop him.

"Let's throw away our guns," Dye suggested, inspecting the flame, "and fight with this . . . the power of the sun." When Emmett didn't respond, the man brushed the torch against the wing teasingly. The scorched aluminum shed molten beads that skipped down onto the floor. Then Dye began rocking the airframe with his body. Fuel sloshed noisily in the tank beneath him. "It'll be like climbing up to the sun once again, Emmett . . . hovering in the light of the—"

Suddenly, his left eyeball fluttered; with a pounding heart Emmett waited for him to pass out.

But Dye rallied. His taunting grin returned. "—in the glory of the fathering sun."

"You have no place in the light," Emmett said, his voice low and raw.

Dye considered this, then said, "You may be right"—he pivoted the torch away from the wing, the pupil of his remaining eye darting back and forth in thought—"but I am unkillable, and that's enough." Dye believed that the spirit survived the body. He'd confided that conviction to Emmett several times. Was the man now trying to figure out which parting act would give him the greatest satisfaction as he soared into the darkness awaiting him?

Yes, Emmett decided. Dye wanted him to watch Turnipseed die before they all vanished in an orange fireball that would brighten the desert for miles.

The stink of gunsmoke brought her around.

And it came back to her. The first lick of the flame, which had felt more icy than hot on her forehead. Once again she was reluctant to leave the comforting blackness and return to the pain, but voices were demanding her attention.

"Drop the torch to the floor."

"Do what you must, brother," the bastard was saying. "But remember the price. I went to market four times, but one little piggie remains for Anna."

That meant something. It had importance. But the significance couldn't break through the thought-muffling fog inside her head. Four and one makes five. *Five what?*

Emmett shifted to the left a few feet, hoping to take advantage of the right engine prop in case Dye fired a quick shot at him.

"Getting restless, Emmett?" the man said. "Then let's make it interesting."

He slowly drew the flame toward Turnipseed's face.

"Damn you!" Emmett cried helplessly. It was a nightmare without solution. A kaleidoscope of horrific choices tumbling on Dye's mad whims. Emmett ached to shoot the man but couldn't bring himself to do it as long as the snub-nosed revolver was hard on Turnipseed. Dye's gun hand was wavering from his shoulder wound, but the muzzle never strayed from the fatal zone between her temple and the back of her head. She stirred, reacting to the approaching heat, and moaned.

341

Her eyelids parted, slitting as her pupils riveted on the nearing flame. "Five," she croaked, sounding almost irritated. "He used one round on the dirt-bike chain."

Emmett's indecision fell away. He fired his last two rounds.

"Turnipseed, can you hear me? Turnipseed . . . ?"

It was like peering through a foggy glass on a scene that no longer interested her. The gunshot echoes had scrambled all thought and memory, and she wanted nothing more than sleep. But a hand gave her a sharp nudge. He was awakening her merely to visit some new torment on her flesh, and she wasn't going to permit that. She'd had enough. "Fuck off," she said.

A hint of laughter followed. Not gloating but stricken-sounding, almost a sob. It made her open her eyes. "Emmett . . . ?"

He was untying her. "Yes."

"How bad did he get my face . . . ?"

When no answer came, she reached out with her suddenly free hand and brushed his cheek. He was crying noiselessly.

Her heart sank at what that meant.

Chapter 21

Emmett reached Kingman, Arizona, at dusk on Sunday. He drove down old Route 66 through a clutter of motels and fast-food joints. Something made him check his office voice mail. Later, he liked to think that it was the sunset that prompted him to do this. A spectacular one, splashing the late March sky with vast feathers of gold and red.

He found a telephone booth.

The air was warm. As he dialed, he left the folding glass door open to the breeze. It flowed out of the Mojave Desert to the west, the ancient heartland of the Chemehuevi. Through the odors of grilled hamburgers and car fumes, he thought he could smell wildflowers. Reportedly, the Mojave was carpeted with a profusion of them, thanks to the ample winter rains.

His machine played back a tentative-sounding female voice to him. She identified herself as head nurse at the county hospital in Barstow, California. *"I'm phoning as you requested, Mr. Parker."* The woman paused, obviously referring to notes. *"Wuzzie Munro told me she saw the blue boy last night outside her window here. That's how she put it.* The blue boy. *He was holding a white horse by the bridle for her. Does that make sense to you . . . ?"* It did. *"Well,"* the nurse went on, *"hallucinations are common at this stage in pneumonia . . . especially at her age."* Emmett smiled at the insinuation. *"All for now, Mr. Parker. Except her lungs are filling with fluid fast. Do what you must quickly."*

He hung up and immediately phoned Ara Kasarjian at home. He explained to the U.S. Attorney that he wouldn't be available for court tomorrow morning, as planned. Kasarjian had decided to use the Racketeer Influenced and Corrupt Organizations Act to tie together the far-flung crimes and combine three separate trials involving three different federal courts into one in Las Vegas. With Turnipseed still recuperating, Emmett was Kasarjian's only means of binding this complicated RICO case together. Since mid-February, Parker had been driving in from Phoenix every Sunday and departing for home when court recessed on Friday afternoon.

Kasarjian said, "Sure, you're excused, Quanah. Give the old gal my regards. But I definitely need you Wednesday morning for Wine's testimony. He's slipperier than whale shit."

"I'll be there."

Emmett sped west along Interstate 40.

Arriving at Wuzzie's shanty that night three months before, as Paul Dye prepared to take to the skies with Anna, Benjamin and Crutcher had found the old woman bedridden, scarcely able to breathe, her lungs were so congested. An ambulance took her off her rancheria.

Emmett opened his side window to the fragrant desert

night. Mostly to cover the sound of his own singing. He'd been rehearsing Wuzzie's hereditary song, a kind of musical description of her clan's territory, ever since she'd taught it to him from her hospital bed in mid-January. Repetition only made him more acutely aware of his tone deafness. If a shaman had to be part cantor, Emmett Parker was a poor candidate. But at least he had the tongue-twisting Chemehuevi lyrics to the Mountain Sheep Song down pat, and Wuzzie would be pleased.

If she was still alive.

The blue boy who had materialized outside her window was no doubt her son, the marine. Only in this roundabout way would she refer to him. He had come to escort her over the chasm.

Emmett reached the hospital in Barstow at 10:17. The head nurse had gone for the night, and the Latina floor nurse seemed prepared to fiercely enforce the no-visitors-after-ten rule until Emmett lied that he was a Catholic priest.

Wuzzie didn't stir when he entered her room. He was too late. Her wrinkled face, mottled gray and blue, looked deflated. Her lower jaw was slack, revealing her toothlessness. An oxygen tube was clipped to her nostrils, and she was propped up in a nest of pillows to ease her breathing. But Emmett could hear no respiration.

Nearing her, he felt as if he were stealing up on a dandelion. The slightest motion—and the puff of her spirit would separate from its withered stalk.

As he took the chair beside her bed, she broke into a deep cough that sounded as if her lungs were stuffed with cellophane. Time passed before she whispered, "What's to become of me?"

"Why do you say that, Grandmother?"

"Sent over the chasm by a witch."

"I'm not a witch," he protested. Mildly. He'd given up trying to convince the old woman otherwise.

"You remember the Mountain Sheep Song, Parker?"

"Yes."

Her blind eyes widened slightly. "How? I sang it just twice for you."

"I remember."

"Sing it."

He did so. Passably well, he thought.

But, smirking, Wuzzie muttered, "Like a mockingbird." The mockingbird was infamous for its toneless imitations of other birds' calls. Her frail hand searched the coverlet for his. Taking it, he gave her a reassuring squeeze. The skin was hot with fever. "Come closer, Parker. I'll teach you my own song. I—" She fought another long, racking cough. It left her so spent, he thought she was finished talking forever. But then she gasped, "I dreamed this song. When I was a girl. I fell over a cliff in my dream. This is what I heard as I fell. . . ."

Anna snapped awake as soon as she heard the key turn in the front door lock. She started to bolt upright, but then remembered and eased back down onto her bed, snuggling her head into her pillow, savoring the feeling of security that came with the knowledge that Parker was in town once again. Although two days late. And with no explanation for his failure to show up Sunday evening other than a FedEx package that had arrived that morning. It had contained a plant-fiber string with a single knot in it. And a note: *I'll come for you Tuesday.*

A mild breeze came through her open window, billowed the curtains out over her. The spring weather had been calling her outside for more than a week. Yet, she still couldn't make herself venture from the condo alone. Even with her pistol.

She could hear Emmett quietly coming up the stairs. His steps sounded tired.

The first week of the trial, he'd stayed at a hotel. But he'd started camping out on her living room couch when she confessed that she slept well only when he was near.

He appeared in the doorway, holding his suit coat over his shoulder. He looked weary but vibrantly alert. As if something large had happened in his life and he was yet too excited to rest. "Wake you?" he asked even though, as always, he'd paused on the landing to listen for the rhythm of her breathing.

"No."

His smile told her that her face was looking better. The bruises from the beatings had faded, but the circle of burn on her forehead had required a skin graft. Fortunately, it was close to the hairline. Still, she'd made no effort so far to hide it. She needed to see how the scar affected people, Emmett especially. Sometimes he looked sad when he gazed at her. But never repulsed. "Em . . . ?"

"Yeah."

"What the hell is this?" She picked up the knotted string from her nightstand.

"A summons to a *Yagapi*. Each knot represents a night before you must appear."

"So I appear today?"

"Right."

"What's a *Yagapi*?"

"It's easier just to show you. Put some clothes on," he said, turning again for the stairs.

"You mean we're going *outside*?"

"Yes."

She thought about that. "You'll be with me the whole time?"

"Like white on rice."

Dressing was still an uncomfortable chore despite the recent removal of the casts from her elbow and ankle. But the prospect of finally getting outside made it easier to bear the twinges of pain as she slipped on a pair of slacks and buttoned up her blouse. The worst part of her recovery hadn't been physical, and she was still ashamed by how badly she'd behaved after her release from the hospital. She hadn't expected to be deeply depressed, overwhelmed by a sense of utter worthlessness. One night she'd come unglued on poor Emmett, saying that she wanted to quit this unforgiving job that pinpointed your every weakness. He'd argued and cajoled, told her that Paul Dye had been no slouch with a handgun, that her blinding him in one eye had probably saved his own life during their firefight. That she had proved herself simply by surviving. When these arguments did no good, he took her receiving cradle down from the wall in her study while she slept and left it beside her in bed. Strangely, it worked. She realized from his gesture that the only way out of her misery was to convince herself that she could be reborn.

To what though? Cynicism? Distrust of everyone around her? She hoped not, but that remained to be seen.

She came down the stairs with the aid of her cane, putting as little weight as possible on her still-tender right ankle.

Emmett was standing at her kitchen window, humming to himself. This newly acquired habit had grown bothersome, although today he had moved on to a new tune.

"Ready?" he asked.

The late-afternoon warmth of the open desert intoxicated her. Among the narrowleaf yucca and blackbrush alongside Interstate 15 were succulent patches of greenery. Many of them were flowering, drifting their scent on the breeze. The greasewood was putting out sap, and she could smell that too. She didn't care where they were headed, as long as they kept moving across the limitless landscape toward the setting sun. A glimpse of the ocean would be nice, no matter how many hours it took to reach such a view.

But in the midst of this uncomplicated happiness, the bottom suddenly fell out of her mood.

They were approaching Halloran Springs. She could see the Chevron station and the hangar in the distance.

Emmett slowed for the off-ramp. Her entire body tensed. "What are you doing?" she demanded.

"Wuzzie Munro died early Monday morning."

After a moment she asked, "Alone?"

"No. I was with her." Adding nothing more, he turned off the freeway and pulled into the gas station. He shut off the engine. "Want a soda?"

"Okay." But she snatched him by the shirtsleeve as he started to get out of the car. "Em . . ."

"Yeah?"

"I knew what a *sodie* was."

"You did," he said somberly.

"My dad grew up at Modoc Prairie in eastern Oklahoma. He always called them sodies too."

"So you pulled me on."

She nodded. Then smiled when he smiled. "Accept my apology?"

"I'll think about it." He got out and went inside the office.

Alone, she struggled not to look across the interstate at the hangar. But it transfixed her. Everything came back. The hiss of the torch. The stench of her own flesh burning. Time standing still because to let her mind race ahead had been an invitation to feel every blow, every crack of a bone.

A click on her window made her jump.

It was Emmett, motioning for her to roll down the glass so he could hand her two bottles of diet Coke. "Hold mine for me. Sodies were on the house. The kid inside was so happy to get his Firebird back—"

"Emmett," she interrupted. His look turned wary, but she couldn't help herself. Something awful had occurred to her. "Dye had some Styrofoam heads in the turquoise mine. On

349

them were . . ." She couldn't make the rest of the words come out.

"I know." Emmett frowned. "They were in a duffel bag inside the plane." Then he yawned as if to erase the frown, as if to remind her that nothing could harm her now. "Everything's back where it belongs," he told her.

They headed up the unpaved road. From the top of the ridge she could see the dry lake across which the bastard had dragged her on the sheet of tin. The sliver of moon like a dagger in the sky. She took a gulp of Coke, and the bubbles stung her nose. "How's the trial going?"

"Okay."

"What happens this week?"

"Kasarjian takes on Leonard Wine. Ought to be interesting."

It was compulsive, this need to discuss the case over and over again after she'd clammed up following her initial statement. "Before he left, Burk phoned to tell me that you turned the Havasupai cop . . . what's his name?"

"Topocoba. And no, he cooperated on his own. Figured he got suckered into something he shouldn't have."

"And Dan Beowawe lost a leg."

"That's right."

"I want to drop him a note, Emmett. He really isn't a bad person."

"That's the bitch of this," he said. "Most of them aren't bad people. Still, no communication till the trial's over, or Kasarjian will have your ass."

"That's absurd. I just want to wish Dan well."

"Yes, it's absurd. But that's the way it is."

They wound down into the arroyo. This time, with no dust storm, the driving was much easier. But she couldn't relax. She'd never wanted to come this way again. Even in her dreams. Especially in her dreams. And bouncing down the same road through the Joshua trees toward the genesis of this nightmare made her start to ask a question she'd promised herself never to ask. "Emmett," she said sharply, "what did you—" She stopped. It wasn't fair.

"Go ahead, Turnipseed."

She shook her head in exasperation with herself, then plunged on. "What'd you ever see in Paul Dye? I have to know."

He stared through the windshield in silence. She watched him over the next minute. He seemed to come up with an answer, only to dismiss it a few seconds later and go on scouring his feelings. He ran a hand over his hair, then exhaled and faced her again. "He was unbowed. I guess I admired that in him."

"Unbowed," she repeated.

She must have sounded incredulous or disapproving, for Emmett quickly added, "I don't expect you to understand. Not after what he put you through."

"No, I think I do."

"Really?"

"Yes, I do." It was the truth, as oddly as the realization now struck her.

"How's Burk taking the transfer?" Emmett asked. To change the subject, she sensed.

"All right, I suppose." She detected no gloating in Emmett's tone, but she didn't want to say too much about Hagiman. Guilt, maybe. As a consequence of his sending her into Spirit Meadows after understating the potential dangers to the undercover operations review committee, Burk's performance rating had dropped from "outstanding" to "fully successful." A seemingly minor detail, but its import had become evident in early March, when he was reassigned to FBI headquarters, where the brass could keep closer tabs on him. Burk had always wanted to wind up his career in Washington, but certainly not under these circumstances.

The sun dipped behind the Panamint Range.

She closed her eyes as they passed the rancheria's no trespassing sign. Here, Stephanie Roper had died. And now Anna knew precisely what those last moments had been like. Imagination did them no justice.

Wuzzie's shanty looked the same, but in the yard the preparations had been made for a large bonfire. Emmett parked and got out, then strolled up to the chest-high pile of brush and wood.

Anna joined him, hobbling on her cane.

Neatly tucked into the pyre were Wuzzie's possessions. Her furniture. Winnowing baskets. A rabbitskin blanket. The framed photograph of an Indian youth in a blue military uniform. "Who's the soldier?"

"Marine. Her son. Died at Iwo Jima in the big war. There was a citation and a medal in the shack. She'd want them burned too, I guess."

The sun was finally gone. "Where *is* Wuzzie?" Anna asked.

Emmett brought a finger up to his lips. As far as she knew, the Comanche had no taboo against speaking the names of the dead; his full name even included that of his famous ancestor. But he was honoring the Chemehuevi way.

She considered another tack. The pragmatic Modoc observed this mourning taboo, but got around it by using descriptive nicknames. "Where's Mehunolush?"

Emmett gave her a questioning look.

"Modoc," she explained. "Means *She Who Is Blind.*"

He nodded approvingly. "I laid her to rest in the old cemetery at the Chemehuevi rez down south along the Colorado. She wasn't one of those river folks. They're the Deer Song People. She was the last of her song group. That's how these Chemehuevi described themselves. This or that song group. 'Tribe' was a European notion that got thrust on them. On all of us." He paused, his eyes distant, mouth a little ragged-looking. "But they can understand each other's dialects, these

Southern Paiutes, so I suppose she'll have company to talk to. She liked to talk."

He looked around and found the darkness sufficient, for he knelt. Touched a butane lighter to a piece of paper. The flame crept over the words *United States of America . . . Silver Star Medal . . .* consumed them, then licked around a spiny stalk of candlewood. The stem gave off greasy driblets of fire that soon set the rest of the heap ablaze.

Emmett stood and sang a song. Earnestly but off-key. The tune he'd been humming for weeks. In fairness to him, it was an eerie melody full of atonal wailing.

When he finished, she asked, "What's it mean?"

"It's a travelogue. Takes you from the hills west of the river all the way to the Bone-Gray Mountains over there. . . ." He gestured at the peaks silhouetted against the last tea-colored band of day. "Places she would have known from her girlhood, traveling with her family. Each clan had a song that gave them title to their country. Told each member who he or she was. She was a Mountain Sheep woman."

"Was that her song?"

"Her personal song? No. That's next." Clearing his throat, he began singing it.

The growing heat drove them back from the pyre. Fat from the rabbit blanket drizzled down through the latticework of branches, spattering and gurgling. The winnowing baskets sent up a flurry of sparks to compete with the first stars appearing in the darkening sky. The picture-frame glass shattered with a pop. As if liberating the spirit of the blue-uniformed marine from the frame. At that instant the fire shot up twenty feet, roaring. Its light spread luridly across the borax-drifted yard, making the parched mineral glisten like snow.

Wuzzie Munro's song was brief.

Emmett translated the refrain, which had punctuated the mournful-sounding lyrics with a note of consolation:

Now I have nothing,
I am nothing.
Now I have everything,
I am everything.

Falling into the Mountain Sheep Song again, he began to shamble around the fire. It took Anna a moment to realize that he was doing the circle dance. Had there been scores of mourners, they would have now formed up in single file and wheeled around the flames in an unbroken unity.

But there was only Emmett for Wuzzie Munro.

He halted and stared self-consciously over his shoulder at her. "Christ almighty, I'm not going to do this alone."

She raised her cane as her excuse.

But he insisted, "Throw it in the fire and dance with me, Turnipseed."

Something rankled. "Is your face going to break if you call me *Anna?*"

Emmett appeared to weigh all the possible implications of doing this before replying. "Probably not."

ABOUT THE AUTHOR

KIRK MITCHELL is the great-great-grandson of a cavalry trooper who fought in the Apache and Nez Percé Wars. After graduating from the San Bernardino County Sherriff's Academy, he was assigned to the Indian reservations of Inyo County, joining an integrated patrol force of Paiute, Shoshone, and Comanche deputies. He later served as a SWAT sergeant in southern California. An Edgar Award nominee for a previous novel, he lives in the High Sierra.